Book Two of
The Dragon Birthmark
Series:

Threats of Tartarus

Jennifer Phillips Russo

FREDONIA, NEW YORK

http://thedragonbirthmark.com

Cover Art Design by Barbara Tackitt

barbaratackitt@yahoo.com

ISBN: 0988294818
ISBN-13: 978-0-9882948-1-3

DEDICATION

This book is dedicated to my Dad, may your angel wings constantly lift me, and to my children, may you always search for the Sunshine in Life and Enjoy the Journey. Also to all of the talented Student Artists who bravely entered their works for this project, I am so proud of each of you, and I encourage you all to continue to create. I believe that Imagination sparks Innovation and our world needs more innovative thinkers.

CONTENTS

Acknowledgments i

1 After the Battle 1

2 Adrastai Council 19

3 Unwelcome Guest 39

4 Violated 55

5 Missing Mage 67

6 Return Visit 81

7 The Map 93

8 Hall of Knowledge 105

9 A Viking Journey 123

10 Message from Beyond 139

11 Meet Ellida 155

12 Cannon Ball 173

13 The Oracle 189

14 A History 203

15 Golden Fruit   221

16 Troubled Waters   243

17 Family Woes   257

18 A Quest   271

19 The Colony   289

20 A Reunion   303

21 The Underworld   319

22 Sacrifice   337

ACKNOWLEDGMENTS

This book is for my children, Giovani, Sofia, Mariella, and Aria, who inspired me to create this tale. I try to encourage them to follow their dreams, question what they know and read, and to have confidence knowing that they can do anything as long as they are willing to work hard for it. With that said, I wrote this story for them. If I did not do everything in my power to see this project through to fruition, then my teachings would be hypocritical. No, is just a word; it cannot physically stop me. Believe in yourself and always search for the Sunshine in Life.

I am grateful to my husband, Sam, as well as, Skye, Scott, Priscilla, Kathleen and Mark for their constant support and encouragement from the earliest draft to this final piece. They believed in me when I doubted myself and were vital in making this happen.

An army of supporters lifted me throughout this process. To my Mom, Dad, Robyn, and Jeff thank you for always being there for me, and to the Jonasse family for sharing their love and zest for life. To Jennifer, Cassidy, Tristen, and Kadence Phillips, thank you for your contributions. To Heather Martin, Susan Wells, Mark Dunlap, Deborah Sellari, Amy Piper, Jodie Walters Korzenski, Stephanie Brash, Jessica Johnston, Corinne Rukavina, Michael Rukavina, Michelle Mathews Gullo, John Gullo, and Kris Dziduch; I value every one of their opinions and professional support. A very special thanks to all of the educators, who supported the Student Artwork contest; I am thankful that we share the same goal to inspire creativity. To Miss Olivia Gullo, who at her tender age was constructive in her feedback and encouraging with their enthusiasm, as always a pleasure to work with.

To Barbara VanEllen Tackitt, whose illustrative talents are greatly appreciated; and to Lisa Kopinski Hogue for your love for written word and kind support, encouraging me to tell the story by getting it onto the paper first.

This adventure would not have been as fun as it was without all of you and I am blessed to have you all in my life. Thank you.

Chapter 1
Illustrated by
Miranda Pavelle

1

AFTER THE BATTLE

Over two months had passed since the darkest day in my family's history. Some days were easier than others were, but the bad days were just dreadful. There was so much bloodshed, right here, in my backyard; so many lives lost. Lives that did not even know me personally, but they fought, valiantly, to save my life and the lives of my family. Some of those who fought, never made it back home to their families, and why? Why did so many die defending my bloodline? What was so important about me? Nothing, for I am no different from anyone else.

Maybe the fact that my ancestors have fought against Evil for hundreds of years played a small role in why the battle took place here, but they all were here fighting for something much bigger than one person was; they were defending all that is Good in our world. They were fighting to stop Evil. I found some comfort in that thought, knowing that their lives were lost protecting something they believed in, fiercely.

I realize that there is always going to be some shade of evil in our world, a constant struggle between Light and Dark forces. There is always going to be someone who thinks that they are better than somebody else is or that their way of doing things is superior and with little regard for others who think differently. They will try to dominate, humiliate, and assert their beliefs onto those deemed inferior by them. Someone needed to protect our world from evil, and that is why The Order was founded, to defend all that is Pure and Light. No one should live in fear and everyone has the right to feel love, peace, and happiness.

Unfortunately, wielding words instead of swords is ineffective when dealing with dark forces. Evil beings, who are trying to rule the world, are not interested in sitting down and talking it out. I am certain that there will be more bloodshed, more pain, and more sorrow. I found myself thrown into this curious new reality; forced to fight to save my family's lives. Now, I joined the fight; the fight for Good and I took a vow to uphold the nine virtues of the Adrastai. Before I learned I was an Adrastai, all I wanted to do was get away from my sisters and live a life of adventure until it dropped into my lap. Now, I carry an enchanted sword and ride upon the back of an amazing dragon named Khai. My new life is cool except for the bloody battles and death part.

All of the warriors in the secret elite fighting force of The Order are branded at birth with the emblem, or birthmark, to those unfamiliar with the world that lives in the shadows protecting all of us. My birthmark was in the shape of a dragon and located on the back of my left shoulder. I always knew I had it, because The Froufrou Crew (my three annoying younger sisters) always wanted to touch it for some reason, but I only just learned about the significance two months ago on my twelfth birthday. My life changed forever that day, when I opened my manual for the first time.

All my life, I have always had a feeling as if I was being watched. I would see things out of the corner of my eye only to look and find nothing there. I have always felt a presence around me that I could not explain. When I learned about The Order, suddenly, it all made sense. There actually were creatures, which live in the shadow world only Adratsai can see, sometimes they were good, sometimes not so; all of those creepy feelings were confirmed. My protectors were the presence that I sensed. They were assigned to me the day I was born to keep me safe from the unknown horrors that would always try to end my bloodline and me. Every Adrastai has their own protectors and there are thousands of warriors all over the world.

I have learned so much about The Order of St. John and its Adrastai warriors over the past two months; thrust into this strange new world. Apparently, not all of the Adrastai birthmarks are located in the same place or shaped alike, although my friend Skye's emblem was in the same place as mine. Hers was an Imoogi. It was in the shape of a dragon-headed snake with wings. We were normal school friends, unaware of each other's involvement in The Order. It was on my first mission as an Adrastai when I learned that she was a Piscisene, which is a being that is half-human half-mermaid, and that she rode a sea dragon. My new life was so cool and terrifying at the same time.

Brochara, my Elven guide, told me that the official emblem of The Order was a dragon and that it wasn't a coincidence that I was branded with one. My manual, an enchanted journal that helped guide every Adrastai Warrior, also wrote about it on its pages. The creature represented the nine virtues that the Adrastai lived by. The tail, Strength; its head, Wisdom. The right wing represented Hope, and the left Nobility. The four feet are Courage, Determination, Justice, and Mercy, and the dragon in its entirety stood for Light, as in "Light over Darkness".

I found myself reading this passage repeatedly during the last eight weeks. Every time I opened my manual to look for some sort of guidance, or to read up on some sort of history, that description of what The Order stood for was all that the manual would show me. It was a bit odd to me that The Order, which had filled almost every minute of my day as we prepared to fight Sukanar, the darkest sorcerer that had ever lived, now seemingly had forgotten me. I had not heard or seen any of my new friends from this world hidden in the shadows. I only had the musings of my three sisters to entertain and annoy me.

Our victory that day, in this very yard, when my new friends and I over-powered the evil sorcerer and his twisted army, was a feat to be proud of, and yet I found myself conflicted. I always longed for adventure, but watching loved ones die was not what I had anticipated. When I would imagine battles in my head, I would crush my opponents, but it wasn't real; I was just pretending. This was real not a story in a book you could put down, or video game that you could turn off whenever things were too hard to handle. Death was final. Suffering was real, pain was excruciating, and, in my case, inevitable. Apparently, I am an injury magnet.

My brief exciting life now seemed to sink back into the ordinary. Well, as ordinary as one's life can be with enchanted creatures running amuck and three younger sisters constantly annoying you. I understood that the magical event that my family endured no one would ever believe, but it was real; it happened. I felt isolated knowing that this new life had to remain secret to protect all of those involved. It's funny how you can go through life, not really *seeing* the wonder around you. I never knew an entire world existed in the shadows and was chock-full of really cool creatures that I always pretended were alive. I suppose now that I have had the chance to reflect upon the idea, all of the magical and enchanted creatures we know of had to be real. How else would so many different people across the world have them in century-old fairytales?

The fact that we battled in my backyard because Sukanar wanted to end my family's bloodline made me think that I was an important part of The Order. But that was it. I haven't heard a thing from The Order since, I haven't been called to defend anything else or warned of any danger. One day I was defeating Evil on the back of dragon and I was the one who defeated him…okay, my sister Sofia may have distracted him a little with her siren song, but still, not one of my new friends has contacted me. Weird. I felt slightly abandoned. *Was this how it worked? Was I to be 'on call' or 'standby' forever?*

At least the backyard was lush again thanks to the tiny fairies and pudgy gnomes. These mystic creatures spent the first few days after the battle working their magic with the flora, erasing the evil that scorched the landscape. Wherever one of the dark creatures had lay slain, the earth had been singed and charred as their evil essence oozed into the ground. It was a war-zone. Whimsical fairies worked feverishly to restore Nature's beauty in the flowers and trees, mending them with their mythical powers; the gnomes worked their magic in the dirt.

Fairies were beautiful creatures with butterfly-like wings exhibiting tiny humanoid features. The little butterflies I thought I had seen in my life have actually been these tiny beings caring for the beauty in Nature and nourishing the flowers with their magic. If ever captured, they changed their fairy features to look like the butterflies that we are familiar with, so not to be discovered. It makes me cringe to think of all of the pinned creatures on display in my science classroom and museums.

The gnomes were awful. They were small, ugly creatures exhibiting very odd, and rather gross, behavior. My face is twisted with disgust as I recall them. They didn't resemble the garden gnomes that covered my Grandma's lawn at all--not even close. These foul creatures looked more like body-building toads on steroids, but without abdominal muscles. Their limbs rippled with muscles, supposedly from carrying their overweight bellies around. When they moved it was gorilla-like, pushing off with their knuckles from the ground. Gnomes stood ten inches and their faces were always scrunched up in a scowling manner whenever they looked at me.

Picture a giant picking up a toad with extra-large muscles, stretching it out far, and then squashing it down between his palms like a amphibian accordion, creating rotund blobs with warts and muscles. Yep, that pretty much covers what they look like, and it is not pretty. It sort of makes me think of my sister Sofia and how she looks at my parents when she doesn't get her way.

Gnomes were not whimsical and kind-like fairies, but rather ornery in nature. They were constantly casting looks of disgust towards people and muttering under their breath how foul the human race was, poisoning the land with pollution and litter. It was crazy to watch them work. The fairies flitted around and looked magical and whimsical bringing a smile to my face, but the gnomes made me raise one eyebrow and glance sideways. They pounded the earth with their knuckles to break it up, swung their stout bodies forward using their grotesque feet like bulldozers, pushing piles of dirt into mounds and then they leaned forward and with large gaping mouths that they used like shovels to engulf the infected dirt. After each mouthful they swirled their portly mid-section, as if they were maneuvering an invisible hula-hoop; after the washing machine-type action, the 'cleaned' dirt either came back up and was spat back onto the ground, or exited out the other end...gack.

This was my reality now. Funny little creatures surrounded me at all times, but I wasn't at all surprised anymore by such wonders. I was forever changed by my place in The Order: Adrastai, noble dragon rider. I never said I was comfortable with my place, not yet anyway, but I did accept it and all of the new complexity it added to my life. Besides, a life of watching fairies flying around like butterflies can't be all that bad.

I remember closing my eyes and listening to the earth heal as I

lay, recovering from my own injuries sustained in the battle. The tree limbs creaking and the smell of green wood and sap filling the air as they regenerated. It reminded me of the dimension door, an enchanted portal that my elven guardian, Brochara, conjured up as it grew before me and the vines intertwined. This magical means of travel was meant to take me back home, but I ended up at Sukanar's lair. It was inside that dismal volcano that I learned of his plot to destroy my bloodline, the very same bloodline that killed his father. I did not start this war, but now it was my turn to fight it.

My three younger sisters had the best time trying to sneak up to catch a closer look at the enchanted creatures. One playful sprite landed on top of Mariella's head, causing the three year old to sneeze and sprout purple posies from her super-power curls. It was nice to hear their giggles again, a welcomed change from the screams of horror and tears caused by the previous terror. They all steered clear of the grotesque gnomes, not because they were not friendly sorts, but as a general rule one should stay away from vomiting, defecating beings.

Maybe the reason I felt abandoned was because I had too much time on my hands without anything to do but heal. Maybe I was overthinking all of it. I have to admit, I really have enjoyed my sisters for the most part. The three year-old, Mariella, was practically glued to my side demanding to hear stories about The Enchanted Realm, Brochara and Elia's home in the cave, and of course, flying with Khai.

Before all of this, all I wanted to do was get away from my house and the girls. I had always felt like I was drowning in their Sea-of-Pink lives and that no one understood me, but when their lives were in danger I could not fathom ever living without them. Tears stung my eyes as I recalled Mom running off of the deck to save me from Sukanar's deadly bolts. And then...when that one death bolt shot passed me and hit Mom's chest, as I watched her limp body slump to the ground, something inside of me shattered. That little selfish child, who demanded his world be only all about himself, who despised everything that took attention off of him and onto the girls, just shattered. Suddenly it became clear to me that it wasn't just about me. My family *was* my world and at that moment I realized that I would do die for them. I guess I should be grateful for the evil that made me feel true love.

These past few months, instead of ignoring my sisters, I've looked at them with new eyes; eyes that were eager to know them, to really appreciate each of them as a person, not just an ankle-bitter annoying sister. The oldest Sofia, who we discovered was a Siren when Sukanar had overwhelmed me and all of the other warriors during the battle, really was a funny person. It was her role that day, her beautiful song, that had entranced Sukanar long enough for me to him. We did together, stronger as a family than an individual. I had never noticed Sofia to be anything more than a drama queen before, but she was really funny. Laughter booms out from every corner of the room when she is entertaining the younger two sisters and she is very quick witted. Her comebacks catch me off guard and stumped for a rebuttal. I can usually think of something witting about ten minutes after she leaves, proud of getting the last word. We have also had a couple deep conversations about what happened; that night changed something inside her too.

I felt an overwhelming desire to want to keep the girls safe to let them live their childhood to the fullest and I loved watching them grow. I wanted to be a part of their happiness and include them in mine. We spent many nights over the last few months together as a family enjoying each other and having bonfires, beach days, picnics, and even just playing in the sprinkler. It has been the best summer yet. Funny what a couple of months and many deaths can do for one's appreciation of their family and life itself can do.

Since my leg had healed, I also have spent more time with Skye and our friends. I felt good to be a child again, instead of fighting for our lives. We enjoyed long days at the shore, hanging out with kids from our school and the occasional vacationers. Rumors started to circulate that Skye and I were dating. Yuck! She's more like family to me than my sisters were at this time. It was really hard when the two of us were around other kids to keep our mouths shut about The Order. Both of us would start to talk about one of our adventures and catching ourselves; we would have to censor the story, making up some ridiculous lie about playing in the woods behind my house, then we would laugh at our own inside jokes. I suppose we probably do look like a couple to people, our relationship is easy; we just get each other.

One evening our friends and we were hanging out in the dunes when Trey, the resident jerk, decided to crash our fun. It was civil at first, but I could tell that none of my friends were thrilled that he was there. But trying to see the good in everyone, I attempted to make the best of it. I guess some people or personalities just do not mesh with mine, because Trey mistook my niceties for sarcasm and decided to pick me up and run down to the water's edge; it was freezing that day and he was about to toss me in. Through my blurred vision from being jostled around and trying to escape, I noticed Skye's eyes flash silver and Trey's feet became entangled in seaweed that appeared out of nowhere. He tripped and we both fell to the sand, but at least I didn't end up in the frigid water. Embarrassed, Trey said he didn't want to hang with us losers anyway and left. Skye was smiling and instantly, instantly I knew that she had used her Piscisene talents to conjure up the tangle of seaweed.

A loud crackling noise over my left shoulder abruptly ended my daydream. I almost fell out of the hammock turning to see what made the sound. With my new knowledge of the world hidden in the shadows, I found myself more jumping with noises that I cannot readily explain; I have experienced too many horrors creeping out of the darkness. I was relieved to find a soccer ball rolling out of the bushes followed by a head of super-power curls sprouting yellow posies this time. I felt my heart smile.

Most of the broken trees were repaired by the woodland sprites; all was green again, except for one spot. The very place, just a few short months ago, where Nature had pulled my Mom's limp body into the earth after Sukanar had killed her. That spot was black as midnight on a starless evening. It was strange how everything else that was charred renewed, but not that area. It bothered me too. Every time I glanced at it, I shuddered and cringed, remembering the feeling of hatred and despair that grew inside of me as I watched the fear in Mom's face before Sukanar hit her in the chest with one of his bolts of death. Its charred black earth seemed to mock me with the memory of what happened that night. I even tried to plant grass seed and then wild flowers, but nothing was able to grow. Dad had placed a birdbath in the center of it to cover the blackness, but never once had a bird landed there. I guess when something that evil happens, there isn't any way of coming back from it.

I turned my gaze to the sky searching for my bald-eagle friend, Boreas, just as I had every day for the past two months. The empty feeling inside me sighed, remembering how his life was also taken by Sukanar's evil. My carefree day suddenly turned dismal, as I recalled how the black smoke dragon's tail pierced his snow-white breast in the black sky, and I watched him plummet to the ground. Suddenly movement caught my attention out of the corner of my eye. I jerked my head to see what it was when something darted behind a nearby tree.

My senses tingled. I grabbed the cool steel hilt of Servo, my elven enchanted sword. I cautiously maneuvered toward the tree line. Immediately, a large root rippled out of the ground, like a murderous arm of the mythical Kraken. My stomach lurched, and fear raced through me as I anticipated the foul stench of trolls when they are within striking distance. Another root ripped from the earth behind me, tripping me, and I stumbled forward. My hands met with the hard earth before my face crashed into the yard, knocking Servo from my grip.

Disarmed in my own backyard by a tree was not very noble of me, so I quickly spun around to grab it, when my actions were thwarted. A thin blade playfully swatted my backside accompanied by laughter that I have heard before.

Relieved, I aborted my defense tactics and collapsed onto the ground as dirt filled my nostrils. I would recognize that laugh anywhere, "Fin! How are you, my friend?" I managed to ask, with my face pinned to ground by the force of his pirate boot donned paw.

"You have much to learn, Sire," he replied, as he used my head as a springboard for his aerial somersault dismount. In typical chivalrous mink performance, he landed firmly on two feet, removed his tiny plumed hat, and genuflected down on one knee. "Felis Ignarus Nescio, ready for duty, Sir Giovani."

Bringing myself to seating position, I was about to protest his entrance, as well as all of his pomp and circumstance, when the mere mention of Fin's full name initiated bubbles of laughter. They were quickly diminished with a stern look from the knightly mink bowed before me, with his paw poised on his sword, ready to defend his honor. Remembering our first encounter, I silenced my urge to laugh at the ignorant cat translation, stood up, and dusted myself off.

"It has been too long since our last meeting friend." I said while smiling warmly. "How are the fledglings?"

Fin had climbed up my arm and perched on my shoulder, just as Boreas had in the past, and a tear pooled in Fin's eyes as he spoke fondly of our fallen friend's children. "They all have Boreas's spirit, and definitely more energy than I." Fin managed a giggle, as he wiped his eyes.

"Will they become part of the Order, like their Father?" I still didn't know much about the Order, after all, I just found out I was a part of it a little over two months ago; I longed to learn more.

As we talked, my eyes drifted back to charred patch of land where the empty birdbath stood, and I was taken by surprise to find a crow, as black as tar, perched on its edge. I had to look twice to convince my mind that there actually was a bird there when my eyes locked stares with the creature's black eyes. A creepy feeling came over me as this crow looked right at me, starring me down. I tried to dismiss the bird's odd behavior and returned my focus towards Fin.

Fin was chattering about baby eagles' eating habits when curiosity took over my brain. I glanced back over Fin's shoulder to find that menacing bird was still staring at me. Purposely, I tried to snake my path through the backyard as we walked, but the Crow's dead, black eyes remained steadily fixed on me. For a brief moment, I would swear on my mother's life, that I saw the eyes glow green. My chest grew warm, my emblem began to ache, and I felt dizzy.

I must have passed out briefly, because the next thing I knew, the birth-bath water was swirling red as the beheaded carcass of the mesmerizing crow fell into it. The splash of the water had brought me out of my trance. Fin was mounted on the edge of the bath, with his blade extended over his shoulder in an executioner's stance. He nonchalantly removed a cloth from his satchel, wiped his weapon clean, and returned it to the sheath. Fin then knelt beside the watery grave, made the sign of the cross across his breastplate, and breathed a silent prayer to the fallen crow.

The sound of a whip cracking in the air behind us caused me to reel around on my heels, ready to defend my family once again. I found Brochara running towards us from the direction of the forest, as a magical porthole quickly closed behind him. He lumbered past me, his tiny green-tinted frame limping from a wound delivered at the battle less than two months earlier. Brochara was visibly shaken and confused as he ran straight by me to inspect the birdbath. He was standing on the very tip of his toes, looking child-like, trying to pull himself up to peer into the blood-stained water.

The familiar feeling that the world was turning around me, while I stood in the middle, watching it all happen, came over me again. Something occurred that demanded the presence of my friends, whom I had not seen or heard from in a couple months. I wasn't sure how a crow could cause so much turmoil. I rubbed my eyes to try to clear the confusion, when a Vision entered my Sight: A picture of a hand reaching up from the depths of an ominous sea filled the backs of eyelids. Confused and unstable, I tripped again and fell to the ground with a force that knocked the wind out of me.

Immediately, and with another whip cracking sound, Elia appeared by my side, cooing in my ear, "Sshh. There, there, Giovani. You are safe now. What was it that scared you so? What did you See?" The scent of her soft breath wafted to nose, smelling of the earth just after a rain, and calming my nerves.

I wasn't sure what my Vision had shown me. I wanted to try and see it again, so I pushed my fists back into my eyes and rubbed again. Nothing but bright colors squiggled across my lids. My mind tried to remember the dark picture first shown to me (something about a hand and water), but it faded too fast.

This was the first Sight I had seen in over two months. I had tried to use my Adrastai gift many times, but it just wasn't working. I would push my fists into my eyes and rub, but only the bright colors would pop and swirl on the back of my closed eyelids; no Vision came to me. I guess I may have even been a little relieved that there was not anything to See.

As a matter of fact, none of my Adrastai gifts were working

since my battle with Sukanar. Maybe his evil bolts of energy that he had tried to kill me with drained my gift. Perhaps the slugleach creature that Elia had used to rid my leg of the evil rot caused by Sukanar's magic could have taken much more than the poison that grew up my leg and sucked all of my special bloodline as well. *Could that be possible? Could I lose this new life that I grew to accept and love just as fast it I had learned about it? Why hadn't any of my new family come to see me, they said they were always there?*

Right after the battle, I could barely walk or move around, due to my injuries. I welcomed the funny performances of my three sisters, The Froufrou Crew, singing at the top of their lungs and dancing around. But, a twelve year boy can only take so much glitter and feathers before slowly going insane. I tried to read for a distraction, but I kept recalling my own adventures with Khai, Brochara, Fin and Boreas; and the book's undertakings paled in comparison.

I spent countless hours in the last two months, just staring at my manual, waiting for it to draw for me, as it had when it sketched me standing on the back of my dragon friend, Khai. But…nothing. The enchanted quill just tapped the parchment, seemingly annoyed with me, while clouds of ink swirled along the paper, slowly settling like dust, and never forming an image. Then the invisible, quilled-illustrator just disappeared into thin air, leaving a tiny puff of smoke behind and no new sketches or bits of wisdom.

I hadn't felt my birthmark either, except for just now. I even tried to squeeze it once, in hopes of gaining super strength and launching my sister, Sofia, into the ocean waves, but still weak, I dropped her on the beach instead. Of course, in typical fashion, more pink drama ensued as a result. She screamed, as if a sharp sword impaled her leg, but she had only landed on top of hermit crab. I quickly shoved her aside to check on the crustacean, when I heard a faint, "Thank You," from inside the shell. I smiled knowing the crab was all right.

I still managed to get in trouble, because I checked on the tiny creature (whom I thought was crushed under the sheer force of my sister's rump landing on it) and I didn't check a member of the FrouFrou Crew first! Talking to certain creatures seemed to be my only gift that didn't disappear. Or maybe it was just an awareness I had gained that all creatures matter. I am not positive if the crab actually spoke to me, or if I heard in my mind, but that is what I would say if I were a crab and someone saved my life.

Then my thoughts shifted to the crow. I never heard the dead creature utter any sounds let alone talk to me before Fin lobbed its head off. Brochara, Elia, and Fin were there. Even through the chaos, I was smiling at the sight of my friends in my backyard again. Brochara was conducting some strange ritual over the black talons sticking out the water, while Fin cautiously stood guard. Fin's head was constantly turning, in a quick-like fashion, like he was anticipating an attack.

Suddenly, I became keenly aware of a tingling sensation, as if all of the cells in my body were colliding into each other at high speeds. It started at my feet and slowly grew up my legs to my chest and arms. Confused, I turned my hand over to inspect the back of it, and was shocked to see my skin rippling, as if my blood was boiling fiercely underneath it. The ground seemed to give away underneath me, and it felt as if I was hovering in the air just above it. I was certain my body was about to explode.

My ears filled with the noise of bubbling thick liquid, and my body began to twitch. I was losing control over my own movements, and suddenly, my body began spinning like a top in mid-air. The world around me became nothing but blurred colors as I circled uncontrollably. Then, just as fast as I started spinning, I stopped with a jerk and my body continued to hover. The thick liquid continued to bubble in my ears, drowning out all other noises, but this time it was accompanied by immense, involuntary, muscular convulsions. The only body part I had control over was my eyes, and I was scanning them, frantically, looking for some sort of assistance or assurance that I was not dying.

Elia was in a trance, standing beside me, with her eyes closed and chanting in her elven language. Her tiny arms and over-sized hands were rhythmically waving over me, in what I could only interpret as a counter spell to save my life.

My eyes glanced back to the bird-bath grave, to find Fin swatting at something I could not see. Brochara was also chanting and waving his arms over his tiny frame. *What was attacking me? Why was this happening again? Where was family? Were they safe?*

A loud, thunderous boom cleared my ears of the muddling sounds, as both, Brochara and Elia, clapped their hands over their head. Simultaneously, my cells no longer collided against each other, but rather sloshed, like water in a pail. Then in a strange, unexplainable way, my body poured onto the ground into a human puddle, with the sound of a water balloon splattering onto a sidewalk. Blades of grass were sticking up through my liquid form and I could feel the grains of sand mixing into what used to be my flesh. The darkness creeped in from the corners of my sight, and just before all went black; wide-open mouthed gnomes surrounded me. Then, the quiet overtook me.

Chapter 2

Illustrated by
Nicole Roth

2

ADRASTAI COUNCIL

I awoke to the familiar smell of the earth, just after a rainstorm, and I instantly knew that I was inside Brochara and Elia's home. Feeling safe without opening my eyes, I nestled my head deeper into the elven-made pillow stuffed with rose petals and lavender. The moss bedding I laid on was fit to burst with milkweed seeds and feathers. A smile grew across my face as I thought of Elia's tiny elf-frame flitting about and tending to her miniature home.

As I lay there, I remembered how this place used to be my cave hangout, before I learned about by my Adrastai placement in The Order. Before any of this new knowledge of another world, hidden in the shadows, this place was just a cave. I spent most of my childhood here fighting imaginary battles and dreaming of fantastic adventures. It was usually just Boreas, my eagle friend, and I hanging out here together. That was when I thought he was just an eagle, unaware that he was part of The Order's elite flying army sent to protect me. I found myself frowning, suddenly watching his death play repeatedly in my mind.

I quickly opened my eyes to stop the horrific replay going on in my brain and spied movement across the room in the shadows. I was excited to sit up and chat with my friends whom I hadn't seen in over a month, but oddly, I still didn't have any control over my body. My attempt to sit caused a reaction through my frame that I can only compare to the gelatinous ripple caused by poking a Jell-O-molded cake. What used to be my body was now waves of involuntary jelly rippling like a thick liquid under my skin, and the sensation made my stomach lurch. The only part of my body I had control over were my eyes, again, and they caught the silhouette of the rabbit-sized Brochara handing something off to a scurrying shadow that darted out the mouth of the cave.

Trying to call out to him, I managed to let out a gurgled noise from the pit of my stomach and Brochara's attention turned to me. He ambled over to my bedside and slowly passed his hands over my undulating frame, all the while, giggling like my three-year-old sister. He always found pleasure in my misfortune. Slowly, the convulsions eased and I felt calmer.

The familiar sound of a whip cracking in the air rang through my ears, and Elia appeared by the bedside. Immediately, her posture became aggressive as she began circling Brochara, growling and snarling in the same manner, they had the first time I saw them. They appeared to be fighting over me once again, shouting in their elven language with their faces twisted in anger. Brochara backed away, as if to motion that Elia won the battle. "I was simply helping, Hag!" he whispered loud enough for us to hear.

Elia quickly shot him a disapproving look, and then she returned her sweet gaze back to me, "Acheyla Giovani, welcome back."

Scorned, Brochara copycatted Elia from in front of the fire, mimicking her voice, "Acheyla Giovani…" He was wrinkling up his nose and shaking his oversized head like a bobble-headed toy, in a manner that reminded me of my almost eight-year-old sister, Sofia, when she copied everything I would say just to annoy me.

"DIN!" Elia shouted as she made a quick arm gesture in the direction of the mocking Brochara. A magical patch, which looked like a piece of bark from a tree, appeared directly over his mouth to stop his childlike behavior. His hands struggled to peel it off as he shot her a horrible look of disgust.

The sight of him struggling, struck me as funny and I felt the laughter bubbling up inside of me. Uncontrollable, jiggling waves took over my gelatinous frame again, and Brochara forgot about his mouth patch and doubled over with laughter pointing in my direction. He was like 700 years old or something like that and he always acted as if he was three.

Elia clapped her hands over her head and immediately all movement in the room, except for hers, abruptly stopped just as it had on the ship, when I found out about Skye's place in The Order. Brochara and I were frozen with only our eyes able to move under Elia's elven spell. "Children!" she shouted. "You both are acting like children! Knock it off!" and with that said, she unclasped her hands and my body rippling commenced. Brochara's patch disappeared and, defeated, he slumped down in the chair next to the fire. With her eleven-husband in timeout, Elia turned her focus to me and repeated the same methodical movement of her hands passing them over my body calming the waves.

"There, there, my love" she cooed in my ear. "It will all be over shortly." Her breath smelled like moss and dirt and made it me smile.

Then she shoved her disproportionately over-sized hands into her smock apron that covered her stout belly. She was rummaging around her pockets looking for something. The sight of my elven friends still brought a smile to my face. They were no bigger than rabbits, and their green-tinted skin seemed to glow in the light of the fire. They were rather round bodied creatures, but their arms and legs were lanky and just didn't seem to match the rest of their frame. Their heads were large with scraggly comb-over hairs sprouting in all different directions.

Elia's large caring eyes grew bigger as her fingers apparently found what she was looking for. She giggled a little looking at me and said, "They tickle." *They tickle? What was she talking about?*

Then I saw them. Fear filled me as I watch a number of large, hairy tarantulas slowly climb up the back of her hand and wriggle, in their creepy way, up her arm. Waves of panic erupted throughout my body, knowing that I could not get away, and the jiggling started all over again. I cannot describe the horrific sound that grew out of my throat, because I have never heard anything like it before in my life.

"That's it, my dear," Elia giggled. "Just keep that mouth as wide open as you can! One wouldn't want one of these beauties to miss their mark. No, indeed not, that would be very problematic." She continued as she wiped her hands on her apron.

Keep my mouth open? What was she talking about? I wondered, but before I could protest or even attempt to close my mouth, the largest arachnid of them all leapt off her shoulder, like a diver off a platform, and landed squarely over my mouth! I could feel its prickly hairs on my lips and my eyes were staring directly at the enormous, sharp fangs poised over my brow.

I was no longer able to emit any sound, because just as quick as the hairy beast landed on my face; its spinnerets began to work. Enchanted under Elia's spell, the tarantula began spewing its silk into my mouth. I felt like hot, stringy material stretching through what used to be my body. Elven magic held my mouth open as a creature that has freaked me out my entire life, stood on my face!

"Spider silk is the strongest material you know. I wish we would have thought of this a couple hundred years ago, when we had shove trees into mouths; imagine trying to keep still for that one." She said, rather flippantly, as she nudged my arm.

The spider tired, or exhausted its silken supply and, nonchalantly, it crawled off my face. I felt myself sigh, which I was unable to feel before, so Elia's efforts must have been working, and just when I thought I could relax, another creepy crawly landed in the same spot. I closed my eyes and surrendered to the fact that this may take a while, and I was too afraid to stare at the fangs all day.

The amazing spider silk was strengthening my bones and building back my muscle. I could feel its web structures weaving throughout my body, and after what must have been seven terrifying encounters, I began to feel the sensation of wiggling my toes. Then I could bend my knees and the rest of my body sensations quickly returned, and just in time for me to nervously flick off the last hairy spider crawling across my forehead! Gack!

"Elia!" I managed to grunt out of disgust. "WHY would you do that…that horrible thing?" My voice had returned and was now crackling, with a hint of little girl. "I HATE spiders! They totally creep me out!"

I was continuing my heebeejeebee dance when she replied, "I bet you appreciate their beauty now. Five minutes ago, you could have been a dish on someone's creepy holiday table and now you can move without rippling, and this is the thanks I get?"

I suddenly felt a tad ashamed for my reaction, and a little grateful for the spider's gift and for my magical friend, Elia. I reached out for a hug from my little protector. It dawned on me that Brochara wasn't rolling in laughter on the floor during all of my misfortune in his usual mocking manner. Glancing around the room, I found him stuck to the side of the cave with a huge tarantula cocoon over his body. Only his head was visible and the bark-patch was back in place over his mouth. He rolled his eyes at me, glanced back towards Elia, bowing his head in defeat. Elia clapped her hands once again over her head and the silken threads untangled, as Brochara fell to the floor. This time Elia and I were laughing at him as he straightened out his clothes and walked over to the table.

It was wonderful to feel their arms around my neck, hugging me, as I knelt before the fire. "I have missed both of you so much." I said while enjoying the warmth of their embraces. "Is this how it will be? Will we not see each other for months at a time? I sort of, you know, got used to you being around all the time and then nothing...you were gone." I could feel my own sadness and hurt in my words. I did feel abandoned by my new friends, and even a bit angry thinking that I helped them accomplish what they needed, by defeating Sukanar, and when that was finished, I wasn't needed anymore.

"You are always needed, Sir Giovani" Elia's voice cooed inside my head. I was starring right at her and her mouth remained closed. I exhaled with relief, comforted that I still had my Adrastai gift of telecommunication. "We were never far, the protective enchantment from the battle remained around your house for several weeks after the battle. We knew you were safe to heal so we could help the families of our fallen brethren."

After hearing Elia's last words echo in my head, I felt completely ashamed. I had been sulking for weeks, pitying myself for not having my exciting new family around to cheer me up or make my life more interesting than The Froufrou Crew, and they were consoling the families of those who died during the battle. *How could I be so selfish? What was wrong with me?*

"More training, you require more training." Brochara was pulling chairs around the table as he barked out his response. He was always an elf of very few comforting words but never at a loss for many sarcastic and gruff words.

24

I was afraid that he was disappointed in the way I was acting, or thinking, and he was trying to busy himself, so not to show me his emotions on his face. I was too ashamed to look him in the eye anyway.

Just then, Brochara and Elia appeared to glow with a soft green light. I had never seen them do that before and wondered what purpose the glowing served. Their abilities continually amazed me. Brochara was right; I did need more training. I dropped my gaze to the floor reflecting on my thought, when I realized that my new friends were not actually glowing; my orb was.

My face lit up with excitement and I glanced around to see if either, Elia or Brochara was aware of my orb's change. Orbs were magical crystals that held the power to deem a chosen soul pure, before it ever entered a child's body at birth. Each Adrastai born, had an orb that was linked to them by magic. They held magical powers that only Elves, Dragons, and Adrastai could detect. They were enchanted tools for Adrastai warriors with the ability to sense danger and worn its keeper. Mine had warned me in the past by glowing red, but I had never seen it glow green. The blue and green ribbons of color have always swirled around on the inside, but never glowed as my manual did.

Noises of commotion echoed from outside the cave, tearing my attention off my green-glowing orb. There were sounds of whips cracking, heavy objects landing on the ground, and crashes of lightning that sent shivers down my spine. I quizzically glanced to each of my elven protectors for answers, fearing that we may be under attack. Many voices and roars came from outside the cave, but my friends were grinning from ear-to-ear.

"Let the Adrastai Council begin." Brochara exclaimed as he straightened out his homemade clothes, licked his hand and slicked his few squiggly hairs down on his ears, and then stood as tall as he could, as he grabbed Elia's hand before walking to the entrance of the cave.

Adrastai Council? I thought to myself.

"Yes, my friend, Adrastai Council. Now get out here and greet me properly!" commanded Khai's voice inside my head.

I had not moved that fast in weeks. Oh how I had missed my dragon friend, Khai. I was oblivious to the commotion surrounding us and just bounded over to his majestic form, as my dragon reared up onto his hind legs and unfolded his leathery wings. His brilliant greenish blue scales reflected iridescent in the setting sun. Such a powerful creature and yet he nuzzled my shoulder with his snout, as gentle as a puppy looking for affection. I threw my arms around his neck, only able to grasp the front of his chest, due to his massive size.

"Where have you been my friend, I have miss…" I stammered to say, but he words fell silent as I glanced around and finally became aware of our surroundings. A bustling commotion of wonderment was commencing all about. Magical creatures greeted each other like long lost friends, while hundreds of people, dragons, elves and other beings wandered in my woods behind my house.

All types of creatures were setting up tents, starting campfires, and playing instruments preparing for this council. It was an overwhelming and joyous sight. A tent city grew out in every direction and as far as the eye could see. The sounds of lightning cracking continued as more elves magically appeared around us, accompanied by slight earthquake-like rumblings every once and a while.

I was more than slightly confused because I was just inside my cave, which was also Brochara and Elia's home. It had always been located in the woods behind my house. Nevertheless, as I glanced around, I found myself standing in the meadow of the Enchanted Valley. The majestic mountains stood like Centurions guarding this magical place. I glanced back at the cave entrance, and found a tent. I just shook my head and giggled at the wondrous magical world that engulfed me.

The entire meadow was bustling with creatures setting up camp, for what seemed to be, for more than one day. The magical tents were all different, reflecting the countries and communities that they represented. Some were adorned with beautiful colors that swirled and depicted landscapes of different regions, and some were plain, but all felt warm and inviting. There were more elaborate canvas structures where colors swirled and popped on the outside walls, and some more humble. Glancing at the tent a few feet away from where we were standing, I noticed that the bottom edge mimicked the grass where it stood; the enchanted meadow flower mural that was painted on the side of it, moved in the breeze. I turned around in wonderment. The differences in tent styles enriched the entire experience, embracing so many differences all of which were equally beautiful.

There was a soft greenish blue light emanating from every tent that cast a soft glow over the valley. I started to look at individuals and noticed that there were many different Adrastai warriors walking around, and each of their orbs were glowing the same as mine. I looked to Khai in amazement. "Wow." was all I could manage to communicate.

"Pretty astonishing, isn't it?" he answered, but truly, I was at a loss for words. It looked like there was an entire tent city sprawled out before us, and up in the sky…dragons. I wondered if they were partners to other Riders. I had never met any other Dragon Riders, but I knew there was a fleet of them. Excitement bubble inside of me as I thought of being part of these honored knights of the sky.

It was evening now and the sun was almost hidden behind the mountains. I had to squint to see, but high in the sky, the dragon silhouettes performed amazing aerial displays. Khai took off with a start, to join the gathering. I couldn't count the moving shadows fast enough to get an accurate account of how many dragons were up there. They were so high up in the clouds, that they almost could be mistaken for large birds. I laughed to myself thinking about all of the things in life that I thought were one thing, now with my new knowledge of this World in the Shadows, could be explained away as another. The flying white fluffy allergens were tiny doctors, blinking fireflies were used as a Morris Code like system or communication, and fairies could disguise themselves as butterflies; and now highflying birds could have dragons this whole time.

I must have been fixated on the surreal happenings in the sky and walking at the same time without realizing it, because I managed to get tangled in someone's tent rope and I fell into the side of it. The canvas shelter collapsed around me with all of its contents scattering about. When I fought me way out the tangled mess, a circle of Adrastai warriors were standing around staring down at me with surprise and bewilderment on their faces.

Feeling my face grow hot with embarrassment, I quickly ambled to my feet, brushed myself off, and clumsily tried to set the tent back up. A tiny elf to my left just shook his head, waved his arm over his head, and commanded the structure back in place all the while looking at me, annoyed.

I tried hard not to make eye contact with anyone as I bowed and gave my apologies to the elven owner, but as I turned quickly to make my departure, I slammed squarely into a girl who was standing behind me. She landed hard on the ground and rolled a few times. Horrified, I ran over to help her up and make sure she was all right. When she turned her face towards me, her white blonde hair seemed to float magically in the breeze, like a curtain on a grand stage opening to reveal the most beautiful sky blue eyes and snow white skin, I had ever seen. I reached my hand out to help her up, when I was hit from the side with the force of a bull, knocking me to the ground.

A very upset and very large, muscular man stood there, glaring at me with the same sky blue eyes as the girl I knocked down. Obviously upset over my carelessness, his face was red with anger, his chest was heaving, he clenched his fists tighter, and the muscles along his jaw tensed. His hair was the same color as the tiny-framed beauty that was now brushing herself off. His powerful frame started to charge toward me again, when I heard the voice of angel shout, "Mateo! No!"

The charging mass of muscle stopped dead in tracks at the sound of her voice. "But-ah Luca, he-ah hurt you!" he replied gruffly and with a very strange accent.

"I am not hurt, just startled that is all. Thank you, but I am fine." Her voice was silken and soft. She walked towards me and extended her hand to help me up, "Please excuse my brother, he is very protective of me." She cooed with a sweet accent I have never heard before. She proceeded to pluck me off the ground, with a surprisingly strong grip. "Are you alright?" She asked.

"Uh, I, yeah, I mean sure…yeah I'm okay, but how are you? I am sorry for all of that." I managed to stutter my words out. I was taken by her eyes, pulled into their beauty and at a loss for words. "My name is…"

"GIOVANI!" screamed a voice from the crowd. "Giovani!" the same voice laughed out another time and then I saw Skye running towards me, full force, and she threw her arms around me. We were laughing and embracing for the first time since the battle in my yard. I picked her up and swung her around, just as I did to Mariella, the three-year-old. I had not seen anyone I was close to except for my family the entire summer, and today everyone was here. I felt complete again, but then I caught a glimpse of the girl's silky blonde hair from the back, walking away on the arm of the muscular bull of a man. I never introduced myself, but somehow I knew I would have another chance.

Skye and I walked back, arm in arm, to Brochara and Elia's tent. It was a meager dwelling, plain grey in color and only around four feet tall, four feet wide, and six feet long. However, I loved how when we walked through the opening, the inside was exactly like the inside of their cave back home in my woods. Perplexed and astonished, I chuckled to myself in disbelief, pondering how all of the space could fit inside this tiny tent.

Skye sensed my confusion and exclaimed, "You didn't expect them to leave home without anything, did you? Come on now Giovani, I know you are new at this, but you have to know that possessing Elven magic definitely has its perks!"

She plopped down in the chair next to the fire and I found another just like it against the wall. The fire was inviting, even on this warm summer evening. There was something comforting in the crackling sounds as the fire burned and the dance of the flames along the logs was entrancing. My mind was quickly flooded with family nights, spent snuggled up by our fire, listening to Mom reading us stories. Life was good.

I guess I had never thought of the possibilities of having magic could present, then again, that was part of the reason The Order was formed, to stop the greedy humans who threatened to use magic to gain supremacy. It unnerved me to think of the power Brochara and Elia possessed, and I could understand how someone would want to harness that power for himself or herself. That thought scared me. I know that, secretly, I thought it would be really cool to have those abilities.

The smell of Elia's stew wafted over to my nose from the hearth, inviting me back from my memory trip. I found that she had the table set for dinner. It was beautiful. A soft, bright green moss served as a tablecloth. Tiny clumps of mushrooms grew out of the center, serving as places for warm dishes. Teeny white flowers sprouted up here and there for a beautiful touch of whimsy, and all of it bathed in the soft glow of the fire.

Nine place settings included different sized plates and acorn cups. I quickly conducted a headcount of friends in my mind: Khai, Brochara, Elia, Fin, Skye, Aluvanim (Skye's elven-guide); and I, but only came up with seven. The largest place setting at the end nearest the tent entrance must have been meant for Khai, but I did not figure out how his large body would fit inside with us. *I really need to stop doubting or questioning what is impossible or normal.* I was still two settings shy of nine. *Who else was coming and why were we here?*

I loved the idea that even though my elven family had magical powers, they did not use electrical devices. Candlelight and fire were used for light, along with the occasional glowing metal, like my sword, Servo, or glowing crystals, like my orb. They didn't agree with the human fascination with electronics, claiming that it made us slowly lose our ability to harness our intuitive powers or use our senses, because we relied on devices too much to do it for us. I am pretty certain they bugged my cell phone, quite literally, because when I tried to use it in their presence, little bugs crawled all over it, preventing me.

Elia must have telecommunicated to everyone that dinner was served, because all at once, my friends filed in through the door with Khai entering last. I stood there with my mouth wide open as the enchanted tent stretched and grew to accommodate our very large friend. I even peeked out of the entrance to see if we knocked down any nearby dwellings, but the tent remained as small as it was when I first saw it. Smiling and shaking my head, amazed, yet again, I sat down next to Khai and patted his shoulder.

Apparently, this Adrastai Council event was a big deal. Khai told me that it only takes place every twenty-five years, because it is too dangerous to have so many of us warriors together in one place at the same time for fear of attack from evil powers. The odds of almost destroying our entire force would be very appealing to one of our enemies.

Elia concentrated all of her efforts on making this gathering something very special, like a holiday, adding so much love into every little detail. She stood at the head of the table and glanced at the two empty seats briefly and with the seven of us gathered around the table, the magical feast began. Like a conductor in front of her orchestra, Elia waved her hand over her head, and her well thought out and choreographed production started.

First, a small dim chandelier appeared at the top of the tent, which now was over twenty feet tall to accommodate my dragon friend, Khai. The crystals seemed to dance and twirl around each other. There was something very familiar and soothing about the lights. I thought for a moment, how odd it was that Elia decided now was the time to add electric. It just did not make sense to me, but just as my thought finished, the chandelier burst apart, like a firework display, and nine tiny lights trickled down from the ceiling.

"Protogenoi." I whispered.

"Proto-what?" asked Skye as she stared with the same look of wonder and amazement that I had. I turned my gaze to see the soft glow that their lights cast on her face and for the first time I saw her differently. Skye's skin looked soft and her expression was gentle, not at all the way she looked when wielding a sword.

"Protogenoi," I answered. "You know, from the Enchanted Realm. They danced through the halls in the Court of the High Mages, don't you remember?"

Skye's focus turned towards me with bewilderment in her eyes, "You were in The Tower?"

"Yes, weren't you?" I asked, now feeling a little isolated.

"No. That is the most *sacred* place in The Order. That is where the High Mages reside, you know, the founders of The Order. They are only the most important players in our fight against evil. I don't even think Aluvanim has been there, and she is over 600 years old. They are under the powerful security measures available." Skye spoke to me with one eyebrow raised, as if questioning my sanity. "Maybe you are mistaken, why would you have been inside The Tower being so new to The Order?." She added.

"Maybe," I replied, confused, "but, I have seen these magical sprites before, when I met Asëa, Laurina, and St. John. It was Laurina, who told me what they were when I entered The Court of Order. I was sent there when my soul was deemed Pure enough to enter The Enchanted Realm. That was scary; I didn't know that there was a possibility I could die if they didn't deem me pure enough." I started to ramble, as I sometimes do, when Skye interrupted me.

"Wait, what?" now Skye's full attention was on me, "You *met* the High Mages? What…when…We spent the summer together and you didn't think that was important enough to talk about? I…I…" Skye was stumbling for words and I could tell that she did not seem to believe me.

An enchanted string quartet, comprise of two violins, a viola, and a cello, suddenly appeared next to the fire and began to play lively music, abruptly ending our conversation. Our heads turned to see the entertainment, when I noticed the instruments were playing without any musicians. "This conversation is not over." Skye added as we watched in wonder.

The bows were magically gliding across the instruments all by themselves and the music was beautiful. Further adding to the entertainment, the instruments possessed personalities of their own.

Every once and awhile, one of the violins would try to change the song and the other instruments would pause, bows pitched mid-air waiting for the rogue player to conform, before continuing the piece. I was thankful for their playing, because Skye and my conversation was getting weird.

The enchanted Protogenoi were busy painting intricate golden vines across the ceiling, as their illuminated bodies flitted around the tent. The gilded artwork demonstrated an animated life cycle of tiny flowers that started as buds, bloomed, and then dropped their golden petals softly, falling like snow, but disappearing before hitting the tabletop. Their production was mesmerizing.

As these amazing sprites of light danced through the air, all eyes stared in wonder. An occasional Protogenoi would land on the head of guest, producing a tiny luminescent firework display around them, while another would dance in between the outstretched fingers of a curious invitee. It was entrancing, and I hardly noticed the leaves on Elia's table that started to turn fall colored and rustled on the tabletop with every subtle movement, but never floated into our cups or plates. The warmth and crackle of the fire was inviting and I glanced around at all of my friends around the table, who all had the same soft smile on their faces. Truly magical. I really enjoyed my new world, and my mind traveled to thoughts of The FrouFrou Crew; they would love to be here.

Elia stood at the end of the table, made a grand gesture with the grace of a ballerina, and her cauldron of yummy goodness, gently lifted from the hearth and glided through the air. We all watched in anticipation, as the enchanted ladle, plunged into the pot, scooped up a thick, gravy vegetable stew, and dished it into large upside mushroom-cap bowls. Cheers erupted from everyone around the table, followed by laughter and chatter.

The smell was amazing and, instantly, my mouth began to water. Aluvanim gestured in the same grand manner, waving her arm over her head, and baskets of hot rolls appeared in front of us. The smell of the fresh baked bread was intoxicating, and just when I thought this evening was perfect; mulled cider filled our enchanted mugs. The spices wafted to my nose and a warm feeling filled my soul. I immediately took a large gulp of the apple and cinnamon goodness, and when I returned the acorn mug to the table, it magically refilled. The thought of never ending goodness filled my mind and I sunk back into my chair, content for the rest of the evening.

We all had been gorging ourselves for over a half an hour, when I was jolted from my happy place. The ground beneath us began to rumble and shake. My thoughts immediately jumped to trolls, who yanked me into the earth, in this very place, two months ago. Khai had to heal me with one of his golden tears from the wounds I sustained.

Worried that our holiday celebration was about to be sabotaged, I grabbed Servo and sprung to me feet. Suddenly, the ground in front of the fireplace began to collapse and, piece by piece, fell into the earth. I stood firm, ready to defend us all, when a hole four feet in diameter gave away in the dirt floor, kicking up a dust cloud that blocked out the light of the fire. Everything went dark.

I stood poised, ready for an attack, with Servo raised over my head. The room was silent and filled with dust. I could hear my friends shuffling nervously behind me. The soft glow of the fire began to show as the dust started to settle and, out of the depths of the earth, a gloved hand grabbed solid ground. Out of the hole crawled a muddy figure wearing an oversized helmet and holding some sort of weapon.

Just as I raised Servo higher over my head to strike, the intruder threw off the helmet and announced "Hey there, Explorer!" I dropped my sword and grabbed my heart, thankful that I had not injured my favorite relative, who was holding some sort of umbrella-meets-eight-shovels looking contraption. "This gadget is amazing!"

She proclaimed!

"Aunt Evangeline!" I shouted as I leapt over to her side, threw my arms around her neck, and hugged her tight. A cloud of dust exploded from her clothing, and the Protogenoi quickly darted through the dirty haze and, magically, the dust turned into cherry blossom petals that fell around us.

The last time I saw her, she had just come back from an expedition in Tibet, where she was working for The Order. Aunt E is a Scholar for The Order. She helps to teach and train young Adrastai in the ways and methods we use against evil beings. She had been preparing me for my Dragon Rider role, all of my life, without me ever being aware of it. All of my birthday gifts, thus far, and her tales of adventure have all been part of her lesson plan for my eventual place in The Order. When I stop to think about our relationship, she always encouraged me to use my imagination and role-play battles with dark forces, which have trained me to be a warrior.

"I am so glad to see you! How have you been? Where…" but before I could finish my question, the earth shook again.

Strange sounds were traveling up from the tunnel in the earth; sounds that made me nervous, and judging by the expressions that were on my friends' faces, they were uncomfortable too. Something was following Aunt E and we were all about to find out what it was. Telepathically, I commanded Servo to me, and quickly it flew back into my hands. I pushed Aunt E behind me and shielded her with my body. Slowly, a large, dark, hooded figure with yellow, slit-eyes glided into sight in front of the fire, emerging from the bottom of the earth and immediately, darkness filled the cave.

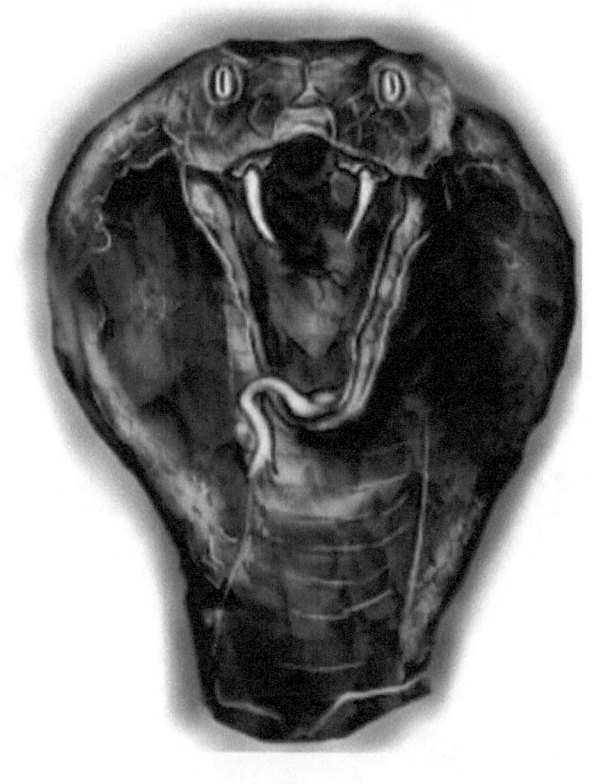

Chapter 3
Illustrated by
Maya Sischo

3

UNWELCOME GUEST

Gasps filled the cave, as the hooded figure's entire body slithered out of the tunnel and into the room. Its' form blocked all of the light from the fireplace and before any of us could react, "Everyone, this is Nak!" Aunt Evangeline said moving her arm with a grand gesture, as if presenting a game show prize.

Nak tossed his head back and the hood of his cloak flipped off, revealing yet another hood of a different kind that slowly grew larger before all of our eyes. There, poised before the fire, was an oversized king cobra, whose hood was three times larger than Aunt Evangeline's frame. His body was swaying ever so slightly from side-to-side, almost entrancing. I shook my head to clear my brain, and I quickly glanced around to assess everyone's reaction to this giant predator in the room to find every mouth gaped wide open in amazement.

This creature was intimidating. Each scale on the serpent's body looked larger than my hand. I could see powerful muscles rippling under its skin. The enormous cobra threw its head back in an eerie snake stretch, when two fangs, each as large as my sword, glistened in the light of the fire. It recovered and focused the yellow, slit-eyes directly at me. A chill shot through me, as if this gaze climbed right into my soul.

"I am very pleassssed to meet your acquaintancssesss," hissed the over-sized cobra, Nak. "It hassss been a very long and dry journey; may I trouble you for a ssssip of water?"

The snake's manner of speech freaked me out. Everything about snakes freaked me out; freaky devil serpent. I found myself still shivering, trying to forget the creepy chill his stare gave me.

Elia quickly moved her hand and a glass full of spiced mulled cider flew over to Aunt E's hand and another full of water hovered in front of the large serpent. The snake reacted to her quick movement, by spreading his hood, his gaze locked onto her small frame, and he hissed with a sound that caused more chills. Elia cowered and Brochara quickly jumped in front of his mate to protect her.

"How rude of me," Elia cooed, "certainly. Welcome to our home." I watched Elia grab, a nervous Brochara's arm with one hand, her apron with the other, and she managed a curtsey; all the while keeping her eye on the snake.

Glancing around the cave, I noticed that everyone seemed a little tense. Eyes were glancing sideways, but always returning to the spot where Nak stood in front of the fire. "Forgive me," he hissed as he deflated his hood, "it was rather frigid in the tunnel and your fire issss sssso inviting. Am I blocking your warmth?"

Nak's question was answered by a bunch of muttering sounds from all of us, with none of us capable of making any complete sentences in our nervous state. Sudden movement from a satchel wrapped around, what I guessed would be the serpent's shoulders, caught my eye. It caught Nak's eye too, because with a flick of his tail, the satchel opened, a tiny mouse jumped from it and darted towards the entrance, screeching a teeny voiced "HELP ME!" before Nak's lightning-fast jaws clamped down on it and swallowed the rodent whole, before it could finish its plea.

Everyone's mouth, with the exception of Khai, gaped wide open at the murderous sight. "Exssscusssse me, many apologiessss my friendssss, but like I ssssaid, it wassss a long journey." Nak exclaimed as he and Khai nodded to each other with a silent understanding.

We all managed to let out a slightly wry, nervous laugh and Aunt Evangeline's, seemingly nonchalant, behavior around this snake, calmed my nerves a little. "Have we missed any of the festivities?" Aunt E asked, taking off her muddy attire and warming her hands by the fire as if there wasn't any over-sized, scary killer in the room. Then she brushed off more dirt and the Protogenoi hurried to her side to turn it into petals before it hit the floor. The flickering sprites twirled and danced around both Aunt E and Nak, until they were sparkling clean. Nak and Aunt E thanked the sprites before they darted back to the ceiling leaving a wondrous light design in their wake.

"No," Brochara managed to bark out of the silence with a nervous crackle in his voice, "Adrastai have been arriving all night."

"Outstanding! This mole-shovel invention from HQ really did the job, hey Nak?" Aunt Evangeline asked as she threw an elbow into Nak's side. Twirling the odd device she was carrying, Aunt E inspected the handle, pushed a button, and the contraption folded in on itself, repeatedly, until it was the size of a quarter. "This contraption and your speed; what a way to travel!" Aunt E flipped the coin-sized shovel thing into the air, caught it, and shoved it into her pocket. I was a little unnerved by her chumminess with the serpent.

Aunt Evangeline knelt down next to Elia and gave one of her

heart-warming hugs, Brochara skipped over to get his, too. Fin sprang from his chair; double front flipped in mid-air and was about the land on Aunt Evangeline's arm, when I saw Nak make a quick move in Fin's direction.

I sprang into action. Leaping from my feet, my hands tightly gripped around the cool steel of Servo's hilt; my body landed in between the cobra, Nak, and Fin's certain death. My feet firmly planted on the earth. Servo was perfectly parallel to the ground, poised ready to slice off the hissing head of the slithering serpent. His fangs exposed and inches above my face, both points with drops of venom pooled at the tip. My chest was heaving with anxiety, "NO!" I screamed protecting my friend.

The serpent snickered at my attempt to defend Fin. I stood, un-waivered, eye-to-venom-glistening-tips of his fangs. Each droplet of venom slowly receded back into his daggers and he relaxed his posture. Nak's hood deflated before my eyes, but his frame continued to tower over two feet above me. He tilted his head down to find my eyes, which were full of purpose. His bronze orbs locked onto mine and it felt like he studied my soul, silently. The large cobra slightly swayed from side to side; as he searched for something in my eyes, the rhythm was entrancing.

I held my ground with Servo still poise in defense, but the weight of my sword suddenly became evident in my hands. A weird sensation was growing over me. My body was becoming exhausted, drained of energy as I tried to remain strong. My sword felt like a ton of bricks in my grasp, and unable to hold on, Servo fell from my grip. My body remained in a defensive stance as I waited to hear the clanging sound of steel crashing onto rock, but it never came. I pulled my gaze off Nak's bronze stare to find Servo poised, firmly, in the grip of his tail. "I ssssee your concsssernssss Evangeline" Nak hissed, as he leaned in even closer, studying me.

Disarmed, my exhausted body stumbled backwards, almost limp, and my bottom landed squarely on the chair. Nak tossed Servo to the ground next to me and the sound echoed throughout the tent. I began to feel my face getting hot with embarrassment and shame. I had intended to defend Fin, but was so easily disarmed.

Confusion and doubt filed my brain. I glanced around the room looking for some sort of support or guidance from my new family, but no one was making eye contact with me. No one was making eye contact period. Everyone seemed to be busying him or herself, deliberately trying to avoid a discussion with each other and me. There was a very uncomfortably tense vibe in the room. Then I recalled Nak's words to Aunt E, stinging my confidence, 'I see your concern'; anger grew inside of me. *What did he mean her concern? Did Aunt E not believe in me? Why was this serpent here with us anyway?*

A loud explosion shook the tent! Immediately, Servo jumped to my hands and everyone ran outside. I was on edge. My confidence was wavering, and I feared I would not be ready for a fight.

To my surprise, the sky was raining beautiful colors of flickering light. Protogenoi of all different colors, were putting on an aerial display of illumination. Everyone gathered outside and watched the beauty-taking place against the dark sky accompanied by 'oohs and aahs' from the crowd. It reminded of warm summer nights on the fourth of July, spend with my family at the shore watching firework displays for Independence Day.

There was laughter and cheers as flowers exploded and soft petals floated down from the sky. I glanced out over the valley and the soft glow seemed to dance and shimmer around the crowd. Then my eyes found her. The small girl, whom I clumsily plowed into and knocked to the ground earlier today. Her eyes were fixated on the sky, her skin radiated in the glow of the lights, and her hair appeared to change color reflecting the different hues from above. She was stunning. I felt my anger and shame melt away.

I pushed my fists into my eyes and rubbed, thinking I was watching an angel and did not want it to disappear when I re-open my eyes. The colors on the back of my eyelids twirled and popped and then it happened…another Vision. A dark serpent-like creature wound its body around my small-framed acquaintance, crushed the life out of her and her limp body lay still amongst its coils.

I quickly opened my eyes just in time to see Nak's huge form rise up behind the angelic beauty. "NO!!!" I screamed and it echoed off of the surrounding mountains!

All heads ripped from their gazes from the sky and found me, the only one screaming like a lunatic, during the beautiful light show. I quickly started over towards the girl to thwart Nak's efforts, pushing creatures out of my way, when her bull-of-a-brother stepped in my path. He stood there, with his arms crossed at his chest, just glaring at me. I tried to maneuver around him, but the crowd was too dense and he was a mountain of a man.

"Look, your sister is in trouble!" I stammered out, while still trying to see around him. His head whipped around to see as well, when the flaxen haired beauty threw her arms around Nak's neck and lovingly nuzzled his chest.

Nak's bronze colored eyes found me, confused, and with my mouth wide open in wonderment. "But, I saw it…my Sight, it…I…" I tried to relay what I just witnessed in my mind, but I realized that the more I talked, the more I must have looked deranged and needed to flee from there as soon as possible.

Why was this happening again, now? After the entire summer of wishing for something magical to happen and nothing had, and now, I was thrust back into a life of everything but normal. In addition, I have made a fool out myself in front of countless members of The Order, on two separate occasions, in less than three hours.

Embarrassed, I hung my head and started back to the tent. A small hand slipped its way into mine and a saw Elia's large caring eyes glancing up at me. We did not need to talk; she just knew I needed a friend. We ducked into the tent together.

Back inside the comforts of her home, I found myself able to smile again, remembering the feast that awaited us. Mockingly, the string quartet played the death march softly in the background. Elia gave them a sharp look and they quickly changed their tune to something more lively. I rolled my eyes at the enchanted instruments sarcasm, and asked Elia if I could help her with any of the preparations. She pointed to two bowls on her prep table near the fire. "Grab one and you can help prepare the dessert." She answered.

I went to investigate my choices. One bowl was full of nuts and berries, while the other contained plump, juicy, wriggling white grubs. My stomach flipped at the sight of the larvae and I grimaced at the thought of eating them. I opted for the first bowl, plunked down next to the fire, and began shelling the almonds.

Elia did not force any conversation; she instinctively knew that I needed space to calm myself. My mind wandered to home. I wondered what the girls might be doing right now or if Mom was making dinner, just like Elia. I missed my Mom terribly right then. She just always knows what to say to comfort me or a simply gave me hug and everything felt right in the world.

"Elia?" I asked. "I had a Vision out there." I continued, but without lifting my head avoiding eye contact.

My dear elven friend had already sensed my nervous hesitation and was kneeling beside me, with her tiny hand on my leg. I felt a bit more at ease, but her magical touch had always had that effect on me.

"I figured that there was something behind your blood-curdling scream during the Protogenoi Dance. Do you want to tell me about it dear; shall I call Brochara too?" Elia cooed.

Embarrassment returned, and Elia patted my thigh as if to say 'there, there, it will all be alright.' "Maybe I could just tell you first?" I questioned lifting my eyes to meet hers.

"Of course darling, just a moment," Elia said as she rose from her knee. Her tiny frame ambled over to the hearth; she wiped her hands on her apron, picked a pinch of something from her pocket, and tossed it onto the fire. The flames jumped higher and brighter, but only briefly before settling and revealing copper teapot above the flames. Elia carefully retrieved the steaming kettle, shook one tiny hip in my direction, whispering "Elea i'dolen." and a small table appeared before me along with a very comfortable looking Elia-sized chair.

Elia gently placed the teapot on the table and the vapors smelled of peaches and roses. She poured each of us a steaming hot cup of tea, sat back into chair, smoothed her apron, and then looked solely into my eyes and nodded. Elia was giving me all of her attention and I felt honored. "I have sensed your disdain my dear, start at the beginning, Sire."

"I'm confused. I have not had any of my Adrastai gifts work for me all summer. I must have opened my manual dozens of times, waiting for it to create for me and all I ever experienced was an annoyed quill and ink dust settling on a blank page. AND, I wasn't visited by any of my new friends…" I dropped my head, because I did not want to offend Elia by revealing my abandonment. "

Elia lifted my chin and just stared into my eyes while tears pooled in her own. "My dear Giovani, my heart aches that you felt abandoned. Please know that we have protected you since the day your soul graced this earth. We will never dessert you. The elven enchantment placed on your home was a strong one. Made up from many different elves it was, which increased the magical powers. You will learn, in time. Giovani, Dragon Rider, is a very important part of The Order. I am sorry we did not communicate clearly, there is always room for improvement, and I shall try to improve. Please continue my love." Her voice was soft, kind, and humble.

"Oh, Elia, I did not mean to make you feel bad. I am sorry if that is" I started to say, but Elia simply held her finger up to her lips and slowly shook head. I understood then, that she was not offended.

I continued, "All I seemed to do was rest, watch the gnomes and fairies, and giggle at my sisters attempts to catch them." Elia giggled and I smiled knowing I could make her laugh. "GNOMES! That's right! All of a sudden, a crow shows up…no wait, Fin showed up first. What happened that day? Why all of a sudden did Fin appear, after two months of being away, just as the creepy crow landed on the deserted birdbath? Wait a minute; Fin must have known something was coming and showed up to help me." I was finally able to start putting pieces of the story together on my own, and Elia was shaking her head in agreement, gesturing for me to continue.

"There was crow, Elia, and I think that it was there just for me." I paused for a moment, once I stopped being so selfish, the actions of my friends became clear to me. "Its' cold dead stare locked onto mine and I even tried to snake around my backyard trying to lose its gaze. I remember the creepy bird's eyes flashed green. The next thing I knew, Fin had chopped its head off, and Brochara and you appeared too!"

I was trying to slow my thoughts down, they were rushing at me so fast and filled with questions. "How did Fin jump from my shoulder and kill that bird without me aware of it? How did you know to show up? Then I lost control of my body…what was happening to me? There was thick liquid bubbling in my ears. I could only move my eyes. My body felt like it was going to explode!"

My eyes shifted from side to side as I journeyed back to that day in my mind. "I sloshed onto the ground, Elia. Sloshed! I could see grass sticking up through what used to be my body and felt pieces of dirt mixing with my flesh! Gnomes! Oh, there were gnomes surrounding my puddled form…with their mouths wide open." I fell silent and shuddered. "Why were gnomes around me, Elia? Please tell me that I did not get swallowed by a gnome."

"Swallowed and cleaned." she responded with a grin of pride across her lips as she smoothed her apron out across her lap. "Very efficient at ridding evil from tainted earth, they are. Very talented indeed, our friends the gnomes." Elia sat before me speaking so matter-of-factly about gnomes swallowing me, I shuddered as I wondered what end of the ornery creature I returned from.

"Wait, what? Cleaned?" I was starting to get very confused. "I don't understand."

"When Sukanar's bolt hit your thigh and he personally touched your forehead, he created a stain. Your body had encountered so much evil, that there was no way of getting rid of all of it. The slugleach was successful with most, but we knew it would only be a matter of time, before dark forces would track you. Dear, you do realize that dark forces will forever try to end you, right?" Elia was looking at me with concern in her eyes, and she every reason to do so. That thought never crossed my mind, but it did now. "That is part of being a warrior, and especially the Dragon Rider who destroyed Sukanar. Our battle was only the first of many, this is real; young Adrastai, not a weekend exercise."

Elia's words stung a little bit. I guess maybe I had not thought if it that way. I just leapt into this exiting role and did not think that it would never stop, like my father's intention to retire one day. I will always be chased by evil, until the day I die or until it catches me. *I am destined to be killed by evil.*

I sipped my tea and stared at the fire for a spell. I didn't normally drink tea, but I welcomed the soothing warm drink. "The crow; it was evil then?" I asked, softly.

"Yes, my dear. Crows are not the most loving of creatures. They like death. Their dark intentions make them the perfect pet for dark sorcerers. This particular one was well advanced in the dark arts." Elia stated.

"Wait, a bird can perform magic?" I questioned.

"Anyone or thing can perform magic. It takes practice, patience and sometimes just a wave of a sorcerer's hand." Elia waved her hand in a figure eight from the top of my head to my feet. I felt the sensation of energy enter my chest and tingle down my arms. "Wave your hand over the bowl you did not choose, and chant Onta Vasa" Elia spoke and pointed to the wriggly grub-filled bowl.

I gave her an amusing look and completed the requested task just to humor her. Light oozed out of my fingertips into the direction of the larvae. I was shocked to see the bowl turn into a toasted grub dish adorned with sugared flowers. "What? Am I a wizard?" I gasped. Amazement was written all over my face and excitement grew inside of me.

"Go on try, my dear; try it over there at the table." Elia cooed.

I moved so quickly that I almost knocked over my first creation. I raised my hands over my head and spoke the words "Onta Vasa" with confidence and pride. I completely expected white lightning to shoot from my fingers and rearrange the table or something, but my fingers sputtered, like and old car out of gas, and I slowly placed them in my pockets, defeated.

"You see my dear; a sorcerer can give as much or as little magic to other creature to aid them in their plight. Creatures of Light know how dangerous this practice can be. It also takes enormous amounts of energy to give away some of your power." Elia's voice seemed tired. I glanced back to her chair and noticed that she was slumped back, exhausted.

I rushed over to her side and poured her a hot cup of tea. "I am so sorry Elia, is there anything I can do to help you? We have a special feast that you have been preparing and you gave your energy to me to prove a point. I feel so selfish."

"You have much to learn, but that is why we are here. Please do not expect to understand a world that has managed to stay hidden from the world for over thousands of years in a mere two months. It takes training; this Council is the perfect place to start that. Do not worry about me, young Adrastai; I will be fine in a bit. Please sit and continue, you haven't told me about your Vision yet..." Elia's coloring was slowly returning.

I tried to sit and gather my thoughts, but I felt just awful about how Elia looked. She patted the back of my hand to assure me that she would be all right, and gestured, again, for me to continue.

"Okay, let me see; this council. I would love to learn more about this. There are so many different creatures walking around outside. I am amazed at the number of Adrastai in this place; it does seem like the perfect opportunity for an attack from Dark forces."

However, as the words fell from my mouth, I recalled Elia just telling me about a stain, my dark stain that allows evil to track me and I filled up with fear. "Oh Elia, I have to leave! I have to get out of here before evil tracks my stain! I cannot allow more Adrastai to die because of me!" I jumped from my chair and paced the room trying to formulate a plan.

"Child! Do you think that this is our first brush with evil?" Elia's voice was firm. She had never raised her voice with me, Brochara yes, but not me and she called me child. That always made me feel like my friends lacked confidence in me, or maybe it was me, who lacked the confidence. I sat back down and she continued.

"Many of the Adrastai outside have also been touched by evil, Giovani, and their guides have worked to cleanse them as well as possible. Everyone here is well aware of the possibility of an attack. This is not a picnic, but a training camp. We all have taken necessary precautions to enchant our travel paths and care for our warriors." Elia sat up a bit taller with that statement and she began to look like she was feeling better.

I sat back down and tried to compose myself, feeling a tad embarrassed about my automatic reaction. *I must try harder to remain calm. Okay, back to my Vision...*

"I bumped into a girl and knocked her down. Oh, she was beautiful," again my words trailed off as I thought of her. "But her man-bull of a brother hates me. She was in my Vision! Nak killed her! He curled his body around her and squeezed the life out her!"

I saw Elia shiver in disgust. "Are you sure it was Nak and Luca?" Elia asked.

"Hold on, how did you know her name? Is that it?" I paused, thinking about her white-blonde hair, "Luca? What a nice name." I could not believe how crazy this girl was making me. "Really, how did you know her name?"

"Giovani, we are always with you, protecting you. I felt your embarrassment from knocking over the tent and stepped outside to see if you required my help." Elia was slightly blushing. "She is very beautiful, and you are correct, and her twin brother is very strong. Can you be certain that it was Luca?" Elia asked again, with a look of confusion and concern on her face, probably because my Visions in the past have always come true.

"Certain? Maybe not certain. It was shadows that appeared to me, but it was a tiny frame in the coils of that cobra, and it looked very much like Luca's." My blood began to boil under my skin just thinking about Nak. "Why is here anyway? It doesn't seem like anyone else likes him?" I added with a disapproving look on my face.

"The Order has sent him with Evangeline. He has a role that we are just not aware of yet. You must trust in things you cannot always see, your gut feelings are intuitive, but he was sent here for a reason." Elia was now smoothing her apron out again and I felt better about her health returning.

"I had another Vision Elia, I just remembered. It was my first Vision, back at the house. There was a hand, reaching out of the depths of dark waters; does that mean anything to you?" I asked.

"Not at this moment, but you must trust your Visions; they are given to guide you." Elia replied, as she glanced back over her shoulder at the beautiful table she created for the feast. I could tell she wanted to get back to attending to the party, so to make my closing statement and walked towards the fire.

"Then I believe that my Visions are warning me to keep this Nak character always in sight. I don't trust him. I cannot trust anyone who tries to eat my friends. And my Vision? It was definitely a cobra, and he is the only one I know! There is something I cannot put my finger on about him, but he makes my skin crawl. I fear for my Aunt too!" Feeling confident in my decision, I turned towards Elia for her support and discovered Aunt Evangeline and Nak flanking her chair. My confidence shrank inside me as I tried to remain standing tall.

"The Protogenoi Dance was breathtaking." Nak commented, with very little emotion, as he looked straight at me.

Perfect choice of words, breathtaking. I am on to you. I raised my eyebrows as I turned away from them and walked back to the table. I decide snarky comments and sarcastic conversations may get my intentions across. "Funny, I didn't see you watching." However, before I could allow him the satisfaction to comment, I turned to Aunt E and asked, "Did you get to enjoy the light display Aunt E? I didn't see you anywhere."

"Oh, it was most enchanting. I watched from the back of a ridge-tail dragon named Sarah! Simply the best seat in the valley!" Aunt Evangeline twirled around with her hands over her head and sank, gleefully, into the chair. I found myself smiling at her love for life.

"Hello Everyone!" Skye's voice called from the tent opening. "I would like you all to meet someone."

We all turned to acknowledge her and her new friend, when my gazed locked onto a flaxen-haired bull-of-a-man at the entrance. "This is Mateo." Skye announced as she slapped me on the back of the shoulder and continued, "Mateo, this is, well, everyone." He smiled at everyone in the room until he looked at me and an audible growl escaped his lips.

"Tula, vasa ar' yulna en i'mereth!" Brochara shouted as he threw his hands up in the air with glee.

Cheers erupted from all of the guests as they hurried to the table. I felt left out, being the only person who did not understand elven phrases. I assumed it must have had something to do with sitting and eating by their reaction. *Great...a killer snake and an angry mountain of muscle that wants to kill me all around the table.* I slumped down in my chair and prepared for a long evening.

Chapter 4
Illustrated by
Edward C. Gallivan Jr.

4

VIOLATED

So far, this Adrastai Council thing had not gone well for me and we had only just arrived a few hours ago. Elia's orchestrated feast was delicious and entertaining, but I sat through the entire meal trying not to make contact with either Nak or Skye's new friend, Mateo.

I was so nervous and anxious that I did not take part in any of the conversations or speak to my dear friends. I secretly hoped that the two of them would leave so I could catch up with all of my friends and laugh the night away. It had been a very long time since I visited with any of them.

I must have been glaring at the man-child Mateo because Skye kicked my shin under the table-hard. "OUCH!" I screamed. "What the-?" I continued in protest, but the look on her face told me that she would do it again if I kept talking, so I slumped back down into my chair.

"I mustta get a-back to my a-sisttah. I needa to protect-ah her during the night." Mateo exclaimed. "My sincerest a-thank yous for a wonderful evening-nah." he continued, as he bowed to Elia and Brochara. "And-dah to you-ah, my dear," Mateo continued as he turned to Skye. "Thank-ah you-ah for including me-ah in this-ah special occasion. I had-ah wonderful time-ah," followed by another bow.

Blah! All I could do was roll my eyes, but he was being respectful to my friends...*maybe I should start over and shake his hand?* I decided to extend my hand; he grabbed mine, and took it in his own. My hand looked like an infant's hand in his enormous hoof. He immediately squeezed down, rolling my knuckles against each other and caused immense pain, all while glaring into my eyes and growling.

A little girl whimper escaped my lips and my body reacted to the pain by curling in the infant position while standing on one leg. Then he followed it up with a double pat on my left shoulder, which astounded me.

"What the heck? I was trying to say I was sorry for crashing into your sister," I said. "I would never knock someone down without a purpose." This time I was trying to squeeze his knuckles, to communicate to him that it was on. I have to admit, that I was not very successful in my efforts to be a tough guy--he was incredibly strong. However, I was successful in putting him on my 'Not A Friend' list. I had extended my hand in peace and he crushed it. Now I had a purpose not to trust Mateo, and to get Skye away from him. *What was with that weird accent anyway?*

"There are-ah no accidents," Mateo answered through gritted teeth, un-waivered by my attempt to hurt his hand.

"I will walk you back, Mateo. There issss much we need to dissscusss." Nak hissed as he slithered after the bull-of-a-man.

I waited long enough to watch them disappear in the crowd before I turned around and started ranting, "What is with that guy?

56

Geesch! It was an accident! Now, every time I see him, he wants to rip my head off! He must be, like, twenty years old and he is after me! And why is the slippery one following him?" I turned my gaze to Aunt E and continued, "And why are you concerned with me? I thought you thought I was 'Old enough to handle' all of this?" All of the eyes in the room were on me, watching my psychotic outburst.

Once the last sentence flew out of my mouth, I immediately regretted saying it. Aunt Evangeline's face was furrowed with apprehension, "Please sit, Giovani," she said. "We have much to talk about."

I apprehensively sat down at the table next to Aunt E with a feeling of dread in the pit of my stomach. For some reason, I thought that she was going to tell me that The Order had made a mistake; that I was not old enough to use the manual yet—her coming explanation as to why I was not able to make it work over the summer. Possibly, I was too unstable, always questioning myself--a risk to The Order. Maybe the snake was brought to kill me. It was not safe for me to live, knowing about The Order and not stable enough to be a part of it. How could my Aunt bring him? She has loved me all of my life and yet she brought the executioner to my side! My chest began to tighten, it was increasingly harder to breathe, and I wanted to be in my own bed, under the covers…safe.

A tiny green hand lay to rest on my right arm and Khai's warm snout nuzzled my left shoulder. "There there, Giovani, it will all be alright. We are here for to protect you, not take your life away." Elia cooed in my head.

"That snake wouldn't get within two feet of you before I would make a meal out of him!" Khai's voice echoed in my mind.

I glanced from side to side sharing a smile with both of my friends, knowing that they felt my distress and read my thoughts. "Thank you" I telecommunicated back. "Hey! I did it! I used one of my gifts again!" I silently shouted.

Elia, Khai, and Brochara all laughed aloud at my regained confidence, and everyone settled in around the table. Skye, Aluvanim, Fin, and Aunt E just shook their heads giggling, realizing that we were telecommunicating, and then everyone turned to Aunt Evangeline, as if she was about to conduct a meeting.

"This is going to be a very important weekend friends," Aunt E began. "We must also be on high alert, and pay close attention to our senses. Word of an attack has been whispered through the Protogenoi vine. Dark Forces are feverishly searching for our Adrastai Council camp. There is a leak, a traitor, in The Order."

Gasps filled the room. I nervously glanced around the table. Fin had already jumped to his feet with his sword drawn, ready to defeat anyone who was giving The Order's secrets away. The room began to buzz with everyone speaking out in detest at the same time.

"Silence!" Aunt E shouted. "We must remain calm. Only the ones in this tent know about the leak. We must keep it quiet as we search for the traitor. If the other Adrastai find out, it will turn everyone against each other and create hate. That is exactly what the dark forces want--to break The Order up. This is the perfect time to investigate with most of The Order in one place at the same time. We must be diligent and precise in our efforts to find the traitor, for we may not get another chance. The Mages are monitoring our every move and all telecommunications. They do not feel the information is leaking via telecommunications, but they are baffled as to how the news of this Council was leaked." I had never seen this expression on my Aunt's face before. She had anger in her eyes.

"The Mages?" Brochara barked. "Hmmm, I cannot remember a time when the three most powerful beings were personally involved." He had lowered his head and was wringing his hands together in his lap. The look of concern on his face made me uneasy. I know that all of this was new to me, but I could tell by everyone's reactions that this was a serious matter.

"We must remain calm. This is not the time to panic, but it is the time to hone our abilities." Aunt E continued. "We must discuss any odd behavior or senses we have experienced in the past few days."

I immediately lowered my head, trying not to make eye contact with anyone. Everyone had every reason to worry about me; I lacked the confidence in myself to be strong.

"Tell them, my dear, what you told me earlier." Elia's soft voice hushed the room.

Again, all eyes focused on me. I glanced up and found her large caring eyes staring at me, "What? About my visions?" I questioned.

"Visions?" Brochara barked, again. The tone of his voice made me jump. "You have had more than one vision? And you!" he turned his focus towards Elia and postured aggressively, "You knew, and did not tell me?" Brochara began to snarl and growl in Elia's direction.

"Enough!" Aunt E shouted as she slammed her fists down on the table and stood up, startling everyone. "This anger is not helping. Please sit down and let us find out what it is Giovani was shown." Aunt Evangeline turned towards me and continued, speaking softly "Giovani, please tell us your Visions."

I nervously recounted both of my visions to everyone. The vision about the hand reaching out from the depths did not seem to bother the group as much as the snakes form killing the small framed girl. More chatter erupted from every creature around the table and everyone shifted nervously in their seats.

"Why does everyone look like they saw a ghost?" I asked, but before anyone could answer, Nak slithered into the room and by my side.

"Did I misssss anything?" He asked.

"Actually, yes." Aunt Evangeline piped up. "Giovani was just revealing some very interesting Visions to us. Let me fill you in."

"What? NO!" I yelled. I quickly dropped my head and avoided eye contact with the snake. The last time we came face to face, I grew weak and lost control. I must remain strong, I told myself, and I really did not mean to say that aloud.

"No bother. I will do thissss mysssself." Nak hissed boldly, and before I could look up confused, his tail wrapped around the leg of my chair, pulled me away from the table, and turned my chair with me in it towards him. Nak quickly undulated his head down to my feet because my gaze was at the floor. I saw his large, bronze eyes and quickly shut mine.

"Get away from me!" I shouted. "You don't scare me!"

"Then be a man and look me in the eyessss." Hissed Nak.

"NO, you just want to make me weak again. I know your tricks. I won't do it! Why are you here anyway? Leave me alone!" I screamed with my eyes still clenched tight.

"You will look me in the eye. Yessss, you will," Nak's voice was calm and creepy sounding. Then he whispered in my ear, "Ssssoul I shall; shall I ssssee? Turn thane eyessss to me."

My eyes began to pry themselves open. I fought as hard as I could to shut them tighter, but the unseen force was too strong. Nak's large bronze orbs found mine as his body snaked under my bowed head. Some sort of entrancing force was pulling my body to sit up. I did not have any control over my motions, but my mind was still under my control. I was telling my body to close my eyes and curl up into a ball, but Nak's power was too strong.

"Please help me!" I telecommunicated to my friends.

"They can't help you. They wouldn't dare try. You will look me in the eyessss." Nak telecommunicated back.

I was seated upright and looking the serpent squarely in the eyes. My will was defeated at the sound of his voice in my head. I gave up all efforts to try to stop Nak's control over me. *How was he able to have such control over me?"*

"Lissssten to me, the lesssss you sssstruggle, the lessss it will hurt," his voice echoed inside my head.

"Hurt?" My eyebrows shot up as I questioned telepathically. "Are you going to eat me?" Though I felt in danger, throughout this entire encounter my birthmark never ached or burned.

"Abssssolutely Not!" Nak answered. "Issss that what you thought?" Nak began to laugh out loud and the sound echoed within the tent walls. "Sssssilly child, let'ssss begin. Do not try to fight me, I wish you no harm." He spoke inside my head.

A vision of my real family flashed in my mind and, suddenly, I calmed. It was as if they were right there beside me and I could endure anything--even the jaws of a mammoth snake.

"Nicssse job, young warrior." Nak hissed in my brain, "An advancsssed tactic. Well played."

I had no idea what he was hissing about. I didn't do anything, but then I felt it and heard the gasps from inside the tent. Something shot me. I was hit directly in the chest. My back slammed into the chair and my head snap backwards. The force was immense, but mysteriously, there was no pain--just a sensation of pressure.

"Remember, try to relaxsss." I heard Nak say but this time it wasn't echoing in my brain as it had earlier, but rather from somewhere deep inside my body. He sounded far away.

I answered with a grunt, but not without tensing and struggling to rid myself of the pressure sensation. I closed my eyes willing the entire event to be over.

Then, just as quickly as my assault started, an explosion of energy shot out from my chest and my body slumped forward. I opened my eyes slowly, but just in time to see Nak's deflated cobra carcass refilling with life. I jerked my head in disgust and confusion as the limp snakeskin began to plump back up.

I attempted to push myself out of the way, but all of my strength was gone. Immediately, pain seared through my skull, causing me to scream and writhe in agony. It felt as if someone plunged a sword through my skull. My body slid from the chair and I fell to the floor.

My fall was cushioned as I was cradled in Nak's coils, like a babe in his Mother's arms. I looked up into his glowing bronze eyes as the dark shadows creeped in from the corners of my eyes, and darkness overtook me.

I slowly came to, and just laid there with my eyes closed. The pain that I felt in my head before blacking out was so fresh in my mind that I did not want to move a muscle for fear of feeling that again.

"He issss awake," Nak's voice filled the silence.

With my eyes still closed, I heard the tiny footsteps of Elia rush to my side. *How did he know I was awake?* "There, there Giovani. I am here. Do not be afraid to open your eyes, my dear." The soft smell of moss filled my nose as she spoke.

"I don't want it to hurt." I whimpered.

"It won't hurt to open your eyessss," Nak announced from

across the room.

Slowly, I opened them. I found myself lying on the floor in front of the fire, exactly where my body had fallen on the re-inflating Nak. My new friends circled around me, and everyone had an expression on their face, as if I had sprouted a third eye.

"Why are you all staring at me?" I mumbled, afraid to move. The floor was suddenly cold against my body. "What happened?"

"You may want to sssstand back for thissss part." Nak hissed, and before anyone could move, immense, bright light filled the room and my body, involuntarily, lifted up off the cold ground. Slowly, I began to spin, methodically, in the air. After a few rotations, my body up righted itself and I was lowered to my feet.

I fell to my knees, still unable to hold up my own weight. Aunt Evangeline ran to my side, slipped my arm around her neck, and helped me to stand. Skye immediately did the same on the other side.

"WOW! That was amazing! How do you feel? What did it feel like? Tell me everything!" Skye was talking so fast that I could not process any of what she was saying fast enough.

"Give him some time dear," Aunt E told her as they gently placed me in a comfy chair in front of the fire.

"Okay, okay, but that was so cool!" Skye replied.

I slowly raised my head to find Skye's face, which looked like my sisters on Christmas morning before Mom and Dad gave us the 'go ahead' to grab our filled stockings. "What happened?" I asked.

"It was CRAZY!" Skye had jumped waving her arms like an animated storyteller. "Nak's body just went limp! His skin fell on the floor in a pile! Then there was this huge bright light and we could see him floating in the air, but it was a golden version of him, uh, made out of light! Then, then like a snake-freight train, he just slammed into your chest! Your body glowed, Dude! It was so cool! Light shot out of your eyes! What did it feel like?" Skye had to stop talking just to take a breath. "Then it was like, BAM!" she continued, but Aluvanim placed her hand on Skye's arm and helped calm her down.

"Please my dear, give him some time to recover." Aluvanim's voice was just as soft as Elia's, but instead of smelling like the earth after a rain, hers reminded me of fresh ocean air.

"What?" I managed to mumble, "Inside me?".

"Ssshhh, there, there. Drink this, my dear. You will feel better soon." Elia cooed as she handed me a familiar wooden cup full of awful smelling liquid with grubs and worms spilling over the edge. Before I could protest, her tiny hand grabbed my nose, promptly tipped my head back, and she poured the hot, chunky goo down my throat.

Laughter and groans filled the room. My body shivered, and I regained some of my strength. I sat up and shot Elia a disapproving look that was answered with a smug smile as she wiped her hands on her apron and walked back to the cauldron over the fire.

"I like your sssstyle," Nak laughed as he placed his tail on Elia's shoulder.

"And I like yours," Elia answered with a wink that made Brochara sit up and take notice. He shot a snarled look in Nak's direction that was answered by a wry smile from Nak.

"Hey there, Explorer," Cooed Aunt Evangeline so softly that it was almost a whisper. The sound of her familiar greeting brought a smile to my face. "How do feel?"

"Um, I'm not sure yet," I answered. "There was such an

incredible pain in my head back then that I am afraid to move," I whispered.

"Do not be afraid, you will not feel that pain again." Nak replied from across the room. "I am no longer insssside your body."

Grossed out and violated, I sat straight up to protest, when to my surprise the giant snake looked kinder than before. I found myself sighing, with adoration, when my eyes found his. It was like looking at one of my sisters for the first time after they were born. *That was weird.*

Chapter 5
Illustrated by
Maya Sischo

5

MISSING MAGE

Aunt Evangeline was sitting next to me and holding my hand, "Do you feel different now, Giovani?" she asked. Aunt E was looking at me as if she was inspecting me. She turned my arm over to see the other side, and then inspected the back of my neck. Her odd behavior was making me nervous.

"Different?" I questioned, pulling my hand from her grip and grabbing my head. "Why would I feel different?" I did feel differently, but I did not want to share that information. I was still wondering why my feelings of anger towards Nak had suddenly changed to feelings of love. It was creeping me out to think that this snake was inside me, but why would that make me love him?

I suddenly felt very vulnerable and violated. Keeping my head down the entire time, I swiveled in my chair to face the table. I could feel everyone staring at me, as if they were waiting for my head to explode or something. I glanced sideways towards Skye and gave her a looked that begged for help out of this uncomfortable situation.

"Would you like to get some fresh air?" Skye piped up as she winked at me. I was grateful for friendship.

"I think so," I answered. "We're going to go for a walk."

"Jusssst be careful not to touch any water," Nak hissed.

"Uh, okay. So swimming is out then." I answered sarcastically.

"Not unlesssss you want to explode," he replied rather matter-of-factly.

I was not sure if Nak was just joking around or if I really could explode, so I decided we should avoid the river. Our dragon friends, Khai and Jock, were resting outside near the tent. They both lifted their heads as we walked past, and Khai questioned, "How do feel Giovani?"

"Right, well, I guess I feel fine, but I would feel even better if you all stopped looking at me, like you are waiting for something to happen!" My chest was heaving slightly with anxiety.

"Dear friend, we are all just concerned for you. This is a very important event in Adrastai history, and we want to make sure you are ready." Khai spoke softly. "Please communicate to me if you feel differently in any way."

The concern in Khai's voice touched me and I began to feel bad about shutting everyone out. I had felt betrayed that no helped me when that serpent violated me, but I guess they were just following protocol. "I will my friend," I answered. "And thank you." Khai gave me a slow nod before he lay back down and continued his rest. I watched my friend settle in and smiled at the singed ground in front of his snout from his dragon snoring that I have come to know in the past.

Aluvanim, Skye's elven guide, was standing next to Jock as she raised her arm over her head. "You may want to back up," Skye said, as she shoved her body in front of mine--just in time, too. An isolated rainstorm formed over the top of her elven guide and Imoogi, and showered cool water down upon them. They both inhaled deeply and the storm stopped. "They need to stay hydrated." Skye continued as she grabbed my hand and we began our walk.

"What was all of that back there in the tent?" I asked, "Why did Nak do that and what did Khai mean about it being an important event in Adrastai history?"

"I really am not sure what it was, but like I said, Nak was inside of you." Skye answered, but I could tell that it made her uneasy. "You were…gone. I mean, it was crazy! Your body was there, but your eyes…they were blank Dude! Nothing but this crazy bright light filled your eyes. And Nak, well, that…" Skye's body shivered with disgust, "that was just the weirdest, creepiest thing I have ever witnessed!" Skye's voice wavered. "I thought he was killing you! I wanted to save you, but Aluvanim grabbed my hand, stopping me. I'm sorry." Skye's excited manner quickly changed to one of shame.

"Thank you for trying anyway." I placed my hand on her shoulder to let her know that I knew there wasn't anything she could have done, but I did appreciate her trying to help me. I really liked how easy it was being friends with Skye. "There was such a pain in my head. It didn't compare to the searing pain of Sukanar's finger on my forehead. This was one hundred times worse than that. What do suppose he was doing?" I asked.

"I imagine it had something to do with your Visions. That was the last thing we were talking about before it all happened," Skye answered.

"I had forgotten about that. So, this snake has the ability to enter people. I have never heard of a snake doing that," I said.

"Well, technically, the snake didn't enter your body. His light form did. I am telling you, it was the weirdest thing. His snakeskin just slide off him, landing limp on the floor in a pile of skin! Then, the bright light jumped into your chest. Your head slammed back and light shot from your eyes and mouth! Dude, it was crazy, like you went away, but your body was still there." Skye was looking uncomfortable retelling me what happened. "Did you hear or see anything while it was happening?"

I was quiet for minute. I was processing what Skye was telling me as I tried to recall what I could about how I felt during it all. "I remember seeing my family, and hearing his voice inside my head, but it sounded far away," I answered, "But then, that pain." I shuddered, remembering.

We both fell quiet and just walked for a spell. The air was cool and crisp. Soft light leaked from every tent door in the sprawling tent city, and one by one, they dimmed. "It looks like most of the Adrastai are calling it a night." Skye broke the silence. "We should get back. Tomorrow is going to be a very busy day. I am really excited to find out what this council is all about." Skye jumped up and down clapping her hands like my three-year-old sister, Mariella, did when she was excited.

With everything that I had just endured, I had completely forgotten why we were all here in the first place. A smile grew across my face as I remembered the feast and Protogenoi's performance. We decided we should get back quickly.

Skye and Aluvanim's tent was right next to ours. The fabric was fluid-looking and tiny sea creatures occasionally swam across the tapestry, woven within its magical threads. We said our goodnights and I heard a splash after Skye entered her tent. *Piscisenes must sleep in waterbeds*, I giggled to myself.

I wanted to look out across the tent city one last time before going in to bed for the night. The sight was unbelievable. The silhouette of the majestic mountains stood strong against the night sky. Dragons curled up outside tents, while puffs of smoke rose with each dragon snore. A smile stretched across my face knowing that every tent was filled with beings all gathered for a common cause: to uphold all that is good and pure in our world. I felt proud and humbled to be a part of it.

A quick movement out of the corner of my eye caught my attention. Before I was aware of this *World in the Shadows*, my protectors caused that movement, but they were all inside the tent. I moved closer to the sleeping Khai and I placed my hand on his shoulder as I peered out into the darkness. Maybe my eyes were just playing tricks on me; maybe I didn't see anything at all. After all, Skye told me that I did just shoot light from them, so maybe my eyes were readjusting from the whole snake incident. But then I saw it again. Suddenly out of the darkness, two small eyes flashed green from the tree nearby. I have seen eyes like those before.

Instantly, like watching a movie in fast rewind, my mind raced back to the day in my yard at the birdbath. I had seen those same eyes on the crow just before it lost its head. Nervously, I jumped, but landed right on top of Khai's tail, waking him and stumbling in the process. "Shhh," I whispered.

I tried to keep my eyes fixed on the same place where the green eyes flashed. Slowly, I leaned into him as I crept my way up to his snout. (Note to self: one should be extra careful when sliding against dragon scales the wrong way…Ouch!) I did not want to look suspicious to the bird.

I telecommunicated to Khai what I saw. I felt his ribcage expand as he inhaled deeply. Immediately, my eyesight changed. Khai and I are connected with a special bond that all Dragon Riders share with their dragon. When connected, we can become one. He can see through my eyes and I through his. Dragon's eyesight is much more sharp then ours. They can see a fish through twenty feet of water while flying hundreds of feet in the air. I was looking at the crow's infrared heat signature through the dark night. Khai's chest instantly became tight, and upon his exhale, a very fast, very thin stream of fire shot from his pursed lips. The charred crow fell to the ground with a thud as embers floated up on impact.

"Fetch the bird," Khai telecommunicated, "Quickly, bring it into the tent."

Inside the tent, the rest of the team already sprang into action. *How did they know? Neither Khai nor I had said anything.* I wondered. I plunked the dead crow onto the table. It landed with a thud as the charred feathers disintegrated into a little black cinder. Elia and Brochara immediately began chanting together, waving their arms over their head. Fin and Khai watched the sky as I waited.

"Nicssse work, Giovani." Nak hissed in my ear, startling me. "You are learning. Well done." The overgrown serpent nodded at me as he slide over by my side.

"Do you think it gave our position away?" Aunt Evangeline's voice came from the back corner of the tent.

"We shall ssssee." Nak answered. "It will only be a matter of minutessss if the messsssage went out."

"Minutes? Minutes for what, an attack? Shouldn't we wake the others? Most of the warriors are sleeping in their tents. An ambush now would certainly be disastrous." I felt my chest starting to tighten as I questioned our plan. "Are we just going to sit here and wait?" I was raising my voice now and anxiously waiting for my shoulder to ache.

"You musssst practicssse patiencssse," hissed the snake.

Patience had nothing to do with it. I could not sit around and wait for an attack to happen. I had friends out there, Skye, Jock, and Aluvanim were right next door. I had to get them up. "I'm getting

Skye." I made the motion to leave, but Nak's tail wrapped around my leg, preventing me.

"Sssstop!" he hissed loudly.

My body froze in mid-step at the door, and I found myself unable to speak. *Why was I this snake's puppet?* I was determined to find a way to resist other beings' control over me. Of this, I was certain. I was getting really tired of it and ready to fight back.

"Now issss not the time to take action. You can sssstart tomorrow," I heard Nak's voice.

Just then, a tremendous thunder-clap boomed just above the tent. Everyone hit the floor, except for my frozen body and Nak. My birthmark did not ache, nor did my orb glow. Nak released his invisible hold over me. I glanced around the room and noticed that the team was now frozen on the floor, like Nak had pressed some sort of pause button.

Maybe this was all happening because of him. Maybe he planned to destroy the Adrastai. Why didn't he want to warn my friends? He needed everyone sleeping, so he would have a better chance of defeating all of us without a struggle. Anger started to boil up inside of me; the same kind of anger I felt when Sukanar killed my mother.

I shot a disapproving look, full of rage and hatred, towards Nak. My jaw tightened and my fists clenched. I was about to dart across the room to defend my friends, when a tiny ball of light began pulsing at my feet. I suddenly remembered what Skye had told me about Nak's possession of my body and how I glowed. I stepped back quickly to avoid another invasion.

The pulsating light immediately grew into a bright column of Light. I had to shield my eyes from the intensity. Then, a wave of calmness passed over me, and a soft voice inside my head encouraged me to step into the column of light.

73

There wasn't any fear associated with this phenomenon, and I felt compelled to obey. As I stepped into the brightness, Nak slithered in from the other side. The body of light I had stepped into instantly washed my anger away. Peaceful was what I felt at that very moment.

Nak and I walked in the Light. There wasn't any odd forces or inertia on our bodies, no super-fast teleporting, or body squeezing of any sorts; just walking. I felt every one of my footfalls and I never blinked. It was as if I just stepped into the middle of the tent, yet I was no longer in The Enchanted Valley. We had transported to a peaceful place.

My feeling of anger returned as I looked at Nak outside of the column of Light. "What are you doing here?" I growled at him. "Why did you leave my friends defenseless on the floor?"

"Why did *you* leave your friendssss defenssssselesssss on the floor?" Nak hissed.

I looked at him sideways, thinking he was crazy for asking or maybe he was mocking me, like Sofia, my oldest sister.

"Welcome back young Adrastai," said a voice a smooth as velvet, "what a wonderful chance meeting." I knew instantly that we were in The Enchanted Realm.

I knelt down on one knee as the figure of St. John, one of the High Mages, glided towards me. His long white beard glistened in the sun. Suddenly, fear for the High Mage's life, took over me and I quickly jumped to my feet to protect him from Nak. To my surprise, St. John gently slipped his arms around the cobra, embracing him. "Hello dear friend, I am always happy to spend more time with you."

Huh? What just happened? I must have been standing there with my mouth wide open, because Nak looked back over, his shoulder and gave me a look, trying to get me snap out of it.

"Our friend issss sssslightly confusssssed, brother." Nak stated.

Brother? What? I don't understand any of this...

"Confused? Good. In my experience, out of confusion rises creativity and knowledge." St. John replied. "Just looked around at what we created during some very confusing times." St. John waved his arms gesturing to the entire Enchanted Realm, that the three High Mages created so be a safe haven for magical creatures during some terrifying times.

"Then we are on the right track," laughed Nak.

"I would recognize that laugh anywhere." stated another voice from behind me that sounded of music: soft, gentle and kind. "Dear Nak, to what do we owe this pleasure?" I turned find the beautiful Laurina, High Dragoness. Her scales were the color of gold, and her eyes the brightest blue. I genuflected again.

"My dear ssssissssster, you get lovelier every time we meet." Nak nuzzled her affectionately, as he slipped his tail under my arm and lifting me to stand up again. My feet came right off the ground and I flailed around a bit before he dropped me to stand on my feet again.

I was turning my head from side-to-side, waiting for Asëa, the third High Mage, to arrive and judging by the way Nak was looking around, so was he.

Asëa was a brilliant elf, with soft green hues that almost glowed under the sun. He was slightly smaller than Brochara, and I was comforted by his presence on my first visit to The Court of Order. I remember, very well, that when he spoke, the air filled with the scent of freshly cut grass in the summertime.

"Asëa is not here." Laurina cooed as she bowed her head, "He has gone to try and reason with Nãga."

"NO!" Nak hissed sharply and his form grew to stand over

twenty-feet tall. "She will kill him!" Nak's eye flashed red and he, immediately froze upright, almost face to face with Laurina.

"Nak, what is happening?" I asked with my voice full of fear. Then I quickly turned my head to Laurina begging for some answers with my eyes.

"Nak, come back." Laurina spoke calmly to his froze form. Nak's skin was making a creaking noise and I noticed it looked like it was giving way or loosening from his tall frozen frame. It was making me uncomfortable.

"Asëa is well aware of her power. He chose this journey and would not have left if he didn't think it was absolutely necessary."

My equilibrium was suddenly shaken. I became extremely dizzy and needed to sit down, before I fell down. Once firmly on the ground, I had the sensation of swimming through water at very high speeds. It was different from when Khai and I had to retrieve the ore from the bottom of the sea; this motion was more streamlined, and agile. An imaged flashed into my mind of large under caves, and then just as fast as it started; it stopped.

"Nak, did you enter this young Adrastai?" St. John's velvety voice questioned, as he stood over me.

"Yessss." Nak replied. His form was back to normal, but he was breathing very heavily. "He ssssaw, just now, I felt him." A tired looking Nak turned his face to me. "Didn't you? You were there."

"I…I'm not sure." I stammered. "There was a sensation of swimming…it felt so real. Dark caves. I saw dark cave, but they were under water; I think." I was confused and felt like they were holding back information that could help make sense of all this.

"I feel our brother, Asëa; he is still with us." Laurina spoke to all of us. "My dear brother, you are weak. Please, go rest and fill your stomach. We need your strength, and so does he." She directed her words toward Nak.

Nak slowing slithered off into the beautiful forest behind us. He never picked is head up off the ground, which was unusual, because he always glided with his head high.

"How do feel, Giovani?" Laurina asked, as she nuzzled me to my feet. Her snout was warm and soft. I reached my hand up, in wonder, to caress the side of her face. Her jaw was incredibly strong, yet there was softness about her. I suddenly realized that she asked me the same question as Aunt Evangeline and Khai had asked me after Nak's creepy invasion.

"Why does everyone keep asking me that?" I blurted out, forgetting my manners. I bowed my head in shame and continued, "Forgive me Laurina, I have forgotten my manners. I am fine. How are you?" I saw my mother's face with a disappointed look in my mind. "Actually, I am very confused."

"Dear Giovani, I am well, thank you, but I am curious as to how your body is responding from a mixing with a supernatural being." Laurina responded.

"Wait, a what?" I asked with a voice full of question.

"Come with us child," St. John said as he crooked his arm around mine and led me through the meadow. "Let us go to the Hallowed Hall and get ourselves comfortable before we discuss this."

I could only manage to nod in agreement. My mind was just given a headful of thoughts to ponder as we walked. I don't even know if I was walking or gliding along with St. John. I never saw his feet touch the ground the last time we met, and he moved with such grace, that I think he is floats instead of walks. It certainly felt like I was floating through the meadow.

The enormity of my situation suddenly hit me. I was back in the presence of the Court of Order, well, two out of the three High Mages. Skye told me that her elven guide, Aluvanim, who was over 600 years old, had never been here, and this was my second meeting with the High Mages in less than six months.

The High Mages created this safe place over two-thousand years ago, when the evil sorcerer, Yfel, set out to destroy all that was Pure and Light. Not many creatures have ever met them, because they had to be kept safe. It is their magic that is so precious that it breathes life and magic into others. Only a few chosen "pure" creatures were allowed to be graced by their presence, and this is my second time. *Why was I here? What was so special about me?*

We found ourselves standing at the entrance of The Hallowed Hall. The grand, platinum gates opened slowly as we approached, and an illuminated cloud rushed towards us. "Protogenoi," I whispered, and hundreds of them rushed forward to greet us. The sprites of light danced upon our skin, tickling us with tiny charges of energy, reminding of the sparklers we waved on the 4th of July. Just being present in this wondrous place was magical. All of my senses were being stimulated with positive energy. Even the air tasted light; I took a deep breath and felt all worries disappear.

"Let us sit." St. John made a gesture to a courtyard in the center of the palace. There was a table set, with a mountain of food in the center that glittered like gold as the Protogenoi continued to add different fruits and pastries. There were five chairs surrounding it, and I found myself breaking away from my hosts and bounding towards the food.

"Why do I keep forgetting my manners?" I stopped and asked. "I truly am sorry."

Laughter followed and I was taken aback by the sound. It was so entrancing and lovely. St. John and Laurina were giggling at my words. My head became dizzy, and I felt light as air. My surroundings started to feel farther and farther away from me like I was floating off, like a helium balloon that slips through a child's fingers.

"Oh, Dear," The sound of Laurina's voice echoed in the air, "It is starting."

I bumped into something warm and hard. I suddenly came back to my senses and noticed that my face mushed against the floor. I turned to look up at my hosts, but found them far below me at the table. I had floated away, and I was touching the cloud-painted ceiling!

"AAAAAAHHHHHHHH!" I screamed. "HELP!"

"I ssssee our friend issss feeling differently, no?" Nak's voice chimed in.

"Yes brother, it would appear so." Laurina giggled.

I was flailing about, at the top of the Hallowed Hall, which from the ground appeared to look like the sky. I was trying to control every fiber of my being so that I would not freak out in from of these enchanted founders, when I felt a gentle tug on my pant leg. The golden jaws of Laurina in flight had, gently, clamped down on my leg, and she pulling me back to the earth, like a mother retrieving a lost balloon.

Chapter 6
Illustrated by
Maya Sischo

6

RETURN VISIT

I must have blacked out, once again, because when I opened my eyes and found myself seated at the table. I really hate that I kept doing that; like I have little control over what happens to me. My frustration must have shown on my face, because St. John placed his hand on top of mine.

"Relax, young Adrastai. Your body is going through many changes and there is much to learn, and I fear very little time to learn it in." St. John's voice was soft, but something behind it made me think that he was worried. "I realize that you have heard those words before, but please rest assured that my brethren and I would not give you these tasks if we did not deem you worthy."

"Changes? I…I just am so confused. My life was completely different a few short months ago, child-like and now…" The voice of a timid boy rose out of my throat.

"There is a plan for you, Giovani, you are extremely important to The Order and our cause." Laurina added. "It tis You, who will restore Light to our world."

"But, I don't understand. Sukanar is gone, isn't he?" I questioned, trying to make any sort of sense out of all of this.

"Yes, Sukanar is gone, thanks to you and your family." Laurina paused and gently bowed her head; and instinctively, I knew she was thinking of those who died during the battle. "But, I am afraid that Sukanar was just one sorcerer. There are many Dark forces in this world, many that you may have thought only to be myth or legend, but they are real. They wait, in the dark, for their time to strike and one has already started to advance." Laurina was visibly worried. Her normally soft face, took on a fierce appearance.

"You must return to the Adrastai Council and learn all that you can. You have only one-weeks' time before you must begin your next leg of this journey. Nak will be your guide." Said St. John, but my brain started to reject his last statement.

"What? Nak? I beg your pardon, but I do not trust Nak. You have bestowed upon me the gift of Sight. My visions showed him crushing a small framed girl." I stood up from my chair, leaned onto the tabletop with both fists clenched, shot a look of hate towards the cobra across the table, and continued to stare into his eyes, "I am sorry to have to be the one tell you this, but he is a murderer."

Nak's hood flared larger than ever, he hissed loudly in protest, and I was certain he would strike for me across the table. He tilted his head back and I closed my eyes and braced for his jaws to clamp down upon me. Laughter filled my ears. Nak was laughing hysterically across the table.

"My dear brethren," he managed to say, while catching his breath between hysterics, "I have not had the chancsssе to sssspeak to him," another burst of laughter, "we jusssst interwove before our journey here." Nak tried to compose himself, but continued to chortle uncontrollably.

"Now Nak, please, let us be respectful of his thoughts. He was simply trying to decipher his Vision." St. John added, but the wry grin on his face told me he was trying to stifle his own laughter.

"Wait a minute! What is going on? I just told you he was going to kill someone. I cannot take him with me nor have him as my guide!" I stood firmly in my decision.

"Young Adrastai, Nak is not a murderer. He would never be allowed to enter The Enchanted Realm, if it were so." Laurina stated.

"But he slithered into my column of light!" I interrupted.

"No Giovani, that column was sent for the both of you." She continued. "Please sit back down and I will elaborate."

I managed to slow my breathing and sit back down at the table, but I could not bring myself to look at Nak. I knew what I had seen, and I was told to trust my Sight.

"It has come to our attention, that there have been spies sent across the sea. Have you noticed anything out of the ordinary?" Laurina asked.

"Everything has been out of the ordinary the last few months," I answered, throwing my arms up over my head.

Laurina gave a soft giggle and continued, "I am certain of that my dear, but has anything that did not feel of Light touched you?"

I remembered the crows. "Yes, there has. Crows; two of them. One, my friend, Fin, destroyed; and the other were destroyed by Khai."

"Did you see any others fly off?" St. John asked, with deep concern in his voice.

"No. Not that I can recall, but I think the first one entranced me," I said, feeling a tad ashamed.

"Entranced? Did your elven guide perform any counter spell? Please Giovani, you must tell us everything." St. John added.

"Um," I hesitated. "I think so. Elia was waving her hands over me, while the thick liquid bubbled in my ears. I thought I was going to explode, but instead, she turned me into a puddle. I poured out onto the lawn. Then gnomes…" I stopped. There was not any need to continue, because my audience all cringed at the mere mention of the gnomes. They all knew what must have happened next.

"That must have been when Asëa first became aware of the situation," said Laurina. "I am sorry about the gnomes…and I presume spiders as well." She added as she gave me a pity full look, which was followed by an uncomfortable silence. I shivered remembering the hairy legs on my face.

"Asëa knows that we stand united. Why would he go by himself? We only had a few discussions in regards to this matter." St. John questioned as he stood up and began to glide through the garden, in a pacing motion.

"The disappearances in the triangle, both at sea and in the air," Laurina directed her words to Nak, "does this sound like…"

"Nãga!" Nak exclaimed, as his hood grew even bigger than before.

"Who's Nãga?" I questioned, feeling like the only one excluded from the conversation.

"My twin." answered Nak, rather gravely, as he sunk to ground and slithered off with his head on the ground into the garden.

84

"Your twin?" breathlessly escaped my lips and I sank back into the chair with an odd feeling of despair. "That must be the snake I saw then, right? So, why do I feel so sad?" I questioned Laurina and St. John.

"No child, they are not identical twins." St. John replied.

"Listen carefully Giovani, Nak has shared his chi, his life-force, with you. You will be forever connected." Her strong jaw appeared soft and her eyes were caring as she spoke to me, "He has blessed you with a sliver of his supernatural soul, but in turn, a sliver of Nãga's soul was shared as well. You feel sad because now you can feel what Nak is experiencing. He knows that he will have to destroy his twin sister, and that pains him." Laurina explained, but I really don't remember anything she said after telling me that he gave me a sliver of his supernatural soul.

"Am I supernatural?" I whispered. "I mean, I floated away." My voice grew louder as my thoughts processed aloud, "How am I going to stop that from happening again? Can I control it? WAIT! Do I have super powers?"

"Giovani, your heart is pure, keep your intentions the same please," Laurina firmly stated.

"Oh, I am sorry, I didn't…I mean, please accept my apologies, I didn't mean it like that." I replied with my head bowed in shame.

"That is exactly how you meant it." She retorted and with that, she stood up and walk away from the table to meet the others in the garden.

I sat there, by myself, left with my thought of shame and wondering if Laurina was second-guessing their decision to put so much faith into me. Immediately, I wanted to be with my family; Mom, Dad, and the FrouFrou Crew, and instantly after having that thought, I felt like a baby. *Is twelve years old too young for such responsibility?* I wanted to go home.

"No brother, twelve issss not too young. I have watched you, that issss why I shared my chi. In over one thousssssand yearssss, I have only shared mysssself three timessss." Nak hissed. He had slid right up next to me and his body was oddly warm for a cold-blooded creature.

"Thank you for having faith in me, Nak." I looked squarely into his large bronze eyes. "Really, thank you. I am honored and sorry for judging you without giving you a chance, but I still do not understand why all of this is happening."

"Thank you. You trusssst your inssssstinct, and I resssspect that. Thissss is my body, but do not judge me by my lookssss. Not all sssserpentssss are bad…or sssslimey." Nak bumped into my side, like a brother who would mess his younger sibling's hair. "We have much to talk about and even more to act upon; come let us eat."

"Eat?" I questioned. "Didn't you just do that over in the woods? To be honest, it freaks me out a little. My food is already dead when I eat it, and yours is, well, screaming." I shivered at the thought.

"I really didn't mean me, I have already ate, and I completely undersssstand where you are coming from. Watching you eat, lifelessss food givessss me the heebeegeebeessss too." Nak said with a shiver. "Ssssit brother and I will begin."

A smile grew across my face at the sound of Nak's voice calling me brother. That was how each of the High Mages addressed each other and Nak. I sat down at the table, and secretly hoped that we would not talk again, at least until after I ate. My stomach was growling, like a troll in pursuit of prey.

Pastries, fresh fruit, gigantic turkey legs and roasted root vegetables were piled high on the table, and I thought to myself, *chocolate-covered strawberries sounds so good…*and, instantly, they appeared!

"Whoa." escaped from my mouth.

"Is there anything else you that would satisfy your cravings, Sire?" came a voice from below the table. My mind wandered to pizza and ice cream, and the voice replied, "As you wish."

I glanced down to find a gnome down on one knee right beside me. I almost jumped up and wrapped myself around Nak's neck at the sight of the ugly creature, who winked at me before burrowing into the ground. Laughter boomed through the courtyard, as St. John and Laurina rejoined us at the table.

I was grateful to dive into the pizza and ice cream, without having to discuss defending all that is Light. My belly was so distended, that I had to undo the buttons on my jeans in order to breathe. I plunked back into my chair and, magically, the table cleared and a beautiful iridescent teapot appeared. The enchanted kettle poured each of us a glass of hot tea and floated a fresh orchid and mint leaf on top. Sipping the inviting concoction immediately relieved any over-indulgent sensations I had. Grateful, I gestured a thank you to the pot, when the invisible gnome-server reappeared at the handle.

I jumped. The remaining hot liquid fell to my lap, and again, the courtyard boomed with laughter. *Why? Why did The Enchanted Realm use gnomes as servers? Was this a cruel joke?* I will forever be creeped out, knowing that I was cleaned inside gnomes and…and…crapped out. GACK!

We all sat, for a spell, with our bellies full and listening to the sounds of the cricket symphony. The daylight sky turned into twilight; painted with brilliant hues of orange and red. I felt like a king, with my feet resting on a large toadstool, my hands behind my head, and the largest grin spread across my face.

The air was sweet with lavender and honeysuckle. The Protogenoi danced and twirled with the fireflies in the warm evening air and all seemed well with the world. I felt myself exhale, deeply. I couldn't remember the last time I felt this content and relaxed. I never wanted to leave The Enchanted Realm.

"Tomorrow marks a new beginning. Another melee between Light and Dark to overcome." St. John's voice broke the silence. "I am more confident now, then ever before, that we made the right decision."

"You know that I am sitting right here, right?" I interjected, jokingly.

More laughing ensued. I began to think that the High Mages and Nak were out of their minds until Laurina replied. "A wise person once said: 'By seeing the seed of failure in every success, we remain humble. By seeing the seed of success in every failure we remain hopeful." She continued, "We are very hopeful."

Laurina's words warmed my heart, but as soon as her last statement registered with my brain, I recalled my own non-winning record.

"Hey, easy, I am new at this." I snickered back.

I really enjoyed being in the Enchanted Realm, digs against my person and all. There was just something about his place that mad you never want to leave. I felt safe here, happy, and content. The last time I was here; I did not want to leave that time either.

"Thank you all for a lovely evening." St. John interrupted the symphony of crickets, by gesturing like an orchestra conductor, "But we must discuss the matter at hand. I had hoped the Asëa would have joined us by now. I am not able to connect with him. I am slightly worried. Has anyone else connected with our brother?"

"I, also, have not had any success connecting with him." Laurina replied with her head bowed in concern.

"It issss time to pay my ssssissssster a vissssit." Nak hissed. "I will go thissss insssstant!" he exclaimed and he stood taller.

"No. Time is of the essence." answered St. John, "This must be a calculated encounter." He turned is gaze towards me. "Young Adrastai, you must learn all you can at this Council. Many there possess the tools you will need to aid you on this journey. Watch and listen carefully; there is something to learn from every situation."

Is there anything in particular I should concentrate on?" I asked. "Sword fighting? Flight lessons? Magic?"

"Just be present in everything that you do and the knowledge will come." Laurina answered, "And Nak, I trust in your judgment, the proper time to connect with your twin is yet to be revealed. You must first have all of the necessary tools."

Just be present…just be present; okay, I can do this. I made a promise to myself that I would keep an open mind and be present during every activity.

"You must learn ALL of the ways of the Adrastai, faulty or not." St. John added, as he looked deep into my eyes. "It is within failure that we see a glimpse of success giving us hope."

"Use your shield, it possesses many helpful elements. The shield can cloak your chi from the crows as well." Laurina spoke softly as the sun set behind the Hallowed Hall walls.

"I never thought to use my coin, I mean, my shield. The only time it presented itself to me was the first night I regained consciousness, after the battle against Sukanar. It revealed a holographic map, and showed where the earth was healing." I responded. "What else can it do?"

"If you are troubled, my brother, simply ask for help." St. John continued, "Nak shall be by your side as well, follow his lead and listen to his council. It was not by mistake that he has joined our forces on this journey."

"I pledge my allegiancesss to The Order!" yelled my scaly brother. "Let this journey begin!"

Suddenly, my body was flung forward and my face smashed into the ground. Nak also fell violently. Stunned, I laid still for a moment. Then I saw him; I found myself looking into the eyes of Asëa. His face riddled with fear, and he was dodging crushing blows from some unseen force. "I see him!" I yelled, "I see Asëa!"

Laurina was already picking me up with her teeth, which were clamped around my backpack. My feet found the ground and I repeated, "I saw Asëa, he is under attack!"

"Mother," Nak sighed. "She will end him."

Silence fell upon the group and concern grew across every face. "We will continue to reach out to him." St. John interjected.

"You must go." Laurina's voice was soft but stern, "Attending the Adrastai Council must be first, and then you may carry on with your journey. No earlier Nak, do you understand? Otherwise, the encounter will be compromised." Laurina directed her words towards the newest member of my family; after all, isn't that who we rely on when things get tough? "Are we in agreement?"

"We are." answered Nak, with a bowed head, "The council first, then some fruit, a collection of siblings, and then off to meet Mum."

"Wait, what?" I questioned. "Meet who?" but before anyone could answer, the world around me started to become a blur of colors. A magical tornado spiraled around me and parts of my body began to swirl with it! I glanced at my hands. The tips of each finger began to unravel, as if a sweater caught on a nail, and my flesh began to blend in with the blur of colors twisting in the magical funnel.

The process was very fast.

Finally, my entire body was caught up in a swirling enchanted vortex made up of all the colors that had just soothed my soul in the evening sky. Then, the pressure became increasing tighter, like being squeezed within a python's grip, until all of my air was pressed out of my lungs. There was a squeaking nose, as if my ear was plugged with congestion, sounding like a squeal from a pig. Amongst the chaos, off in the distance, I heard the High Mages whisper "Be well Brother." and then, everything went black.

.

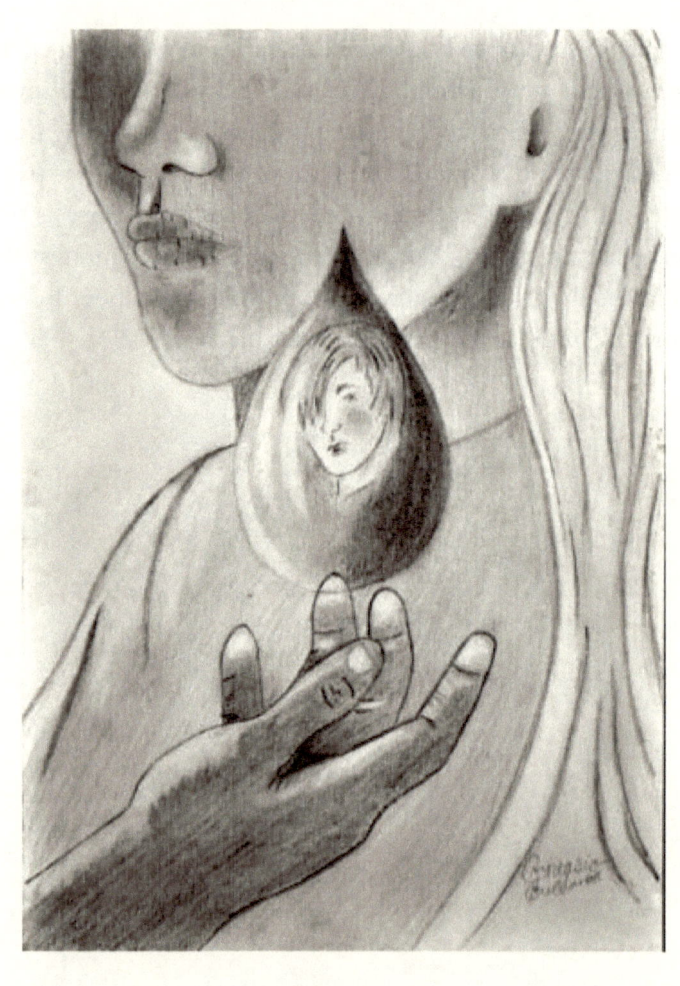

Chapter 7
Illustrated by
Dontasia Buchanan

7

THE MAP

The swirling vortex stopped and Nak and I found ourselves back inside our tent. Our friends were still frozen on the floor, as if time stood still while we were in The Enchanted Realm. Just as our feet hit the ground, their bodies began to move, finishing the motion they started before frozen and their suspended state was un-paused.

"Are they coming? Did the crow send a message?" Brochara voice was shaking as he spoke.

"What caused that thunder?" Aunt Evangeline was also visibly upset, "Are we under attack?"

"My dear friendssss, we are not under attack. Pleasssse, let ussss ssssit. There issss much to deliberate." Nak was calm as he slithered over to the table.

Everyone brushed themselves off and followed Nak's lead. Elia's enchanted teapot sprang into action and fresh baked muffins filled the center of the table.

"Why do I smell The enchanted Realm?" Aunt E questioned looking at both, Nak and I, with one eyebrow raised. *How can she smell the Enchanted Realm?*

"That issss what we need to talk about." Nak answered. "Giovani and I were ssssummoned by the Laurina and Sssst. John." He was very good at making eye contact with each person as he spoke.

"Wait, why not Asëa? Was he not there?" Brochara rose from his chair and nervously glanced around, "He is always there; it is not safe for him to leave The Enchanted Realm alone. Was he or was he not there? Why wasn't he there?" Brochara was very upset and started pacing the floor.

"Please Brochara, we will explain." I put my hand on his tiny shoulder and could feel his heart pounding wildly under his skin. I continued, but made certain that I chose my words carefully, "Laurina said that he would not have left if he didn't think it was absolutely necessary." The tables had turned; it was my turn to ease Brochara's anxiety; when it has always been the other way around.

Tension filled the room. Fin sharpened his sword, seemingly calm, but the sporadic twitching of his whiskers on only the right side of his face, gave away his nervousness. Elia was constantly wiping her hands and wringing them on her apron, but she was not touching any food, while Brochara continued to pace. Aunt Evangeline just sat there, quietly, on the edge of her seat, as if she were waiting to shoot her hand up in class wanting to be the first one with the right answer.

Nak sat at one end of the table and I, directly, across from him. Surprisingly, his serpent accent was not as strong as usual as he began, "Dark forcessss are on the move, growing stronger and must be stopped. That is why Asëa hassss ventured outside of the protection of the Enchanted Realm. He hassss gone to try and reasssson with this enemy."

"Outside the protection? He will be killed!" Brochara shouted as he grabbed the few scraggily hairs on his head and pulled down, like a knit cap.. Elia buried her head in her hands and was obviously weeping.

"Nak, this has never happened in the history of The Realm, why now?" Aunt Evangeline asked. She remained calm, but I began to fear that maybe she was in shock.

"I think he hasss gone because he feelssss a sense of responsibility in all of thissss." Nak's voice briefly waivered. I tried to catch his eyes with mine, but he was staring into the fire.

"Responsibility? We all signed up to be responsible for fighting evil and dark forces. Why did he choose this one to go out on his own? There has to be more to this." Aunt Evangeline was asking all of the right questions; I found myself wishing I had asked them.

"I am ssssorry, I cannot explain further. Laurina and St. John have instructed me to enlist your help with another matter," Everyone settled down a bit and was seated back at the table while Nak continued, "We have been asked to ensure that the newest Adrastai, Giovani, completes all of the training offered within this Council'ssss time. He will need every bit of it to help ussss on our quest."

I nervously shifted in my chair. Even I didn't' know what our quest was, but if it had anything to do with the fact that one of the High Mages had left the protection of The Realm for the first time in history; it was going to be difficult. Everyone's eyes were shifting back and forth, searching for answers in one another's faces.

"We have been given a direct order from the High Mages; we should be honored and, as always, perform to the very best of our abilities to succeed at this mission." Fin didn't finish speaking before he jumped onto the table in a chivalrous gesture and continued, "We shall make them proud!"

"Here, Here!" Everyone cheered in agreement.

The mood in the tent changed. The tension lessened and there was a sense a sense of pride among my friends, a sense of honor. Everyone wore a smile.

Brochara abruptly pushed himself away from the table and jumped to his feet. In a jester-like fashion, he jigged across the room hopping from one foot to the other; he danced out of the room. Giggles erupted as we watched him disappear into the shadows. A few moments later, he returned carrying something that was taller than he was. As he approached the table, he clumsily swiped his hand over his head, briefly throwing him off balance. The table magically cleared itself from the baked goods and dishes, and Brochara plunked his package down with a thud. Tiny grunts and odd noises escaped from the item.

"This is the agenda of events for the upcoming Adrastai Council," barked Brochara in a rather commanding voice as he made a grand gesture with his arm, like a game show host presenting a prize. An old, leather scroll lay before us and slowly unfolded upon Brochara's command, "Study we will, and then we shall develop our course of action."

Fascinated, I bellied up to the table and leaned in closer to have a look at this agenda, but I was not expecting to find such an amazing site! "Whoa." Was all I could manage to say.

This scroll was a map, but not just any map. It was alive! A three dimensional map, with buildings and mountains stretching up toward our faces adorned the table. It was an animated diorama of the week's events, complete with teeny creatures milling around. My eyes didn't know where to study first. I was amazed and full of wonderment.

Tiny warriors, no more than an inch tall, were sword fighting in one area of the map while the title 'Swordsmanship and Defensive Tactics" waved within the leather on the lower left-hand corner. They were performing acrobatic feats while wielding swords in the heat of combat. Fin's eyes lit up with excitement and he leaned in towards the map get a closer look. Fin pulled his head back quickly and grabbed his snout, as we watched a tiny portion of one of his whiskers float to the table. Just as a teeny pair of Adrastai rolled off the scroll in combat, they paused, acknowledged Fin with a tip of their tiny helmets, and jumped back onto the map to rejoin the action.

Suddenly, something whizzed past my eyes, like a hornet, and dove back towards the map. My gaze caught up with a glorious red dragon, two inches long, which was performing aerial maneuvers. Upon closer inspection, I noticed a tiny Dragon Rider standing in a harness on its back and holding leather reins. The Rider was girl with long red hair that resembles flickering flames as the wind blew through it. Her gaze met mine and she banged her fist upon her breastplate, acknowledging my presence. I instinctively did the same gesture in return, forgetting the fact that there were others standing around me, and I almost punched Aunt E in the process. The tiny rider smiled sweetly, and they dove back towards the map to an area titled 'Flight Maneuvers". I found myself smiling from ear to ear.

Booming laughter erupted from my friends and brought my attention back to the rest of the room. Pulling my eyes off the magical map, I looked to my left and found the few hairs on Brochara's head entangled with seaweed and a tiny fish flopping out of his ear and back onto the map. I could not stifle my amusement, and I banged my fist onto the tabletop in my hysterics. Another splash from the lake in the lower right-hand corner, shot up and splashed over the top of his head again, immediately created fits of more laughter.

A one-sided water fight ensued from the scroll, while Brochara just stood there soaking wet. "Caela ie'lle!" He shouted, when the splashing stopped, and we noticed a tiny Piscisene playfully diving in the water. Brochara shook his fists at the mermaid, but the silvery beauty just giggled, flipped her tail, and splashed him yet again, before diving back into the portion of the map titled 'Aquatic Training'. I bet if Brochara wasn't so wet, steam would blow from his ears!

My stomach muscles and cheeks hurt from laughing so hard., and I decided to investigate the rest of the map. A very curious building, which reminded me of a museum, stood in the upper left-hand corner titled 'The University'. Aunt Evangeline leaned in, very closely just centimeters from the tiny stoned structure. She closed one eye, and peered into a window, "The Hall of Knowledge." She whispered. "So much scientific information gathered in one area." I couldn't see what she was looking at, but tiny 'Shhh' noises came from inside the building, and Aunt E promptly apologized.

"Ah Yessss," Nak whispered beside her as he also peered into the building. "I have many fond memories of this magical place. My ssssister and I, sssspent many wonderful eveningssss learning between those wallsss."

Aunt Evangeline gently placed her arm around Nak's neck, as if she was comforting him from some painful emotion. He leaned his head in closer to snuggle her with a silent thank you. My heart sunk, remembering what the High Mages had told me about having to destroy his twin. I longed for my family.

Elia and Brochara embraced each other, as a group of very tiny elves waved their arms over their heads, enchanting the tiny forest in the center of the map. Trees changed from season to season right before our eyes, and then morphed into different animated shapes under their elven charms. One oak tree was enchanted into doing a cartwheel, when half if its nuts fell onto the map and rolled off the edge, before disappearing into thin air.

"That's a full schedule, my friend," Khai's voice filled the room, as he gently pushed the back of my shoulder with his snout. "I can't wait for Aerial Maneuvers! I have only had the pleasure of watching other dragons train with their Riders, until now. We are going to light up the sky! It is going to be fantastic!"

Excitedly, I patted his muscular shoulder. I loved flying with Khai, the feeling when I am standing on a dragon's back, high up in the clouds; it is powerful and freeing.

"Tomorrow marks the first day of training. You must start at 'The University'. This will be the longest portion of your teaching. It is extremely important that you learn all that you can and remember the information. Do not question if you will ever use the knowledge acquired; you surely will. Nak will work with you this evening on study skills and techniques. He is very educated and will guide you through your course." Aunt Evangeline's voice was full of energy as she spoke.

"No disrespect to you, Nak, but why aren't you guiding me through this one? You have been there since the day I was born, secretly filling my head with guidance for The Order. Why not continue?" I questioned and then turned to Nak, "Please know that I am very happy to work with you, it's just…Aunt E and I, well why can't she teach me?" I had true respect in my eyes while I gazed into Nak's. The noble snake simply nodded his head, signaling he understood.

"Things are different now, Giovani. You have been chosen and must move on to the next level." Aunt E cradled my face in her warm hands, the room seemed to shrink down to just us, and her eyes filled with water as she continued, "I am so very proud of you, my little Explorer. You are destined for greatness and I consider myself blessed to have guided you thus far. Your training, from this point on, is crucial. There are certain practices that I just do not have the understanding to teach; certain supernatural realms that I can't even begin to understand. Nak will lead you well, learn all you can."

A single, large tear fell silently down her cheek as she spoke. I watched it gently caress her face as it slid and then pooled on the edge of her jaw. Mesmerized and touched by this symbol of love, I felt the impact of her emotions deep inside my heart. Staring into this love-filled gesture, I noticed my reflection staring back at me from inside the droplet, but I saw myself as a small boy, innocent and pure, unstained by pain and sorrow. Noticeably too heavy with love to hang on, the tear gave way, and began falling to the floor.

Saddened, I felt the need to catch it; to save that little boy in the tear from crashing to the ground. I outstretched my hand to save my reflection trapped in the falling droplet, when memories from my childhood flooded my mind. Just then, a Protogenoi swooped past and caught the tear. The brilliant sparkle of light turned to me cradling my memories in her illuminating embrace, winked at me, and ascended towards the sky. Tears rolled down my face as I watched the enchanted sprite carry a piece of me up to The Enchanted Realm. My heart sighed watching the Protogenoi disappear; keeping my memory of the child I was, tucked safely in its arms.

I flung my arms around Aunt Evangeline and held her tight. The faces of my Mom, Dad, and the FrouFrou Crew flooded my mind and I felt disconnected from them. It had only been a matter of days since we played in our backyard, but it felt like years. My heart grew heavy and I felt my body sink into Aunt E; missing my family and mourning my childhood.

"I know Buddy." She cooed, trying to console me, "I know, and I love you too."

"I know this isn't a very grown thing to say Aunt E, but I want my Mom." I whispered into her ear, still weepy.

"Your parents are so proud of you, and you should be very proud of them. You have been chosen, out of millions, to be a very important player in this constant struggle between Good and Evil. Your parents have raised you well; you are ready to fulfill your destiny. Everything that you do from this point on is to protect all that is good in this world. What an honorable life you lead. There isn't a parent alive who would ask their son not to fight for what is right, even if it means not seeing him as often. You will forever remain in their hearts and them in yours. Love never stops, it is what motivates us." Aunt E's voice was comforting and she was right; we fight because we love them. We fight so our loved ones may live free and happy.

"Find the sunshine, Giovani; find the Light." Elia's tiny voice came from in front of the fire. "Your young age isn't a con in this situation, it is a pro! Think of all the glorious years all of our kinds will have you fighting for what is right. Protecting all of us. There, there is your sunshine. You are a ray of hope to me."

"Here, here!" Fin shouted from across the table raising a glass of mulled cider. "I second that, and thank you for choosing this fight!" Fin's grin made me giggle. There was something about the way his newly, lop-sided whiskers twitched that brought a smile to my face.

"With all of you on my side, how could I fail?" I asked as I stood up and made eye contact with each one, "you all give me strength and I am honored to stand beside you."

"You are brave and worthy of the title Adrastai, my friend." Khai's voice boomed inside the tent.

"Thank you, brother." I replied, bowing my head with mutual respect for my dragon friend.

Brochara also stood up, rather regally, like a leader about to address his subjects. He raised his right hand, extending only his boney pointer finger, and inhaled deeply to begin a grand speech adding his take on this powerful moment. Just then, the tiny Piscisene on the map flipped her tail once more and a giant wave slapped Brochara, squarely in his face. There he stood, arm still raised, mouth wide open about to make a proclamation, with seaweed and water running out of the corners of his mouth, and tiny fish splashing around inside. He closed his jaw, crunched down, and began to chew, "Hmmmm, not bad. Not bad at all!" Brochara slicked back the few wet hairs he had atop his head, and gestured a thank you to the diorama.

"Leave to Brochara to bring the comic relief!" Fin exclaimed. "Come to think of it, I am rather hungry myself."

And just like that, Elia waved her arm over her head and the enchanted string quartet re-appeared and began playing lively music.

Brochara hooked his arm inside of Elia's and they began to dance and sing in front of the fire. Nak swayed back and forth and Aunt Evangeline shimmied alongside of him. Fin performed an aerial dismount off the tabletop and joined the dance.

Khai bobbed his head from side-to-side, keeping time with the music and I looked around and smiled, taking it all in. In an odd way, watching my new friends reminded me of watching my sisters perform in our living room. At that exact moment, I realized that Life *was* good. Joy and happiness was important to enjoying life fully and that was what we needed to keep sacred. Love for friends and family, happiness and laughter for all, and realizing that the Adrastai helped to provide that…to make a difference. *I will make a difference.*

"Hey! Who's having a party?" Skye's announced as she and Aluvanim burst into the tent.

"Apparently we are!" I said as she flung her arms around my neck and spun her around.

"Ooooh! You have your scroll, too?" Skye asked as she spotted my map on the table. "Aren't they cool?"

"Amazing." I answered. "I couldn't take my eyes off of it. Wouldn't it be cool if all of our textbooks were interactive like that?"

"Are we in any of the same classes?" Skye asked.

"Uh, I don't know. I guess I didn't realize it was a schedule." I managed to say before she yanked my arm so hard, that I thought she dislocated it.

"Come On! Let's check it out!" Skye's enthusiasm was contagious. I bounded over to the table with her, hand in hand.

"Whoa," was all she managed to say.

"Yeah, that's exactly what I said." I laughed

Chapter 8
Illustrated by
Miranda Pavelle

8

HALL OF KNOWLEDGE

"Rise and shine, Explorer!" chirped Aunt Evangeline as she shook my body from a deep sleep. "Today we continue to build your brain!"

"What? Why are you over-the-top cheery this morning?" I managed to ask through my first invigorating, morning stretch. Aunt E had a very unique way of conversing.

"Today, my dear, you are going to The University!" Aunt E plunked herself down on the side of my bed, like a schoolgirl about to tell me her secrets. "You will have an entire day of learning, and filling your brain with knowledge you will need to become the best Adrastai you can. Isn't that exciting?"

Aunt E looked like a love-struck Juliet with her hands clasped at her heart and a far-away look in eyes. Her excitement over education made me giggle. That is why she is a Scholar for The Order. She is so passionate about learning and sharing her knowledge, and in doing so, fulfilling her part in the battle against dark and evil ways. Aunt Evangeline loves finding and nurturing the potential of young Adrastai, promoting integrity and respect. "Knowledge is Power!" she constantly exclaimed, while balling a fist and staring off into the imaginary battlefield in her head.

"Okay, okay, I'm getting up." I mumbled. "Hey, Master Explorer," I called out from buried in my pillow, "I love you and, truly, I appreciate everything you do and have done for me."

Peeking out at her, Aunt E bit down on her lip and her eyes began to mist, but she playfully reached out and tousled my hair before giving my lower sheet a gigantic tug, causing my body to spin. I caught my balance, executed a perfect double twist dismount off the bed, landed with my feet firmly on ground, and gestured like a super hero.

"Bravo!" Fin shouted from the doorway, clapping his hands at my performance; "Bravo!" He repeated, as he removed his feather cap and made a sweeping bow.

"Thank you, thank you, kind mink. Your adoration is much appreciated." I mused in a very thick, over-dramatized, English accent.

When I walked into the living quarters of the tent, I was greeted with a table was full of pastries, fresh fruits, nuts, a huge stack of blueberry pancakes, and bacon. I love bacon and Elia was well aware of that. She has protected me since the day I was born, watched me grow, and knew what all of my favorite things to eat were. Warm mugs of mulled cider accompanied each plate and the sweet smell was intoxicating. *Today is going to be great!*

I was thankful for my little elven caretaker for creating an environment that reminded of home, that I ran over and scooped

Elia up in my arms. I had never picked her up before, and my actions caught Elia and myself of guard. I swung her around like had done to my baby sister, Aria, and her squeals of joy were just as infectious. We bellied laughed and continued to giggle for quite some time.

Today just felt right. Everything foreshadowed greatness. Today was going to be the start of something amazing; I could just feel it.

I plunked myself down, giddily, and reached for my pancakes, when my stomach suddenly lurched. I spotted a box made of bark with whiskers and tiny eyes staring out at me; pleading for their release.

"Good Morning, Everyone," Nak slithered into the room. He noticed me disturbed and staring at the wooden cage, "I assssked Elia to producsssse a ssssilence charm sssso you would be more comfortable." A wide smile grew across Nak's face, as he reveled in his cleverness. I was impressed at his thoughtfulness; remembering my comment about how his dinner runs away screaming.

Fin bounded into the room and sat next to Nak, he briefly lowered his head and placed his paw on top of the box of bark. After a brief moment of silence, he twisted hands over each other and fixated his eyes on the wooden cage, looking quite sinister. I had completely forgotten that mink enjoy fresh meat. Again, my stomach turned. "It is all a part of the glorious circle of life, my friend. I have given thanks for their sustenance." Fin could feel my look of disgust upon him and then glanced at the plate in front of me, "Enjoy your bacon." He added.

"Ouch, touché Mon ami, touché." I giggled to myself, thinking of all the different personas I was playing today and enjoying myself.

We all fed our bellies and had enjoyed a long nights rest. The

107

time had come for us to embark on training of The Adrastai Council. I was excited to start. I grabbed my backpack, not sure, if I would require the use of any of my trinkets from aunt E, but I felt like a part of her was with me then. Nak joined me at the entrance of the cave, and with the nervousness and anticipation of a child about to leave for school for the first time, we ventured outside together.

The morning air was crisp and light. Each inhale refreshed and invigorated my body with a sense of awakening. I was ready to tackle a day of learning; keeping an open mind about how everything was important to The Order's success; and ultimately, to my success.

Khai was talking with Jock, Skye's Imoogi, when we walked outside. Both dragons turned their head at the same time. Skye must have been on the same schedule as I was. She, too, was grinning with a sense of excitement. We met over by our large dragon counterparts and began speaking at the same time.

"University?" we asked each other in unison.

"Yeah, me too." We both answered together.

"Perfect! We can sit by each other, and help each out," Skye said as she threw her arms around Jock's neck. "Have a great time in the lake," she added, focusing her attention to her Imoogi partner. Jock was a sea dragon; they do not possess wings, but more like elongated fins running the length of their backs. Imoogi can travel, with lightning-speed, through almost every form of water except ice.

Apparently, all different types of dragons, elves, and other guides also had training. A giant stadium was situated off in the distance to encompass classes in aerial tactics. This enchanted arena simulated different weather conditions and created circumstances that dark-forces could conjure, allowing the dragons to maneuver through "real-life" situations. Khai was jumping out of his skin with excitement.

"Go friend, enjoy your training." I told Khai as I patted him on the shoulder. He and Jock took off with a start. Skye and I just stood there laughing.

The scene was remarkable. I was reminded of the first day of school after summer break with all of the different groups moving off in every direction and everyone excited. The elven guides headed into the forest. Fin and some other creatures had already begun their fencing exercises. Aunt Evangeline left, right after she woke me up, for The University to teach her classes, and Nak, Skye, and I needed to hurry over there to start our training as well.

As we hurried towards the magnificent Hall of Knowledge, I was awestruck by how grand the structure was. It looked exactly like the miniature one on the scroll, yet it was not there yesterday. The Enchanted Valley had been transformed into a massive training campus. I secretly hoped that, throughout my years, I would continue to take the time to pause and be amazed by magical things around me.

"Nak! Wait up!" shouted a voice from behind.

We all stopped and turned around to see who called Nak. My eyes immediately spotted her long, white-blonde hair flowing out behind her and rippling like a sea of sunlight in the breeze. The brilliant morning sun glistened off her skin, casting the soft glow of daybreak on the path before her. She was beautiful. Then a very large silhouette of a bull quickly shadowed her golden radiance. The huge form of her brother, Mateo, stepped in front of her tiny frame and bounded right up to Skye.

"Good-dah Morning Skye. How-ah are you this fine-ah day?" Mateo had hooked his arm around Skye's and was patting her hand as he spoke to her. All I could do was roll my eyes and shake my head.

"Nauseating, isn't it?" Spoke the voice of an angel.

I turned towards the voice and found myself lost in her sky-blue eyes that seemed to smile back at me. Mesmerized, I was at a loss for words, stunned by her beauty. *Why did this girl have this effect on me?*

"Do you know that you almost glow in the sunlight?" she asked.

"What? No." I quickly looked at my arm, turning it over and trying to see if something weird was happening to me. "I actually thought the same about you. My name is Giovani."

"Yes, I know who you are," she replied as she rubbed her hip.

Remembering our first encounter, quite literally, I suddenly felt very embarrassed, "Oh yeah, I am so sorry. Did I hurt you? Are you okay? Is there anything I can do?" I realized that I was beginning to go all-lunatic on her, so I slowed my words down, and took a deep breath, "I am terribly sorry about that. It was very clumsy of me."

"It's okay, it really isn't that bad, just bruised." Her soft voice floated to my ears. "My name is Luca. It is nice to properly meet you."

"Let ussss hurry, young Adrasssstia. We musssst not be late to The Universsssity." Nak broke up the awkward meeting and hurried us over to the grand stone structure.

The Hall of Knowledge reminded me of a cross between a medieval castle and one of the old magnificent churches. There were large stone steps leading up to two over-sized wooden doors that were intricately carved with carving of various vines and creatures. Stained glass windows graced every wall of the building, each one telling a different story within the glass artwork.

A large, three-paneled window rested above the doorway, shaped like the outline of a simple house. It had the square bottom with a pointed, two-sided triangle top. The stained glass artwork was a view into The Court of Order, which housed the three different sized thrones of the High Mages; and each Mage was sitting upon them. The golden scales of Laurina, matched her coloring perfectly. Asëa's green-hued skin was spot on, as well, and St. John's brilliant robe adorned with the same golden, magical vine that created my shield.

"Whoa, that looks just like them!" I managed to mutter out of amazement.

"I know." Replied Nak "Isn't it breathtaking?"

"Laurina sparkles, just like she does when standing next to her; and, and St. John's vines…" I grabbed the coin-shaped object from my pocket and turned it over in my hand, "They are perfect. Look at Asëa's coloring." I pointed to the window and looked to Nak with amazement in my eyes.

"Magnificsssent! I have alwayssss loved thissss window." Nak responded.

Suddenly, I became keenly aware of six large eyes blinking at Nak and I, and mouths gaped open. I had forgotten that not many other people had ever seen the High Mages, let alone met them, and here Nak and I were carrying on about it, "Uh, shall we go inside?" I quickly said to redirect everyone's focus.

The heavy wooden doors swung open slowly revealing the splendor that waited inside. Each one of us in our group gasps in wonder. This truly was a special place. Even though we were the only ones standing in the grand entranceway, you could feel the presence of greatness surround you. Calmness settled over me and I stood tall, and confident. I looked around, and the others were doing the same.

My eyes glanced upwards to find large glass windows, wedged in between enormous, carved, wooden trusses. The rays from the sun filled the room and I followed their path to the cream-colored marble tiles on the floor.

"This is the same floor as in the Court!" I exclaimed, nudging Nak with my elbow and twirling around taking in the grandeur of the Hall.

Nak just chuckled to himself as he guided us down a long corridor to another set of giant wooden doors. A brass plate, above the doors, read 'Lecture Hall'. There was a low buzzing sound coming from behind the door that sounded like a hum from a bees hive.

"Giovani, Pleasssse do the honorssss." Nak gestured for me to open the doors.

I pushed the heavy wooden handles and the low humming sound became quite loud as hundreds of Adrastai chatted, awaiting the lecture to begin. All eyes turned towards us, and immediately, the chatter stopped. You could have heard a pin drop and the sound of it echo through the space. Not a soul spoke or moved for what felt like forever. The five of us slowly entered and the sound of our footfalls boomed through the room. There were only four seats left in the front row, but there were five of us. I turned to look at Nak for guidance, but he had already slithered up the lectern. Dumfounded and confused, I just stood there staring at him.

"You may take your sssseat, Giovani," Nak announced.

I snapped out of my confused state and realized that my other friends had already sat down, and I was the only one left standing. My hurried steps echoed through the silent room as I scrambled to my seat. My swivel desktop created a horribly loud squeak as I flipped it into place, I felt most uncomfortable. All of the Adrastai around me covered their ears to try to block out the heinous noise. Embarrassed, I felt myself sink as low as I could, into my chair.

"Good Morning, Adrassssstai!" Nak addressed the room, "and welcome to The Hall of Knowledge!"

Nak looked very authoritative standing in front of hundreds of warriors and commanding all of their attention. The room was completely silent. I turned my head around to take in the view of all the Adrastai in one place. Everyone seemed to be sitting at the edge of their seats with eager expressions on their faces.

The audience consisted of so many different people of all ages, races, and gender. There had to be over one thousands of us warriors staring at Nak. One man in particular caught my eye, because of the length of his snow-white beard; it had to touch his belly button. I wondered what a man of his age could do in a battle against dark forces, and I was slightly concerned for his safety.

"It is my privilege to be selected to share my knowledge with all of you. I have many fond memoriessss of thissss Hall from my youth. Many a night, I found myssssself in the ssstudy, curled up by the fire, assssleep with a book." Nak was telling his story, but my mind wandered to how a cobra could hold a book; they do not have any hands. Nak's quick movement of his head, turning it to give me the stink eye, snapped me back to the present.

"It issss imperative that everyone pay attention and lissssten clossssely to what I teach you today!" Nak continued, starring right at me, with a twinge of anger on his face. I sat straight up and tried to focus as hard as I could.

"I would like to begin by ssssaying "thank you." Thank you to all of you, who are on the front line, every day, fighting for all that issss right and jusssst in our world. It issss only by your effortssss that we can live in hope." Nak bowed his head showing a grand gesture of respect, "Thank you. We, the High Magessss, mysssself and the world are depending on all of your collective effortssss to keep up the fight againsssst the dark forcessss that loom in every shadow."

I glanced over to Skye, who had a grateful smile. She looked at me and nodded, slowly, as if to say "thank you" without any words. Mateo and Luca were also smiling at Nak. Then, something odd caught my eye. Just beyond the huge shoulder of Mateo sat three scruffy men, all scowling in Nak's direction. Nak's voice started to drift off into the background as I focused in on the angry men.

They looked war-torn and tattered. Their clothes were made with different animal pelts sewn together and strips of tanned leather. I found myself staring at the exposed flesh on their strong arms, which told a story of a savage life with faded wounds woven through their skin. They reminded me of Vikings, wearing metal helmets, large straps of leather holding their armory of weapons to their bodies and heavy shields lying at their feet. Each one of them bore distinct scars of battle. One of the men had long slash marks on his large forearms, which appeared to be made by a blade. The man in the middle had claw marks across his chest and thigh, that matched the scariest man furthest away. He wore a scar that started at the top of his head, dragged down diagonally across his face, tucked under his chin, and continued onto his shoulder. *What could have made wounds like that?*

Unexpectedly, he turned quickly and glared straight at me, surprised, I flinched. His right eye was gone! Not even a patch, just a grotesque, red, splotchy-socket, where his eye used to be. He growled at me, like an animal, and slammed his fist onto the desk. Startled, I jumped in my chair and knocked Servo, my sword, to the floor. The sound of crashing steel and animalistic anger filled the Hall of Knowledge, and once again, all eyes were set on me.

"Did you get good look?" growled the one-eyed man. "Would you like a closer one?" he belted out as he quickly stood up posturing in my direction. The force of his large frame knocked his desk over, as he lunged towards me.

Nak's oversized hood quickly slid between me and intimidating, one-eyed Viking thrusting in my direction, "I wouldn't do that if I were you." Nak hissed.

"Get out of my way, Serpent, or I will gladly shred you to pieces!" growled the angry man. I heard the sound of his sword drawn from its sheath as he made the motion to push Nak out of the way to get to me. A sinister laugh gurgled up from his throat, as he turned his attention toward Nak. The other two men stood up on this cue and began to surround Nak. "Our time for vengeance is upon us, my brothers." He sneered, and they all drew their weapons.

"Servo!" I yelled and my enchanted sword leapt into my hands, as my body left the ground, executing a perfect flying somersault over the top of Nak. I landed firmly on the ground, between the Vikings and Nak, with my chest heaving in anticipation of a battle. To my surprise, Lucca and Mateo had automatically stood up as well, poised to defend.

A flash of white light filled the room, temporarily blinding everyone. When I re-opened my eyes, the three Vikings were hovering in a bubble of light, six feet above the floor. They were pounding their fists in protest against the clear barrier, but no noise penetrated their enclosure.

Gasps filled the Hall. Every Adrastai stood up and then genuflected down on one knee with their heads bowed. I was the only one, besides Nak, still standing. Confused as to why they would be reacting to my aerial flip in this manner, I looked to find an answer in Nak's eyes.

"Please lower your defense, young Adratsai," cooed a voice as soft as silk, from over my shoulder and I immediately recognized whom it belonged to.

"Laurina!" I gasped in excitement, quickly returning Servo to my left shoulder harness. "It is wonderful to see you again." I rushed over to the golden dragon and threw my arms around her neck, completely forgetting where I was and whom I was standing in front of. A wave of insecurity washed over me, and I slowly released my hug, letting my arms slide awkwardly down her shoulder and I began to genuflect, like the others.

"It is good to see you too, Brother." She nuzzled me with her snout, restricting me from kneeling, and gave me a surprising wink. Her actions were followed by more gasps from the crowds. "Our sincere apologies, brethren, I am Laurina and this is a place of peace, tranquility, and learning; not hate, distrust and battle. We are ALL here for the greater good, let us not forget that! Those who enter with a heart of hate will not be tolerated! Do I make myself clear?"

Laurina's voice was very stern as she spoke, directing her words to the three Vikings hovering above us. Humiliated, each of them quickly removed their helmets and dropped to one knee inside the floating bubble of light. The sternness in her voice sent a shiver down my spine. "Please Adrastai, return to your seats. Forgive my intrusion Nak," Laurina spoke as she nodded to Nak.

The Viking bubble popped and the three fell to the floor, with a crash. "You four will follow me." Laurina growled through clenched teeth. The muscles on either side of her jaw were rippling, tensely. I felt nervous for the Vikings as they collected themselves and followed her. They bumbled about, running into each other and stumbling, as Laurina stopped her exit and turned to look at me. "You too, Giovani," she commanded.

Me? What? My nervous anxiety returned and I first glanced at Skye, who had horror in her eyes, and then to Nak, whose gentle smile gave me the confidence to collect my things and follow the group. As I walked to the door, I hear the room erupt with mummers and the squeaking sound of desks shuffling as the occupants returned to their seats. I longed to join them.

I tried to keep my distance from the very large and angry men. No one spoke a word as Laurina lead us down a large marble-floored corridor. The rhythmic clicking of her talons on the tile was entrancing. Her soft golden hue reflected off the walls, bathing the rest of us in her glow. It was beautiful and extremely uncomfortable at the same time.

The one-eyed tyrant glanced back at me in silence. His glare told me everything I needed to know about his plan to inflict pain upon me.

Suddenly, before I could even take a breath, a flash of gold blurred my vision and a horrible growl echoed through the corridor. In a blink, it was over and the chaos of what just happened came into my view. In slow motion, the severed lower-half of the sinister Cyclops stumbled in my direction! I scurried back avoid the horrible scene, when it toppled onto me, slamming me into the wall! I slid down the cool marble as the one-eyed Viking's severed, bloody legs lay on top of me, still twitching. I glanced up in horror, to find Laurina spitting out the top half of the man. The other two Vikings were pinned against the other wall by her powerful tail, and a sound of fear, that I have never heard before, grew out of my throat.

Laurina's open jaws were heading straight towards me. I closed my eyes and tucked up as small as I could with half a man in my lap. Then I heard the awful sound of bones crunching, but I did not feel any pain. Upon opening my eyes, I saw Laurina's jaws setting the legs next to the other half of the body. She proceeded to kneel next to the dead Viking and whisper a prayer, and when finished, she stood, turned, and looked back to me. With a golden tear in her eye, she said, "His heart was no longer pure."

That was it. She turned slowly and solemnly continued her descent down the corridor. The three of us watched, stunned, as the golden executioner proceeded down the hallway. Protogenoi jumped into action, and surrounded the severed, lifeless body. The sprites

117

danced upon the corpse in a choreographed and caring way. I stood there, not knowing how to react, as the Protogenoi carried the dead man to the sky.

"Come, Giovani." The sad voice of Laurina beckoned.

I tried to snap out of it, as I stumbled down the hall. My body covered with the blood of a man, who wanted to kill me. The other two Vikings were scampering, nervously, behind her.

"I am sorry Giovani, that you had to witness that, but we cannot shield you from the reality of what is happening." Laurina's voiced cooed, but not in my ears; oddly, I just felt it.

"I am here. I am listening." I responded, but not with words; just by simply feeling what I wanted to say.

"You are stronger than you know, Brother. We have watched your powers grow in just one day." Laurina replied, but she never looked at me as she continued down the hall.

"Please, this way." Laurina spoke to the three of us in the Hall, as she pushed open two large double doors to the left.

The two Vikings hurried into the room, in fear of receiving the same fate as their brother. I followed them into the room; walking with confidence. The room was lit with only the flames from a fire in an extremely large fireplace. It looked like a library of some sorts, with three story high walls, filled with ancient looking books. This must have been the study that Nak spoke of. The woodwork as dark as walnuts, and the area rug was a dark cranberry color, that matched the bloodstains on my clothes. I shivered in disgust of wearing another man's blood.

A ball of light descended from the ceiling and surrounded my body. Tingling sensations of little shocks of electricity tickled my body, as the Protogenoi worked feverishly to rid the stains. When they suddenly shot back towards the ceiling, I looked as if I had gone through a laundry-carwash. My clothes were sparkling, and so was my skin. The Viking pair stood there watching with their mouths gaped open.

"Wonderful, aren't they?" I addressed the men. They only shook their heads in agreement. I assumed that they were terrified in regards to what was going to happen next. They just witnessed the death of their brethren, and found themselves sitting in the same room as his murderer.

"What is this hate all about, Adrastai?" St. John asked as he glided into the room starring at the Vikings. "Hello Brother Giovani." He added, casting a smile in my direction.

I was really enjoying that the High Mages not only called me by my first name, but also always called me brother, just as they did to Nak.

My thoughts drifted to Nak. He was the Adrastai teacher in my first lecture and never told us. I suppose that Aunt Evangeline was right, if he was worthy of teaching all of the Adrastai then having him as a personal mentor must be a big deal. *I wonder what Nak is doing right now?*

Immediately after finishing my thought, a strange new sensation came over me. I felt an odd pull, like my three year-old sister was tugging at the back of my shirt trying to drag me into a play. The room started to stretch out before me then, suddenly; my body was racing backwards through the long corridor we just traveled. It was like a strange roller-coaster ride stuck in reverse. Then I heard a commotion behind me and before I could turn to investigate, my body passed right through a crowd of Elves walking in the hall; right through them! I did not knock any one of them over and not one of them moved to avoid me, but two elves removed their hats in a gesture to say hello. Confused, I waved back. *Could they see me?* My short journey abruptly stopped and I found myself standing next to Nak who was still in front of the Adrastai Council. He was lecturing the audience, schooling them on the different aspects of The Order.

I shuffled nervously, but no one reacted to my presence. I leaned forward, putting my entire upper body in front of Nak, trying to block his view, but he continued on with his teaching. *How couldn't he not see me?* So in the spirit of my sisters, I decided to do a crazy jig in front of the audience,   and still, no one reacted. *What was going on?*

"Do you mind?" Nak's voice boomed inside my head, startling me. "I am conducting a classsss, and your dancing issss horrendous!" He giggled in my brain.

"Why am I here?" I asked, as I straightened out my clothes from my wildness.

"You willed yoursssself to me, but you are not actually here; just your ssssoul, which issss intertwined with mine. Your body issss where you left it, mosssst likely in a pile on the floor." Nak's voice spoke inside my head, but I could also hear him continuing his lecture to the Adratsai in the background.

"Wait! Like the time I saw your snake skin in a pile on the floor, when you were, you know, inside of me?" I started to freak out a little bit and shook out a hee-bee-gee-bee dance.

"Yessss. You may want to get back to the High Magesssss, brother." He hissed, "I believe they are waiting for you."

"How?" I asked.

"Jusssst think it, and make it sssso. Now, kindly leave sssso I may educate thesssse warriorsssss." Nak hissed, rather agitated.

Think it? Make it so? What the heck, why is all of this happening to me? I tried hard to tell myself to return to my body. In a flash, I was standing back in front of the enormous fireplace with two very freaked out Vikings just blinking at me with their mouths gaped open.

"Sorry about that." I sincerely told them, knowing full well how freaked out I was when Nak re-inflated, even though I didn't feel a thing.

The two, burly men, scurried themselves backwards, like rodents trying to escape death, until their backs slammed against the wall and a pile of books landed on top of them.

"Oh, gosh. Sorry about that too. Here let me help you." I went to move one of the books off the men, but when I reached to grab it; it flew off them before I could touch it. "What?" I questioned aloud.

I reached out to grab another, and, that book also flew off before I physically touched it. I stood straight up, bewildered. Then I had the overwhelming urge to perform my pretend karate moves, to see if the books were actually following my arm movements. Waving my arms like a sensei, all of the books went flying off the huddled Vikings in every direction! It was awesome! I was laughing so hard at my cleverness, that I did not see the one book land squarely on top of St. John's head!

"I do believe it is time to seek the Oracle." He said dryly, with the pages of the book flopping down on either side of his head, looking like a really bad wig.

Chapter 9

Illustrated by
Kyoko Inagaki

9

A VIKING JOURNEY

The Oracle? What was an Oracle and was this Oracle going do for me? Maybe it was for me, or maybe it was for the Vikings. I wonder what an oracle would look like. My head was filled with so many questions.

"Sit down, Sensei Giovani." Giggled Laurina, "That little comedy show of yours was quite entertaining."

Blushing, I grinned and sat in the oversized, leather chair by the fire, which dwarfed me because of its enormity. "I practiced those moves in the forest behind my house, Ninja-style. They ward off any member of The FrouFrou Crew." I sheepishly replied. "I miss my sisters. They would have loved to see that." I picked up my chin and took a deep breath to snap courage back into my heart.

"You will be reunited again, Giovani. There are matters at hand that you need to attend to first. You must go on a journey to seek The Oracle." Laurina's voice was gentle but firm; now was the time to be strong.

"Where shall I find such a thing, and what am I looking for? I have no idea what an Oracle even is." I asked. I was honored and confident knowing that the High Mages hand-chose me for this quest.

"You must travel to the Ethiopian Mountains, but be warned: this is not an easy task. Your journey will be dangerous. The terrain is unforgiving and filled with terrifying creatures, some the likes of you have never seen before. Many strong warriors have entered and never returned." St. John glided across the room to a window looking out at the mountains surrounding the Enchanted Valley.

"But some have returned, right?" I nervously chortled.

"You must leave as soon as possible. Belac and Ttensir will accompany you." Laurina added while casting a stern look towards the Vikings.

What? Them? "Um, forgive me please, but are they the best choice?" I questioned. "I, uh, I..."

"They are noble warriors, who have navigated those mountains before. They will most certainly be of assistance. You must work together to find the Oracle." Laurina added. "Get up, I do not enjoy the taste of Viking blood, do not force me to try it again!" she growled in the direction of Belac and Ttensir.

Both of the Vikings jumped to their feet and quickly collected themselves. They stood very tall, over six feet, and their bodies rippled with muscle. This was the first time I was able to get a good look at them. Their skin was war-torn with scars; claw marks, and their faces were hard. I questioned whether their hearts and intentions were true, and I was very nervous about traveling with them.

"How shall we travel there?" barked Belac.

"I believe that you have a noble ship, do you not?" St. John answered.

Both Ttensir and Belac immediately slammed their right fists onto their strong chests directly over their hearts. The force of their noble gestures echoed through the chamber accompanied by their guttural war cries.

I glanced at St. John and shrugged my shoulders, questioning their integrity; after all they did want to harm Nak just a few moments ago. "Huh?"

"They are Vikings and very capable sailors." St. John replied.

"I love to sail, but are we to accomplish the quest quickly, or does time not matter?" I asked, but I suddenly became keenly aware of the fact that I continued to question the High Mages decisions. St. John did not look pleased with me.

"We are most capable and our ship is the finest on the seas." Ttensir replied and he glared in my direction sensing my concerns. "May we enlist the help of the Sylphs?" he added, speaking directly to Laurina.

"Seek out Clerah, if she obliges, then you are certainly welcome to try." Laurina replied. "And you, Brother," Laurina turned her attention to me, "remember your shield, elven and dragon forged sword and what you have learned. Be strong, do not waiver in your courage, and uphold the nine Virtues of Adrastai."

I felt the need to genuflect down on one knee, like the knights before kings, "I pledge my Life to The Order!" The Vikings followed my lead and did the same.

"Dear Brother, be safe." St. John had glided over to my side and laid his hand on my shoulder. "This is not a game in the woods behind your house; you will need to focus."

A strange sensation made my dragon birthmark on my left

shoulder, jump at his touch. I suddenly began to feel very light-headed and disoriented. I stood up, uneasy and stumbled to the chair by the fire. I searched the room for some sort of answer in one their faces, but St, John and Laurina seemed affected by the same strange illness.

Laurina collapsed onto the floor and St. John grabbed the book shelve to try to steady himself. The Vikings were bewildered. Ttensir ran to Laurina's aide, "Laurina! What is going on? Are you all right? Laurina!" I saw Laurina's eyes go completely white, she was not responding to Ttensir at all.

Belac had run to help St. John, catching him just before he buckled to the floor. His body was limp in Belac's arms. His head swung lifeless to the side, revealing the same strange white eyes as Laurina. "Help! Somebody help us!" Belac screamed.

I was useless. My strength was being pulled elsewhere. I felt myself crash to floor and my soul ripped from my body. A white light filled my vision and I was blinded by the brightness. *What was happening?*

"Ssssilence!" Nak hissed in my mind. "Just let it happen! We have been called; we musssst remain quiet and calm to remain undetected!"

"We? Called? Help me," but all of my breath was leaving as my chest tightened with an incredible pressure. I felt, again, as if a giant snake was wrapping around me, constricting, and crushing all of my air out of my lungs. I surrender to the light and slipped out of consciousness.

The sound of rushing water filled my ears, and it was all too familiar to me. When I opened my eyes, a wall of bubbles rushed past me in an upward motion. I was being pulled down into the depths of some body of water by an unseen force.

Our decent suddenly stopped. My feet landed onto what felt like sand; it moved beneath me. My hair swayed, fluid-like in the water above my head, but I was not prepared for what I saw next. Soft glowing light grew out of the darkness behind me. I turned slowly, and was confused by the lack of effort it took, considering I was underwater; there was no resistance.

One by one, each my friends began to appear in a ghostly manner; literally, like the tales of apparitions, spectral and white. Their figures grew from darkness into light, right before my eyes, but they were not the bodies I was used to seeing. I swayed there in the depths with my mouth wide open in wonder.

Laurina, St. John, and Nak were all with me, in ghostly forms. They were brilliant looking, all colored in golden light. I felt peaceful in their presence. I could not see through them; they were made of solid golden light. Every detail of their physical body was present, but made of this magical light.

My eyes were torn from their splendor by quick movements darting through the depths behind them. I raised my arm and pointed off into the dark abyss; the golden glow of my own arm caught my attention. Amazed, I quickly patted my own body, which felt solid, but I was made entirely of the golden light too. I looked just like the others--just like one of the High Mages. They continued to call me brother...*why was this happening?*

"Silence your thoughts, brother," Laurina whispered inside my mind, as she tucked her arms and legs to her side and began to snake through the water in a serpentine manner, with St. John riding on her golden back, tucked down ready for speed .

Nak slithered alongside them, and instinctively, my body began to slither too. I was confused about all of these new experiences and changes I was going through, but Laurina had asked me to quiet my mind; I was going to have to think about all of this later.

Suddenly, a sharp pain seared through my left shoulder! My birthmark! We were in danger! Laurina faltered in her swimming and St. John slumped forward, seemingly affected as well. Nak, too, was laboring in his path. An eerie feeling came over me and all of my senses tingled, alerting me of lurking threats.

Immediately, something knocked into the side of me with the force of a train, sending me tumbling through the water. A flash of silver rushed past me, and my golden body slammed into Nak.

Laurina quickly turned to snap at the shimmering assailant, but it moved through the depths with lightning speed. She, too, tumbled over herself after being hit by another silvery aggressor. The sheer force of the impact knocked St. John clear off her back.

I up-righted myself and unsheathed a golden Servo. It was magnificent. I was in awe of the brilliant light that emanated from the golden sword, and then, just as it had in the charred forest of Sukanar's Lair, Servo began wielding itself in my hands, slicing through the water in every direction and hitting its target. Through the bloodstained water, I watched decapitated snakes fall to the ocean floor and I never even saw them around me! They were sea snakes; I recognized them from my studies, the most venomous species. I was grateful for my elven-forged sword.

St. John was in front of me, battling another unforeseen force with golden balls of energy that formed between his magical hands. He made rhythmic motions, reminiscent of a tai-chi master, defending himself in every direction. Laurina, too, was fighting the unseen--snapping her jaws and thrashing her tail. Out of the corner of my eye and off in the distance, I saw the glowing body of Nak swimming into a large dark cave.

"GET OUT BRETHREN! LEAVE ME!" shouted a voice inside my head! I quickly scanned my friends to see which one was directing me, and searched for some sort of direction from them.

"NO! WE WILL NOT LEAVE YOU!" St. John's voice screamed back inside my head. I had never heard such panic in his voice before, and suddenly concern overwhelmed me.

"WE ARE COMING Asëa! HOLD ON!" Laurina roared.

"NO! SAVE YOUR..." but Asëa's voice was replaced with a horrible scream of agony and his breath escaped him, as if some force crushed it out of him.

"Asëa! Asëa, NO!" cried the pained voice of Laurina, who's golden light seemed to dim.

Instinctively, the three of us shot towards the cave as fast as we could following Nak's path! Jagged rock ripped at the flesh of my hands as I crawled my way up the underwater rock wall, towards the cave. Our heads emerged into a large underwater cavern, just in time to find Nak cradling the limp body of Asëa in his coils.

My Vision! My Sight of the small-framed girl being killed by a snake! It wasn't a girl; it was Asëa! Did Nak...no, he couldn't have, he wouldn't. I pushed the thought out of my mind before even thinking it. Nak didn't kill anyone. However, if Nak didn't kill him, then who did?

"Nãga!" roared Nak in a guttural crescendo as Asëa's limp body lay in his coils, "WHY?" he cried dragging the word out until it ended in sobs.

I stood there, not knowing what to do next. I was in shock. One of the High Mages, one of the founders of The Order, one elven brother, who meant so much to everyone fighting for the Light; lay slain.

Numb, I fell to my knees and cupped my head in my hands. St. John also fell to his knees and with his head slumped down. The long golden hair of his beard now looked tattered and worn as it lay in the mud on the cavern floor. His body was heaving with sighs of sadness.

Everything was happening in slow motion. I turned to find
Laurina, looking for some sort of explanation or solace. A large
golden tear was slowly sliding down her cheek. Instantly, I jumped
up remembering how Khai's golden tear healed my wounds from the
Troll attack!

I darted towards the majestic dragon, who was wrought with
sorrow. My eyes fixated on that healing tear that appeared to fall
faster as I neared.

"NO!" was all I could manage, as the tear slipped off her jaw just
out of my reach! I dove towards her, with my arms out-stretched to
make a diving catch. The warm liquid filled my hands, but then
continued to seep through my fingers.

Turning hand over hand, I tried to keep as much of the golden
tear cupped within my grasp as I could; as I ran to Nak. I clumsily
scaled his coils, just in time to let the last remaining drop of tear fall
from my hands and land on the forehead of the lifeless Asëa.

"Please," I pleaded, "please work." I felt myself holding my
breath and body anxiously shaking.

St. John and Laurina were suddenly right beside me, each one of
us waiting expectantly, for a miracle. Abruptly, Asëa's tiny green
chested jutted forward, grasping for life, and violently inhaling a deep
breath. It was horrifying, but when his body settled back down,
Laurina gently nuzzled his little shoulder and whispered, "We are
here, brother. We are here."

Asëa, slowly opened his eyes halfway, but I could tell that just
doing that took too much energy. "I...I," he stammered to speak.

"Ssshhh, don't speak brother, we have you. We will take you
home." St. John spoke lovingly, as he gently took Asëa's hand in his.

"I love you all." Faintly whispered Asëa inside my head, but he sounded weak and far away. "What a beautiful family, look inside your heart, for I will forever dwell there." A tear gently slid from Asëa's closed eyes. Laurina pressed her tear-stained cheek to his forehead and turned her face from the rest of us, Asëa tried to reach up and caress her face, but his arm fell limp.

A long silence followed, no one spoke or made eye contact. Asëa's chest heaved again, filling his lungs with breath that escaped as he struggled to push his words out, "Giovani, I knew we were right to put so much faith in you. Thank you for giving me the energy to embrace all of you one last time." His voice was slow and shaky, but he managed to open his eyes and look into mine; I felt his love deep inside my heart, "You are destined for greatness brother, if you always follow your heart and..." but his words trailed off, his eyes slid shut, and he fell limp again.

Without hesitation, Laurina quickly bent forward as Nak placed the body of Asëa, High Mage, into her mouth. I was a little concerned about the ritual, but did not have time to think about it. Straight away, our bodies just exploded showering gold dust throughout the cavern.

Instantly, without the rush and squeezing transport we endured earlier, I found myself back inside my body next to the fire in the study. Ttensir and Belac rushed towards each of the Mages' sides, and Laurina gently lowered Asëa's tiny limp body onto the soft white fur rug next to me. The Vikings gasped at the sight of the fallen Mage. St. John kneeled down beside us, and Nak coiled his tail around me in a fatherly way.

No one spoke. Sadness filled the room, pressing down on me like a weight upon my shoulders. I reached to hold this marvelous being's hand, and he stirred at my touch. "Rest, my brother," I whispered. "You are safe now."

Asëa struggled to open his eyes, he looked directly into the eyes of St. John and then to Laurina's, "Thank you for loving me." His last word trailed off and floated away on his last breath as he eyes softly closed, forever.

Laurina's head dropped in sadness, as St. John gently folded Asëa's tiny arms across his chest and bent to place a kiss on his forehead.

A soft glowing light filled the room. Peering through my tear-filled eyes, I found millions of Protogenoi lining the perimeter of the study. They were not dancing or twirling; just simply there hovering with their tiny bowed heads. It was very somber feeling, they, too, were mourning the loss of this great being.

St. John slowly stood up. Laurina pulled her head up high and sat back on her hind legs, looking very majestic. Nak nudged my shoulder and gestured for me to rise. Silently, we all acknowledged the reality of Asëa's passing from this realm and united we stood around him.

Encircled by the four of us, Asëa's lifeless body stopped glowing. Tears streamed down my face. With a silent nod from both St. John and Laurina, the Protogenoi gently approached us, softly flying in from all angles and in a choreographed ritual; they gently surrounded the fallen elf. They did not cover his body quickly, as they did the one-eyed Viking, but simply lifted him up, cradling him in their soft light.

Slowly and with the utmost respect, the Protogenoi ascended to the ceiling and disappeared into the sky, just as they had when they carried my youth-filled tear.

Laurina and St. John both let out a terrible, rage-filled roar that shook the very foundation of the Hall of Knowledge. I fell into the chair, startled. The stained glass panel above the door, with Asëa's portrait on it, shattered into a million pieces and rained down onto the floor of the Hall of Knowledge. The tinkling sound of glass hitting the stone floor filled my ears.

Instantly, Nak's skin dropped to floor! His bright essence grew stronger before me until it exploded into thin air. My body involuntarily began to move in the oversized chair, and the entire room was bathed in a bright golden light.

I found myself thrust into his actions, going through them as if they were my own. My birthmark seared hot with pain, and I could not move. We were traveling with intense speed and I could feel Nak's rage building like it was my own. I was conscious that my body was still in the Hall of Knowledge, but I was seeing through Nak's eyes and experiencing through his body. The pain of being in two places at the same time was immense and it felt as if I was being torn apart. My nails dug into the arms of the chair, as everything was flying past me at alarming speeds. I was losing control of my body again, and just when I thought my body would tear apart, everything came to a halt!

We were back inside the cavern again, but only through Nak's eyes; I could still feel my grip on the arms of the chair in the study. He was engulf in anger and growled with all of his being, "NAGA!!!!!"

The stone floor of the cavern began to shake, violently. Stalactites fell from the ceiling, crashing on the ground. One shard pierced Nak's tail, pinning him to the floor and he yelped in pain. Something large approached, each giant footfall trembled the earth. Nak's face was twisted with hate, as he focused on the largest tunnel leading off of the cavern. He stood strong and without fear, but I could hardly breathe, full of anxiety.

"Nak, get out of there!" I screamed inside his head. "Whatever that is, it is much larger than you, NAK! Can you hear me?"

"Leave me be!" he hissed back full of rage, with his eyes fixated on the mouth of the gaping tunnel and approaching terror.

I felt my heart race and my chest grow tight. My dragon birthmark burned hotter than ever before. I could have sworn I smelled my flesh burning. Then, in slow motion the horrifying figure slowly emerged, snake-like from the mouth of the darkness.

A giant, silvery-grey colored Dragon's head grew from the blackness. This creature stood twice as high as Khai, and the room grew cold from the sheer hatred and evil emanating from its soul. As its full body came into sight, it was more than a dragon. Two large fins with enormous spikes on the tips and jutted out from just behind the powerful jaws. Its body was sleek and long, perfectly designed to stealthily maneuver through the depths of the sea, and lined with an entire row of spikes down its back. The tail was serpent-like with a gigantic fin at the end.

Nak growled a guttural roar, full of rage, "NAGA! I WILL END YOU!" and he postured aggressively, and appeared to be larger than he ever was, almost as tall as Khai.

"Why, hello little brother." The beast calmly sneered. "How nice of you to drop by for a little family reunion. Father will be most pleased." She continued, spitting her sarcastic words out through clenched jaws. I could feel the hatred in the cavern.

"Let's go see him, shall we?" She chuckled as her gigantic tail lifted and slammed down on the floor of the cavern. The ground immediately began to shake, causing both creatures to stumble. Immediately, the earth between them split apart and molten lava shot up over twenty feet in the air!

"I am here for you, you wicked beasssst! How could you?" Nak hissed, and then he turned his head to the giant fissure that separated the twins and shouted into it, "Typhon! This has nothing to do with you!"

"I see you haven't corrected your lisp in the last hundred years." She retorted, tossing her head back with a sinister laugh and exposing her fierce jaws. "Look at your little boy, Typhon, trying to bring good to the world. Aren't you proud?" Her voice riddled with sarcasm again, and she too, spoke to the crack oozing lava.

"Unfortunately, one cannot pick the family they are born into." Nak's words stabbed back at the ferocious creature. "We have a score to settle! You killed my brethren! We had an agreement!" Nak lunged towards Nãga, ripping his tail free from the stalactite that nailed him to the floor.

More lava exploded up from the center of the earth, just as Nak's words finished. The ground trembled again. A giant bolder broke away from the ceiling of the cave, and crashed down landing on the serpent-like tail of Nãga! The creature shrieked in agony and her hind legs collapsed to the cavern floor. With a powerful flick of her tail, the bolder shot off and headed towards Nak, who slide out of the way, just in time.

"Well played Father!" She screamed down the fissure in the floor. "So sorry that Zeus pinned you under that nasty volcano, because it would be my pleasure to bite off every serpent digit you have!" Nãga shook her head from side-to-side seemingly trying to shake way her pain, "You certainly have a funny way of showing your affection and gratitude for the only child trying to help you!" The wicked Nãga regained her footing and turned her attention back to Nak after yelling at the crack in the floor, "Get out of here before I bite you in half, dear brothersss." She added the lisp and spewing spit, mocking the way Nak speaks.

"Helping Father and murdering Asëa? What happened to you? Destroying you would be a great service to The Order! I'll have your head!" Nak screamed!

I felt a stirring inside of me, and my birthmark seared with pain. A strange sensation that has never happened before grew from my stomach out to the farthest points of my body, when two bright rays of light shot from Nak's eyes, causing my eyes to burn with pain and blinding me. I pushed my fists into my eyes to alleviate the pain, when I heard blood-curdling screams of agony, but was unable to see who was making them.

Shortly, my eyesight recovered and I was able to see through Nak's eyes once again, revealing a horrific scene. Green liquid shot out of a large gaping wound on Nāga's neck, spewing everywhere and covering everything within twenty feet of the beast. The creature roared in pain, regained its footing, and glared straight at Nak with pure hatred in her eyes. Instantaneously, the beast sprung over the lava-spewing crevice with the quickness of a tiger on its prey.

Nāga roared as she sprang through the air with razor sharp jaws honed in on Nak's head. He swayed and slithered out of the way just in time, she slammed into the cavern wall, sending boulders careening in every direction! One struck Nak in the head, knocking him onto the ground. She chuckled, sinisterly, and wiped more green fluid from her jaw with her front paw. "Still quick, I see." She quipped before, nonchalantly, picking a piece of boulder out of her teeth with her talon and flicking it at Nak.

My eyes started to burn again, Nak's eyes flashed white before the blindness took over, and more screams of agony ensued. A horrifying roar rumbled up from the molten depths, followed by Nāga's cynical sneers, "Guess who's mad!" she giggled out in a sing-song sort of way before lunging to attack him again. Nāga faked her move to bite him, flicked her strong tail up from behind Nak, and hitting her mark. A loud clunk thundered inside my skull, as the serpent-like weapon struck Nak on the side of his head, crashing him into the rock wall of the underwater cavern. Darkness creeped in from every corner of my sight, followed by Nāga's maniacal laughter, and then everything went black.

Chapter 10

Illustrated by
Lydia Lanski

10

MESSAGE FROM BEYOND

My life essence shot back into my body and I gasped for air, frightened. The process caused me to fall off of the chair, landing onto the fur rug in front of the fire, where Asëa took his last breath.

Laurina, St. John, and the Vikings quickly ran to my side. "What happened Giovani, where's Nak?" Laurina questioned me with much concern in her voice.

"Isn't he back?" I managed to ask through the fog in my brain and the tingling inside my body. My hands flew to cradle my head, which felt like it was being squeezed in a vice.

"No!" Laurina barked at me and quickly pointed her head in the direction of the limp cobra skin lying on the floor.

"He's hurt! It was Nãga! They fought." It was always difficult to talk, the pain in my head was severe. "There were earthquakes and lava...the beast was enormous...so strong and their father. I don't know how he can fight her alone. Her tail...her tail, it slammed into his head just before I was pulled back here." I was struggling to shake the fog from my brain, and for some reason, my right shoulder ached.

"Earthquakes and lava?" St. John repeated. "Their father? Are you sure? What did she say?" Alarm filled St. John's voice.

I tried to answer him, but immense pain grew inside my skull. The pressure felt like my head was going to explode, and I collapsed back to rug, curled up in agony. All I could do was grab my head, hoping to keep it from bursting open. I couldn't think or speak, just moan and writhe in pain.

"Giovani! Take a deep breath and let it happen! Nak is calling you; he needs you." Laurina's voice echoed behind the pain in my head.

Nak needs me? I wanted to vomit from the agony.

"Go to him!" Her voice was sharp but growing faint and far away as if I was traveling away from her, even though she was just beside me a minute ago. Nak needed me. That was all that I could concentrate on. I had to help him. The desire to save him was overwhelming and consuming.

Then, just as I had moved through time and found myself in front of the Adrastai class he was lecturing, I was traveling back to scene in the underwater cavern. The sound of rushing bubbles filled my ears and tickled as they passed over my skin. I was willing myself back to Nak. Just then, I found myself back inside the cavern. I quickly surveyed my surrounds and hoped I would not find Nãga.

My birthmark ached and I checked my protective orb that hung around my neck, to see what color it was; oddly, it was transparent. In extreme danger, it always glows red, but maybe because I wasn't inside my true body, it was transparent. I was just a fraction of myself, ghostlike. I didn't have time to ponder this; Nak needed me.

Something moved out of the corner of my eye. I jerked my head to find Nak lying under a pile of rubble dangerously close to the lava-oozing fissure. I ran over to him faster that I have ever moved before!

"Nak! Nak, are you okay?" His body was limp. "Answer Me!" I screamed!

"I thought I killed you!" boomed Nãga's voice throughout the cavern. The ground shook again, with each rushing footfall as the beast returned to finish Nak off.

"Nak! Get Up! She's coming!" I was frantically trying to get him to stand, move, or slide! Nothing. Maybe I did make it in time. "ANSWER ME!" I shouted into his ear.

Just then, the giant form of Nãga crashed into the cavern. Stalagmites shattered as her back collided with the top of the opening. I shielded my face to avoid being struck with flying debris. With a single leap, she landed beside us. The earth trembled so violently, I lost my footing and crashed into the wall of the cavern. Pain shot through the side of my leg! The colonies of oysters and mollusks with their razor-sharp shells had sliced through my flesh.

Nãga kicked her brother's body, "Why aren't you dead? I felt you walking around out here. Stop playing and get up and face me you coward!"

Felt him walking around? He hasn't moved. I looked around to see if there was anything I could defend us with. Rocks; nothing but rocks. Lava oozed out of the ground, but I could not grab that. I had to somehow outsmart the beast in order to get us out of here alive.

Nãga turned and spoke to the gaping crack in the floor, "See, Dad? He is not worthy of your blood. The weak must be destroyed."

Lava shot up through the crack like a geyser, as if in agreement. Nāga's behavior seemed psychotic, the way she constantly spoke to the fissure as if it actually was her father, but Nak did too. *What did he say?* I tried to remember, but suddenly Nak's eyes opened and locked onto mine.

"Brother, help!" he screamed.

"Brother?" Nāga questioned, as her head jerked towards Nak and glared at him out of the corner of her eye. "So there is someone else here with us, is there?" the sinister tone returned to her voice, as she scanned the cavern looking for me.

"Show yourself, Brother!" She sneered. "WHERE ARE YOU!" she y three year-old sister during a game of hide-and-seek.

I didn't know what to do. *How was I going to help him?* If the entire class in the lecture hall could not see me then Nāga couldn't, right? I decided to run to Nak's side. I made a break for it. My birthmark seared with pain and I reached back to grab it. I felt the warm tingling sensation grow up from my feet and the strength of ten warriors fill my arms!

"Then I will end him, right in front of you. COWARD!" Nāga quickly opened her jaws and made a move to swallow her brother's limp body.

Instinct took over. With incredible speed, I maneuvered the ghost of myself between the two siblings and turned to face the beast. Her gaping jaws and enormous teeth were mere inches from ripping us apart when I reached up with one hand and grabbed the top mandible to keep it from clamping down on us. Her large fang-like incisors narrowly missed piercing through my flesh. I crammed my feet in between her lower teeth to prevent her lower jaw from biting us in half. Pain shot through my stomach. I looked down to find one of the enormous spikes that jutted out from her lower jaw

142

pierced through my abdomen. I faltered at the sight of it but, somehow, I found the strength to hold her at bay.

The ferocious monster was stunned and stopped in her tracks, as she tried to process what just happened. Her yellow eyes shifted from one side to the other, trying to focus in on me, and discern what thwarted her advance. I could only assume that she could not see my light form.

The pain in my stomach was unbearable. My grip on her jaws was slipping and I felt my knees begin to buckle. The dragon birthmark on my left shoulder burned, as if a molten rock shot from the fissure in the floor and melted through my skin.

An eerie creaking sound echoed through the cavern, as if all of the rocks were shifting over top of each other. Six-foot wide stalactites twitched on the ceiling like twigs in the wind, and the stalagmites Nak was propped against, swayed under the pressure of the sliding earth. Nãga released her bite, shook my body from her spikes, like a dog shedding water, and backed away with concern riddled on her face.

I immediately sank to the floor and grabbed my stomach. My hand sank inside a gaping hole, where my bellybutton should have been. Chaos ensued around us. The ground shook with a force of an earthquake. Rocks shattered sending shards off in every direction. I needed to shield my eyes from the debris.

A terrifying guttural growl gurgled up from the depths, filling the cavern, and sending shivers down my spine. Nãga stopped dead in her nervous tracks, frozen in fear. I could feel the rage of this unseen beast's voice, full of pure evil, and it rocked me to my core. I laid, fearful for our lives, on the rocky floor that grew hotter to the touch every second.

"NAGA! RELEASE ME!" growled the dark voice. The water's

edge started to bubble up along the cliff entrance, forcing the depths to rise and fill the cavern, as if something gigantic was pushing it towards us. 'I COMMAND YOU TO DO IT NOW!"

Nãga reeled around on her heels and faced the crack in the floor, looking for something. I took this split second to throw my body on top of Nak's. The instant our bodies connected, bright light exploded into the room and golden flakes fluttered down from the ceiling!

Confused, Nãga didn't know how to react or where to turn her focus to. Whatever lies in the depths of the molten crack, commanded her attention and she gave up on eating us and walked towards the fissure, peering inside. Nãga quickly glanced at us, and I would swear she actually saw me. She looked right into my eyes and I felt her evil deep within my soul. Undeterred, she slowly turned her face back to the fissure, ignoring us, and I heard her speak to the ground, "Typhon, I am at your service."

I reversed the process and willed us back to Laurina and St. John and our bodies took off like a shot! The familiar feeling of being sucked back through a path I had already traveled, but in reverse came over me. I felt Nak with me, but he wasn't standing or traveling beside me, but somehow, magically attached to me, by some invisible bond. I didn't need to carry him, he was just ...there.

"Thank you brother," Nak's exhausted voice whispered inside my head. "I owe you my life."

Blocking out the agony in my gut, I quickly turned all of my conscious thoughts to the study. The wood-paneled walls lined with leather bound books, the gigantic fireplace with a crackling fire and the white fur rug that lay in front of it. Just as soon as I completed my thought, our bodies tumbled safely onto the soft rug.

The High Mages and Vikings were already at our sides. "Well

done, Giovani!" St. John exclaimed as he caught my drained body, when I collapsed into his arms.

We were safe. The fire warmed my cold skin. I kept my arm over the Nak's shoulder, not wanting to let go and, immediately, I drifted off into a pain-induced deep sleep.

I awoke to the familiar smell of damp soil and moss. I smiled with my eyes shut, knowing that Elia was there caring for me back in our tent. The fire crackled and Brochara and Fin chatted across the room. I sunk my face farther into the lavender and rose petal-filled pillow wanting to drift back to sleep, safe and sound, but the events that just occurred flooded my mind. I nervously reached up to my stomach, sinking my hand into a cool, wet patch of goo that Elia must have applied to heal my wounds.

I slowly tried to sit up, but it quickly became clear that I had sustained injuries in the cavern. Elia made her way over to me carrying a large mug. Instantly, I knew that it was going to be full of the chunky concoction that she hands me every time I get hurt, which seems to quite often, and I plunged my face back into my pillow. Fighting off Elia's remedies was pointless. I guess the medicine would be okay if it wasn't for the awful smell and worms spilling over the lip of the cup. I didn't even argue, I just sighed deeply, reached out, plugged my nose, and drank it down with my eyes closed. *Gack! I felt every wriggling worm as it slid down my throat.*

"Well done, my dear." Elia cooed. "Now, how do you feel?" she asked with a smile.

"I have had better days, to be honest." I answered. "How's Nak?"

"Nak is healing; being the child of two different Monsters has its advantages," barked Brochara, as he climbed up on the side of the bed, pulling the weight of his over-sized belly up to sit beside me.

His large eyes looked at me with anticipation, darting from my stomach to my face and back again, like the three year-old did as I told her a story. "Well, what happened to you?" he finally asked.

"Monsters?" I questioned, "Nak is a Monster? I knew he was supernatural, but a Monster?"

"He is the offspring of two very nasty mythological monsters; that is what Evangeline told me last night." Brochara added looking proud as if he figures out a piece of a puzzle. "I don't really know what that means." He continued, nonchalantly, shrugging his shoulders and giggling.

"Is that why she kept asking me if I felt differently after he took my body over?" Suddenly, I was very intrigued about whom he was and I wanted to know more. "I need to speak with Nak."

"He will talk to you when the time is right, my explorer." Aunt Evangeline walked into the room and sat down on the bed next to me. "How are you feeling, Buddy?"

I always loved being around Aunt E. I threw my arms around her neck and she felt like home. I wanted to be home right now, the FrouFrou Crew singing, Mom's hugs, and playing catch with Dad. I tried not to let my mind wander back home too often, because it just made me feel sad. The only thing that kept me going was the fact that I felt like I was protecting them being a part of The Order.

"I'm okay, I guess. I mean physically, I am a little sore and drained, with a huge hole in my stomach." I slid back onto my pillow and I was going to tell her that my mind wouldn't rest, but she could already tell.

"Do you want to talk about what happened? Nak has been healing, so we have chosen not to disturb him; you know, with the whole trance during molting thing." Aunt E playfully nudged me with her elbow but I could tell by the look on her face that she was anxious for answers.

"Um, sure" I hesitated, "Where do want me to start?" Tired, I reached out and took her hand into mine.

"Well, how about starting at the part where you were removed from lecture this morning." Aunt E said with one eyebrow raised, as if she was questioning why?

"Oh yeah, that seems like it happened forever ago," I paused briefly to recall what happened earlier today, "that was extremely intense as it unfolded, but it paled in comparison to how the day ended." I added.

"Well there were these Vikings, scary guys, and the one with one eye wanted to hurt Nak…I think." I hesitated to recall earlier that day, because so much had happened. "Then he wanted to hurt me, that I can swear to. Anyway, Laurina interrupted with this really cool bubble-cage that she held the angry men in and then pulled the four of us out of class. Oh yeah, then she killed the one-eyed guy in the hallway." I shivered with the hee-bee-gee-bees again, remembering the severed pair of legs that pinned me to the floor. The look on Aunt E's face was priceless as I spewed out the morning's events.

"After that, Laurina told me I had to go on a quest, with the two remaining Vikings, who previously wanted to rip my head off, to find some Oracle that St. John thought it was time for me to seek." I shrugged my shoulders, questioning the statement.. "They said something about traveling by ship and a Clareh?" I was just rattling of the details as they came flooding back to me, but I was certain they thought I was delusional.

"Wait, They who? Who are the 'they' you are talking about?" Brochara, rudely, interrupted. I turned to answer him, and found his faced contorted with confusion and his left ear involuntarily twitching trying to follow my babbling. I couldn't help but laugh at him.

"Oh sorry, St. John and Laurina. Okay," I took a deep breath, collecting myself, and ready to spit out the rest of it, when Elia walked back into the room and interrupted.

"Wait, dear. My apologies for interrupting, where was Asëa?" she questioned with her oversized hands anxiously writhing inside her apron.

I quickly averted her stare and lowered my head. I had forgotten that part of the day, or possibly blocked it out. I didn't know if I should continue to tell them that he wasn't with us anymore. Didn't they know? I started to get extremely anxious and worried, when I felt a slight buzzing in my pocket. Startled, I jumped and heard the sound of metal landing on the hardwood floor followed by the distinct sound of a coin rolling before it landed on its side. My shield was rolling in a spiral, making smaller and smaller loops as we all just watched it circle, absorbed.

"Is that your shield?" Brochara barked, scaring us out of our trance.

Just then, Fin cartwheeled into the room, grabbed my shield just before it finished the spiral to the floor, and tossed it back up to me. The shield flipped over itself, repeatedly, until it met the palm of my hand.

Once the heavy coin landed in my hand, it fanned open, like a metal spiral repeatedly, until it grew as big as a shield. I set in my lap and brought myself to sit up. Elia magically appeared behind me and was already fluffing pillows to support my back. I smiled lovingly at her. The large shield was almost weightless in my lap even though it was made of metal. The underside was as shiny as a mirror and reflected all of my new family's faces back at me except for Nak. Even Khai had joined us inside this magical tent, which always stretched to accommodate all of us.

We all stared into the shield in wonder, when green rings started to ripple out of the center of it. The metal in the center appeared to look fluid, as if someone had cast a stone into the shimmery silver metal...

We were all mesmerized by the rippling metallic pool that lie within the curve of the shield, when an outline of a figure started to appear, or rise up from the center of the shimmering liquid. After the moving settled and the metal smoothed out again, Asëa, the High Mage, was staring back at all of us.

Quickly, all of my friends genuflected down on one knee and bowed their heads in respect. I just sat there on the bed, not sure of what was going on or how to react. *Why did his face appear when I was thinking about him and how?*

"Hello dear Brother, Giovani." Asëa's reflection spoke to me.

I dropped it quickly to the floor and tried push myself as far away from the talking vision as possible. The apparition of Asëa landed face down on the floor of the tent. *He was dead. I saw it. How was he talking to me?* Brochara quickly leapt from the bed, scrambled over and picked up my shield, cast a disapproving look at me, and flipped the shield upright so we could see his face.

"One thousand apologies Sire. Forgive him; he knows not the ways of our kind." Brochara spoke to the enchanted reflection with his head deeply bowed. Brochara's hands were shaking at the sight of the High mage and more ripples careened across Asëa's reflection in the metallic pool.

"Thank you Brochara, you are most kind. I do appreciate your assistance very much." Asëa replied as his reflection made eye contact with Brochara. My elven guide bowed lower than I had ever seen him bow before at Asëa's kind words and some of the enchanted liquid spilled over the edge. The nervous Brochara overcorrected his mistake and more of the High Mage sploshed over the other side of the shield onto the floor.

Elia quickly grabbed her mate's elbow to steady his hold, when Asëa cast her a look of appreciation and continued, "His apprehension is quite understandable. He tried to save my life, but I was gravely injured. There was not anything anyone could do to save me. Although, I must say, it was a most gallant effort and quite intelligent of you to try, dear brother."

I didn't understand how all of this was happening...his voice was real, but I saw him die. My mouth must have been wide open and my face white, because Elia was now standing at the foot of my bed and placed her hand on my thigh. "Just breathe dear."

"I don't understand, I..." I stuttered.

"Our world and its ways must be confusing to you, Brother, but one day you shall be knowledgeable enough to teach others. Shall I continue the telling of the details for you?" Asëa asked with a caring smile. The elven to English translation was always just a bit off. I was still in shock and could not answer with words; all I could do was nod my head in agreement.

"I had left the protection of the Enchanted Realm and my brethren Mages, on my own volition, fully understanding what may come of me, to see if I could persuade Echidna to stop her daughter." I looked around the room to find some sort of explanation from one of my friends, but everyone was staring into my shield.

"Is that one of the mythical monsters?" I naively asked, to which Asëa simply nodded a yes.

"When she refused to discuss anything with me, I knew I had to confront Nãga. I feared that she was the monster responsible for the recent deaths near the Bermuda triangle, and with the recent earthquake activity, I figured that she was working with her father." Asëa told us.

"Typhon." I interrupted. Everyone in the room shifted nervously, and their eyes darted from me to the shield and to every other face in the room.

"Yes, Giovani, that is correct; Typhon." Gasps filled the room, at the confirmation, but I didn't understand why. *Who was Typhon?* Asëa made eye contact with me. "I raised Nak and Nãga after Echidna tossed them away. I believed in my heart, that she would be rational with me because I raised her children. I was gravely mistaken. I am afraid that the Nãga I reared for 700 years exists no longer. She has been dissuaded by her father, and craves nothing more than to gain power and greed."

All of the creatures in the entire room just stared into my shield, hanging on his every word.

"That was when I summoned you all." Asëa bowed his head and continued, "I only regret not summoning you sooner. I thought if we all talked with her, maybe she would change he mind and stop listening to Typhon. I deeply apologize for what you had to witness and endure on my behalf." Asëa's voice waivered, but he raised his head and a smile grew across his face, "You, young Adrastai, did not leave me to die alone. Thank you brother, you are very brave, and we were correct to put our trust in you, Giovani."

All eyes turned to gaze at me in awe and a bashful smile grew across my face. Proud smiles grew across the faces of all of my friends.

"You should all be very proud of this Adrastai. He is of pure greatness." At the sound of Asëa's voice, everyone glanced back to the talking reflection in my shield.

"A vengeful Nak then went to destroy his sister, but she overpowered him as well. She has grown very strong under her Fathers guidance." Asëa added, and the smiles immediately turned to frowns of concern.

"Giovani had to travel by essence, of which is something he has no understanding of, and attempted to rescue his soul-linked brother, Nak. He succeeded once again." Asëa turned a proud face to look at just me again, "You must complete your quest with the Vikings, it is imperative to our cause. I am just a toss of a coin away, and send you with my love and strength. It is now time I bid you adieu, take care of Laurina and St. John, and give them my love. You are our Hope and our Light. I bequeath you my knowledge of our ways."

The shimmering metallic pool suddenly rippled fiercely and connected with my hands. We all watched as the liquid traveled up the backs of my hands and found its way into my veins. My eyes grew large as I traced the cool liquid snaking up my arms and onto my shoulders. I felt it travel up my neck and a sudden pop noise filled my ears. Just then, Asëa smiled broadly, bowed his head, and then faded away in a brilliant green glow. My shield returned to be just that, a shield, but oddly, there was still a green glow filling the room.

Everyone in the room ran over to me and knelt before me. I looked over my shoulder expecting to see another Mage behind me but found no one. "Get up! What are doing?" I questioned.

"The High Mage, Asëa passed his knowledge to you. That is the highest honor that any Adrastai has ever received. We have never had to deal with the death of a High Mage, nor understand what would follow, but a bequeathment of his knowledge? I am honored to be in your presence." Brochara exclaimed, bowing so low that his head bumped into the dirt floor.

Just then, Nak slithered into the room looking refreshed and

152

strong. "Hello Brother, Thank you. I owe you my life." He humbly said and then added, "Why are you green?"

"Nak!" I sprang to my feet, ran to him, and threw my arms around his neck. "I am so glad to see you looking healthy. How do you feel? Wait, I'm green?" I turned my hand over to look at the back of it, and there was a greenish tint to my coloring. But, as I looked, the green sunk into my skin and my normal coloring returned. I shrugged and turned my focus back to my friend, Nak.

"Almosssst perfect, thankssss to you. I am so proud of you, but we have another tough journey ahead of ussss. Let'ssss go eat so we can leave this morning." Nak's eyes were shining and I was so glad he was all right.

We all cheered and walked out into the dining area. My friends walked a tad further behind me than usual, rather than arm-in-arm, which was odd but I was so pleased to see Nak up and slithering that I chose not to care.

Elia clapped her hand over her head and, instantly, the room was warm and smelled of decadent baked goods. In typical mothering fashion, Elia had conjured up fresh berries, nuts, pastries, and much to my dismay, rodents.

Chapter 11

Illustrated by
Ronan Murphy

11

MEET ELLIDA

The atmosphere in our tent was different this morning; not different in a bad way, just off I guess. Maybe it was just me. I glanced around at my friends and everyone was playful but no one's eyes connected with mine for too long and I figured it must have had something to do with Asëa. It had only been about 30 minutes since I woke up to Elia's healing worm juice, our ghostly encounter, and my green-tinted skin, but I felt as if an entire day had passed already.

My friends were acting goofy, giggling and waving at me even though we had all just gathered around my shield and listening to Asëa discuss his death. "Why are you all acting crazy? Did I miss something?" Laughter erupted from every corner of the room.

Confused, I shrugged at Elia looking for answers. With a wave of her tiny hand, she created a reflective pool of water right before my face, floating on thin air. It hung vertically, just like a mirror, but the water didn't spill out onto the floor. After catching a glimpse of my serious bed head, I looked at my face. Apparently, I must have slept so hard while I was recovering from my injuries, because my cheek had an imprint of my hand on it. All five fingers and half of my palm were present. I guess that explains why no one looked me in the eye for too long.

Elia gently licked her thumb and swiped it across the red handprint in the reflective pool, like my Mom did when trying to clean the dirt off of Mariella's face. Like a magic eraser, the imprint on my face disappeared. Then I realized that it had to have been there while Asëa was communicating to us and embarrassment washed over me.

"Thanks." I said, while rubbing my face where the imprint used to be. "I guess traveling by essence takes a lot out of a person."

Elia winked back at me and smiled sweetly, "I packed you some food in your backpack, dear." She cooed. "You have a long journey ahead of you, and I know that you are not very fond of herring."

"What? Herring?" I looked at her sideways. "That was a very random statement." I snickered and shivered at the same time because I could not stomach the thought of eating pickled herring.

I also packed you some of my poultice, should you need it to help heal wounds." Elia added.

I giggled wryly, but she didn't change her response; she stared directly at me, expressionless, "Oh, you're serious? Wounds." I turned my mood from joking to serious with one word, swallowed hard, and continued, "Okay, wounds. So, if I happen to acquire one, I just apply the goop and fasten it with a leaf and vines bandage, right?

"Yes dear, but try not to get one." She winked, smiled wryly, and nudged my knee with her elbow, enjoying her own whit.

"Uh, thank you for being so thoughtful Elia." I bent down and gave her a big hug but refrained from squeezing as tightly as I wanted to, for fear of crushing her tiny frame.

Nak was waiting for me in front of the fireplace staring off in deep thought, "We musssst travel today Brother. Nãga has grown stronger, and I fear father has employed her help. She musssst be ssssstopped." He had bowed his head and his words trailed off to the floor. My heart ached for him. He tried to save the man who raised him, but instead watched him die; his twin sister just tried to kill him, and now we all know that his parents are evil monsters.

"Nak?" I put my arms around his shoulder, "Something was commanding her attention from that crevice in the floor; something evil, I could feel it." My serpent friend's body twitched at my words. "I am sorry. There must be an awful lot of pain in your heart for your sister; your twin." Snakes are coldblooded creatures, but Nak's body was piping hot up under my arm, "Are you feeling alright? You are burning up."

"I am fine. I am not burning up due to injury; I am just extremely angry." He spit his words out in reply. "I come from a very long line of Dark relatives." Nak lifted his head to look me in the eye, but his normally bronze colored orbs blazed red, "My parents are evil and so are all of their offspring! And now, we have to journey to seek out and visit the whole lot of them, which is something I have avoided for centuries."

Before I could ask for further explanation, a thunderous knocking banged on the tent door, startling all of us. The flaps blew open and there stood the enormous forms of Ttensir and Belac.

"Ellida awaits us. We must go." barked Belac in a gruff voice. "Two days travel on foot to get to her"

"Who's Ellida?" I asked Nak from the side of my mouth. I did not want to make two Vikings angry with me again.

"Let'ssss not make hasssste then, time issss not on our side." Nak replied. Then he turned his focus to me and continued in a commanding voice, as he appeared to grow taller, "Ellida issss very sssspecial and highly ressssspected among ssssea-faring people." Nak then added a slight tilt of his head to the side, as my Mother had done many times in the past when she was silently trying to urge me to use my social graces.

The Vikings, full of pride, stood up a little taller after hearing Nak, and Nak gave me wink, "One catchessss more rodentssss with honey than with vinegar." He hissed into my brain.

Catching on, I added, "Oh please, Belac and Ttensir; I would love to hear all about her. She sounds fascinating." I grabbed my backpack, said my farewells to Elia and Aunt E, and out the door we went. My pack was much heavier than ever before. *How much stuff did Elia cram in here?*

The Vikings walked with long strides and it felt like I was running to keep up, or maybe it was the weight of my pack slowing me down. I didn't think the care package that Elia made for me could weigh that much. I flipped it over to the front of me to open it and inspect the contents, when a tiny green hand reached out from the inside and snatched the pack closed. "Brochara, what are you doing?" I whispered into the bag.

"Silence, we have been your protectors since birth, we will not stop now that you have been gifted by Nak and Asëa. No, absolutely, we will not stop!" He shouted back in a whispered voice from inside the pack full of pride.

"We?" But before I could finish my inquiry, my pack began to rustle about, as if a struggle was taking place. I heard moans and grunts; followed by low mutterings of "get off", "move over" and "ouch!"

I pulled the top open, and found both, Brochara and Fin, entangled and struggling to get comfortable inside my backpack, "Really?" I questioned with one eyebrow raised.

"Sshh!" They both immediately stopped their commotion and shushed me at the same. Each one extended a tiny hand, grabbed the sides of the flap cover, and pulled it back shut simultaneously. I chuckled to myself, hoisted the stowaways onto my back a little more forcefully this time. The thud of my bag on my shoulder was accompanied by grunts and murmurs of "he did that on purpose," and "that's the thanks we get?"

We had been walking in silence for over two hours, and all I could think about was how Brochara and Fin were probably playing cards or some magical game to pass the time all snug and rested in my pack. I was getting more resentful with every step. "Didn't you say two days walking?" I questioned, as my back started to spasm, "Wouldn't it be easier to fly there?" I cast my gaze to the sky and a smile grew across my face.

"Why, Yessss it would." Nak smiled back.

I grabbed my dragon birthmark on the left shoulder and called Khai's name inside my head. Moments later, the wind picked up tossing my hair into my eyes and then the ground shook as he landed directly in front of us. The large Vikings both yelped and drew their weapons, as fear flashed in their eyes. "Hold on! Hold on fellas, this is Khai; my dragon brother." Khai took a bow but the Vikings looked uneasy. I forgot that the last time a dragon was in their presence; their brother was bitten in half. Suddenly fearful for my friend, I walked as fast as I could past Belac and Ttensir, carrying the heavy pack on my back, and hugged Khai's neck.

"Good Morning Giovani." He nuzzled me affectionately with his snout over my shoulder, but Khai began to sniff around, like a dog detecting a strange scent, "Why does your pack smell like

Brochara and Fin?" he asked.

With their cover blown, the closed flap of my pack flew open and both Fin and Brochara struggled themselves, each spitting out words of "We're going", "You can't stop us", "Like it or not.", and "Ouch, get off of me!", but not at the same time. It was comical to watch, and the rest of us just stood there guffawing at their attempts to exit the pack with dignity.

Brochara broke free first, and tumbled out grabbing the string that pulls the neck of the bag closed on his way down, ultimately cinching Fin around the waist. Fin let out a tiny scream as his air was forced from this lungs. Brochara was holding on and swinging around trying to spit out his intentions of going with us, completely unaware of the fact that his efforts to be galiant were hurting poor Fin. Khai lowered his snout under Brochara's feet and helped him gain his footing on top of his nose. Fin drew in a deep breath, turned towards Brochara and drew his sword in anger.

"Sirssss, you both are welcome to join ussss on this journey, but let it be known, that there will be dangerssss of thosssse you have never witnesssss before." Nak quickly interrupted, thwarting Fin's protest. "It issss entirely posssssible that some of ussss will not return."

Both of my protectors collected themselves and stood up straight trying regaining their composure. "I accept!" they proclaimed and bowed at the same time, followed by "Thank you." The rest of us just watched the fiasco unfold, perplexed.

After an awkward silence, I turned to Khai and asked, "Friend, would it be possible to carry all of us on your back for a journey that would take us two days to walk?" I didn't know how much weight a dragon could carry, but it never hurts to ask.

Khai surveyed the group, "I believe that it is possible. You all will have to distribute the weight evenly along my back, in order for me to fly."

Everyone agreed to Khai's conditions and Khai lowered his head to the ground. My leather harness magically appeared with Brochara's infant car seat carrier already in place. I told Nak to place himself next to Brochara and Fin in the harness. To help balance the weight, the large Vikings, Belac and Ttensir, needed to be placed one on each front shoulder, so Brochara waved his hand over his head and, magically, two platforms appeared. I climbed up the spikes along Khai's spine and stood on the very top of his head, holding onto the two enormous spikes. What an amazing sight we all must have been, cargo'ing on top of this majestic dragon.

"Hold On!" Khai yelled, but his voice was full of struggle, trying to lift all of our combined weight off the ground.

The Vikings both had a look of apprehension in their expressions. Brochara sat perched in his seat, with a gleeful look on his face and kicking his feet, like Baby Aria. Nak and Fin sat regally, taking in the birds-eye view and I just smiled at my place in the world at that very moment. I patted Khai on the top of his head and telecommunicated, "Thank you brother."

With a grand roar, Khai shot through the sky pumping his wings with such a mighty force. His normally smooth take off, was choppy and laborious. A twinge of regret entered my brain as I felt my friend struggle to carry all of us, but it did feel amazing to be flying again.

We had already walked for hours, but Khai's flight pattern had quickly brought us back over top of the Enchanted Valley and the tent city of the Adrastai Council within minutes. The entire view of the land below looked exactly like the scroll map of the Adrastai Council! Glancing back at the Vikings and my friends, I saw their faces relax and everyone smiled.

We soared for about an hour, up and over the mountain range that stood tall protecting the Enchanted Valley. In front of us, a large body of water stretched out on the horizon. The sun was welcoming on warmed my skin. Khai slowly started to descend through the clouds and the cool mist on my face was refreshing. I looked below to see the blue of the water, when a magnificent ship came into sight. It was a huge vessel in the shape of a dragon anchored just off the shore.

"There she is!" yelled Belac, excitedly, and he pointed toward the dragon ship.

I followed the direction of the Viking's outstretched arm with my eyes, but I couldn't find any woman or girl in sight, but the ship was amazing! The front of the vessel was shaped like a dragon's head, which was proudly held high, and the throat was painted gold reflecting the sunlight off it illuminating the water is rested in. The body of the ship was shaped like Khai's body, and large leather and wooden wings were tucked all along the bulwark, or railing around the ship's deck. The aft, or rear of the ship, was shaped like a coiled tail of a dragon with the rudder trailing off behind it. She was beautiful, strong, and majestic!

Khai landed softly on the deck of the magnificent dragon ship. The enormous deck could house two of Khai's bodies lying head to tail across it and at least five Khai's stretched the length of this vessel. It was floating fortress and as soon as Belac and Ttensir touched their feet on the wooden deck, the ship seemed to come alive!

The two black wings that were tucked along the bulwark unfolded and stretched out fifty feet on each side. The outside of each leathery wing was outlined in a brilliant burnt-red coloring. The enchanted main sail hoisted itself up the mast, which was over seventy feet tall, and as the wind filled the sails billowing them out like giant pillows, I could have sworn I heard the ship inhale!

"This is Ellida!" Ttensir proclaimed as he made a grand sweeping motion with his horrifically, scarred arm.

I reeled around to meet this person, when it dawned on me that Ellida must have been the name of this grand ship. "Wow! She certainly is magnificent!" I was in awe of beauty.

Fin was having a blast exploring the ships details! Brochara was just turning in wonder taking it all in, but then I saw Khai collapse in the front corner of the ship with his head slumped. Concerned, I ran to him.

"Are you alright friend?" I asked stroking the side of his neck, like a rider to his horse.

"I will be." He replied, "Just exhausted…that flight took a lot out of me, but nothing a little rest won't fix." Poor Khai never lifted his head while he spoke to me.

"I am so sorry, did I ask too much of you?" I was beginning to feel guilty, that we made his life harder in order to make ours easier.

"It had to be done, for The Order." His answer was breathless, "Please leave me. I just need to sleep." and with that last word, his eyes shut and his snout fell to the deck. Khai began to snore, heavily.

Whenever Khai snores, two even spaced burn marks are carved straight out in front of his nostrils. I was worried about the deck of this ship and disrespecting the Vikings. I tried to stir my friend awake by skaking him, but that was not going to work. He was just too exhausted.

I quickly looked to check for the damage to the deck of the ship. As I predicted, after each one of Khai's snoring exhales, streams of fire charred two grooves in the deck's surface. I began to sweat nervously, as I looked up to find the Vikings; they were headed right towards us! Their pride in this vessel scared me, because I knew they

163

would defend it to the death. Nervously, I glanced back down to assess the damage, or find something to cover it with, but the sounds of their footfalls were fast approaching.

Afraid to look them in the eyes, I kept my head bowed trying to muster up the courage, when the charred boards magically healed right before my eyes! New wood simply grew over the burnt spots like a giant eraser! I shook my head and rubbed my eyes, thinking I must be mistaken, when booming laughter grew from the Viking men.

"Ellida was gift from the Aegir, God of the Ocean and King of the sea creatures, to my family!" Ttensir proudly proclaimed. "The Sea Giant of the North!" At the mere mention of that name, every member of the Viking crew, who were milling around the deck dropped to one knee, banged their breastplates twice, with their right fist, and shouted "Skål!"

"Our Norse God took kindly to my relations, and gifted her to us. She has no nails fastening her together; her boards are enchanted. They are grown together! If she is destroyed by the sea or in battle, she simply regenerates herself!" Belac explained. "She has just recently returned to us…" but his proud words trailed off as he bowed his head.

"We were sent to destroy the beast that has been terrorizing the Devil's Triangle when we were attacked." Ttensir words were full of anger, "Our Father was taken from us that day, by the jaws of that beast! Our Ellida; smashed! The crew, all dead! Only my brother's and I escaped!" Ttensir lifted his shirt exposing the obviously recent claw marks that I noticed in the Hall of Knowledge.

"Our eldest brother's heart turned black that day and he vowed revenge on the beast, who took our father and his eye!" Belac's voice was full of fury as he lifted his head and glared directly at Nak. "He vowed revenge on the beast and all of its family! We floated adrift for days not knowing if we would live to see another!" His audience of guests shifted nervously at this tale.

"The beast, I understand; but all of its family, I do not." riddled Brochara as he positioned himself between the Vikings and Nak, followed by Fin and myself. "Was the beast's family present at the attack? Did they hurt any of yours?" Brochara was taking a defensive stance and I was trying to make the connection that everyone else already had.

"What does this have to do with Nak? Hey, why were you glaring at him during the lecture?" I questioned the Vikings.

"It issss becausssse of Nãga. She issss the Beasssst! The evil of my twin and my family tree proceedssss me wherever I go! It is my cursssse!" Nak answered. "But, Brochara is right. I may be her blood, but I am nothing like her! I am very sorry for your loss and pain, but I did not inflict them. Together, we have been chosen by the High Magessss of The Order, to embark on the journey. It is our heartssss that are Pure, and we will ssssucceed." Nak was standing taller than I have ever seen, as we were stood in the shadow of his enormous cobra hood.

"What is our quest?" Ttensir asked, but I had been wondering the same thing.

"It issss our duty to keep Ssssir Giovani ssssafe." He hissed.

"Me? All of you are here to protect me?" I was shocked. "I thought we were all sent to fight Nãga, not for my protection."

"Brother, you are far more valuable to our causssse than you know. It issss our duty to make sure you ssssurvive. You musssst go find the oracle to hear the prophecsssy. That issss your quesssst and your ssssafety isss ourssss." Nak was looking directly into my eyes, and I felt his concern in my heart.

"Then, let us go find the Oracle," I stated. "I believe our course should take us to the Ethiopian Mountains, correct?"

"CLERAH!" both Vikings shouted together in a drawn out manner. The giant dragonhead, which made up the entire front of the ship, let out a tremendous roar at the sound of the Viking's cry; even the sleeping Khai woke by the sound.

The sky quickly changed and the air turned cool. Clouds twisted and swirled at a rapid pace, pulling together from all corners of the sky by some invisible magnet. An eerie feeling came over me as I watch the splendor. I shuddered. The last time I witnessed clouds act this way, they crashed through my bedroom window and I was almost devoured by them. I managed to walk away with just my face and forearms cut up by shards of glass. I took a deep breath and stood firm, bracing myself for what might happen.

The clouds continued their dance high in the bright blue sky, twisting and turning over each other, until they formed the shape a beautiful woman, made entirely from fluffy white clouds. She was long and slender, with wispy flowing hair. The beautiful being glided across the expansive blue background and floated down to the dragon ship. Her movements looked as though she was swimming through the sky, like a mermaid of the heavens. Her cloudy form continued to swirl as she settled next to Ellida's dragon figurehead and hovered there, "Who summoned me." She spoke softly, her voice sounded of music, and her breath was a warm, caressing breeze. I was in wonder over her billowing beauty.

"Clerah, we did." Ttensir and Belac were standing proud on the bow of Ellida. "We are on a quest for The High Mages, and have been given a blessing to solicit your help." Both Viking's gently bowed in her presence. "Will you please assist our sails to the Ethiopian Mountains?" Ttensir asked.

"The High Mages? Which one?" her warm breath was

intoxicating as it blew against my face.

"What is she?" I whispered to Nak, feeling mesmerized by her beauty. "She is amazing" I was entranced with her hair of clouds that gently swayed as the winds blew through it.

"Clerah is a Sylph, an elemental of the air." Nak answered, "Do take care not to look her in the eye."

"Why? I whispered, but before Nak could answer, a burly Viking crashed to deck, motionless, just a few feet away. I was could see his face, riddled with deep lines from a hard life of battles. He wore a vacant expression and far-away look in his eyes. "Is he dead?"

"Air elementals are very sensitive beings, they perceive eye contact as a direct challenge, and they will fight. Looking one in the eye is almost always certain death, not of the body, but of the mind. A Sylph can destroy your brain by filling your head with clouds." Fin's whispered, then he removed his plumed-hat and added, "Rest in peace warrior."

The wind began to swirl around each of us, as if individual tornados were sent to destroy us. The Sylph was getting irritated that no one had answered her question and her once bright-white clouds turned violently grey. Everyone was focused on the poor Viking, who lay motionless on the deck with his eyes open. "WHICH MAGE?" screamed Clerah, and her voice boomed through the skies, groans of fear emanated from the crowds of Vikings.

"Laurina." whispered a nervous Ttensir, as he bowed his head to avoid making eye contact with the angry elemental.

"Laurina," the Sylph dragged her name out, calmly, on the wind. Her temperament changed quickly, like the wind on a stormy day. Soft, warm breezes replaced the turbulent tornados that circled each of us, and her quiet white demeanor returned as she softly spoke, "She is most kind to ask for me. I would be honored to assist you as a favor to Laurina. Are you ready?"

The Vikings looked at all of us and then simultaneously yelled. "Hold On!"

Everyone within earshot hit the deck and grabbed onto something to anchor them to the ship. I flung my arms around side rail and Brochara and Fin each grabbed one of my legs. Nak slithered to the main mast and curled his tail around it three times then nodded at me indicating he was ready. Khai continued to lie, exhausted, in the front corner of the ship.

The seemingly gentle Sylph, Clerah, drew in a deep a breath that pulled Ellida's sail and anything else that wasn't tied down quickly towards her mouth. Cargo flew through the air and soared off the ship upon her powerful inhale.

In awe of her power, I glanced towards the elemental, who had inflated to three times her original size full of wind. The clouds that made up her frame were growing dense and violently swirled around her midsection. Clerah's long flowing hair of mist, grew out behind her, like a gorgons head of snakes, into spiraled clouds of curls. My eyes continued to drift up this ever-changing cloud formation, when, accidently I looked straight at her face. An alarming whistle noise filled my ears, I let go with one hand, pushed my ear into the opposite shoulder, and tried to plug my ears to stop the horrifying sound.

The strength of her inhale was too great. My arm began to tingle and I lost my grip. I was sailing through the air, with Brochara and Fin dangling from my legs, as we whipped around in the vortexes of wind. The whistling wind in my brain was replaced with my own screams of terror at the sight of Clareh's pursed lips. Our bodies crashed into what can only be described as a cool, misty pool of fog and rain, which absorbed us, like landing on a trampoline. We were no longer careening across the sky; we were in the large cloud-made hand of Clerah.

Immediately, Brochara and Fin clenched their eyes and buried their faces into my legs to avoid making eye contact with the Sylph, but instinctively, I turned to thank her and our eyes met. Swirling clouds, the color of the bluest skies, stared softly back at me. "Thank you." was all I could manage to say.

A soft gentle breeze encircled my head as I heard her whisper, "Hold on tight this time, Brother." And she winked at me and placed my friends and I back onto the dragon ship.

I nodded in a silent agreement, smiled at her beautiful face, and wrapped my arms around the rail again. Suddenly, a mighty exhale, with the strength of a hurricane, blew from her cloudy lips. The sheer strength of the wind forced my eyes shut to protect them and I felt my fingers slipping from their grasp. I tried to weave them together tighter, heeding her warning.

Fin's hat flew off his head so quickly; there wasn't any time to grab it. Thankfully, it slammed into the side of Khai's jaw and lodged within his teeth, just before he started rolling across the deck, like tumbleweed across the desert sand, motionless. I feared for my friend. How could he not realize what was going on? He looked unconscious.

Two of the Vikings crewmembers lost their hold, their bodies shot through the air, and plummeted over the side of the ship, but their screams for help faded quickly due to the speed of our travels. Anything that was not tied down flung through the air, slamming into crewmembers, busting through gunwales causing injuries and damage, like being in the center of a hurricane, completely unprotected.

My eyes shut tight, trying to avoid damage by the flying debris. I squinted through the chaos andwatched Khai's back slam into

Ellida's dragon figurehead, which roared out upon impact and turned its wooden neck to grasp onto my friend. Splintered wood flew off in every direction as the ship frantically chomped at Khai. I couldn't tell if the enchanted dragon figurehead was trying to help Khai, or if it was trying to defend itself from the crashing weight of my dragon brother. Then Khai's motionless body slid into the first mast, crushing three Vikings and snapping it off twenty feet high from the deck. He still did not respond.

"Khai!" I screamed full of fear, "HOLD ON!"

Suddenly, my grip gave away. Brochara, Fin, and I started to slide across the ship's deck, tumbling over each other, unable to stop ourselves. Nak outstretched his hood to catch us as we careened past, but we were just out of his reach. Fear filled my body and I, instinctively, wrapped myself around my tiny friends, cradling them with my frame, to protect them from any impact our bodies may endure. We came to an abrupt stop when my back slammed into the chest of Ttensir who scooped us up close into his body, with one strong arm.

"HOLD ON!" he yelled again, laughing at the same time. He and Belac seemed to be enjoying the ride immensely, with smiles on their faces and the salty breeze whipping through their long beards.

The Sylph's wind was relentless. Ellida skipped across the water, as if a stone cast from a giants hand. We were traveling at a tremendous speed that continued for over an hour. Suddenly, as if a leaf caught in a whirlwind, Khai's exhausted limp body flew off the ship, tumbling through and out of sight!

"NO!" I cried, but my own screams could not be heard through the roar of the Sylph's exhale.

Chapter 12

Illustrated by
Laura Korn

12

CANNON BALL

Our dragon ship, Ellida, suddenly slowed down to a normal sailing speed on a light wind. The enchanted breath of the Sylph, Clerah, had ceased to blow, allowing everyone still left on board to release his or her grasp and, slowly, stand up.

The damage to the ship from flying debris was extensive. Ellida looked as if she had been through a battle, with holes the size of shopping carts riddling the ship. The sounds of wood creaking and vines twisting over themselves filled the air as the magical ship, immediately, began repairing herself.

I slumped down to the ship's deck, exhausted and distraught. My heart was heavy with guilt and worry for my dragon partner, Khai. After all, it was my fault he was too weak to hold on. If only I hadn't asked him to carry all of us, he would have been strong enough to hold on.

Vikings wandered around the deck of the ship, bleeding, dazed and confused. There were injured people lying around, screaming for help, but I was too absorbed in my own self-created horror to notice. I tried to telecommunicate to Khai, but he didn't respond.

"Giovani! Snap out of it!" Brochara yelled as he was violently shaking my leg.

"What?" I shook my head trying to come back to reality.

"Giovani, we need you here, now! Khai will be just fine. Now, grab your pack and come on!" Brochara was stern, almost angry sounding, and I did exactly what he asked without any more questions or hesitation.

"Elia's poultice! Give it to me, now!" he commanded as he knelt down next to a Viking with a horrible gash on his back that exposed his bone. My stomach lurched and I almost threw up at the sight.

I raised my head and glanced around at the horrible scene surrounding me. "Brochara, I don't have enough for all of this," I thought aloud.

"Just give it to me!" he demanded!

I nervously fumbled through my backpack and produced the healing goo Elia had made for the trip. Brochara quickly grabbed it from me and laid it on the surface of the deck. He proceeded to wave his arm over his head and chant something in Elvish, and the poultice began to bubble and grow right before our eyes.

"A duplicating charm, I should have known," escaped my lips.

We ran from injury to injury, like triage nurses in the middle of a war, patching up Viking after Viking. When the last injury had been tended to, we both collapsed, side by side, forgetting our own exhaustion to help the others.

I sat there with my eyes closed and my face turned to the sun. Its rays warmed my skin, like a hug on a cold, chilly day. "That was the strongest wind I have ever felt." I sighed.

"It has been hundreds of years since I have been in the presence of a Sylph, and I must say that Clerah has the strongest gusts. Laurina was spot on, recommending her." Brochara giggled.

"Issss everyone alright?" came a soft hiss from under a wooden box, "Any chance one of you might remove this from my tail?"

Exhausted, Brochara waved his arm over his head and the box flew off Nak's tail. For some reason, this struck us all as funny, and we all began to laugh. We must have been to that point of exhaustion, where you are either going to laugh or cry or we chose laughter.

Heavy footsteps approached from behind us, "Thank you for helping the crew." Belac stood, like a mountain before us, blocking the sunlight.

We just smiled through our exhaustion, acknowledging their gratefulness. My dear friend, Fin, was walking towards us, rubbing is exposed head, and searching for something. I quickly remembered his plumed hat that lodged in Khai's teeth during our travels.

"You must gather your strength. We are here." Ttensir added as he plucked me off the deck with the same strong hand that saved me from flying off the ship.

"Thank you Ttensir, for saving us." I had a new found respect for the savage man.

"It is my quest to keep you safe." He nodded.

"LAND HO!" rang through the air from one of the Viking crewmembers.

With nervous excitement, we all ran to side of the ship. There before us stood a large region of jagged mountaintops jutting out of lush green forests, like a rooftop sheltering the African continent.

"Wow," was all I could come up with in response to our destination.

"Don't let its beauty distract you. This is one of the most dangerous terrains we have ever traveled. Sheer cliffs, jagged rocks, dense forest that will swallow you up and never spit you back out. Venomous snakes, and man-eating predators all await us, not to mention all of the horrifying creatures lurking in the shadows." Ttensir added, nonchalantly, while giving me a slap on the back that knocked the wind out of me.

"Well then, what are we waiting for?" I replied reluctantly. "Bring on the adventure." I added, with absolutely no enthusiasm in my voice.

"Atta Boy! Embrace the excitement! Is there Viking blood in your veins?" barked Belac adding another Viking slap to the back, causing me to lose my footing. I was thankful for the ship railing keeping me from falling overboard, as I flapped my arms like a dodo, trying not to lose my balance, to no avail. I plummeted over the edge and careened to the blue waters below.

"Well, that's one way to get off a boat." Belac laughed.

The drop from the deck of the ship was well over thirty feet, and I felt my stomach move into my throat on the way down. The cool ocean water was actually a welcomed relief to the intense African sun. When I resurfaced, I had to quickly swim out of the way of the cannonballing Belac, who was headed right for me.

I giggled at the sight of this enormous tough Viking, tucked childlike in a ball, plugging his nose with one hand, and holding his metal helmet on top of his head with the other, all the while squealing with laughter.

Suddenly, the sky was raining friends, all shrieking on their descent to the cool ocean waters. It felt like summer vacation; playing with friends in the ocean and enjoying each other's company. We all laughed and joked the entire length of the swim to the shore.

The enormity of our situation hit us when we climbed up the shore and out of the Red Sea. Miles of sand and dirt stretched out before us all the way to the jagged mountains that loomed over the land. There wasn't much shade or lush vegetation to hide a foreign group filled with an elf, a mink wearing musketeer clothing while walking upright, and a giant cobra.

I looked at my friends for guidance, "How are we going to find this Oracle? Does anyone know?"

"I believe that the Oracle already knowssss we are here, and the game issss afoot!" hissed Nak.

"Game? What kind of game?" I asked, but something deep inside me already knew the answer. *We needed to find it, before It found us...*

"That issss why we are here, to protect you." His large bronze eyes looked right into my soul, "You are my sworn duty now and forever more. I will lay down my life you Brother, and you will carry mine on."

"No, you will stay alive and stand right by my side. Now, where will we find this Oracle? Wait, carry yours on?" I asked, but before he could answer, the Sea behind us began to bubble furiously.

Everyone grabbed their weapon and turned to the water on high alert. Fin was poised directly in front of me, sword drawn. Brochara by his side with magical elven hands ready to defend and our new Viking friends were sheltering me as well. At the same time, the ground began to shake. "Is this the Oracle?" I shouted over the roar of the fast approaching danger.

"NO!" Nak was perched high on his tail and stood almost twenty feet tall and turning his head from side to side, trying to make sense of what was happening.

"Nãga?" I questioned grasping for any sort of explanation.

"NO! It issss neither. Get behind me!" he yelled as he flattened out his neck producing an enormous hood. I was completely shaded in his shadow. I felt confident that my friends would protect me from the Sea, but what of the vast desert behind us and its inhabitants?

Nak's actions and words made me even more uneasy. Something large and powerful was emerging from the Sea at a rapid speed. Then the thought crossed my mind, *Why am I to cower in the shadow of a snake? I just defeated the most powerful sorcerer, and Nak wants me to hide?*

I pulled a Fin maneuver and dove out from behind the swaying Nak, just as the emerging form shot out of the Sea. Salt water and spray clouded everyone's vision, but streaks of white, silver, and black passed over all of our heads, blocking out the sun.

The entire group reeled around again, ready to strike. Servo was poised over my head, Belac and Ttensir appeared to welcome a battle by the look on their faces, and both Fin and Brochara looked as anxious as I felt.

Not one giant form, but three separate beings crashed to the sand and tumbled over. We rushed forward to thwart any efforts from the intruders and surrounded them immediately. Confusion formed on all of our faces. There lying on the sand before us, was a bright white dolphin, a shimmering silver mermaid, and an enormous black wolf? *What?*

Nak immediately reduced his size and pulled his hood back in. A look of excitement filled his eyes as he quickly coiled his body around the dolphin and wolf, "Luca! Mateo!"

"Mateo?" I echoed, questioning his sanity. We were staring at a mermaid, dolphin, and wolf, which the wolf didn't make any sense to me since the other two belong in the water.

Before anyone could comment, the three creatures began to recover from their landing. The wolf yelped as it up-righted itself. The mermaid, whose hair was made of a tangle of glistening silver strands that reflected the sun, temporarily blinding was, began to push herself up to sit. Her hair slowly slid back, uncovering her face, and revealed "Skye?" I was shocked!

"Hi." She managed to breathe out on a sigh of exhaustion.

I quickly fell to my knees next to her to help. "How? Why? I mean are you okay? How did you find us?"

"Giovani, please, I need a minute." Her voice was weak, and she turned away from me and pulled her knees to her, as if she was nervous to look me in the eye.

"Oh sure, sure." I stuttered as I plopped down in the sand next to her. Confused to find her here, I thought back to the first time I found out about Piscisene "We have got to stop meeting this way." I giggled.

A tiny laugh bubbled from under her hair. She had her back turned to me, as if she didn't want me to see her for some reason, so I tried to glance away, when it dawned on me that Skye was a mermaid! An actual mermaid was lying on the sand in front of me. I looked at her legs. They were definitely a fish tail, with brilliant silver scales that glistened like diamonds in the sun. Her hair was silver, the skin on her back was slightly tinted a soft hue of bluish-green with boney-nodules protruding like some prehistoric fish. "OH, oh! OH." I shuffled away from her, kicking sand all over her by accident as I tried to flee. She was naked! Skye was a half-naked fish-lady!

Suddenly, I was completely embarrassed for the both of us. We were like brother and sister, but I was so blind to why she needed a minute, and I sat right next to her…she must have felt so violated.

"Calm Down!" she said sharply as she turned to me.

I threw my hands over my eyes, not wanting to see her nakedness, when my friends all began to laugh. "What is so funny? Can't you give a girl, Fish, I mean mermaid…whatever, a little privacy?"

"Giovani, what are you talking about? You pyscho!" she sounded confused.

I slowly uncovered my eyes, and saw Skye sitting on the sand in front me, wearing a thin, silver metal warrior bikini top of some sorts. I let out the biggest sigh of relief. "Phew, I thought you were naked."

"Giovani, I just swam over a thousand miles, as fast as I could…I just needed a minute to catch my breath before I could change back." She added, "My legs and eyes need a minute to adjust."

I quickly looked into her eyes, which she had been hiding from the bright sun; they were all silver except for a tiny black pupil. Then she smiled at me, revealing a mouth full of three rows of wicked sharp teeth.

I screamed like a little girl. She quickly closed her mouth, her shoulders slumped forward, and she cocked her head sideways looking at me, "Really?" she said, "Did you think I was going to sing you a beautiful song in my Piscisene form?"

Brochara doubled over laughing, and fell into Fin, who was trying really hard not to crack a smile.

"You have a mouth full of shark teeth! That's scary!" I replied.

Then I muttered under my breath about how anyone would be afraid to run into her in the water, as I brushed myself off and stood up. "Don't EVER do that again."

Skye let out a noise that I have never heard before. It sounded like twenty screeching owls all at the same time! I had to plug my ears, and so did the others. When the sound faded, I looked back towards Skye, and her human body was back.

"Are you alright?" I asked.

"Transforming is always the hardest thing to do. I am sorry if I frightened you." My Skye was back; I threw my arms around her neck and then re-spit out all of the questions I asked earlier about why she was here.

"Giovani, we…" she started, but a chilly howl interrupted her and sent shivers racing down my spine.

We turned our focus to the wolf and snow-white dolphin that were still lying on the beach. The black wolf reminded me of the werewolves that I had seen in movies. The upper body was oversized and extremely muscular, and even though it wasn't snarling at us, it looked ferocious. Suddenly, the animal stretched out all four legs, like it was shocked by electricity. Right before our eyes, this horrifying creature reanimated into the bull of a man, Mateo.

Brochara rushed to his side, as he spat out water like he had almost drowned. "Easy Mateo, you are safe. Shallow breaths, my friend, breathe slowly." Brochara's teeny frame looked much smaller in comparison the Mateo's massive form.

"Luca!" He spat out, "Help her!" Mateo continued to choke on the seawater, coughing up large amounts as he tried to crawl to the bright-white dolphin, who lay there, lifeless. "Nak, please. Do it again!" he cried.

"I can't." Nak softly whispered. "Thissss time it issss up to her." The giant cobra was cradling the white dolphin like a child. "Come on Luca, follow my light," he whispered to her lifeless form.

I didn't understand what was going on, but I could tell that it was serious by the look on Nak's face. The brilliant white coloring began to dull and fade to gray. I was certain she was transforming just as the other two had, when Mateo jumped to his feet and screamed "NO!"

His eyes immediately became bloodshot, his veins pumped up to twice their normal size, and all of his muscles tensed. He looked as if he was going to explode with energy, and he opened his mouth and roared her name with such force, we covered our ears once more to protect them. He was deranged and psychotic! It was the same way he looked at me when I accidentally ran into her at the Council, before she commanded him to stop.

He shot over towards Nak, and didn't show signs of slowing. "MATEO, DON'T!" Nak screamed!

He was a human freight train, unable to stop and he plowed directly into Nak, knocking him to the ground, and sending Luca flying through the air. The dolphin landed with a thud about twenty feet away and he continued his path in her direction. I was certain he had lost his mind by the way he looked and was acting. I couldn't get to her fast enough to save her from his rage, and I had no idea how to stop him. "Brochara! Do something!" I yelled.

It was too late. Mateo grabbed the limp dolphin's tale and swung her around in a circle three times over his head, and then launched her into the Red Sea, like a discus. After her body hit the salty water, we turned to Mateo with shock and horror. His chest and shoulders were heaving, and he just looked mad, unhinged.

"What happened? He just went Berserk!" Skye asked. "I should get her." Skye was ready to plunge back into the Sea.

"Exactly," replied Brochara. "I could smell it on him when he came to dinner that night. He is a Berserker; it is what his kind is known for."

"A what?" I questioned, but a large wave of water splashed over me, pulling my gaze up.

"A Berserker," sang a soft voice from above, "He gets it from our father."

Luca was walking towards us from the desert. Her white-blonde hair flowing out behind her in a breeze that I didn't even feel blowing. She passed all of us, and walked straight to her brother, who was still in a psychotic state, heaving uncontrollably with each breath.

"Breathe slowly, brother. I am alright now, thanks to you." She cooed softly while stroking his hair, "Just breathe. I am right here." Her voice was soft and slow. She was trying to control Mateo's breathing with her own slowed version.

Mateo calmed down with her touch and soft voice. His eyes returned to normal and he grabbed his head and shook it like a dog, or wolf, shaking of water. "Are you-ah okay?" he asked her.

"I am thanks to you." She replied. "I love you, brother."

The siblings embraced and everyone exhaled. Then, I blurted out my questions once again, "What are you all doing here?"

For the next fifteen minutes, the three of them rattled off how the news of Asëa's death had buzzed through the camp. Classes postponed, every elf joined forces to create a stronger enchantment of protection around the Valley for fear of attack. Skye had gone to find me in our tent, and Aunt E told her about our journey. Luca and Mateo joined Skye to try to find us, but none of them knew where to begin.

"Luca fell into a trance and astral traveled!" Skye blurted out, and then hee-bee-gee-bee danced at the thought of it.

Nak immediately grew a large smile across his face, "Issss that true?" he asked Luca.

She simply nodded her head quickly, and dropped her gaze to the ground, blushing.

"I am proud of you, ssssister." He hissed.

Sister? What? Why did he call her that? I wondered, but then I recalled what Mateo asked Nak, before he went all berserk. He pleaded with Nak to help her, to do it again. "Did you..."

But I didn't get to finish my question, "Yessss." He answered, "Two yearssss ago."

I reverted to my selfish childhood ways, briefly, thinking *how was it, every time I started to think I was special, someone comes along and brings me back down.* Nak cast a sideways look at me, scolding my thoughts and I quickly stood up straight.

"Issss everyone back to normal?" Nak asked.

"I am not sure about Khai," Skye began to say, but she quickly remembered that I was right there.

"Khai? You saw Khai? Where? How is he?" I felt panic returning.

She turned her gaze to me, "We came upon him, floating face down." Her words drifted off as horror sank into my soul. "Jock dumped me off and I had to transform. He stayed with Khai, but that is all I know. We rushed to be with you." Skye could not look me in the eyes. I felt her worry deep inside my heart.

"Giovani, we need you here now!" Nak hissed, knowing that my thoughts were focused on Khai. "The Order needsssss you to be here! We have been ssssent on the journey by the High Magessss for a direct purposssse; now clear your mind and focusssss!" Nak's voice was commanding and stern. "Khai issss in good handssss. Thisssss wasssss not your fault!"

I took a slow deep breath and stood up straight, but I would be lying if I didn't admit to feeling guilty. If Khai died, it would be all of my fault. I asked him to carry us all to the ship. It was because of me he was so exhausted. If he dies, I will no longer be a Dragon Rider. If I am so important to the order, how could I continue without my Adrastai placement of Dragon Rider? This was horrible, and it was my entire fault. The slight breeze tossed my hair into my eyes and I tossed my head back and regained my composure.

A tremendous roar echoed from the mountaintops off in the distance. It almost sounded like entire pride of lions growled Nak's name at the same time. Startled, we all jumped!

"Hurry, we musssst go, now!" Nak commanded. "She knowsssss I am here." And with that, he slammed is oversized hood onto the sandy beach, and created a large tunnel. "Follow me!"

We all jumped in behind him. The tunnel was cool and dark. Nak was traveling at a high rate of speed and we were all running behind him. I had to pick up Brochara and place him in my pack and Mateo grabbed Fin. No one asked any questions, we all just followed Nak into the darkness.

I was not comfortable underground. That was where the trolls lived, and where they tried to drag me to my death. The attacked that was frightening and painful. I had dirt impacted so far under my fingernails; it took weeks to get it out, not to mention I almost died but Khai's golden tear saved me.

Suddenly, Nak came to an abrupt stop. He quickly flared his hood and we all knew to be silent. Heavy footfalls from something enormous echoed from above us. The ground suddenly began to shake, dirt and rocks started to cave in over top of us. My feet grew extremely hot, and my birthmark burned! The tunnel began glowing red with all four of our orbs on high alert. I wanted to squeeze my shoulder and call for Khai, but I didn't even know if he was alive and if I did, the trip would just exhaust him further. I was on my own, and hopefully my friends could help me.

Nak's gaze was not to the surface but rather at the ground beneath us that appeared to begin to melt, "DIG UPWARDSSSS!" Nak yelled. Darkness was closing in.

Chapter 13

Illustrated by
Mikayla Reynolds

13

THE ORACLE

My friends and I were trapped underground. Something was rising from the depths of the earth, oozing steam through growing fissures, and the earth above us was caving in. Something was digging down towards us. The awaiting danger above apparently was our best option, because Nak had told us all to dig upwards.

Belac was directly behind me and his efforts were incredible. His arms were digging at amazing speeds, pulling large chunks of the earth out with each stroke, and slowly, the ground started to open up. A tiny, hopeful ray of sunlight leaked through a small crack. Belac lead the way and all the others quickly ducked behind me as we followed Belac's climb to the surface.

The strong Viking gave a mighty punch, and broke through the remaining earth with a proud Viking cry. He looked back wearing a proud grin and dangling by a root with one arm. I smiled back at him feeling his satisfaction with his performance as he beamed. He reached for a handhold to pull himself up, when for a split second a something blocked out the light. Without warning, an enormous clawed foot, twice as big as his head, slammed down on top of Belac's hand. Instantly, the muscular warrior was yanked out of the hole with supernatural strength and speed; we heard his cries for a brief moment, but they were quickly silenced.

Frozen in fear, no one moved. The dangers from below still advanced and now, terrors from above waited. I could hear Ttensir sniffling somewhere in the dark, and my heart ached for him; two brothers and his father gone. I was next in line to exit the hole. *What was up there?*

"Stand tall, brother! You carry with you a part of me. Use that, and walk proud," Nak's voice was quiet inside my head. I felt Fin grab my leg to climb up and go first, but Nak stopped him with his tail.

I had to be brave, what other choice did I have? Slowly and cautiously, I began my ascent grabbing roots and stepping on rocks, pulling myself out of the darkness. With Brochara still in my pack, I followed Belac's last mortal handhold. My entire body was shaking. I tried to control the fear, but fear was winning.

I closed my eyes, swallowed hard, and reached for the boulder that jutted out of the earth, but before I did, I grabbed my dragon birthmark. The familiar warm, tingling sensation started at my feet and coursed up my legs. My confidence grew and I decided to move quicker than I had ever moved before. I leapt with the power of a leopard. Cautiously, my feet hit the ground and I heard Brochara moan.

"Stay still." I telecommunicated. "We're being stalked."

All was dark due the cover of the canopy. Rays of light stretched through tiny openings in the leaves, illuminating the woods just enough to see shadows darting through the darkness or doubt your brain's perception of what was there. I could feel the beast's

190

eyes on me, and hear the low, guttural snarls. I turned around quickly, scanning in every direction. The growls seemed to come from everywhere, echoing off the surrounding rocks and trees. The hair on the back of my neck stood up straight and I shut my eyes to use my senses. *To the Right!* I heard whispered on the wind.

I turned with a jerk, to find two large, green, glowing eyes peering at me from the brush, just before the beast lunged for me. I spun out to the left, narrowing escaping the murderous claw that grabbed Belac. I quickly stopped my momentum and beheld at the beast, which tumbled across the dirt.

Anticipating an enormous lion, my eyes grew large with disbelief when before me rose a creature I had only seen in my Greek mythology books, a giant sphinx. It stood about six feet tall on all four legs and possessed the body of a lion with two large cream-colored, feathered wings jutting out from its' back. As the creature shook off the dirt, a long serpent-like tail with the head of a snake on the end of it slithered out from behind it and hissed at me. When the creature turned its gaze towards me, I expected to see the gaping jaws of a lion, but the face of this creature was that of a woman surrounded by a lion's mane.

The beast snickered at me as it aggressively postured in my direction slamming its forepaws into the dust revealing its mal intentions. I remained tall, never breaking eye contact. The two of us circled around each other in slow motion, menacingly, in a confrontational show of strength. "I see my brother has brought me a feast!" she said as she tossed her head back and roared like a lion, "How very nice of you Nak. Show yourself, fool."

"Issss that how you greet your only loving brother?" Nak hissed as he slithered out of the tunnel. "By eating my friends?"

Brother? Nak's other sister is a sphinx?

The beast lunged towards Nak, who stealthily slid out of her way. "Tisk, tisk, you should have waited to eat if you knew I wasssss here, Dissyca," Nak remarked, snidely. "You know, good manners and all."

"Oh, very nice baby brother. I see you have silenced your lisp. You said my name so well." Dissyca mocked him by speaking like a baby, as her face twisted and she tossed her head from side to side.

"I ssssee you haven't changed a bit, still juvenile." He retorted, "Aren't you ssssupposed to give your mealssss a fighting chancssse?"

"Not when I am starving." She bantered, "Thank you, by the way; your gift was delicious!"

Ttensir emerged from the tunnel in a shot with his ax raised. Nak's relations had killed his entire family, and he wanted revenge. A primal yell pushed from his lungs as he leapt to kill the sphinx. Nak whipped his tail and tripped him. The Viking tumbled and landed hard on the ground, rolling over himself before coming to a stop. He turned to Nak with rage in his eyes and barked, "I should have killed you in the Hall!"

"Hall?" snickered Dissyca. "So it's true? The big bad Adrastai Council is underway." The creature threw her head back again and laughed maniacally. "Such a sweet idea, isn't it? Protect all that is Pure and Light. FOOLS! You will never rid the world of Evil!"

The sphinx darted towards Ttensir, who was still on the ground on the opposite side of the tunnel opening. I dove over top of the hole, landing firmly between Dissyca and Ttensir and stood tall, just as Nak had told me to.

The sphinx outspread her wings and stopped her attack mid-air directly in front of me. The force of the wind from her wings blew my hair back and caused my stance to waver. Her human face with a gaping mouth full of razor sharp was a mere inches from my face. I could smell Belac's blood on her breath; my stomach lurched, but I did not weaken. I simply glared into her angry green eyes with disgust on my face.

She slowly lowered her massive lion-shaped body to the ground, never once breaking her stare. A commotion behind me, briefly, tore my gaze away from her face. Her serpent tail struck out from behind, traveling over my shoulder as the cool scales slid against my cheek. Ttensir screamed in agony, and, instantly, I knew the strike had hit its target. I remained tall, never showing fear even though every fiber of my being wanted to run. The evil face just smirked at me and she raised one eyebrow in silent reveling. Her tail started to recoil scraping skin of my cheek with it, but the venomous head stopped abruptly at my backpack, sniffing around.

"Brochara! Don't Move!" I shouted inside his head.

I felt the serpent tail lift off my shoulder and hover above my head, ready to deliver another toxic bite. "What is your purpose?" I barked in Dissyca's face! It was all could think of to try to save Brochara's life.

I never took my eyes off the creature's face, watching her smug expression of enjoyment as her tail made its mark on Ttensir. But now, her face suddenly turned hard with anger as she glared back at me stepping in even closer, pressing towards my face. Her tail swung back over her body, turned its snake eyes to me, swaying from side-to-side as Nak had done in the past.

"I see we have a worthy warrior." Dissyca addressed me, as she sat back on her haunches, "What is your name, Adrastai?"

"Why is my name important? Do you wish to know the name of the warrior who will destroy you?" I calmly questioned, adding just enough of my own smug to mock her.

Dissyca lunged towards me again, but I stood my ground and

did not flinch at all. She stopped so close, that the fur surrounding her face touched my right ear and she whispered, "I will end you."

Suddenly, my brain turned in a different direction. It became clear to me that all my life I had been trained for this; trained to be an Adrastai warrior. My childhood play was always a part of a bigger plan. I studied mythology, legend, and lore. Aunt Evangeline had given me book years ago, and then clearly, it all made sense to me. That was part of my studies, my preparation for this very moment. I knew all about sphinxes and recalled the myth surrounding them. My confidence was now genuine.

"Aren't you supposed to ask me to solve a riddle? Funny, I didn't hear you offer my friend a chance? What kind of sphinx are you?" My voice was full of judgment.

"Well played," Nak telecommunicated with a nod of his hood.

The beast flipped her head back and boomed with laughter. "You amuse me. Ah, very well. Your sarcasm shall be my dessert when you fail to answer correctly," Dissyca snickered.

The beast circled me, sizing me up while she developed an appropriate riddle to end my life. Nak had slithered around from behind the crater and was looking intently into my eyes. I could feel his concern. My other friends were still below ground and I had hoped everyone was all right. "Well? Get on with it," I demanded.

Dissyca glared back at me and then sneered, "Alright, Adrastai," she spoke sarcastically as she sat back down, "I shall enjoy this. Your fatal riddle is: On your travels, you will come to a fork in the road, forcing you to make a choice. One path leads you to a place of darkness, where everyone always lies and leads you to certain death. The other path is one of Pureness and Light, where everyone tells the truth and you get to live. A snake from one of the villages stands in the middle of the fork, but there is no way of telling which village he

194

is from."

Dissyca turned her head at smiled at Nak as she continued; she raised her eyebrows, silently, questioning his integrity. "You are allowed to ask this snake only one question. One question is all you get to place your fate on the line, by the advice of a snake. What is the question you ask?" Her head turned to me, as she finished delivering my riddle.

The beast stood up and walked around me, licking her jaws in anticipation. Nak wouldn't look me in the eye. *Would I trust a snake? Should I trust a snake?* I decide in order to think of this riddle reasonably, I needed to change the word "snake" to "man". Why would she use a snake in my riddle instead of a man anyway? A twinge of doubt crept into my brain as I looked at Nak, which I am certain, was Dissyca's intentions. *What would my question be?* I paced, back and forth in front of the hole. Ttensir was writhing in pain, alone in the dirt. My friends were just under my feet. Nak was glaring at his sister on the other side. I was alone with my thoughts.

"If the one village must always lie, and the other must always tell the truth…Hmmmm…if I choose incorrectly, then I shall die." I was thinking aloud.

"State your question to the snake, Adrastai, or soon you will die," Dissyca, mused seemingly annoyed.

I looked to my brother, Nak. His expression had turned from concern to acknowledgment. His look gave me the confidence to solve the riddle.

"Then my question to the snake in the fork can only be: which way to your village? Because the truthful snake would point to the truthful village, and the lying snake would also point to the truthful village; either one would point in the same direction." I stated.

Dissyca roared so ferociously that I had to cover my ears!

Immediately, she sprang from her haunches. Her front paws hit me in the chest and I was knocked to the ground on my back. The beast stood over me, leaned in to bite my neck with her razor sharp teeth, but stopped just in time to bring her eyes inches from my own. Her long warm tongue licked up the side of my face. She tossed her head back and laughter boomed out of her mouth. "Well done, Adrastai. Lucky for me, I already fed today."

The beast raised her head and slowly walked forward. The entire length of her underbelly passed by my eyes and as the serpent tail passed over my head. It too, reached down and licked my face. "Get up and walk with me." Dissyca growled. "There are questions you need answered, I am told."

What? I slowly stood up, but not before removing my backpack. I gave Nak a look and glanced back to my pack, hoping he would understand that Brochara was inside. I am certain he was injured. Nak nodded, and I walked off into the forest with the beast.

I walked alongside Nak's sister, who just moments before wanted to make a meal out of me, but now I saw her in a different light. The sun illuminated her tan coat and danced on her cream-colored feathered wings. She was magnificent! Even the serpent tail glistened in the sunlight. Her long lion's mane gently waved in the slight breeze.

"It isn't polite to stare, young Adrastai." She spoke, looking straight ahead on our walk.

"I...I'm sorry." I stuttered, "You just, I mean, you're beautiful."

Dissyca stopped in her tracks and turned her human face to me, "Thank you." She nodded slowly, showing appreciation for my words. Then in an instant, she sprung off from all fours and landed on a large boulder. She looked majestic and glowed in the sunshine.

"I am the Oracle you seek." She proclaimed.

"You? You're the Oracle?" I managed to ask, in my confusion.

"You have been sent to seek out prophecy. I asked you my question, now ask me yours." The sarcasm had left her voice and only softness remained. Her fierce demeanor was replaced by a peace that calmed me.

I didn't know what to ask. I wasn't told by anyone. I found myself wondering why the Mages would send me here. What sort of information was I supposed to retrieve? I wished my friends were here to guide me. "I am certain there are specific questions others wish for me to ask, but I have not been instructed by anyone. I was only told that it was time to seek the Oracle, and the journey would be a dangerous one." I was really just talking aloud; I didn't know where I was going with my conversation.

A sudden burst of energy shot out from the center of Dissyca, like an electric charge that caused every one of her hairs stand on end and then softly float back against her skin. She was disconnected from reality and transcendent as her prophetic powers overtook her. When she began to speak, her soft voice traveled on the breeze, tumbling to my ears like a dandelion seed, aloft, and heavy with hope:

"Your journey has already been dangerous,
And it will not become one of leisure.
You are destined for greatness,
But will require the help of others.
Golden fruit shall quench your thirst
And giant tasks are required.
Family gives strength,
But can betray when victory is desired.
Tread every so softly and with wit,
When dancing amongst the fire.
For truth be told, your heart is gold,

But heat can melt bonds sired."

Dissyca's eyes had rolled into the back of her head while she continued to prophesize.

"This shall play amongst your heart
Forever to be heard.
Amidst the Dark and with the Light,
Alliances converge."

"Wow," was all I could manage to say. That was beautifully confusing and well delivered. I was in awe of what just happened, and not quite sure what it meant. I was afraid that I would forget it all before I even stood up.

Dissyca's eyes rolled forward again, and I assumed her prophecy was complete, but once again, her gaze then locked onto mine, and she continued,

"Young Adrastai, you will go you will return never in war will you perish. It is up to you where to place the commas."

"Wait, what? What does that mean?" I was completely confused. She had just poetically delivered my prophecy, and then she added another riddle about my death? "Is that a part of my prophecy? I don't understand."

"Write it down and you shall see what I mean," and with her words an eerie darkness set in, covering the warm sunlight. I looked to Dissyca for further guidance, but she was scowling back at me and her ferocious demeanor had returned. The beast's terrifying teeth were exposed and her lip curled up in a snarl. The fur along her back stood up and she crouched down on her front legs poised to attack.

She began growling and nervously snapping the air with her ferocious jaws in every direction.

Confused, I stepped back quickly and noticed that Mateo, Luca, Skye, and Nak had all surrounded us. "Ssssorry our vissssit musssst end thissss way darling, but you have broken your promissse. You ssssee, you never gave our friend, Belac, a fighting chancssse." Nak's expression on his face was full of anger.

"A fighting chance?" growled Dissyca "Is that what you are offering me right now? Mother would be so proud."

"Mother hassss nothing to do with thissss." Nak hissed back.

"Oh, but wouldn't she be proud to see her little snake boy standing up to his big sister. She always liked a good fight." Dissyca retorted. "An unfair one at that! Well played, brother!"

I looked to Nak for guidance, and his large bronze eyes flared red. Something wasn't right. I felt darkness surround him and hatred bubble up inside. For a moment, I thought back to the riddle. Why did she choose to say a snake instead of man? Did she intentionally mean to plant a seed of distrust between Nak and me or was it just a coincidence? Did he falter in his path? Should I trust a creature from such evil beginnings? How can I keep my sense of certain expectation strong even when the world around me suggests I would be wiser to pay more attention to my current state? The High Mages trusted Nak, Aunt E trusted him...That is exactly what she wanted. Doubt. With doubt, it is impossible for confidence to exist, and Dark cannot be replaced with Light if doubt exists.

"You will die!" I shouted as confident as I could, standing tall, just as Nak had told me to. Servo leapt to my hands and I lunged towards the beast.

Suddenly, the serpent head of her tail struck out with lightning speed, and Skye fell to the ground in pain.

"NO!" I screamed. Dust filled the air, blinding us. The sphinx shot up to the sky leaving us in a powdered cloud of soil and filth. I stumbled through the haze, following the screams of my friend. I tripped over Nak's slithering tail and slammed my head into the boulder. As the darkness creeped in, Skye's cries for help echoed in my brain.

Chapter 14

Illustrated by
Cassidy Rasmus

14

A HISTORY

The dust cloud settled revealing a grave scene. Skye was slumped over on the ground with her back against the boulder Dissyca prophesized on just moments earlier. She was very pale and she appeared to be having a hard time breathing. I ran over to her side and it became apparent that Sphinx venom is very powerful. The skin around her mouth and eyes had a greyish hue around them and her eyes looked sunken deep inside their sockets.

"Skye! No, no, no, no, no, no. You have to be okay. Come on Skye, tell me you are okay!" I ranted.

Skye laboriously turned her eyes to find mine, which were drowning in tears. She tried to reach for my hand, but she was too weak and it fell to the dirt. There was a look of sadness and fear in her half-opened eyes. I quickly scooped her into my arms and without hesitation; I stood up and took off running towards the ship.

"KHAI!!!!" I screamed at the top of my lungs! "HELP ME! Please help me." My voice was shaky and desperate. There was no way I could lose her! Was Khai still alive? My brain was swirling and

I was only acting on instinct. Things were just happening so fast and I didn't know if I was acting irrationally or doing the right thing; I just had to try to save her.

I had to sit down. I had to get it together. After all, we tunneled here, and I was running aimlessly through a dangerous forest, carrying a dying friend. I had to stop and think. I found a mossy patch that reminded me of home, and what better place is there than home? I laid her down on spongy patch of earth, closed my eyes, and took a deep breath trying to clear my head. Something shifted in the air.

Apprehensive about what horror I may find, I opened my eyes. An enormous mass of the most brilliantly colored butterflies I had ever seen encircled us. A column of color with a center filled with a puffy cloud of white, gently descended toward Skye. I remembered that flying doctor thingies that took care of Khai after I had cracked some of his ribs when I slid of the cliff at Sukanar's lair. There was tiny chatter in a language that I did not understand as the medical allergens fussed over her.

One of them flew up to the butterflies and communicated something to them because suddenly, they dispersed and flew off to cover every surrounding tree. The entire canopy began to rattle and shake under their touch, and then the familiar sound of creaking wood filled my ears as each tree bent away from the mossy patch that Skye lay on, clinging to life. The butterflies were African fairies, speaking to the flora to create a giant window for sunlight to reach us.

It felt like hours had passed, but it was only minutes before a group of the fluffy doctors flew up to my eye level, hovered there for a moment, and then shook their tiny heads from side-to-side indicating there was nothing more they could do to save her.

"NO!" I cried and stuffed my hand into my pocket and pulled

out my coin. There had to be something I could do. I couldn't just stand there and watch her life slip away…not Skye. I needed her. The High Mages gave me this shield for a reason, maybe there was something it could do. The sun reflected brilliantly off of the metal as I held it in the palm of my hand, and I felt its warmth. The last time I looked at it, Asëa spoke to me from another realm.

Then, it all became clear. Well, not clear, but I had an idea. I held the shield in both hands and it sprung open to the size of a dinner plate. I knelt beside Skye's weak body and held the plate up over my head, closed my eyes, and wished intensely for Asëa to appear to me again; to guide me. I put all of my energy into calling him. Maybe he could give me some advice or direction.

My hands began to shake involuntarily and the shield grew heavy. Excited to see Asëa again, I lowered my hands and peered into it. To my surprise, my elven brother was not there, but a familiar golden liquid was. It sloshed around the inside of the silver shield, coating the sides like a thick broth. "A golden tear! Thank You Laurina," I whispered with my eyes wet with hope and my heart full of gratitude.

I carefully raised Skye's head and brought her lips to my shield, but she was too weak to realize what I was trying to do. "Drink Skye, this will help you." I tried to pour the tear into her mouth but it ran down her chin and onto her shoulder, which I noticed was bleeding. Her shirt had two circular holes torn next to each other and anger bubbled inside of me realizing that that must have been where Dissyca's tail struck her.

There was no response. I could feel her slipping away and taking a piece of my heart with her. She was fading fast. "You have to drink! Skye!" I screamed and shook her shoulders, but her body went limp in my arms.

Instinct took over and I plunged my in to the shield and gulped the warm healing tear into my mouth. Bright lights popped and exploded before my eyes as the liquid filled my mouth. I felt a power come over me; every cell in my body felt strong, healthy. Intuitively, I brought her mouth to my lips and slowly released some of the tear into her mouth; her lips were cold and stiff.

Her body was icy, and very heavy in my arms. I looked to see if the liquid made it into her mouth or just ran down her cheek. When I pulled her from my lips only a thin golden trickle of tear snaked down her chin. Some had to make it in. I had to try again.

I took an ever-larger gulp and the same incredible reaction took place within my body. This time, I pressed her to my lips longer and made sure not to waste any healing powers of the tear. Slowly and cautiously, I released the liquid into her mouth. Her body twitched and grew warmer in my embrace. Her eyes slowly opened and met mine. A look of surprise grew across her face as she realized that I held her against my lips, but then her eyes rolled back again and her body went limp.

"Thank You Laurina!" I shouted to the sky. The tear was working. I couldn't stop now, not until every last drop had been administered. I slurped up another dose and raised her to my lips again. As I delivered the healing tincture, something caught my attention out of the corner of my eye; there was movement in the tree line. *Not again.* How was I going to fight off an attack? I needed to give all my attention to Skye.

Suddenly, the foliage burst apart, and Nak was charging through, slithering in our direction with a limp Ttensir on his back. He slid over to us, and plunked his gravely injured passenger next to Skye. I knew I had to share the tear, it was the right thing to do, but a little piece of me wanted to be selfish for Skye. Brochara and Fin hitched a ride on Nak's tail carrying my backpack, and Mateo and Luca kept their distance and stayed by the tree line.

I quickly grabbed my pack and retrieved my pirate spyglass. I used the eyepiece end as a cup and poured a small amount of the tear onto the lens. We lifted Ttensir's head and poured some into his mouth. No response.

I quickly scooped up some the golden tear and shoved my hands deep into the snakebite wound on his leg. Ttensir's body tensed up rigid and went limp just at fast, but I was getting a reaction. I had to keep trying!

Just then, the ground shook. Startled we turned to find our next obstacle. Khai's body was skidding and tumbling across the clearing towards us. He was obviously not doing well. "Khai!" I screamed filled with emotions half-full of fear and half-full of relief to see my dragon brother once again.

I ran to my majestic friend and threw my arms around his neck. Khai opened his eyes and feebly blinked them again. "You needed me?" he faintly whispered inside my head, unable to muster up enough energy to speak.

"Oh Khai, I am so sorry." I answered, "Be still, I have a tear." A sudden calm rushed over me; I was exactly where I supposed to be. My friends needed me, the High Mages knew that I needed my friends, and I was given this tear to help them. I just knew that this was supposed to happen this way; I felt it deep in my bones. I ran back to the others and carefully grabbed my shield. I gave a grateful look to Brochara, who was methodically passing his hands over both, Skye and Ttensir's bodies performing his elven healing that I have witnessed more than once; together we could do this. I poured a little more of the golden liquid into the spyglass, gave it to Fin, and he dripped it into the Viking's mouth. I delivered another healing kiss to Skye, before gingerly carrying the shield, so not to spill and of the contents, over to Khai.

"Please, give it Skye," he whispered.

"There's enough." I told him, "Don't be stubborn. I can't do this without you."

Khai managed a snort of laughter and looked caringly into my eyes. "You are noble, Sir Giovani."

I poured the last remaining liquid into Khai's mouth. Instantly, his wings unfolded, he sat up on his hind legs and roared tremendously. Exotic birds fled the tree tops in every direction and the sky filled with the bright colors of the African fairies.

Ttensir's body jumped, startled, and Skye sat straight up. The tear was working. Khai's strength quickly returned, and Skye's coloring slowly seeped back into her face and she still looked a little dazed, but Ttensir remained unconscious.

"We have to get him back to the ship." Nak hissed.

"I am strong again; I can carry all of you." Khai proclaimed.

"Absolutely not!" I yelled. "We are not dong that again. Ever!"

Khai shot me a disapproving look. "Giovani, it must be done this way."

"No, I am sorry. I need you, and you need me. We cannot afford to put you in danger again. You take Skye, Ttensir, and Brochara to care for them. The rest of us will meet you there." My voice was commanding. Secretly, I was proud of myself.

Khai nodded in agreement, and I was relieved. With the help of Nak, we were able to get the injured onto his back. Brochara delivered a charm to secure them to the harness, before he climbed into his car seat. The rest of us watched as the majestic dragon flapped his mighty wings and disappeared on the horizon.

"Be safe," I telecommunicated to my friend.

"We need to talk about your meeting with Dissyca," Nak interrupted the silence.

"I had almost forgotten about that," I responded, "It seems so long ago."

"Did she give you a prophecsssy?" Nak hissed.

"You knew she was the Oracle?" I looked towards my cobra friend with confusion on my face.

"She issss my ssssissssster," he replied, still glancing to the sky. "What did she ssssay?"

I had to sit for a moment and clear my mind of everything that just happened, so I could recall what she said. All of my friends welcomed the rest, and sat in a circle with me on the soft, spongy moss. I smiled at each of them, and then closed my eyes.

Sitting still, I listened to the sounds of the forest and just allowed my mind to drift away on the warm breeze. I traveled back to the encounter when I was at peace with the sphinx. The scene flooded my memory vividly; the smells and colors rushed back to me, and then I heard the prophecy again, as if Dissyca were telling it for the first time.

I repeated it so all of my friends could hear and help me remember, "Your journey has already been dangerous, and it will not become one of leisure. You are destined for greatness, but will require the help of others. Golden fruit shall quench your thirst and giant tasks are required. Family gives strength, but can betray when victory is desired. Tread every so softly and with whit when dancing amongst the fire. For truth be told, your heart is gold, but heat can melt bonds sired. This shall play amongst your heart forever to be heard. Amidst the Dark and with the Lights, alliances converge."

I opened my eyes, and saw the looks of each one of my friend's faces. Mateo just looked confused, and Luca wore a warm smile. Fin also was smiling at me and Nak seemed to be in deep thought over this.

"Issss that all?" he questioned, "Wassss there anymore?"

How did he know? I purposely left off the part about my death. "More?" I questioned. "Why would there be more? Do you understand what the first part meant?"

"Firsssst part? Giovani, you musssst be honessssst with me if I am to guide you well," Nak spoke and I looked to the ground ashamed. Both at the fact that I tried to hide something from him and that I wasn't clever enough to do so.

"Yes, there was more." I spoke to the dirt, "She told me to write the next part down." I grabbed my backpack and took out my manual. "This is the only thing I have to write it in." I glanced up to my friends, the twins seemed surprised that I would write in the Adrastai manual. I knew they each had one of their own and was fully aware of its importance to its owner.

"I think that issss a grand placssse to write a prophecsssy from the Oracle. After all, it wassss the High Magessss who ssssent you on thissss journey," Nak's voice was soothing and kind. "Write away brother.

I placed the manual in my lap. I didn't even have to open it, because, just like in the past, the manual flipped open by itself. The smell of parchment brought a smile to my face and the worn pages turned by themselves, creating a slight breeze. When the pages stopped turning, the manual lay open in my lap with blank parchment. In a teeny puff of smoke, the magical quill suddenly appeared and tapped on the pages, poised, ready to create. I took a deep breath and exhaled, preparing myself to share, when the quill began to spin, vertically, in the path of my exhale.

Right away, the invisible illustrator began scribbling and twisting along the parchment, without any guidance from me. The usual clouds of ink covered the pages while the quill worked its magic. Then, just as quick as it started, it stopped.

When the ink clouds settled on the left-hand side page, a beautiful drawing was revealed, depicting Dissyca on the rock with me alongside of her, listening intently. The words of the prophecy that I had just re-told everyone was scrolled out, captioned under the sketch recording my memory.

The quill was tapping impatiently, as it had all summer, waiting for some sort of direction from me. I glanced at each of my friends, shrugged my shoulders, and they all shrugged back unsure of how to offer guidance. I blew on the feather again and it spun around collecting my memories from my exhale.

We all stared at the right-hand side of my manual as the quill feverishly created yet another ink cloud. When the dust settled, the remaining portion of the prophecy, the one I tried to keep secret, was scrolled out and read, "You will go You will return never in war will you perish. It is up to you, where to place the commas." My friends wore the same confused expression as I did.

The enchanted illustrator paused indecisively for a moment and then placed a comma in between the words "return" and "never,. but suddenly, it erased the comma, and then placed it between the words "never" and "in". Like a student unsure of the answer on a test, the quill erased the comma again, and placed it back into the first spot, only to erase and place it back to in between "never" and "in" again.

"What is it doing?" Mateo barked, seemingly annoyed.

"I believe that the prophecy is trying to tell Giovani that his fate depends on him," Luca's soft voice interpreted her perception of the confused quill's actions.

Nak wrapped his tail around her, and gave her a snake-tail hug, in a fatherly sort of way. "I think you nailed it." He said, lovingly.

To be honest with myself, I didn't like it that Nak and Luca thought they understood the deeper meaning of the latter half of my prophecy. I still didn't get it. Why would she not know whether I was going to die in battle, or not? I didn't want the two of them to find happiness while I sat confused, so I focused on the first half of the prophecy.

"What about the first part? What did Golden fruit and giant tasks and all the other stuff mean?" I questioned with my annoyance reflected in my tone.

"I am afraid I undersssstand the golden fruit part. I had a feeling it would come to thissss." Nak hissed.

"What-ah do-ah you mean-ah, come-ah to this?" Mateo interrupted. I gave him a look of disgust. I wasn't happy with him butting into my business. I still didn't trust him.

"His is required to meet, yet another, one of my ssssiblingssss." Nak answered.

"Really?" my shoulders slumped forward. "Will this one try to kill me too?"

"Yessss." Was all he said.

"Ladon." Mateo whispered.

"Oh no." Luca added.

"Who is this Ladon?" Fin jumped to his feet and drew his sword.

"Wait a minute, are you talking about the one-hundred-headed dragon that protected the God, Hera's Golden Apples in Greek mythology?" The thought suddenly popped into my mind. I shoved my hand back into the pack and found the book I was looking for, *Greek Mythology Monsters.*

"No need for the book, Giovani. I lived it, and bessssidessss, the bookssss only give you half of the sssstory," Nak mused.

"May I tell the story, please?" Luca's eyes were bright and full of excitement as she questioned Nak.

The large cobra looked upon her like a father to his daughter and replied, softly saying, "Of coursssse you may, dear. I will fill in the partsssss that may be unclear."

Luca threw her arms around Nak's neck and gave him a loving squeeze as Mateo looked on with a smile across his face. She excitedly turned to me and began a tale that blew my mind.

"Everything starts with Chaos!" she started, with a look like she was going to jump out of her skin!

"I've heard that somewhere, just recently." I responded, but I couldn't remember where.

"Saint John reminded me of that back in the Enchanted Realm, when you didn't trusssst me. Remember now?" Nak gave me a wink as he jogged my memory. I nodded, sheepishly, and felt my cheeks burn hot with embarrassment.

"Okay, I love this story, so I am just going to blurt it out! Here goes," Luca was very alluring. I was attracted to her excitement and wanted to give her all of my attention.

"Like I said, it started with Chaos known also as Confusion. Chaos was the first immortal to come into existence, followed by Gaia or Earth, and then Tartarus; you know, the Underworld. Are you following me?" she asked. I found myself smiling at her use of hand gestures as she told the story.

"Yes, I am. What about Love? I mean Eros." I replied and felt my cheeks flush red again.

Luca giggled as Mateo grunted and moved closer to his sister in a protective sort of way. "Yes Giovani, Eros was next. Speaking of Love, Gaia and Tartarus created Typhon, Nak's father. Are you familiar with Typhon? Do you know his story?" she asked me. She was speaking really fast in all of her excitement. Fin was also right beside me, and we both looked at each other with amazement and then turned back to Luca. We were fascinated with Luca's story telling.

"Um, I am not that familiar with Typhon, no. Sorry, Nak." I looked at Nak, but he seemed uncomfortable and slithered away from the circle. I looked at Mateo and Luca and shrugged my shoulders.

"Nak is-ah Pure soul-ah. Most of his-ah family are not-ah. He gets-ah very uncomfortable when we-ah talk about his-ah family." Mateo explained, and I was surprised by his gentle approach.

"Anyway, Typhon is wicked! He is the most deadly monster of all! Some have called him the Father of all Monsters. He and his wife, Echidna," she paused and gestured towards Nak, "Nak's mom, she has been called the Mother of all Monsters!" Her excitement with this story telling was infectious.

"What happens next!" squeaked Fin's voice, which I had never heard happen before.

"Okay, so Typhon is a sibling of the Titans, and Zeus had imprisoned all of them. Gaia, Typhon's Mom and Nak's Grandmother," Luca giggled again as she acted out parts of her story and continued to talk incredibly fast, "asked Typhon to destroy Zeus. Can you imagine the battle that the two of them must have had?"

Luca was now unable to contain her excitement and belly laughed out-threw herself dramatically backwards onto the moss. The sound of her giddiness drove the rest of us to laughter.

"I am sorry, I just love this story!" she managed through her enjoyment, and I couldn't wait to find out where this was going. I felt like my three-year-old sister must have when I told her stories.

"Okay, okay." She calmed her merriment, took a deep breath to continue, and stood up now incorporating arm movements to re-enact the battle. "A massive battle; Typhon destroyed cities and hurled mountains. All of the Gods of Olympus fled in fear, but not Zeus! No sir, he stood his ground. Typhon won some battles and Zeus won others, but in the end, Zeus overpowered Typhon. He cast him into Tartarus, and pinned him under Mount Etna! Ha, ha! Wait, did you know that every time he struggles, earthquakes occur and/or volcanos erupt? Isn't that so cool? All because of Nak's Dad."

"Wait, volcanos?" I interrupted, and turned my focus to Nak suddenly serious. "Nak, he was there...with Nãga, wasn't he? The ground shaking, the lava...She mentioned him. Teasing you." I paused between each thought as I processed them in my own mind, while Nak remained silent. "Nak, when I had to go and find you... Nãga almost ended us, but she was pulled away by something more important in that fissure in the floor..." My words trailed off as I made the connection that I was very close to the Father of all Monsters!

"Yessss. He wassss there. I felt him, and that issss why I paussssed long enough for Nãga to make her move." There was anger in Nak's voice. "I should have known." Nak's hood deflated and his head slumped over.

"What do you mean, you had to go and find him?" Luca asked. "You met Nãga?"

Suddenly, I felt her mood shift from giddy to put out and confused. "Nak?"

"Luca, ssssissssster, we have not had the chancssse to chat." Nak's voice had softened when he turned to address her, "I was inssssstructed by Asëa to share my essencssse with Giovani. The High Magessss have put their trusssst in him." Nak had then coiled his tail around me, hugging me as he did Luca earlier. "You both share a part of me."

"WHAT?" Mateo shouted, "HIM-AH? COME-AH ON!" and he threw is muscular arms up in the air frustrated, stood up, and stormed off.

"Enough!" Nak scolded Mateo and whipped his tail catching the man-bull on his backside.

"Owe-ah!" he cried as he grabbed his fanny, "I'm-ah sorry." He spit the words at me and quickly glanced back to Nak, shrugging sarcastically.

"Nãga is helping Typhon?" Luca sank down, hung her head, and shook it in disbelief; her excitement faded, quickly, "This can't be happening. What about Echidna? Oh, this is bad."

"That issss why we have sssset out on the journey, my friendssss. Giovani wasssss to hear his prophecsssy in the hope of giving ussss direction to sssstop Nãga. Sssshe musssst be sssstopped." Nak wore a pained expression as he spoke to all of us.

"Then, a visit to-ah Ladon is our-ah next stop-ah," Mateo added. "Golden fruit for all-ah!"

Nak quickly slid over to Mateo and rose up, alongside of his body; towering over him, with his hood flared wide, "NO! You will not be going with ussss. I fear that your heart issss turning. You have shown me nothing but jealoussssy and animossssity!"

"But, but…Nak, I'm-ah sorry." Mateo had hung his head in shame, "I was-ah blinded by rage and-ah jealousy. Please forgive me."

Nak reduced back to his normal size and looked Mateo directly in the eyes, "I forgive you, but I do not think it issss wisssse for you to join ussss."

Luca's eyes filled with tears watching the two of them argue. "Please, Mateo. Remember what we are fighting for and why."

"I am-ah sorry sister, I was-ah wrong to judge and act that-ah way. Sometimes I feel-ah more Berserker than-ah human." Mateo was sincere in his words and he hugged his sister.

"Ladon is a good guy," Luca proclaimed as her eyes beamed with excitement once again; "This should be fun!"

"Let's get back to Ellida." Nak dove back into the ground and began to tunnel towards to the shore.

Fin jumped onto my shoulder and I followed the siblings into the dirt passageway. "Are you sure you are up for this?" Fin whispered into my ear.

"The Order needs me. I have to be." I had to squint through the darkness. The only light was a dim greenish glow that illuminated from our orbs. The soft light reflected off Luca's white-blonde hair and made her a vision of light. She turned quickly, stopping in her tracks and I, again, plowed into her.

"Did you know that Aphrodite, the Goddess of Love, and Ares, the God of War, had a daughter? Her name was Adrestia." Luca was inches from my face and holding my hand in the darkness while she continued, "She was the one who helped form the Adrastai Warriors. Warriors of Love. Isn't that romantic?"

The impact of our collision stunned me, and I found my face

covered with her hair, which had flopped over my head. She smelled like a meadow of wildflowers. Nevertheless, I was unable to answer because her overprotective brother thumped me on the top of my head, and everything went black.

Chapter 15
Illustrated by
Caroline Powell

15

GOLDEN FRUIT

When I awoke, I was sitting on the deck of Ellida, which was completely repaired from Clerah's damaging winds. Skye was lying next to me and the healthy coloring had returned to her face, and Ttensir was swinging in a makeshift hammock of nets above us. The gentle waves of the Sea rocked him back-and-forth like a baby in a cradle. Luca noticed my stirring and ran over to be by my side.

"UGH! I am so very sorry, Giovani. My brother can be such a jerk when it comes to me." She laid her hand on my shoulder and my skin tingled at her touch. I tossed my disheveled hair out of my eyes and found hers; the bright sky-blue coloring entrances me every time.

"Uh…wait, what?" I said as I rubbed an extremely sore spot on the top of my head. Why do I get lost in eyes every time? I can't speak correctly, I fumble over myself, and I must look like a jerk.

Fin and Brochara's laughter boomed from behind me. I turned to them, shrugged my shoulders, and shook my head, confused.

"Hey! You found your hat." I exclaimed, smiling at Fin's plumed brown Cavalier hat that was back on top of his head, which he tipped in my direction while still laughing. Luca giggled, stood up playfully, and then marched down the deck of the ship with a purpose towards Mateo, who was sitting by himself in the corner.

"I am beginning to think that this girl is hazardous to my health." I told Fin and Brochara over my shoulder. They both laughed harder. Skye's, who was lying a foot away, stirred in response to the loud amusement. "Sshh," I whispered through a giggle to avoid waking her.

I turned back over to sit when I bumped directly into the muscular legs of Mateo, who had replaced his sister's small frame. "Sorry, again-ah." he barked; his deep sharp voice startled me and I flinched.

I looked directly into his eyes, but found myself drawn to the grotesque, black bruise that covered his left eye. I leaned back to regain some of my personal space, when the long thin cut above his right eye became visible. "What happened to you?" I asked.

"Your protectors-ah, they-ah do their job-ah well," he replied without any emotion. "Again-ah, I'm-ah sorry." Mateo rose and turned to walk away when I noticed a large slice in the back of his shirt. A giant welt, the size of Nak's tail peeked through the torn fabric. I giggled to myself, thinking about what must have occurred in the darkness.

Just past the exiting form of Mateo, I saw Khai and Jock conversing with the dragonhead of Ellida. I was so happy to see him that I jumped to my feet and ran towards them. Mateo spun around at my approaching speed and yelled, "I'M-AH SORRY!!!! Geesch!" and he sat back down, rather hard, on his crate in the corner and crossed is enormous arms across his chest.

"Okay," I answered, looking at him sideways, and questioning his sanity, "I'm just going to see my friends. Wacko." I finished the last part under my breath.

I had planned a sneak-attack hug on my dragon partner, but Mateo's outburst caused everyone to stop what he or she were doing and look. "Hey! How are you feeling?" I asked running my fingers through my windblown hair trying to keep it out of my eyes.

Khai giggled, rolled his eyes around in his head, and fell to the ship pretending to be knocked out. After his dramatic mockery, he opened one eye, looked up at me, and chuckled, "I'm-ah great! How about-ah you?" Jock, Ellida and Khai all roared with laughter.

"Ha, ha, ha. Very funny. What is up with that guy?" I plunked myself down next to my dear dragon friend; his iridescent scales were shimmering in the sunlight.

"I don't think he likes you," the dragon ship's head answered which was accompanied with more booming laughter.

"Really? Whatever gave you that idea?" I joked.

"Khai, let's get out of here for a while. What do think?" I jabbed my elbow into his side. "I could really use from fresh air."

I didn't have to ask twice. Khai jumped to his feet and in one swift maneuver I was on top of my harness. With a gigantic roar, we took off like a shot through the warm salty air.

Freedom. I stood with my face to the sun and closed my eyes for some peace and quiet. It was heavenly, and I could sense that Khai felt at peace as well. We soared silently for over twenty minutes, performing aerial maneuvers and spontaneous dives. It was one of those moments in life when everything feels right in the world. All of our friends were healthy again; life was good.

"Are you ready for the next leg of your journey, Giovani?"

223

Khai's voice was soothing inside my head.

"I really don't know what to expect. Luca said that Ladon is a nice one, so I guess I am not that worried." The cool mist of a cumulus cloud wet my face and, like a cold shower, it thrust me back into the present.

"Really? Is that what she said?" Followed by another dragon giggle, "I do believe that girl *is* hazardous to your health!" He pulled a corkscrew maneuver, and I was forced back on top of my game.

"That's what I said!" I chuckled. "Wait, what do mean?"

"Ladon may be one of the good ones, but he still has orders to follow," Khai boomed, performing a triple loop-de-loop.

"Orders? For what?" I was struggling to hold, and began to think that Khai was deliberately trying to knock me off.

"To protect the Golden Fruit." Khai came to an abrupt stop and I tumbled forwards, through the air. My arms jerked in the reins, and I plunked down backwards onto Khai's snout. I ended up facing my friend, eye-to-eye, and we both laughed uncontrollably.

"Owe!" I said in a voice slightly higher than usual.

"Why do you suppose I need to go there?" I asked as I scooted up his snout, climbed over the extra-large spikes on the top of his head, and performed a handstand move back into the harness.

"Very nice," Khai complimented as he watched from the top of his eyes. "Fin would be proud. My guess is that you are going to have to steal some fruit. Why else would you be sent there?"

"What? Really?" I stood there, thinking about what Khai had just said, "Why is the fruit so important?"

"It is said that those who eat it gain immortality." We coasted through the brilliant blue sky and the sun danced on the Sea's surface.

"Whoa." I plunked down on the harness now, digesting the information that Khai just handed me. "I do not want to hurt Nak's nice sibling, nor do I want him to hurt me. What am I going to do?"

"I don't know friend, I don't know." Khai's voice had lost its playfulness.

"LAND HO!" shouted Ellida from the Sea's surface.

Khai and I glided silently back to the dragon ship. He executed a perfect landing, and I executed the perfect dismount. I leapt from the harness, slid down his front leg and gracefully glided onto the deck. I caught a glimpse of Luca's face, which lit up with a brilliant smile upon our landing. Just past her small frame, I watched Skye sit herself up. I ran past Luca and plunked myself next to my dear friend, Skye anxious to finally speak to her.

"Skye! How are you feeling?" I eagerly shouted, not aware of how close I was to her ear.

"Oh, I could have done without that shout," she answered as she rubbed her ear, and I knew right away, that she was feeling better. "Maybe a little sore," she added, grabbing her left shoulder. Then Skye swatted my elbow that I was leaning on, out from under me and I fell back. "Show off!"

"Oh, you saw that did you?" I chuckled, as I threw her an elbow to the arm in jest, forgetting about her injury and she let out a tiny yelp. "Ahhhh, I am so sorry. Does it hurt? Is that where her tail bit you?" It bothered me to see my friend in pain, but I was so glad she was alive to talk about it.

"It is all kind of hazy. I remember feeling the bite, then the searing hot pain, like lava traveling through my veins." Her eyebrows

225

furled as she tried to remember, "But then everything went cloudy…Hey, did you kiss me?"

Skye turned her questioning gaze to me. "I, uh, well, kind of." I stuttered to explain. "There was my shield and a golden…" This was all very awkward.

"It's fine. Thank you, I think." She interrupted my fumbling for words, and spared me any more embarrassment.

"Well, I think I have to go pick some fruit now," I sighed. "Rest, and hopefully, we can talk more later."

"Oh no. I am definitely going with you!" she demanded. "I may have been unconscious, but I heard some things that made me realize that you need me."

I cast her a look of disapproval and confusion. I was about to protest, but just as I opened my mouth and raised my pointer finger, Skye interrupted again.

"There is no arguing this point. Let's go." She firmly stated.

I went to help her up, but stubbornly, she did it without me. Then she walked straight towards Jock and Khai, passing Luca, without even acknowledging her, giving her the cold shoulder.

Fin and Brochara flanked both sides of me. I looked to both of them for some sort of explanation. But for once, neither of them had anything to say. They both just shrugged their shoulders.

"Girls. I am not even going to try to understand them," I said, and we all walked to the front of the ship.

Nak was waiting for us by the head of Ellida. I was pleasantly surprised to see Ttensir by his side. He looked fine, maybe a little gruffer than before, but I suppose such is the life of a Viking.

"Thank you." Ttensir removed his horned helmet and bowed his balding head, "I owe you my life." Ttensir took his respect one-step further, and genuflected down on one knee. The entire Viking crew followed his lead and banged their weapons upon the deck all at the same time. The roars of all three dragons echoed with a thunderous sound.

No more words were required. Brochara, Fin, and I jumped upon Khai's back. Skye, Nak, and Luca climbed onto Jock's, and Ttensir scaled to the top of Ellida's woodenhead. Like a giant slingshot, Ellida pulled her head to the side, as far as it would reach, and flung Ttensir through the air. But the grounded Mateo watched from the ship's deck.

All of our jaws would have hit the deck if they weren't attached. We all stared in amazement, as his large body soared through the air, as if he were just shot from a canon, and he squealed like a child on an amusement ride. Khai took to the air and Jock dove into the sea. Just before Ttensir was about to crash-land on the shore, Khai grabbed him in his talons and gently guided his feet to the ground.

We all arrived at the shore together, but something just didn't feel right. A thick fog was hovering near the ground, just inland, and it had been full sun all morning. Very unusual weather conditions, indeed, the fog should have evaporated with the heat from the sun. My birthmark was tingling, and the other Adrastai seemed agitated as well.

Skye stopped dead in her tracks, frozen. I grabbed her elbow, and she yanked it out of my grip. "What's wrong?" I whispered.

"Ssshhh!" she responded, very quickly. Skye was turning her head slightly from side-to-side, as if she were hearing something we couldn't. "We're not alone."

She quickly climbed back onto Jock, and I could tell they were telecommunicating. He moved so suddenly into the fog, it was as if they disappeared.

My orb began to glow red. Luca grabbed her orb at the same time. She whispered something into it, and the red light ceased. Quickly, she ran over to me, took my orb in her hands, and brought it to her lips. The warning glow of my orb stopped, too. Our eyes met, and she nodded without words. Then, right before my eyes, she transformed into a white dove and flew into the mist.

Nak slowly slid over to Brochara and whispered something into his ear. My elven friend waved his hand over his head, and then he disappeared right before my eyes.

Nak then slithered over to Ttensir and proceeded to give him secret instructions, like a commander on a covert operation. Ttensir then snuck off in the opposite direction, and soon was engulfed by the fog.

I turned back around, just in time to see the feather on Fin's hat swallowed up by the eerie cloud. I waited for Nak's direction, but he was gone. *Gone?* "Hello?" I telecommunicated, "What about me?"

"Giovani," whispered Khai's voice inside my head, "remember who you are and what you stand for. Uphold the nine virtues and defend them! Be Safe."

"Where are you?" I asked twisting my head from left to right, but I didn't see anyone, nor did anyone answer.

I couldn't see past my arm in front of me, and the strange mist was heavier than water. It felt more like a wading through a pool than walking on land. *Maybe it was meant to exhaust me?* Instinctively, I thought of my sword, Servo, and it leapt to my hands.

Something rushed past me streaking a trail of silver in its wake. Startled, I reeled around to find it, but I did not see anything.

Screams rang through the air and chills shot down my spine. Another silver flash streaked by me heading in the other direction, followed by more cries of pain. Then, a horrible roar grew out of the mist and stopped me dead in my tracks.

We were under attack. I turned to run, but I slammed into something and was knocked to the ground. My vision was blurred from the contact, but squinting through the thick mist, I saw a large branch of a tree stretching across my path. I had walked straight into a tree. Smooth. I stood up and almost bumped my head again, when something flickered on the branch. My eyes quickly glanced to the light, squinting through the fog trying to focus on what was glimmering. My eyebrows rose as my brain deciphered what I saw: a Golden Apple, only one, and it hung there, just out of my reach.

Just then, another streak of silver shot past me, crashing into the left side of my body, sending me twirling like a top, and I fell to the ground again. A weight of a boulder landed on my chest pinning me to the earth, and I found myself face-to-face with a dark-haired boy. He couldn't be no more than ten years-old. His face leaned in closer to mine, staring at me with his silver-colored eyes, as if he was studying me. My eyes shifted from side-to-side, nervous from his stare, when I noticed that in one hand he was holding the Golden Apple, and in the other, a trident.

We both held our breath, waiting to see what the other would do. I didn't feel threatened by him even though he was kneeling on my chest. Then the dark-haired child leaned in even closer, looking straight into my eyes, when I sensed that we had met before. I thought for a moment that he was going to get off of me and help me up, but he smashed the metal fruit into the side of my head instead, and then shot through the mist, so quickly that a trail of silver streaked out behind him.

The pain in my head was secondary to my confusion. Another sound screeched through the fog--one I had never heard the likes of before in my life. I had to throw my hands over my ears, which felt like they were about to burst. Instantly, with an explosion of white light, the fog was forced outwards by some unseen power and it dissipated, evaporating within seconds.

I found myself standing alone in the middle of an apple orchard. A whip-sound cracked through the air, and Brochara suddenly appeared by my side with his back to me in a defensive pose. Startled, I jumped. "Where are we? Is this it?" I telecommunicated.

"Hera's Orchard, in The Garden of Hesperides," he whispered inside my brain. "Who was that boy?" he added.

"You were here? I don't know, but something feels familiar about him," I answered.

"We need to move quickly," Brochara barked inside my skull. The Hesperides do not take kindly to trespassers. They may look kind and gentle, but will bite your head off if the need be."

"Hesperides? What do they look like? What am I supposed to be looking out for?" My head was turning, quickly, from side-to-side, waiting for another ambush. The quick movement caused my head to pound.

"The Golden Fruit," Brochara answered. He was creeping around all hunched over, and he looked like someone trying to break either into or out of a high-security operation.

"That boy had it. Didn't you see that in his hand?" For a brief moment, I questioned Brochara's sanity, but then I began to question mine. My hand found its way to spot where the boy clunked the metal fruit against my head. *He did have the fruit in his hand, right?*

Another howl of pain rang through the orchard. Instinctively, I took off running towards the sound, leaving Brochara behind. I stopped quickly when I saw a beautiful fairy hovering three trees in front of me. She was much bigger than the fairies I was used to, about the size of an elf. Her delicate, golden wings shimmered in the sunlight, and her skin sparkled like diamonds. I was mesmerized. My eyes suddenly fell to the ground just beneath her, because something moved in the tall grass--a white dove.

"Luca!" I screamed as I ran to her side. The golden nymph spun around and her delicate features instantly turned to fury! A mouthful of sharp teeth lunged towards my head, snapping continuously like a crazed animal. Then she made her moved and shot straight at me. The Hesperide's advance was stopped as she slammed into an invisible barrier and fell to the ground. Confused, she lunged at me again, but golden glitter exploded from the fairy when she crashed into the invisible shield. I reached for Luca, who was motionless on the ground. This agitated the nymph even more and she lunged towards my arm, snapping at me again and again!

Brochara appeared and shot a ball of green energy from his hands, freezing the nymph in mid-air. "Get her out of here!" he yelled aloud.

The wind suddenly began to blow harder through the trees, as if the orchard exhaled a roar. I could hear tiny grunts and growls heading towards us. "GO!" he barked.

I took off running. I didn't know where I was going, only that I needed to save Luca. I was dodging limbs that appeared to reach out for me as I passed. I leapt over roots that ripped from the ground to trip me up and pull me back into the ground. The orchard was trying to capture me. Finally, I burst from the apple orchard into a meadow. The only cover in sight was a small grouping of orange trees in the center of a grassy field. Animated vines and roots reached out from the orchard after me, like a long tentacle reaching for its prey.

I had to hide her. I needed to make sure she was all right. I darted for the trees, and slid beneath the branches, which touched the ground heavy with fruit. It was the perfect place to hide. I was whispering to her tiny white-feathered head, but Luca was not responding to any questions. I felt her heart beating and could smell her sweet breath, but she was unconscious. She needed water, but there wasn't any in sight. Then I reached up hoping to pluck an orange, and drip some fluids into her beak.

"I will slash you to ribbons," rumbled a voice from the darkness. "Touch one of my oranges and you will draw your last breath," growled and unseen beast.

I picked up Luca and tried to duck back out into the meadow. A tree branch aggressively bent to the ground and blocked my exit. Laughter echoed through the trees bouncing off each branch, but I could not see where it came from--it sounded like it was right next to my ear.

"Leave me alone!" I shouted, hugging Luca closer, "I won't touch your stupid oranges, you grumpy fool, just let us pass."

"Well now, I am afraid I can't do that, brother." I paused in my tracks and tried to focus my eyes to find the owner of the voice. Then, right before my eyes, a serpent-like dragon appeared out of thin air! Its body was wrapped around the trunk of the tree, guarding it with his life. His scales were the color of the bark, allowing him to blend in perfectly without detection, and his eyes glowed orange, camouflaging with the fruit.

"Brother?" I tried to stand strong, although I instantly knew by the salutation, that I was standing directly in front of Ladon. "I am certain you are confused." I retorted.

"Put her down, NOW!" the dragon made a quick lunge in my direction displaying a mouth full of large pointy teeth. I pulled Luca even closer to my chest and tucked her inside my shirt.

"NO! She has no part of this! I was merely trying to help her!" I was strangely confident, "We wandered into this orchard, purely on accident, fleeing the chaos from over there."

"You came to steal my fruit!" Ladon growled back at me, slithering down branch with amazing agility, and snapped again mere inches from my face.

"No I didn't!" I stumbled backwards trying to avoid his fangs, "Hang on, how did you know this bird was a girl?" I asked aloud, but really didn't mean to. The beast was slowly slithering closer to me and his flickered orange. I stammered, "Well, wait...maybe I did mean to steal your fruit, but a silver child got here first. He took your Golden Apple, not me."

Ladon threw his head back and laughed, "Fool! Then he is a dead child!"

"How can you wish death on a child?" I interrupted his maniacal laughter with my question, which abruptly brought Ladon's laughter to a halt. The thin dragon twisted himself higher up the tree, hanging by his lower body; he dropped his upper body down towards my head, sniffing and inspecting the goose egg-bruise that had now formed.

"I did not make him steal, that was on his own volition. He just so happened to pick the wrong fruit." Ladon was chuckling to himself, "Funny how sin works...just like that silly girl, who couldn't resist the apple after I taunted her...What was her name? Oh never mind, that was thousands of years ago."

"Uncle Ladon, is that you?" sang a tiny voice from under my shirt reminiscent of a dove's coo.

"Uncle?" I questioned aloud.

"Luca darling, are you alright?" Ladon had quickly shrunk his size to that of a small lizard, dropped to my shoulder, and shimmied inside my shirt much to my dismay.

"Hey!" I shoved my hand into my garment and pulled the tail of the small dragon, "Get out!"

Luca had started to wriggle and my shirt began to expand. I heard threads ripping and, somehow, I twisted my way out of the shirt, just before she shape-shifted back to her human form but she grabbed her right arm in pain.

Ladon was back to his former size, slid to her side, and nuzzled the white-blonde Adrastai. "Are you alright, child?" He asked, standing upright on his hind legs and hugging Luca.

"I think so." Luca tucked her head under his dragon jaws, and snuggled him. "I have missed your smiling face."

"Can someone please tell me what is going on?" I interrupted their little love fest.

Ladon scowled over her shoulder, but she threw her elbow upwards, closing the jaws of the dragon.

"This is Ladon, our Uncle." She addressed me. The small dragon, who resembled more of a snake with legs donning a dragon's head, nodded in my direction.

"What happened over there?" Ladon asked Luca, as he turned her face to look into his. Flashes of gold flickered out of the corner of my eye, and I saw the golden nymph creeping up behind them.

I lunged towards the two of them, to protect them from the Hesperide, when my body did a backflip in the air, and I crashed hard on the ground. Immediately, I felt the weight of Ladon's land on top of me as his talons dug into my chest. "I will kill you!"

"NO!" Luca screamed.

"Behind you!" I managed to choke out, pinned to the ground with the weight of his body crushing my chest.

Ladon reeled around by twisting his overly flexible body while still pinning me to the ground and found the nymph. Just as she was close enough to bite his head off, she grabbed his snout and kissed both sides.

"Aegle darling, we have guests." Landon spoke lovingly to the crazed fury, and the Hesperide just glared in my direction with anger in her eyes.

"We've already met," her soft voice cooed at Ladon as she looked lovingly upon him, but her expression turned cold as she glared down at me, "in the Garden."

"You were going to eat Luca!" I protested quite loudly, but Landon had pressed down harder making it difficult to talk, "I couldn't let you hurt her!" Luca quickly turned to look at me with a questioned expression on her face that softened to a gentle smile.

"I was trying to help her," she growled back at me, showing her terrifying teeth, and flaring her wings larger while golden glitter rained down to the fresh green grass.

"Everyone, stop!" Luca commanded and stretched out her arms to hug the golden nymph. "There is a much more pressing issue we need to discuss, and besides, it appears that you were both trying to do the same thing. Uncle Landon, please let him go."

The air rushed back into my lungs as the talons lifted off my chest and I brought myself to sit up. Luca sat down next to me in the grass, made a gesture to the others, and they followed suit. "Nak is here with us." Ladon and Aegle clapped their hands in excitement. "I wish it were under much happier circumstances. We did not come for a family reunion, unfortunately. We came to stop one."

The mood under the orange tree turned somber as Luca retold the past week's events. Ladon had stood up, walked away from the circle, and wound himself back up the tree.

Aegle cringed when Luca recalled the meeting with Dissyca. "See?" She called over her shoulder, "I always told you your family was crazy." She scolded Ladon. I shook my head at her last comment, because Aegle was quite crazed the last encounter I had with her.

I felt the need to explain why we were sent here on our quest so I produced my manual from my backpack, and shared with them my scrolled prophecy.

"So that is why you are here? Golden Fruits shall quench your thirsts?" Ladon asked. "Well, then I am sorry you made such a long journey for nothing. I am sworn to protect these fruits with my life." Ladon was wrapped around a branch above us gazing at the oranges growing from it; his eyes looked like he was counting them. It was quite impressive how he could twist his form three times around the limb.

"Oranges? Am I the only one not following this? The orchard is over there," I pointed across the meadow. Confused, I looked at Luca for some sort of guidance.

"Giovani, do you know what the scientific name for oranges is?" Luca asked me. *Why can't I ever get a straight explanation from people?*

"Citrus?" I answered, unsure and half annoyed.

"The Greek botanical name for all citrus is hesperidoids. You are standing in the Garden of Hesperides, Garden of Oranges." Her voice was strong and she wore the same soft grin as she did whenever she revealed her intelligence.

"Oooooh." It finally made sense, after Luca spelled it all out for me, but I felt like an entire mythology class was snickering behind my back. "But, if Ladon won't let me quench my thirst, what are we supposed to do now?" Our journey seemed for naught, and I lay back on the grass starring up at Ladon and the golden oranges. *Very clever,* I thought, pondering the orange as the golden fruit and placing an orchard with golden apples right next door.

"Let me talk to him, dear." Aegle whispered softly to Luca as she fluttered up to the treetop. "You know how he gets," Aegle added, tilting her head to the side she winked at her, and nodded with a wry smile.

Luca gave me look that said, 'trust me' without any words. Just then, Nak slithered under the branches. "Ladon!" There was love and excitement in his voice. "Aegle darling, how are you?"

Ladon immediately dropped from the heights and hugged his brother. The sight of the two brothers embracing warmed my heart. It was so refreshing to see Nak genuinely smile, but it was short lived. Unbeknownst to the rest of us, when the brothers reached in to embrace, Aegle fluttered up to the treetop and plucked an orange from the highest branch. Ladon roared ferociously, like someone had just stabbed him, and snapped towards me! "Now I have to kill you!" he bellowed quickly advancing!

"What? What did I do?" I was taken completely by surprise and Luca placed her body between our Uncle's and mine. "I promise…I didn't do anything." Fear and confusion filled my voice. The tree's branches grabbed me from behind, pulled me to the trunk, and tied me to the tree with its limbs. Ladon had already twisted around me and his gaping jaws were inches from my neck. It all happened so quickly that even Nak was stunned, trying to figure out what just happened.

"Ladon, NO!" cried Aegle. "It was me! Darling, it was me…I did it! I picked the orange!" Landon's grip released a little on hearing her voice and his eyes filled with angst. "Dear, look at me. It's right here, in my hands." Aegle's voice was shaking as she presented the fruit that looked oversized in her tiny hand.

Ladon's anger quickly turned to sheer horror, he slid off of me, and looked upon his Hesperide wife with tears in his eyes, "Aegle, no." he desperately cried. "I can't...I can't kill you."

"Darling, you don't have to. Please listen to me," Aegle cradled Ladon's snout in her hand, "that is why you were sent here, because of us silly nymphs. We just couldn't stop eating the fruit, right?" Their love for each other was endearing, "Well darling, we've stopped eating them and I don't plan to eat this one either. You have done a great job for thousands of years. If this fruit helps to keep your father stay pinned under that volcano where he belongs, then I am certain Hera will not be angry. You have protected this Garden fiercely and I am confident she will understand why I had to do this. Besides, I nursed you back to health so you could continue to protect it; she will have to show mercy on me, right?"

Landon was distraught and he just sat there with his gaze to the ground. The golden nymph flew over to me, with dazzling tears in her eyes, and gently handed me the orange. "Welcome to our crazy family, dear. Please use this well." She fluttered in closer and planted a soft kiss on my forehead, which felt like the softest sunlight of the dawn. She smiled at me and there was both love and fear in her eyes.

"Thank you." Was all I could manage to say. I wanted to say more but I could not find the words. She plucked this orange that rested in my hands knowing that her husband would have to kill her for it. That unselfish act brought tears to my eyes. I glanced at the Fruit of Immortality in my hands which put her mortality was at risk.

There wasn't an easy way of making our exit, or saying goodbye to such friends. We all hugged each other, knowing that we had overstayed our welcome. I felt sad for Ladon, Nak, and Aegle. They never spent time together and, now it was cut short because of me.

We all walked back to the ship in silence. When we reached the shore, all of our friends were waiting. Some were nursing small wounds that must have been inflicted by the silver boy and I reached up to my own lump on my head. Skye was sitting off by herself on a large boulder jutting out of the water, kicking her feet in the surf, and hanging her head. I ran over to her to make sure she was all right.

"Skye!" I yelled, but she didn't even turn to acknowledge me. "Skye, I have it! I have the orange!" But she didn't budge, like she was ignoring me for some reason. I plunked myself down beside her, "Are you okay?"

All she did was shrug her shoulders while she searched for something in the water. She never even looked at the Golden Fruit or shown any interest in how I obtained it.

"Oh yeah, guess what else? The craziest thing happened to me, when the fog covered the Garden." Skye still didn't lift her head to make eye contact with me. Every now and again, she would kick at the surf looking for something under the sea foam. "There was a silver boy! He knocked me down and stared right into my soul! It was really weird, like I knew him or something."

Skye immediately stopped kicking the water and, hastily, turned her eyes to me. She had obviously been crying. Her eyes were swollen and red. She grabbed my arms so tightly, that I winced at her strength. "What did he say? Did he talk to you?" Skye was forcefully shaking me as she spoke and she looked frantic.

"No. Ow! You're kind of hurting me." Skye released her grip and returned her stare to the foam-covered sea kicking to clear the water's surface.

"Ryan…where are you?" I heard her whisper to the waves.

"Ryan?" I pulled her shoulder to force her to look at me, "Who's Ryan?"

"My brother." She replied still searching the waves.

Chapter 16

Illustrated by
Giovani Russo

16

TROUBLED WATERS

Skye and I sat on the boulder, just staring into the water, for what felt like hours. I didn't know how to comfort her. Ryan, her brother, had been lost and presumed dead for almost three years.

He was swept away by a tornado in our hometown when he was nine. The entire community searched for him for days. It was a sad time for our all of us, but I cannot imagine how tough it must have been for the family. To see him again must be stirring up all different emotions.

My shoulders slumped forward as guilt ran through me. I hadn't thought about or missed my family at all the last couple of days. They were all I thought about before. I was always either trying to get away from them or protect them, but now, nothing. *Was that a part of growing up? Does life get in the way, and you forget about your family?*

"He didn't talk to me." Skye finally spoke, but there was confusion in her tone. "He just knocked me down." She was rubbing her left thigh and I noticed three puncture wounds.

"Hey! You're hurt." I grabbed my backpack and rummaged around inside to find Elia's poultice. "Let me put some of this on it."

"NO!" I jumped at her sharp response, and she pushed herself backwards trying to flee.

"Skye, we need you; and we need you whole, not injured." I assured her it wouldn't hurt.

"My brother gave me this." Her eyes were full of tears as she looked into mine, "It's all I have from him. I know it was brief, but I knew it was Ryan right away. Why didn't her recognize me?"

My heart was so heavy and aching with her pain. I didn't have any words of comfort or explanations for her; I was just as confused as she was. All I could do was hug her. I wanted to hug her and take her pain away, just as I remember Mom doing for me.

"We need to get moving," Nak had slithered over and interrupted.

Skye and I followed our serpent leader to the dragon ship. I was still holding my Golden Orange. My mind replayed the scene between Ladon and Aegle repeatedly. The Hesperide, knowing that her husband's job was to kill anyone who plucked the sacred fruit from the tree, plucked one for me. Me.

More sadness filled my heart, thinking of how that situation may end. Aegle willingly gambled her life to protect the lives of others. The love within people, for others they don't even know, amazes me. I believe that is why she sparkled; she was shimmering with love.

The first half of the morning, we all went our separate ways on the ship. I climbed all the way up to the crow's nest or lookout station on the mast. I found it peaceful up there in the sky, just like flying on the back of a dragon. Perhaps we needed space to process what had happened over the last few weeks. It had been stressful for all of us.

I must have fallen asleep. The salty air, slight rocking motion of the waves, and sounds of the water lapping against the ship created the perfect lullaby for my tired body. The sun was warm, like a soft towel, fresh out of the dryer. I awoke and just lay up there with my eyes closed, listening to the sounds of the sea, when an eerie feeling crept over me.

It was a very familiar feeling, as if someone were watching me. I was a nervous to open my eyes, because I feared someone was going to be with me. Slowly, my right eye peeked open. Relieved, I didn't see anything. I sat up with both eyes wide open, refreshed, and recharged.

I glanced around to take in the view of the open Sea when my stomach dropped! Over to my left, perched on the side of my elevated resting spot, was another sinister crow. The sunlight beamed off his feathers that were black as a starless night. The crow didn't react to my startled reaction; he just stared at me, motionless. I wanted to run, to shout for help, but I was too high above the ship's deck.

Fin made quick work of the crow on the birdbath and Khai did the same in the Valley. It was my turn. I had to dispose of this myself. "Servo!" I yelled, and my trusted sword jumped into my hands.

The crow's eyes flashed green, and it just floated off the edge of the wooden nest, just out of swords reach, mocking me. "Help!" I yelled down to the deck, as I continued to slice out in the air at the menace. Then I remembered to telecommunicate. "Help, a crow!"

Brochara immediately appeared in the crow's nest with me, and Fin was already scaling the mast, sword drawn.

Fin's pirate boots landed on the edge of the lookout just as the black bird dove backwards, like a diver from a platform, and plummeted toward the Sea's surface. But just before it entered the dark abyss, a flash of silver momentarily blinded us, followed by the sound of something heavier than a crow entering the water.

Skye immediately dove of off the ship's side and threw herself into the sea. She was frantically diving down and resurfacing all around the ship. "Where are you?" she screamed before descending again.

I began to get nervous. I knew that she was half mermaid, but she was underwater for a very long time. I made it halfway down the seventy-foot tall mast before Skye resurfaced screaming her brother's name. She had a look of panic on her face before she dove down into the dark water again.

I had made it to ship's deck and was leaning over the bulwark, before she resurfaced again. "Skye! Skye! Where are you? Climb aboard!" I yelled as I flung the buoy over the side.

Defeated, she slid her arm through the ring, and Ttensir began to pull her back through the water to the ladder on the side of the ship. Tears were streaming down her cheeks as she gave into the reality that Ryan wasn't there, clinging to the buoy with her.

With my heart heavy, I bowed my head for my friend's sorrow. Suddenly, Ttensir grunted and I saw his body lunge forward and slam into the gunwale while the rope burned through his hands, as if pulled by something enormous. Luca screamed and Mateo leapt over the side.

I quickly turned my focus to the water, but Skye was gone. Desperately, I asked what was going on, but no one could answer me. Everyone was calling her name and asking Mateo if he saw her.

"What happened?" I yelled scanning the water's surface for

some sign of her.

"Something pulled her under!" Brochara screamed.

I made a move to jump overboard to help Mateo search for her, when Nak wrapped his tail around my ankle. "I am ssssorry, I cannot let that happen."

"LET ME GO!" I yanked my leg, but Nak yanked back and I landed hard on the deck. "Nak, I have to help her!"

"We can't rissssk lossssing you too!" Nak hissed, "Mateo issss looking for her."

I ran back to edge, but an invisible force pulled me from behind. I looked over my shoulder, but there wasn't anything to see. Nak's eyes were focused solely on me, "I am ssssorry brother, it hassss to be like thissss."

I watched the commotion in the water; Mateo and Jock dove in and out of the water, repeatedly. Brochara was in a smaller lifeboat, waiting to pull her to safety. There were no sharks or black hands made of water that attacked us like last time--just sea foam. Thankfully, there wasn't any blood to be found either. After an hour of looking, the exhausted members of our crew called off the search.

Skye was gone. I just couldn't bring myself to talk to anyone. I stared out at the open water, waiting for her smile to pop up from the depths. I waited for hours. She didn't come back.

I wept for the loss of my friend, and I wept for her family. Tragically, within three years of each other, they lost both of their children. It just didn't seem real or fair.

Dream-like, I was staring out into the vast watery horizon, but everything moved in slow motion. Waves crashed along the surface, but it was as if I was watching a silent movie. I could only hear her laughter and words she spoke to me, echoing inside my head.

I spent the night out there, staring into the abyss. The full moon reflected on the water, like a lonely street of light that stretched for miles across the shimmering surface. Peaceful is not the correct word to describe it; numbing worked best. My friend was gone.

Emotionally exhausted, I finally closed my eyes to rest. Khai walked over to my side and curled up around me. I welcomed his comfort without words, and drifted off to sleep, sad and numb.

I don't even remember falling asleep. Then I found myself walking through the cream-colored corridor that led to the Grand Hall of the Court of Order in the Enchanted Realm. I was conscious that I was dreaming and welcomed the escape.

The air was warm and smelled of jasmine. The floors were polished to a sheen that the sun reflected off them, brilliantly. The magical golden vines grew inside the marble, twisting and twirling like an invisible artists painted right beside each footfall as I walked down the hall, drawing golden flowers that appeared to sprout from under my feet…Happiness filled my soul.

Suddenly, the air grew cold, the sun ceased to shine, and a foul stench filled the hallway. I tried to wake myself up to stop this nightmare, but I was unsuccessful. A chill raced down my spine and I paused to glance behind me. Darkness was creeping down the hall, crawling along the walls, and leaving nothing but emptiness in its wake. Clouds, like those of the darkest storms, began to swallow up the cream-colored walls at alarming speeds billowing in my direction. The enchanted golden vines turned black and shriveled up before my eyes, as if a terrible rot was invading the Court of Order. The black vines coursed through the marble tiles, like black blood through evil veins.

The beauty of the Enchanted Realm was crumbling before my eyes. A small ray of light at the end of the hallway was beckoning me, pulsing light a lighthouse to a ship in stormy weather. The swelling, jet-black clouds grew up the walls, and encompassed the ceiling, and an ominous feeling filled the Grand Hall. Darkness was coming for me.

All of my senses screamed for me to flee. I turned and ran towards the only source of light that remained in the once bright palace. A tiny speck of light glimmered at the end of the long hallway. No matter how fast I ran, the corridor seemed to lengthen as I fled the darkness. The light at the end of the tunnel grew farther, farther away, and dimmed with each step. Then a horrible roar echoed from behind me sending chills through my body.

I ran as fast as I possibly could, but the jet-black clouds grew past me on the marble walls frightening me and the sound of water splashing filled my ears. I slowed down and gathered up enough courage to reel around and face my fear. A wall of jet-black water, that filled the entire corridor, was rushing straight towards me, like an invisible dam broke. There was no way to escape the looming doom; the water was too fast. Black, watery hands reached out of the depths, grabbing for me.

I couldn't get away; there was no way to escape. I drew my last big breath of lightness and the darkness swallowed me whole. The walls and floor fell away, and I was suspended in a cold, dark abyss. Emptiness filled my soul. I didn't hurt. My chest did not tighten with the lack of oxygen. I was just floating in what felt like a sea of sorrow. The hopeless feeling of being numb returned.

It felt like I was drifting for hours without any change until something caught my attention out of the corner of my eye. I paddled through the dark sea of loneliness, turning myself towards the movement in the water. Images began to form in the cloudy abyss, like movies made of black ink. Dark silhouettes of crows and mutated creatures developed in the ink-colored clouds. I reached out to smear the ugly scene before me when the strangest thing happened; my arm and hand were jet black just like a shadow. I quickly patted the rest of my body, which was also black as night. *What was happening? This was the weirdest dream ever.*

Suddenly, the tent city of the Adratsai council stretched out in front of me, then, like a black flame licking the back of a parchment, charred embers grew from the center out, engulfing the tent city and destroying it. Black flames burnt the trees of the Enchanted Valley. A horrific scene of silhouetted Adrastai figures scrambling to escape the black flames formed in the clouds of ink. Screams of horror filled my head.

I was helpless, adrift in a sea of death and destruction, watching it all happen. Then, with the force of acceleration, like a downhill ride on a rollercoaster, I was pulled through the black waters. Tumbling over myself, caught in the undertow of crashing black waves.

I up-righted in the murky tunnel of death to find myself in a different ink-like movie scene. This time I was rushing towards a shoreline, like a black tsunami. My body crashed and tumbled over the beach, never touching the ground. I was suspended inside the evil wave and horror filled my soul, as I recognized my surroundings. I was home!

My childhood forest with my cave hideout stretched before me. A wall of billowing blackness, like ash from a volcanic eruption, consumed and destroyed everything in front of me. I was riding the top of this evil; seeing it all unfold through its eyes.

My house came into view. We were headed directly towards my house! I felt the powerful pull of the darkness that dragged me here suddenly slow to a crawl, and we came to a stop. We towered over my house and glared down at it, as if it was searching for something.

Another watery black hand stretched out of the darkness and towards the window of my sister Sofia's room. The protective charm that Elia and Brochara created was still in place, and the hand splattered against the shielding dome. I tried to scream, but my voice couldn't travel through the billowing darkness.

Sofia, startled by something, came to her window. A look of excitement grew upon her face and I followed her gaze to find a beautiful black stallion rearing up playfully in the backyard. Sofia's eyes lit up and she darted away from the window. An eerie snicker echoed through the darkness.

I was still floating, aimlessly in the wall of watery ash and soot, confused and unable to scream to her. Sofia slowed her running as she emerged from the house and stood on the deck with wonder in her expression. The enchanted black stallion stood, majestically, before her out in the yard.

"That's it little one; follow the pony. Every little girl wants a pony," whispered a maniacal voice in inside my head.

I watched in horror as this black beauty of a horse lured my sister outside of the protective charm. She reached to stroke its mane, and the horse backed away and stopped a few feet from her. She reached out again, but the stallion retreated once more.

"NO!" I screamed, but the ash rushed down my throat and I began to choke.

I watched my eight-year-old sister excitedly step across her protection, chasing a mystical stallion, and as soon as her leg crossed the enchantment, the stallion transformed back into the black watery hand. It grabbed ahold of her ankle, knocked her to the ground, and dragged her with brutal force into the darkness! Frightened, she screamed, but the ash quickly muffled the sound.

I tried to swim down. I frantically pulled through the watery ash and soot to reach her. It was completely black. I could hear her cries muffled in the darkness. The force of acceleration began again, and I tumbled over and over in the turbulent energy of the waves. The sound of Sofia's screams drowned out by the thunder of the surging darkness.

Just as fast as this nightmare started, it stopped, and I was alone. Blackness surrounded me, void of any sound. Nothing. Nothing happened, everything stopped. No more inky silhouettes or black flames. No more waves or billowing clouds of black ink. No sounds of horror or little girl screams, just nothing. I was drifting in a sea of sorrow, alone.

Hours later, I was still adrift. No sound, or movement, just drifting. Filled with sadness and despair, I couldn't even formulate a thought. I was drained and I just wanted to close my eyes and drift off to sleep, forever. At that very moment, when all seemed lost, a faded memory of my family flashed before my eyes. Immediately my body began to spin, like the funnel travel I had experienced in the past, and I was whirling like a vortex and spiraling downwards.

Something inside me woke up and decided to fight. I pulled through the water, reaching for an imaginary surface I knew did not exist. Spinning faster and faster, my body sank down to the very tip of the watery funnel, like something pulled the plug on this watery misery. I was losing strength, my feet kicked, trying to avoid the black drain. The strong cyclonic currents were too much. My body was circling at high rates of speed, my brain couldn't handle the swirls of darkness, and I started to lose consciousness.

An ice-cold splash hit me squarely in the face, like unforgiving hand, and immediately brightness returned. My eyes clenched shut it so was so bright, and I curled myself up into a little protective ball.

"Giovani! Snap out of it!" barked a concerned Brochara, who was holding an empty wooden pail he had just emptied on my head.

I flailed around trying to escape the horror I just witnessed.

Sheer terror filled me. I wasn't sure where I was, but hearing Brochara's voice made it all a little clearer.

I opened my eyes afraid of what I would see: but I was back on the ship. Nak's enormous form was gliding straight towards me, larger than I had ever seen him before. His eyes flickered and stopped mere inches from my face.

"Where did you go?" his voice was short and commanding, "ANSSSSWER ME!"

His tone and inflection scared me. I cringed and cowered away from him, still recovery from the horror I just experienced.

"ANSSSSWER ME NOW!" he shouted again, right in my face.

"Nak, give him some room," Fin's called from behind him, "he obviously is shaken."

"DO NOT INTERFERE WITH ME OR I SHALL HAVE YOU FOR LUNCH!" Nak turned to Fin, the shade from his hood disappeared and the light burned my eyes again.

"Ssssee? He can't handle the light!" Nak hissed. "Tell me now!" I had never heard this side of Nak before; he was extremely agitated.

"Okay, okay…hold on just a minute." I mumbled, still noticeably shaken.

"We don't have a minute." Nak responded, spitting his words at me. "Quickly, what happened?"

Sensing his urgency, I spat out my entire dream, starting with the destruction of the tent city, the wave of ash, Sofia, and ending with my drifting. I don't even think that I took a breath.

Nak hung his head, and slumped into his coils, defeated. "That wassss what I afraid of." His voice was weak.

"Afraid of?" I questioned. "Nak, it was just a bad dream. I right here." *What did he mean? It was a dream, right?*

I glanced around to the rest of my friends, trying to assess what just happened. They were all staring as me, shocked and confused. Even the Viking crew off in the distance peered around each other and seemed to tremble and avoid eye contact.

"What?" I asked, without really wanting to know the answer.

"Astral travel," Brochara said, staring at me with his large eyes.

"What?" I directed at him, but something sank in the pit of my stomach.

"You did it again: astral travel," he answered, as he caught himself as his knees buckled underneath him.

"Brochara! Are you okay?" I was too weak and unable to go to him, "What do mean, I did it again?" Something physically affected my guide, something was terribly wrong, and I was beginning to feel insane, "I don't understand, I have never astral whatever'ed in my life."

Suddenly, a strange sensation grew up my legs, that I was too confused and scared earlier to realize. I looked down at them just in time to watch my feet re-inflate, like human balloons.

"Hey!" I tried to push myself away from the freakish sight and scurried backwards, grossed out. Now I knew why the crew looked horrified. They must have watched my entire body re-inflate. "Wait. I didn't do that travel thing." I gasped, making connections to the story in my brain, "I couldn't have. Everything was black. There was no light at all, only shadows."

"I am afraid it issss true." Nak hissed with his head still looking to the deck and his hood drooping. There was a horrible sorrow in his voice.

"No." I shook my head not wanting to believe a word they said or the fact that my re-inflating body wasn't proof enough. "It's not true. It can't be true." I was stuttering, "There was no light…I, I am telling you, it wasn't like the past couple times." I looked at Nak, almost pleading for him to agree with, "Nak, look at me! I wasn't glowing like I did when we went to Nãga's cave with the Mages. I was dark as night not golden! It was a nightmare. What else could it be?"

Nak raised his head and his gaze found mine. There was tremendous sadness in his eyes. "Brother, you did travel by essssencssse, but not mine." He turned his face to the deck again, "It wasssss Nãga."

"What?" anxiety filled my voice, "It was real? No. No it couldn't be. It CAN"T be." horror filled my soul; again, "The Council…burning…Adrastai running…and, and she has Sofia!" Uncontrollable sobs overtook me.

"I am afraid sssso, and I am sssso ssssorry." Nak sighed and he wound his tail around me, trying to comfort my distress.

"She's just a little girl." I sighed, "just a girl."

Chapter 17

Illustrated by
Paul A. (Alex) Williams

17

FAMILY WOES

"Nak, how did this happen?" My cobra friend was still staring at the deck, when Brochara broke the silence. "How did she get to him?"

"I don't understand. How did I astral travel with Nãga?" None of this made any sense to me, "She never invaded my body like you did! The only time I ever came close to her, was when I came to get you, and she didn't touch me..."

He finally looked into my eyes, "Twinssss share sssspecial bondsss. I have only mixed my essencssse with one other. This hassss never happened before." Nak's expression was full of remorse as he continued, "Nãga ssssummoned you."

"Summoned me? What does that mean?" Anger started to boil up inside of me, "Do you mean that she can call me whenever she wants and my essence just leaves? Can you? Am I like some crazy astral travel servant to you and your twin?" My chest was heaving and I was getting angrier with every passing second.

"Essentially yessss, but there are wayssss to block ussss." Nak answered, but returned his gaze to the floor. "It is not something that I did, and I never thought that she would do it either…Father must have told her how to do it."

"Tell Me! Tell me NOW! How do I block you?" I was really angry; I felt violated and used. "How dare someone manipulate me like a puppet. That is unfair! Tell me how this works!" I did not want to experience that ever again. "Wait a minute, if you can summon me, can I summon you?"

"We need to go ssssee Laurina and Sssst. John. They can help explain. I am not really sure how thissss all happened, but…" Before Nak could finish his sentence, a column of light appeared between us. We looked at each other, like siblings about to be spoken to by angry parents. We stepped inside the light, knowing that transport to the Enchanted Realm awaited us.

The Court of Order was as brilliant as ever, but it was strange walking these halls since they just crumbled before me. The walls were bright cream and the golden sunlight reflected off the sheen on the clean marble tiles.

This was the very first place I had ever seen in the Enchanted Realm, the day I passed the Purity test. The three grand thrones of cream-colored marble and gold stood before us, with their respective Mage in each one. We were in front of the Court. Excited, my eyes traveled to Asëa's throne, but, sadly, it was empty.

"Nak, what happened?" St. John's voice echoed through the large marble chamber, with a hint of fury behind it as he quickly glided into the chamber.

"I am not ssssure." Nak, again, was looking at the floor, "I believe she summoned him." St. John gasped at the suggestion.

"What?" A strong gust of air tossed my hair into my eyes as Laurina landed abruptly beside us. "Giovani, I need to know EXACTLY what happened, leave not one detail out!" Laurina shouted. She was very agitated and suddenly my mind traveled to the one-eyed Viking, and fear struck me.

"Laurina," I started, but I felt very nervous. My gaze went immediately to the floor, just as Nak's had, avoiding eye contact. "I...I, think I may have led Nāga to the Adrastai Council." Tears of sadness and fear began to stream down my cheeks. "I am so sorry. I don't how it happened...I am so sorry."

I was wracked with grief. The enormity of the situation hit me. I had somehow forgotten or repressed the part about the tent city burning, I was focused on Sofia. I fell to my knees, "Did the entire Adrastai defense force die?" I sobbed.

Quickly, our surroundings changed. We did not physically move or transport anywhere, but it was like the room spun around 180 degrees and I found myself kneeling on lush grass. Looking around us, I realized that we were inside the courtyard of the Hallowed Hall, where we ate the last time we were here.

"Giovani, please rise. We need to know everything that happened." Laurina cooed. "Do not be afraid, we are not angry with you; it is just that this situation is dire."

Feeling a little more at ease, I stood up. Laurina escorted me to the empty table and we sat down. I began to retell what happened to St. John, Laurina, and Nak. I started with my dream of being here, in the Enchanted Realm. How I was walking down the hallway, which became consumed with darkness.

Laurina's eyes grew larger than ever before; she turned to St. John, "How did she know?" and then they both looked at Nak.

"I am ssssorry. Sssshe hassssn't done that in hundredssss of yearsssss. I never thought sssshe would after the lassssst time." Nak continued to look at the ground.

"What? I don't understand, what are you talking about?" I interrupted.

"Nãga invaded my mind." Nak looked at me and his cheeks were stained with tears. "She went through my memoriessss and learned about you." He turned his gaze back to the High Mages, "I don't undersssstand, the lasssst time, we were ssstuck together for weekssss, sharing thoughtssss until Asëa could sssseparate ussss. We were jussst kidssss."

"She is much stronger and wiser than we thought." St. John stood up from the table and glided a few feet away in thought.

"Wait, so was I really here? Did Nãga come and take me from here? How did she get in?" I began to ramble off questions as they popped into my mind.

"Giovani, focus." Laurina spoke sharply, "What happened next?"

I told them about the images of the Adrastai Council, like silhouetted movies in the ink, and how I tried to reach out and smear them, only to find my arm was jet black in color.

"Dark astral travel." St. John said as he glided back to the table.

"Yessss." Nak answered, "I am sssso sssssorry."

"The rest of the encounter, please." St. John looked directly into my eyes; concern furled his brow

The severity of our situation was evident on all of their faces. I didn't leave out a single detail. I told them all about the dark undertow and the turbulent, crashing waves. Of how I tumbled out of the black ocean and onto the shore by my house, traveled on a wave of ash, and then hovered above my house. I told them of how the black hand reached for Sofia, but was stopped by the charm. The High Mages looked pleased at the mention of something magical working. I recalled the black stallion used to lure Sofia away from the charm, and how I could hear her in the dark water, but I couldn't find her. Finally, I elaborated on how I drifted in sorrow forever, wanting to just close my eyes, until the funnel pulled me down the drain.

"This is not your fault, Nak." Laurina's voice was soft again as she spoke to Nak, "Nãga is very strong, and under the guidance of the most vicious monster ever known."

"Father." Nak interrupted. "I felt him again, when we went to vissssit Dissyca. He reached out for me when we were traveling underground."

"Were you traveling underground?" Laurina asked.

Nak shook his yes, and then turned his gaze back to the ground, as if he were ashamed.

"You had no way of knowing. Clear your conscious, or I will clear it for you." Laurina snapped; her voice stern once more. I was just watching, confused about what they were talking about.

"I have jeopardized our mission, and I have invited my family in." Nak picked his eyes up to face her.

"Enough!" Laurina growled, "Your family IS evil, but that is not your fault. Giovani is here with us. He is safe and that is because you. You are doing your job."

Nak's hood seemed to stand up a bit higher than earlier.

"It was you who saved him from death, adrift in the black abyss." St. John laid his hand on Nak's shoulder.

261

"I was dying?" I finally interrupted.

"Yes. Nãga left you adrift in his family's dark sea of essence. You felt like drifting off to sleep and didn't want to live until Nak came to get you with the funnel." St. John explained. "Nãga used you to get your sister and then drained you of your will to live. That is pure evil at its best."

The mere mention of her name brought tears to my eyes. "Why Sofia? She is just a little girl and how did she know to take her? How did she know about me? And, why haven't I thought about my family at all? They were all I thought about, and now, I don't think about them at all! I mean, I know I have a family, but I just never think about them..." that was the first time that I let myself acknowledge how I had been feeling, ashamed.

That last question opened the floodgate of emotions that had silently built up inside of me. Why hadn't I thought about my family? I must have been mourning the loss of my memories, somewhere deep inside of me, without even realizing that they were gone.

"I think I can explain that." Nak interjected. "When I entered Giovani, to begin the processsss of essence exchange, he tried to fight me off with hissss love for hissss family."

I cocked one eyebrow and looked at him quizzically, "What? I don't remember doing that."

"You used your family to ground you, to resist me; an advanced move." Nak reminded me of his intrusion, and then I remembered thinking of my family and feeling stronger.

"Hey, that was the last time I thought about my family." That thought just dawned on me.

"I can explain that one too." Nak sighed. "Because you used them as your defense, I placed the memories of them in limbo, lost, partly, inside of me."

"Lost? Will they ever come back?" Sadness started to grow inside of me. I missed them all terribly right then. I began to feel anger bubbling inside of me. Nak shrugged his shoulders, but didn't answer.

"My memories of my family are gone?" I was looking at the serpent sideways and felt the urge to strike out at him.

"Giovani, I am sorry, but we need to move on." St. John had glided over to my side and placed his hand on my shoulder. "Why does Nãga want Sofia? She is talented indeed, but she is not ready. She doesn't even know about her gifts yet. Why now?" The High Mages were pacing around each other, sharing their thoughts and concerns, and working together to figure this out.

"Brother," Laurina's eyes sparkled with an idea, "the crows."

"The crows!" I echoed, "That's it! There was a crow on the birdbath at my house…and another one I saw at the Council from the trees." The connections were coming to me fast and I was just spitting out my thoughts. "And Skye! There was another crow, just before Skye di…" My words stopped abruptly. Finishing that thought would mean, that inside my mind, I believed that it was true, but I couldn't bring myself to finish my last word. My heart stopped me.

"Nãga has used the crowsssss to gain information." The expression on Nak's face was one of wonderment. "Well played ssssissssster, well played."

"Why are you excited about that?" My eyes shot anger in Nak's direction; I was upset with him for honoring her evil move.

"It wasssss a carelesssss move." Nak grinned. "Nãga issss using her minions to relay information, but we have dessssstroyed two of

263

them already. She can't have many more in her army."

I couldn't follow what he saying. I continued to get more and more confused. "Minions?" I questioned, "but she did get information, even though we destroyed them. I'm not following you."

"We battled them outside of the watery cave." Laurina added, "The quick flashes of silver. We must find out how strong and how many her guards are."

"Wait a minute," more connections were made inside my brain, "Flashes of silver? Like the one at the orchard? Skye's brother moved in flashes of silver and knocked me down. Skye recognized him! Do you think the crow that was there just before she was dragged into the Sea could have been her brother?"

Excitement grew inside of me! "If that was Ryan, and he was the one who took her, then maybe, just maybe she was still alive! We have to save them!" Led by my emotions, I jumped to my feet. Nak and the Mages silenced themselves and just stared at me, making me slightly uncomfortable.

"Giovani, please sit down." Laurina asked politely without any signs of emotion on her face.

"But, if they are still alive, we need to go get them, come on!" I retorted.

"SIT DOWN NOW!" she growled this time with her entire face furled in anger.

Immediately, I sat down and looked to the ground, ashamed that I had questioned one of the High Mages. "I'm sorry."

"Do not be led by your emotions. You must listen to your heart and your mind." St. John stated sternly. "We understand your love for Skye and Sofia, but there are reasons they have been taken.

Reasons that we must try and figure out, logically, so we may be prepared for what lies ahead of us."

Love for Skye? Did I have love for Skye? "You are absolutely correct; I did let my emotions lead the way." I replied. "It was foolish of me."

"Luring you to your csssertain death." Nak interjected, driving his point that I am reckless.

I thought about Nak's last statement, and he was right. I would run to save my sister and my friend, and running into a war that Typhon and Nãga have schemed together on, without any sort of plan, would lead to certain death.

"I do not believe Nãga has any need for Giovani." Laurina added, "She left him to die and probably thinks that he is gone already. She needs a Giant."

"A Giant?" I questioned, "Giant tasks are required..." I whispered aloud as I recalled my prophecy. "Dissyca told me that giant tasks are required!"

"Then, it is so." Nãga's plan seemed to become clear to Laurina. "Nãga needs Sofia to gain entrance into Tartarus." The golden dragon stopped pacing, sat down on her haunches, and sighed. "It is so; ours worst fears are coming true."

"She must be stopped!" St. John added. "If he is freed, it will be a reign of terror! The mighty Zeus fell in battle with him."

"Please, tell me what to do. I will stop her." My mind was swirling with thoughts of Skye still being alive and Sofia going to the gates of Hell, and then to my family...my family memories lost.

"Did you get the Golden Fruit?" Laurina quickly asked.

I had forgotten about the fruit. I plunged my hand inside my backpack and produced the orange, presenting it to her in the palm of my hand.

"Clever." She laughed, when she saw the orange instead of an apple. "So witty. You must eat half of it now." Laurina's instructions reminded me of another part of my prophecy (come to think of it) I was hungry.

I dug my thumbs into the top of the fruit and began to say how Laurina just reminded me of something, when I was interrupted by a sharp, "BE CAREFUL!" St. John nervously made a move for the orange. A glass magically appeared in his hand as he caught the juices that fell from the orange's wound. "That is why you were sent to retrieve the Golden Fruit, to quench your thirst."

"Hey…how did you know that?" I asked. Taking the glass from St. John, I was very careful to catch all of the juice that dribbled down the side of the punctured orange.

"Your manual, Brother." St. John offered his explanation, "You wrote it in your manual, and it was written in the scrolls of our halls."

"So you already know my prophecy foretold by Dissyca, the sphinx?" I should have known that, and felt a little sheepish playing catch-up.

"Yes, young Adrastai, we are aware of your prophecy, and it is very important that you only drink the juice from half of the fruit now." Laurina answered.

I removed Servo, my elven-made sword from its sheath, and produced my shield as well. I place the Golden orange in the shield and with one sweep of my sword, sliced it in two. The orange juice collected in the curve of my shield, like a bowl.

I plucked one-half of the fruit up from my shield, and the sliced fruit sparkled like diamonds in the sunshine. Its fleshy center was golden in color and it oozed liquid gold, which St. John was nervously making sure that none of it fell to the ground.

"Careful," whispered Laurina, "Do not squeeze any more of the juice out."

Judging by their reactions, I froze in place, afraid to move, "What shall I do with it?" I whispered, worried to set it down in fear of losing more of the liquid that the High Mages were so concern about.

"Just be still for a moment, I need to call someone." Laurina closed her eyes, and I exhaled. I tried my hardest not to wiggle as the air in front of her snout shimmered with heat, like the air above hot pavement on the hottest summer days.

I almost leapt out of my skin, when before my eyes, Elia appeared. "Elia!" I shouted, but she turned to the High Mages and genuflected down on one knee. She looked under her arm, in my direction and gave me a loving wink.

"Please rise, Elia," cooed Laurina, "We have summoned you to the Enchanted Realm to utilize your charms."

"I am most honored." Elia stood up and bowed her head at the Mages, "How may I be of help?"

"We need a seal for Golden Fruit." Laurina continued and gestured her snout in my direction. I remained frozen in place, cautious not to lose a single drop.

"Elia! I am so glad to see you." I felt tears of joy pooling in my eyes; Elia always made me feel better.

"Hello Dear," she cooed. The familiar smell of her breath, calmed me. "Hold still please, Love."

Elia waved her arm over her head and chanted a charm in

Elvish. I watched as a waxy covering began to grow over top of the sliced Golden Orange in my hand. She tapped her foot, impatiently, with her hand out-stretched under the fruit. I understood that she wanted me to drop it into her hand, and once I let go, the wax grew over the spots where my fingers held it. Elia caught the fruit and handed it St. John before bowing again.

"Well done, my dear." He nodded to Elia, whose smile grew from ear-to-ear.

"Now Brother, you must drink the remaining half of the juice." Laurina instructed. I looked to Elia, her eyes were larger than I had ever seen them before, full of excitement. Then she gently nodded assuring me it would all be all right.

Picking up my shield, I raised it to my mouth. The Golden Fruit's juice was cold when it passed my lips, but as soon as it hit my tongue, an intense heating sensation burst inside my mouth. Popping warm sensations filled my body and felt amazing. I wanted more. I never wanted that feeling to end. I quickly shoved the remaining half, peel and all into my mouth and was chewing and sucking like a wild man, draining every last drop!

It wasn't until all of the liquid was consumed and I dropped my shield frantically looking for the other half, when I noticed the look of horror on my friends faces.

"What was that?" I asked with both eyebrows raised, invigorated and still searching for the rest of the fruit.

"Easy, Giovani." Laurina voice was sharp again, "The Golden Fruit is not to be abused. It is highly addictive and very dangerous if consumed too quickly."

"WOW! That was amazing!" I lunged out to grab the other half from Elia's hand, when Laurina's tail knocked my feet out from under me, and I rolled across the ground. With a slap of Elia's hand on my cheek, I was thrust back to reality.

"Please forgive me." I looked at Elia, pleading with my eyes, and then to Laurina. "I do not know what came over me."

"How do you feel Brother?" Laurina asked.

"Amazing." I simply stated. I did. I felt amazing. I felt strong and more confident than I ever had before. My mind was clear, and I looked at my friends and said, "We must travel the Styx." Very matter-of-factly.

"We have our next move. The River Styx it is. To the gates of Tartarus," St. John remarked, nodding his head with confidence.

A look of horror flashed across Elia's face. "The River Styx? Who shall travel with him?"

"The entire team," replied St. John, "and you must take Ekadenc with you."

I was glad to hear that all of us would be together on this quest, but was concerned with the expression on Elia's face at the mention of the name Ekadenc. I could not wait to hear who that was.

"Go back to Ellida and inform the others." Laurina cooed, "You all are strong Adrastai. Our hope lies within you and will bring you strength. You must believe in yourself and in others, and only then will the bonds be sired out of love." Her stare was directed at me.

I quizzically cocked an eyebrow in her direction at yet another reference to my prophecy, but before I could ask, we were standing on the deck of the dragon ship.

Chapter 18

Illustrated by
Tiffani Woods

18

A QUEST

It was a grey sort of day. The clouds were dark and close to the ground, heavy with potential rain. The air was crisp and chilly, a little too cool for me, but the Viking crew seemed to perk up under cooler temperatures.

Nak and I gathered up all of our friends below deck to the captain's quarters, in the belly of the dragon ship, to give our orders and explain our recent trip to the Enchanted Realm. There was an enormous round table in the center of the room, adorned with dragons, wolves, and vines hand-carved out of it all along the edge. Oversized chairs as tall as I circled the table, and each one had a long Norse drinking horn, slung of the back by a leather strap, made from a large animal antler. The décor was very dark and masculine with animal pelts, antlers, talons and oversized iron works all around. Massive candles were the only form of light save the tiny windows near the ceiling, and hours of drips collected on the waxy sticks.

Elia, Brochara, and Fin were small to begin with, but seeing them sitting in the huge wooden chairs was almost comical. A particularly plump Viking, seemingly in charge of the ship's food, brought a tray of cheese and fruit and plunked it down on the table before us. Another tray full of oversized poultry legs and racks of ribs bounced across the table as the large, non-friendly Viking cook plunked it down before disappearing into the shadows. A large wooden stein slammed down in front of me in the grasp of the cook's meaty hand riddled with burn scars and lacking part of a finger; the liquid inside sloshed out across the table. I muttered a "Thank you" without making eye contact; I could feel his eyes glaring at me and feared an angry retort.

The smell of roasted meat was making my mouth water, but I was afraid to grab anything in fear of what the annoyed cook might do. I turned to Nak, who I knew would prefer a fresher meal, but he assured me that he was single-handedly keeping the ship's rodent problem under control. Brochara and Elia waved their arms over their heads and produced their own meal of grubs and worms which the sight of twisted the face of the portly cook. Finally, the Viking cook grunted loudly, throwing his hands out at the delivered spread of goods, like a hairy game show host over the prize. There was an awkward pause until we figured out his intentions. We all clapped and thanked him, but no one relaxed or ate anything until he left the room.

Everyone giggled and laughed, admitting that we all feared the round chef. It was nice to just sit and eat with each other, forgetting briefly the quest we were about to embark upon. There was an empty chair, directly across from me, and I kept picturing Skye sitting there, joining in the laughter. My heart sank a little further into my chest.

"Everyone, fill your bellies and drink up!" I said, "We have a long and dangerous journey ahead us."

"Nãga issss doing Typhon'ssss bidding." Nak's hood expanded out large. He really was an amazing creature. His beautiful shades of brown and blacks glistened in the candle light, as he swayed from side to side. "He found her and hassss destroyed all that oncssse wasss right and jusssst within her heart. She issss a Monssssster!"

Nak held his chin high as he spoke. In the past, he would stare at the floor in defeat or sadness for the loss of his sister, but today, he stood determined. Determined to end her reign of terror, "We ssssail to the Dead Sssssea!"

Gasps filled the room, and Brochara began choking violently on an inhaled grub. Elia quickly whacked him on the back and the obstructing larva shot out of his mouth, hitting me in the cheek, and slowly slid off my face.

"Amin hiraetha," Brochara giggled, "I'm sorry." The room boomed with laughter, except for Nak.

The cobra stood, silently still, waiting for everyone to calm himself or herself down. An awkward silence filled the room. "This is no laughing matter. Nãga has been destroying creatures for her own amusement down in this triangle for centuries, playing with other's lives to curb her boredom. She crossed the line when she murdered Asëa, one of the Purest Beings to ever grace the Earth; the kind being who raised us as his own when our evil parents tossed us away like garbage. Now, she helps the one who threw her away. This is what we are up against."

Nak made a grand gesture with his hood, and with that, a funnel of smoke grew from the center of the table. Grey billowing clouds undulated and turned reaching up to the high ceiling. The enchanted cloud started to take form while Nak's voice resonated in all of our skulls, "The mosssst horrifying, powerful monsssster of all, no other beasssst issss more feared than he!"

The smoky figure took form before our eyes, and Nak continued, "He issss a giant! Hissss head touched the starssss. Hissss hair was made up of one hundred snakessss with red glowing eyes that drew fear into the heartssss of anything that looked upon them." Everyone shifted, uncomfortably, in his or her seats.

"Hissss body issss that of man, but each leg issss an enormous viper tail that coilssss and hissessss as he walkssss." Nak's large bronze eyes flashed red as he described his father. "Instead of fingerssss, he has venous snakessss. Wings grow out all over hissss body, and beware of hissss vicious jaw that breathessss fire." Every mouth around the table gaped wide open as the clouds of smoke formed into a moving replica of the monster Nak just described. This terrifying model of the monster lunged, and swiped at all those in attendance.

Cloud-made viper fingers grabbed Luca's hair. Mateo sliced threw them, only to watch them regenerate right before our eyes. Horrifying screams escaped the smoke figures mouth, causing us to plug our ears in fright. "Thissss issss Typhon!" Nak's voice was harsh and full of rage.

A shrieking scream, followed by a loud crash, came from behind me, causing everyone at the table to jump in fright. I turned quickly to see the enormous backside of our Viking cook fleeing out of the room, and a mound of desserts crashed on the floor.

"Thissss issss what liessss ahead of ussss if we do not ssssstop Nāga!" Nak was standing taller than ever with his hood outstretched.

Unexpectedly, the smoke-made Typhon took on animations of its own. The eyes glared red and it stepped from the center of the table, walking towards Nak. Nak waivered in his stance, surprised by the uncontrolled animation. "Protect Giovani!" Nak's voice muffled through the smoke-made model of his father.

Every step it took sent hisses throughout the room that seemed to echo from every corner. A demonic voice rose up from the belly of the smoke beast, resounding off the walls of the room, and sending shivers down everyone's spine. "YOU UNGRATEFUL CHILD! I WILL DESTROY YOU!"

A sudden crash of lightening and clap of thunder shot through the room. The smoke version of Typhon exploded. Nak's enormous form flew backwards through the air, crashed into the wall, and fell to the floor. Terrified members of the Viking crew ran from the room and threw themselves from the ship to escape the upcoming horror. And in the middle of the table, where the cloud figure once stood, was a small burning hole.

I ran over to Nak, scooped his head up in my arms, and he lay there, lifeless. "NO!" I screamed!

Elia quickly removed Servo from his sheath and raised him over her head, poised to strike Nak, horrified as to what she was about to do, I grabbed her tiny arm. "What are doing?"

"Move your arm, dear!" Elia politely shouted and I magically flew backwards.

"Elia, NO!" I screamed! "We need him!"

"I know, now MOVE YOUR ARM!" there was anger towards me in her voice. She struck Servo down and hit the floor directly next to Nak's head. Three golden drops flew from my blade and twinkled like diamonds as they tumbled through the air above Nak's face. Elia quickly dropped Servo, the crashing metal echoed through the chamber; she threw her hand up in the air, and spat out something in Elvish.

The three golden drops responded to her arm motions, stopped in mid-air, and hovered above Nak. "Open his mouth," Elia's tiny voice was calm and soothing once again.

Not even thinking twice about his venomous fangs, I reached in and pried his jaws open. With the precision of a surgeon, Elia maneuvered her hands through the air and, one-by-one, the droplets and the fell into his mouth and down his throat. Nak immediately began to spit and sputter, breathing life back into his lungs.

I collapsed to the floor, relieved. "How did you know what to do?" I asked my tiny protector.

"The Golden Fruit," she replied with a wink, "and dear, don't ever doubt me again."

"That's right!" I had forgotten that I used Servo to cut the fruit in half, but thankfully, Elia remembered and she hoped there was some liquid left on the blade. She was so incredibly clever and suddenly her stinging words hit home. "I promise," I bowed my head in shame for doubting my tiny protector. Then Dissyca's voice echoed inside my head saying, "Destined for greatness, but will require the help of others…"

Nak sat on the floor against the wall for quite some time, gathering strength. Our friends had all sat down in a circle beside him. He thanked Elia with gentle eyes and then addressed the group with labored breath, "My Father has the power to kill his own son with an enchanted cloud, and one that I created as a visual. I do not blame you if you wish not to accept this quest." His voice was weak and his complexion was pale.

"I'm-ah in!" Mateo blurted out, without any hesitation as he pounded his fist on the floor. I respected his courage.

Every friend sitting on the floor, in the belly of a dragon ship, agreed to join us on this quest. They agreed not because Nãga abducted my sister, Sofia, and not because our friend Skye was gone, but for all of us. For every creature who hoped for a life of love and laughter. For all that is Good and Pure in our world. I was in awe of the noble army that sat before me. I was and will forever be grateful for each and every one of them.

"I think I know where Nāga is going." Nak said as he struggled to upright himself. Luca and I quickly ran to each side of his large serpent form and helped to steady him as he slithered back to the table.

The charred center of the table was an eerie reminder of what just happened. Nak shuddered, briefly, and then regained his composure. "Gather around, and please take your seats again."

Ttensir and Fin helped move Nak's chair back into place. Brochara was sweetly holding Elia's hand; it had been some time since they were together. Mateo and Luca were also side-by-side; I sat on the other side of Luca, across the table from Nak. Aluvanim sat beside Nak, and there were now two empty chairs between us. We were all there, minus Skye, and I think we all realized it at the same time, but who the other chair was for I wondered.

"Skye will be there. She is present in all of our hearts," Aluvanim interjected, calmly soothing our wounded hearts. "I pledge to walk with you all, every step of the way." Everyone nodded a silent thank you to Aluvanim, understanding that her heart was heavy from the loss of the very Adrastai she was sworn to protect, Skye.

"Let me explain my heritage," Nak began. "I am the sssson of the two mosssst awful creaturessss ever created! You have already met Typhon, now let me introducssse my Mother, Echidna."

"Oh please Nak, no more cloud illustrations," pleaded Luca, and by the looks on the rest of our faces, we all agreed.

"Not thissss time." He smiled warmly at Luca before continuing, "My Mother, Echidna, issss half nymph, and the other half issss snake. She issss jusssst asss beautiful asss she issss deadly. Mother controlssss corruption, rotting and plaguesss and feasssstssss on flesh.

She hassss grown very powerful over the lasssst one hundred yearssss." Everyone around the table cringed and made expressions of disgust.

"Mother livessss in the lower dregssss of the earth. It explainssss, partly, why I am proficient underground," Nak added, rather smugly. Fin nodded his head with the explanation, as if he just figured out a riddle that has been tumbling through his brain.

"Echidna and Typhon gave birth to many monstrous offspring. You have already ready met Dissyca and Ladon, but alsssso Cerebussss, the three-headed dog who guardssss the entrance to Hadessss, Orthrossss, Chimera, Hydra, and Gorgon!" Nak's hood grew larger and larger with every horrible sibling mentioned.

"There are many more, but I do not have the time. As you can tell, I am the outcasssst! I fight for all that issss Pure and Light in thissss beautiful world! Thissss infuriatessss my family." Nak was bursting with pride at his moral stance. "Typhon tried to overpower Zeusssss. A terrible battle raged on as Typhon tried to avenge hissss brothersss. He plucked Mt. Etna from the earth and wasssss about to hurl it at the Greek God, when Zeus hit the mountain with one hundred thunderboltssss, trapping Typhon underneath it. He hassss been trying to free himsssself ever sincssse."

My friends and I all sat around the table hanging on Nak's every word. In my life, I had to deal with annoying sisters, but never ones that tried to kill me.

"Nãga hassss alwaysssss tried to win the affection of whomever would pay her attention; ssssad really." The giant cobra slithered around the table as he continued his story, "Typhon will ussssse her to free him, and then he will dessssstroy her and everything we know and love."

"We musssst travel to Tartarussss." Nak then made a sweeping gesture with his head and called to another room over his shoulder, "Ekadenc, bring the map!"

Ekadenc? St. John mentioned that name. He said we had to take Ekadenc with us on the quest. I was excited to find out who or what this Ekadenc was.

All eyes turned to the doorway. The room was completely silent with anticipation. Strange sounds grew from the hallway, a slow cadence that sounded like a peg-leg step, followed by a heavy object being dragged across the wooden planks. Whatever was making the sound was not moving very fast; in fact, it was painfully slow.

Everyone's eyes shifted back and forth, looking for some sort of answer. No one spoke. The noises grew closer, and closer, bang…slide…bang…slide…bang…slide. Then they stopped all together, what sounded like just outside the door. We all held our breath. The door began to creak open, ever so slowly, with the same approaching speed. Every eye in the room grew twice its size!

There in the doorway stood a sight that nightmares are made of. An over-sized, ancient-looking scroll was being used as a crutch for an equally ancient-looking creature that didn't look like it should be standing at all. A creepy, old, decrepit woman peered over the top of the scroll and from under her tattered hood. She was cloaked in dark, leathery looking garb and smelled like death. Only one of her eyes opened wide; the other looked as if the eyelid was too heavy with warts to open.

My eyes traveled down her body, wondering how she was standing at all. This thing didn't have complete legs! Her entire lower half, from under two wrinkly knees, belonged to a bird! Her worn-out frame was supported by two over-sized, broken talons, barely bird-like in their twisted grotesque shapes. She was a hideous sight.

"Everyone, thissss issss Ekadenc." Nak introduced the hag, who didn't say a word; she only grunted, loudly. Then, with the same painfully slow pace, the creature maneuvered through the doorway, like death walking.

Once through, two leathery brown wings slowly unfurled from her back in a grotesque stretch. There were hooked talons on top of the wings, and flesh in-between was thin and vein-riddled. Groans escaped my friends, and the crowd cringed. Then, in a bat-like fashion, Ekadenc slammed the hooks into the wood, creating the peg-leg sound from earlier. Balancing on her clawed wings, she swung her legs forward, dragging her talons across the floor, in a creepy walker-like manner.

Ekadenc slammed the scroll down on the round table, startling myself and my friends, and a strange wheezing sound escaped her lungs. The baggy skin on her arms flapped back and forth for a while, like the ripples on a pond after a stone was cast into it. I was certain she would drop dead any minute. "The map," she growled, with a breath so foul, I gagged.

"Uh, um…thank you," I managed to say. Part of me wanted to laugh, in disbelief of what I was witnessing, and the part of me wanted to run screaming from the room. *Why would St. John request this thing?*

The smell of rotting flesh and decaying teeth emanated from her body. She quickly turned her head, surprisingly fast, and made eye contact with me. "Styx!" she growled again, so forcefully that my hair blew back off of my forehead, "Must travel Styx!" Ekadenc slammed her fist onto the table and the dishes bounced. The half-woman, half-bird creature plunked herself down in the empty chair next to me. *Great.*

"Thank you, Ekadenc," Nak nodded to the hag, "Ekadenc issss a Harpy." He further explained. "She hassss traveled to Tartarussss many timessss."

"Aren't-ah Harpies ah known-ah for stealing peoples and-ah they are-ah nevah seen again-ah?" Mateo asked in his weird accent, that his beautiful sister did not possess. My mind traveled to my mythology books, remembering that harpies were considered the hounds of hell; seeking out evildoers and carrying them off to Tartarus.

Ekadenc threw her demon-like body against the table, shoving it inches into Mateo's chest, pinning him between his chair and the table. I was caught off-guard, because the table was constructed out of a redwood tree trunk that was ten inches thick; it had to weigh a ton yet this haggard old woman pushed it with ease. Her wrinkled up neck then extended almost a foot and one half, stretching across the table, leading her good eye closer to the trembling bull-of-a-man. Her good eye moved rapidly, scanning him. No one moved or spoke a word, and I found myself hold my breath.

The grotesque sight gave me the shivers, and I was glad I didn't ask the question. My stomach couldn't handle much more; I had to look away, but as I did, I spied a tattered satchel, strung over her shoulder, and the resting on the front of her hip. It caught my eye, because something inside of it was wriggling. In a half-inch gap between the top of the leather sack and flap closure appeared to expose a part of creature.

Curiosity took over and I leaned in for a closer look. The smell of death grew stronger the closer I got to Ekadenc, but I just had to see what was in that satchel. Whatever it was sensed that I was coming, because it abruptly stopped rustling around. I was inches from the Harpy's hip. But the creature had backed further into the shadows of the bag luring me in for a closer look; my curiosity begged me to peer inside.

I reached out to open the gap, just a little further, so I could see what that was. Slowly, and full of nerves, my finger approached the bag, but my face wasn't far behind it. I could see something! Something was moving towards the same gap, slowly emerging from the shadows. My finger touched the worn out edged of the sack. Just then, my eyes focused on the rim of the bag, picking up details I didn't notice before. Scratches. Tiny tears in the leather that were clearly made from the outside in, as if the enclosed creature was trying to claw its way out, viciously.

It was too late; I was too close. Whatever evil was stored in that bag, waited for my stupidity. Before I could retract my hand, a tiny, clawed appendage, quickly reached through the opening, striking my finger and slicing a gash in my flesh. The excited creature jumped inside the bag and made noises I had never heard before, almost laughing. Pain immediately coursed through my digit, causing me to catch my breath.

Without warning, Ekadenc's grotesque face pressed against mine, forehead to forehead. She screamed at me with a mouth full of tiny teeth that resembled snake fangs, poking out in every direction with bits of fleshy morsels stuck in between them. Her breath burned my eyes, and I thought I might get sick from the smell of rotting flesh stuck in her jaws. She was surprisingly fast, when she wanted to be.

"WHAT ARE YOU DOING?" She growled into my face with a devilish voice. "DON'T TOUCH THAT! WHAT BUSINESS DO YOU HAVE SNEAKING AROUND MY STUFF? RUDE CHILD!"

"I...uh, I mean..." I was terrified she was going to bite my head off with one bite. The pain in my finger was so intense that I closed my eyes for a second, hiding my hand in my lap. But an eerie laugh grew from inside the malicious satchel, and Ekadenc stiffened upright!

"Did he scratch you?" she barked at me, but her tone changed from the angry sounding devil back to the old decrepit Harpy. "DID HE?" The devil voice was back, but before I could answer, Ekadenc punched the satchel with incredible force. The hidden creature squealed in pain, and then under her breath, Ekadenc murmured, "Stupid boy." And she turned back to the table, and grabbed the large scroll.

The mouths of my friends were wide open as they stared at me questioning my behavior. Their eyes returned to the table and the oversized scroll that the Harpy clutched in her wrinkled, old hands. Her knuckles were gnarled and bulging out from top of her hands, thick veins protruded from under her thin skin, like tiny snakes under a skin blanket. My one hand ached, and I glanced down, trying not to draw any attention to the finger I was hiding.

The tip of my finger, where the creature scratched me, was completely black and charred. It reminded me of the wound I had on my leg from Sukanar's deadly bolt. Then, right before my eyes, I saw the rot absorb into my skin and my finger returned to normal. It was as if it just drained into my veins. I watched in horror, as the blackness ran through the veins on the back of my hand. It felt like ice water was running through me. I turned my arm over and could follow its course traveling through my body, using my bloodstream as a dark highway. It didn't dissipate or fade away, but came to rest in about a three-inch section of ice that was now by my left hip.

All of the light in the room, unexpectedly, extinguished. A soft red glow filled the chamber, emanating from the center of the table. The unopened scroll was radiating red, like a hot iron in the fire. The foul Ekadenc leaned over the scroll and, slowly, in a cloud of hazy breath, spoke the words, "mihi revela." dragging them out in a long disgusting whisper.

The scroll began to slowly unfurl, on its own, at the sound of Ekadenc's voice key. We all stood up from our chairs and leaned in closer to see the marvel that lay out before us. It was a map, very similar to the one of the Adrastai Council, but dark and gloomy. The label that burned in flames at the top of the map read THE UNDERWORLD.

Everyone's eyes were scanning the map, excitedly. It was exciting. It was also unnerving. Until now, I had only been warned of this place. 'If you do this, or act in a way that hurts others, you will end up down below.' Conditioned to lead a noble life or pay the consequences in The Underworld after death. There was always doubt if it ever existed, because no one has ever come back from it to tell us if it was real, yet there it was mapped out in front us.

The map was almost exactly what I would expect a chart of The Underworld to look like. The parchment was grey and charred, with areas of darkness and doom all around. Five separate rivers snaked their way into the center of the map and dumped into a large marshy area, and an eerie fog hovered over this section.

I was surprised to see a lush green meadow and forest area on the western portion of the map titled, ELYSIUM. Trees and flowers grew out of the parchment, but darkness loomed in the forest, darting between the trees in the form of shadows.

A grand palace lay on the outskirts of Elysium, off to the east and it looked out onto the lush grounds. Its diorama was constructed of marble and iron, with raised lettering that spelled out HOUSE OF HADES.

Below the marshy wetlands, in the southeastern portion of the enchanted scroll, lay a land called PLAIN OF ASPHODEL. Ghostly figures flew over this section of the map, circling around over and over again, lost. I had an empty feeling as I stared at this part; all too close to the numb feeling I had adrift in the dark abyss.

The only portion of the map that noises were present was the lower left hand, or southwestern portion. Larger flaming letters were hovering above a deep abyss spelling TARTARUS. Screams of agony and suffering grew from this region of torment, and it was the River of Styx that flowed closest to it.

"STYX!" the devilish harpy banged her gnarled, boney finger onto the river. Her ugly wrinkled face quickly changed from hag to hunter, and her eyes flickered with an intense determination. She started to sniff deeply, taking in huge amounts of air, as if trying to pick up a scent. Her actions seemed to electrify the demonic creature in her satchel, which chortled with excitement.

"Ekadenc! Focussss!" Nak demanded, but his voice wavered and I detected uneasiness in his tone.

The hound of death appeared to shake it off and calm herself down and she glanced back at the map. "Travel Styx to Tartarus," she grunted, but her eyes began to change again. The Harpy, Ekadenc, started to undergo a creepy transformation; the decrepit hag no longer existed, and a force to be reckoned with replaced her meager persona. A creature that nightmares are made of stood next to me, drooling, and twitching. Then she growled the words in a crescendo, "hate and destruction will come your way!"

Ekadenc's wings forcefully unfurled. Her face smoothed out into a face of horror, and a terrifying roar screeched from her pursed lips. With amazing agility, she leapt onto the table; her talons puncturing the scroll as she stumbled uneasily. Again, she began to smell the air, inhaling deeply, tracking some unseen scent. Ekadenc was no longer a feeble old harpy; she was a horrifying hound of death!

Her teeth snapped at each of us, as she sniffed out her prey. All the while, the creature in her bag giggled with excitement. Nak was weaving from side to side, ready to defend anyone of us, and trying to reason with the creature that no longer resembled Ekadenc. It snapped ferociously towards Luca. Startled, all of us jumped back, stumbling over chairs, and I fell to the floor. Ekadenc's wings were scraping the ceiling and chips of wood were splintering everywhere.

Abruptly, the creature locked onto her scent and honed in on her target. With an enormous inhale, which pulled my hair forward into my eyes, all commotion stopped. We all held our breath, our senses on high alert. The Harpy immediately stopped lashing out, stood erect, and slowly ambled her way in a circle following the scent in the air.

Everyone froze. *What did she smell?* Ekadenc's circular motion ceased and her terrifying form came to stop directly in front of me. She inhaled deeply again, and then let out a roar with such force, my hair blew back tight against my skull. My orb immediately turned red and my birthmark seared with pain. I tried to scurry backwards across the wood-planked floor, but in a split second, the creature had leapt off the table. I turned to right myself and run, but she snatched me up in her talons piercing through my flesh. Excruciating pain, like hot pokers penetrating my back and sides, made my body contort.

"NO!" screamed everyone, but I could barely hear them through my own screams of agony, and the laughter from the satchel, the screeching from the hound of death, and the beating of its wings.

Adrastai sprang into action! Mateo instantly went Berserk, flailing his arms in a windmill action trying to knock the creature down. Luca transformed into a white bird and began trying to peck out the eyes of the beast.

I couldn't see the others. I was wincing in pain but I was keenly aware that the beast was building energy. She tightened her grip, crushing my ribs. My screams of agony were replaced with mere attempts to scream. I felt a rib crack. She was crushing me.. There was a sudden surge forward, and she smashed right through the wall

286

of Ellida's side.

We were a flight, soaring through the skies that once welcomed me. She was fulfilling her duties as a Harpy. It was her job to deliver me: she was taking me to Tartarus! I called for Khai. He answered with a tremendous roar as he soared off the ship! Within seconds, he crashed into the side of Ekadenc. The sounds of their growls were deafening. I threw my hands up to shield my ears.

"Servo!" managed to escape my lips. The beast screamed in pain as my sword sliced the bottom of her claws as it flew into my hands. The Harpy's hot blood ran down her talons and into my wounds. I tried to inflict a blow, intending to chop off her legs, when she gripped tighter. Like a constrictor squeezing the life from its prey, air pushed from my lungs and I lost my hold on Servo.

Without oxygen, I began to lose consciousness. Through half-closed eyes, I watched my weapon plummet to the ocean below. I tried to glance to the sky to find Khai, but my eyes met two yellow eyes peeking out of the satchel over the top of six creepy claws. It let out a belly laugh, just before Khai slammed into Ekadenc again. The force jolted me from her talons. I was careening to the ocean's surface, tumbling from heights unknown.

I was dying. I couldn't get air. My ribs and spine were crushed. There was no way I would survive this fall. My thoughts went to my family. For the first time, since Nak invaded my body, I thought of my family. I managed a laugh and a smile just before my body shattered upon impact.

Still semi-conscious, I felt the cool water engulf me, covering me as I sunk down into the abyss. I couldn't move. I couldn't swim. There was no more air…streaks of silver began to light my eyes. Then nothing.

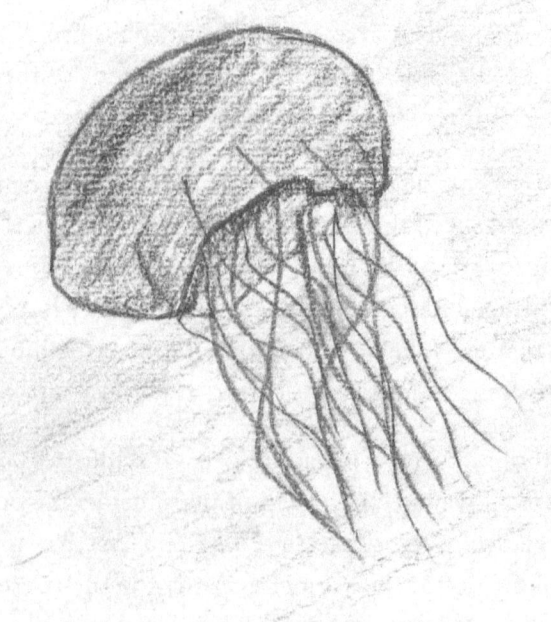

Chapter 19

Illustrated by
Jordyn Guziec

19

THE COLONY

The sun was so bright squinting was required. I was swaying in the warm breeze, snuggled up inside the hammock, like a swaddled child. Mom and Dad were playing bocce ball, and the FrouFrou Crew were turning cartwheels and jumping all over the back yard. It was so nice to be back home.

Home, what a great concept. Surrounded by the ones you love, all together sharing, laughing, crying, arguing, but building bonds that last lifetimes. I felt myself smiling, which hasn't happened in very long time.

Mom was up to something. I saw her whisper something to Dad, and he smiled in agreement. She walked off towards the house and Dad was heading over my way. "What are you getting at?" I called out laughing.

Dad just smiled. He was almost to me, when Mariella, my three-year old sister, snuck up behind me and giggled, "Oh, you better run!"

Then I saw Mom. She was heading straight for me with the nozzle on the hose aimed at me, like a prisoner on the execution wall. "Wait!" I laughed. "Give me a fighting chance, would you?"

Squeals of laughter rang through the yard as all three members of the FrouFrou Crew tried to push out of the hammock from behind, but Dad was flinging them around like a giant.

Mom was still advancing. That hose has the coldest water ever running through it that takes your breath away. I have seen many a FrouFrou lip turn blue from running under the sprinkler attached to that hose. The weather was so warm, and I was so comfortable; I didn't want to be sprayed.

My attempts to flee were not successful; I was tangled up in the hammock, laughing to myself, because I just couldn't get away. Suddenly, something changed. The birds stopped singing and the girls no longer giggled. Confused, I looked to the sky and noticed a grey clouds billowing in from all around. The sun darted behind a cloud, and the vibrant summer colors started to drain out of my surroundings leaving ominous greyscale colors in their place.

My tangled hammock tightened around my waste. I glanced down and found it had morphed into scaly arm and hands that were keeping me from fleeing. I screamed to Mom for help, but she just kept walking towards me, without any emotion on her face. I was pleading with my eyes, when Mom's beautiful frame began to contort, stretch, and bulge in ways a human could achieve. Something was pushing on my Mom from the inside out. Then her shoulders stretched out more than twenty feet wide by some invisible force, her back hunched throwing her upper body forward, and talons grew from her hands and feet. Nãga! The bluish-silvery creature was rushing towards me. I could not bust free from whatever was holding me back.

The beast opened its terrifying jaws, and I peered into the mouth of death. A spark ignited at the back of her throat, as if someone was using a flint to start a fire. The fire was coming! A bluish-green glow grew from deep inside her gullet. Struggling was useless. I bit at my restraints and tried to rip flesh away, but my teeth only crashed together, never biting through anything. *What was holding me back?*

Blue flames shot from her throat! I tried to scream, but I was too late. Flames engulfed me! My brain swirled uncontrollably and my flesh burned. I dropped to the ground, defeated. Nãga's booming laughter accompanied by others filled my ears. Struggling to roll to put out the fire, I saw what was holding me back, the arms of my friends.

I was slapped in the face by icy hatred. Then, I was slapped again. I woke up sputtering, in a pool of ice water on a slab of rock. Coughing, choking, and finally free from the hating hands of those I loved; I frantically tried to scurry away. Anxiety filled my head; unaware of where I was, or who was around me.

"Ssshhh, there, there, dear," cooed a soft voice that smelled of the seashore in the summertime. "Don't struggle."

I recognized that smell, and knew instantly that Aluvanim, Skye's elven guide, was by my side. I opened my eyes and cried at the sight of her. I tried to speak, but I just didn't have the energy to produce any sounds and pain shot through my back when I tried to struggle.

"I know dear," she softly spoke. "I am right here, and we will fix you right as rain."

We? I tried to bring myself to sit, but the agony in my back and side was just too much, and, I couldn't move my legs. I tried to drag my lower body around on my elbows, when I realized I was paralyzed. My elbows gave way and I collapsed onto my stomach, with my face pressed against a cool wet surface. The pain was excruciating.

"Brochara? Khai? Are you there?" I telecommunicated. No one answered. I tried to speak; the words just would not come out.

"They are not here, dear," Aluvanim answered. "You are safe for now, but you will have to rely on us for a couple hours. I have pledged to protect you."

I slowly turned my head to her, smiled acknowledging that I trusted her, and telecommunicated, "Where am I? I take it I am not dead."

The little aquatic elf giggled, "Oh heavens no, dear. I dove from Ellida when Ekadenc carried you off, and good thing I did, too." As she finished her statement, she nodded her head gesturing off to the left, and began stirring something. I had forgotten about Ekadenc; that seemed so long ago.

My eyes tried to focus on where I was. The floor was damp and cold and it smelled of the sea. The previous events came flooding back to me; watching Servo plunge out of the sky to the depths, Khai crashing into Ekadenc attempting to save me, and then my body crashing into the watering depths. A tiny crab scurried over my arm and I watched it plop into a little pool. My eyes traveled up the side of a rocky wall adorned with oceanic crustaceans. I must have been in another underwater cavern. A glimmer of light caught my eye and I glanced over to find Servo leaning against a rock wall. I was so relieved to see it that I tried to sit up again, crashing back onto the rocky floor.

"Giovani, stop doing that!" Her voice was stern this time. "You have been gravely wounded, and if you do not lie still, you will die."

Die? I decided that maybe I should just wait. "How did you catch me and the sword?" I asked using our minds. "By the way, thank you. Thank you for Servo and saving my life." I looked to Servo again; the wall it was leaning against was alive with crustaceans, mollusks, and something slimy that slithered in between them. Fear immediately filled my body. "Nãga! This is her cavern!"

"Oh aren't you so sweet," she said aloud, "But, it was not I who saved you." Her tiny frame flitted around the cavern, "And darling, there are many caverns in the ocean. We were just lucky enough to be close to a colony of Piscisenes!"

"Piscisenes? Is Skye here?" but I immediately knew the answer when Aluvanim bowed her head and turned away. "Aluvanim, I...I'm sorry. I didn't mean to upset you."

I kept forgetting how others were affected by her death. I was too wrapped up in my own emotions, but Aluvanim was even closer to Skye than I was. She protected her from the day she was born.

"I feel her, you know," she replied with her back turned to me. "I just know, in my bones, that she is still with us."

"What?" Emotions started to stir inside of me, "You think she is still alive?"

"I know not. I only know that I feel her. I cannot go to her for she does not call, but I feel her." What a helpless feeling that must have been, not being able to do anything to help the ones you love. Aluvanim turned back to me with tears in her eyes, and a conch shell full of some liquid in her hands.

"Oh no," I knew instantly what she had created. "Please." I pleaded with her.

"I am not a stranger to the pinching of noses to make Adrastai drink!" She chortled.

I couldn't fight her anyway. The healing concoction did not taste anything like Elia's, but it was equally as disgusting. I am pretty certain I saw a fish eye bobbing in the concoction before she poured it down my throat. It felt like fish guts going down, and tasted like it too.

The reaction to the fish goo wasn't as violent as Elia's. I felt all fluttery and flopping on the inside, kind of, like when a fish flops around on land. I was able to stand right up and get back to my quest.

"Wow! Don't tell Elia, but yours is much better than hers." I told her with a wink. Aluvanim belly laughed and it warmed my heart. "What do you mean a colony of Piscisene?"

Aluvanim bowed her head as she spoke, "Nãga destroyed many Adrastai and their protectors, when she attacked the Council. Many died in their beds! They didn't even have a chance to fight. Nãga is a coward! Our numbers are not strong."

I didn't know what to say. Guilt filled my mind. I had watched it happen. I thought it was a dream, but Nãga had pulled my essence with her. She used me, and my knowledge, to kill many good people and capture my sister. There wasn't anything I could do to stop her. I could feel hatred and anger build up inside of me.

"We will rebuild, and we will stop Nãga!" Cheers erupted from all over. Startled, I looked around because I thought Aluvanim and I were alone.

About twenty Piscisene revealed themselves. Some stepped out from behind coral and others standing mere feet from me; the dim light reflected off their silvery surface as they moved, illuminating their bodies. They had been standing right before me the entire time, but camouflaged with the sea environment. Amazing.

"We will help you." A tall man with brilliant green eyes stepped forward, "Nãga has killed our people for many years, and stolen our youth. She has created an army of Piscisene, children, who have turned against us." His voice wavered with pain.

A beautiful silvery woman walked up behind him and put her webbed hand on his shoulder. They were an amazing species; not at all what I was expecting. They looked incredibly similar to humans; besides the obvious silvery hue of their skin, they had webbing between their fingers, toes, and under their arms. An odd bone protruded out of the top of their skulls, sort of like a boney mohawk. Gill slits were on the sides of their necks, and they shimmered, like the scales of a silvery fish in the sunlight. Up close to them on land, I could detect their scales just under the surface of their skin. A couple of Piscisene were in the water at the edge of the rocks; their skin disappeared and brilliant scales replaced it.

When the tall beautiful Piscisene spoke to me, her eyes were also a brilliant green and they appeared to shimmer. "Our son and the children of others have been taken. That horrible beast has used her magic on them! Can you imagine how it feels to have your own children strike out to kill you? The child you cradled, loved, laughed, and cried with suddenly doesn't remember you, and only feels hatred towards you!" She burried her head into the shoulder of her mate and wept.

"I am so sorry." Was all I could think of to say, "What a horrible feeling that must be."

"She has your sister?" The tall man asked.

"Yes." I suddenly thought of a world where Sofia might not recognize me. A couple months ago I would have laughed at the thought, but now, now, my heart ached.

"We pledge our allegiance to The Order and you, my friend. We will help get your sister back!" As the man spoke, the others stood behind him. I felt their pride and welcomed their help.

"We need a plan." I proclaimed. "I have to get back to Nak. How do we do that, Aluvanim?"

"We will need to get you to the surface first," she answered. "Once you surface, you must call Khai right away. The oceans are not safe anymore, and you cannot be floating in them for too long."

"I can help." A young Piscisene child walked through the adults and said, "I've helped him before."

The Piscisene group all looked at each other confused. The couple, who spoke earlier, knelt down and looked the child in the eyes.

"No!" cried the boy's mother, "I will not lose all of my babies to that monster!" She threw her arms around her son and the webbing under her arms created protective blanket about him.

"What are you talking about, son?" The father asked.

The child looked a little nervous, as if he had been keeping a secret and could not any longer. He was trying really hard to avoid his mother's eyes. "You can tell us anything, my love. We won't get angry." She added, lifting his chin to look him in the eyes.

The child starting sobbing. My heart just ached for him. Through his sobs, he managed to tell a story about the day his older brother was taken by Nãga. They were playing outside a kelp forest, when something curious entered the ocean. It was dragon, with a boy on his back.

"Wait, a dragon and a boy?" I interrupted, "How often does a dragon with a boy rider enter the oceans? Do you mean me?" My memory of finding the meteor to forge Servo with at the bottom of the ocean flooded my brain. Khai and I had to retrieve it from an ocean cave that Sukanar had enchanted.

"Yes," he answered, "It was you. We were trying to help some of friends escape Nãga. She trapped them in that cave and put a spell on it. When the rock dragon went for you, we saw our chance to free the others. Then I saw you float away and you looked like you were in trouble, so I called my jelly friends." My eyes lit up, with the realization that this boy was the one who saved my life, but his head hung down and he finished, "When I went back to help my brother, he was gone…along with the others."

"You saved my life." My forehead was deeply creased while I processed this crazy turn of events, "but by saving me, the others were lost; I am so sorry."

"Why didn't you tell us!" the father demanded, taking his son by the shoulders and forcing him to look at him. "Son, you have been carrying a horrifying secret for many months. Why have you suffered in silence?"

"I didn't want you to hate me for losing my brother." He wept, standing in front of his parents.

Both Piscisene parents threw their arms around the boy and held him tight. "We could never hate you, never. You are our baby; your intentions were most honorable and your actions saved your life, allowing you to swim back to us."

I found myself weeping watching them, but then guilt filled me again. Those children might have been saved if it wasn't for me. They would be safe with their families, not under Nãga's evil spell. I always thought Sukanar cursed that cave…evil is everywhere and it always seems to find me. Well this time, I was going to find it. For Sofia, the lost Piscisene children, and because now, I was mad.

"The giant jellyfish! That was your idea?" I asked the boy, full of determination.

He nodded through his tears.

"Brilliant! Can you call them? Can we do it again?" I continued my fast-fire questioning.

"Yes," he answered without tears, and his spirit appeared lifted, "I just need to call them."

"Then let's go get your brother and his friends!" I yelled. The jumped with excitement and darted to the water's edge. He dove in and proceeded to produce snapping and clicking noises that reminded me of dolphin communications. I was smiling with pride for the boy's assertiveness.

I didn't have a plan, but I knew this had to be done. Being part of The Order means protecting all kinds, not just my family. I needed to help this colony, and that was exactly what I was going to do. Besides, finding the lost Piscisenes meant I would find Nãga.

Aluvanim's smile beamed from ear to ear. "Brochara will be so proud of you, just as I am. You will make a great leader one day."

Leader? "Uh, umm, thank you, but I think anyone would do the same thing in this situation, at least I hope they would."

"You would be surprised, Giovani. I have lived for hundreds of years, and have watched humans slowly become a greedy race. Helping others is becoming a thing of the past. Humans are more concerned with themselves, individually, than the greater good of mankind, or all the creatures on this earth." There was much sadness in her voice, and her words made me sad too. "We can make a difference. Sometimes it just takes one good deed." Her smile was genuine, and I felt it all the in my heart.

"Well, I promise to do my part. Do you know where Nãga can be found? I have only ever gone by astral travel." I still didn't know how I was going to do this, but Servo was there and the Piscisenes were behind me. Now I needed to get to the surface and find Khai.

"Giovani, you cannot go and do this now." Aluvanim's words stopped my courage's momentum.

"What are talking about? Now is when we need to do this!" I was confused, "I thought that was the plan."

"We will help you to the surface, but you must continue the journey the High Mages set you on." Aluvanim's voice grew harsh, and I saw the boy's spirit crush. "That is your destiny, and by fulfilling it, you shall set them free."

"Aluva..." but she interrupted my rebuttal.

"No! It must be so, and there is no time to waste." I had never seen Aluvanim so stern, "I must go help the fallen Adratsai in the Valley. Be safe my friend, and remember the waters are no longer innocent. You must call Khai immediately!"

I threw my arms around her tiny frame and hugged with all of my might. "Thank you for saving me," I whispered into her ear.

"I could not save my Skye; I am honored to have helped you." With tears in her eyes, she waved her teeny arm over her head and disappeared in a tiny puff of green smoke.

"They are here!" called the boy, excitedly, from behind me. "Three will help you to the surface. If your air becomes too thin, then swim into the next one."

"You have already helped save us." I placed my hands on the Piscisene boy's shoulders and looked inside his silvery eyes, "Your bravery will never be forgotten. Thank you so much for your help, friend. What is your name?"

"Thyak," the boy replied with pride in his eyes, "My name is Thyak." His smile grew wide, he dove towards me with a flying hug, and he buried his face into my chest.

"We shall swim beside you, to defend your ascent," the boy's father added, and then he called out in their native language what must have been a battle cry, because all of the older men and women grabbed spears and dove into the icy waters.

I climbed in and drew my last breath of free air. Swimming under the tentacles and then up into the body of the jelly, used most of that breath. I was slightly apprehensive of taking another breath once inside, but my chest tightened and my brain made me. I gasped with apprehension. I was breathing. The same way I did the first time. I laughed to myself. This life sure was odd and exciting.

The view from inside the jellyfish was a little unclear, like looking through clear Jell-O, with the sporadic streaks of bioluminescent lights passing in front of my eyes. It was the way the jellies communicated to each other. The other two took their positions alongside of us.

Surprisingly, these invertebrates were very fast swimmers. Peering through the gelatinous forms, I saw my Piscisene protectors beside us. In the water, their skin changed to scales, and their legs fused together creating a tail. Every now and again, one would swim off with speeds that made them disappear quickly into the blue. Their silver coloring camouflaged them well. They were really hard to see in the water; just the occasional flicker of silver caught my eye. Their agility in the water was impressive.

All at once, many of the Piscisene darted away, leaving three back with me, looking very nervous. Silver flashes flitted through the water. I felt the jellyfish increase their speed, but the faster they went, the less air was available for me. My brain was starting to cramp from lack of oxygen. I remembered what the boy, Thyak, told me and I drew in a deep breath and swam for the next jellyfish.

The air-filled jelly just kept on swimming, much faster than I could. I was trying to notify them that I could not catch up, but none of them could hear me telecommunicate. They didn't notice me leave. My chest was starting to tighten again. I was running out of air and the jellyfish lights were far away, barely noticeable. I had to swim up on my own.

Suddenly, something grabbed my ankle! Whatever had ahold of me, yanked me downwards so powerfully that some of my remaining breath escape my lungs. I looked down, and saw a human hand. Then with a force greater than a rollercoaster ride, I was being pulled to the bottom of the ocean. Confused. No more air. No way to fight. "Someone save me!"

Chapter 20

Illustrated by
Giovani Russo

20

A REUNION

My lungs burned. I wasn't sure if it was from the lack of oxygen, or because of the pressure from the ocean's depths. My head felt like it was going to explode, and I just knew that I was dying. My thoughts trailed off to my family. I hope that they were proud of me, and knew how much I love them. Unable to hold my breath, I decided to inhale before whatever had a hold of me decided to kill me. I made my peace with dying and lifted my face to surface that I could no longer see. Just as I opened to my mouth to inhale the seawater, my assailant launched me forward thwarting my efforts.

I zipped through the depths with amazing speed, like a torpedo. The resistance of the water quickly stopped as my body shot out of the water and into air. Instinctively, I gasped. Air filled my lungs as full as they could grow, just before I crashed onto a rocky surface, knocking the wind out of me.

Sputtering out seawater and trying to catch my breath, I rolled over as a silvery figure shot from the water and headed straight for me. Amazingly, this thing changed its course, mid-air, adjusting its path to avoid me, but I had already rolled to get out of the way, choking again, and the creature plowed right into my chest.

I slammed onto the cold hard surface with a thud. When I opened my eyes, the same black haired boy from The Garden of Hesperides was kneeling on my chest again. He was acting in the same way he did before; looking at me like there was something familiar, but he just couldn't figure out what.

Before I could respond, something started to crawl out of the sea that caught his attention. With supernatural reflexes, the boy spun off me, sliced through a mutated crab-like creature, spun back around, and landed back down on my chest.

"Ryan?" I looked into his eyes, and they seemed to respond upon hearing that name, "Is that you?"

Suddenly, I heard steps running towards us. The boy turned his head and sat up, still pinning me to the ground with only one hand. He gestured to something and smiled as he pointed down at me. It felt like I was some kind of offering.

"GIOVANI!" Skye's voice echoed through the cavern and was like music to my ears. My emotions were so intense that I bucked off the boy, and ran to her. We threw our arms around each other half laughing and half crying. "I thought you were dead! Everyone thinks you're dead."

"I'm not." Skye's sarcastic humor was still intact. "Ryan grabbed me. I knew I saw him in the water, following us."

"Wait a minute." The memory of the crow, perched on the Ellida's crow's nest, flooded back to me. I pulled myself away from Skye and looked her in the eye, "He works for Nãga. Skye he was a crow. You know, one of the bad crows…remember? He dove off and then he, you know, he turned back into himself before hitting the water."

"That wasn't Ryan," She exclaimed in a tone that made me feel like I was crazy. Skye shook her head no, "I saw that crow change into a Piscisene before it hit the water. That's when I saw Ryan again. He was looking up at me from under the waves. There were others too. Once that Piscisene dove back into the ocean, the rest of them took off. I couldn't lose him, not again. I had to jump in and find him." Sadness filled her voice, but then she looked at her brother and a smile grew across her face, "He's alive."

"I am so happy YOU are alive!" I scooped her up and spun her around, "And you found your brother. Your family will be complete again." But sadness creeped into my heart, remembering that my family was no longer whole…Nãga had Sofia.

I glance around my surroundings, and realized that I was in another cavern. An eerie feeling came over me; something was very familiar about this place. To my left stood a wall full of crustaceans that looked like the one I fell into once before. There were many large tunnels leading off in different directions, and in the middle of the large cavern, was a gigantic fissure in the floor that was oozing lava. Anxiety filled me as I realized where we were.

"Skye!" I shouted in a whisper not draw any attention, "This is Nãga's lair!"

Ryan flipped towards the water's edge, and with reflexes that reminded me of a Ninja, he intercepted another mutated-crab creature that was climbing out of the depths. The slain creature made me nervous, its pincher claws looked like it could slice me in half. I was thankful that Ryan was talented with the dagger strapped to his leg. He made quick work of the creature and kicked the remains back towards the water, but it landed right at the water's edge. Ryan looked at Skye with a concern on his face and pointed to the ocean.

"Come on," she said as she grabbed my arm, "We've got to get out here, fast."

With that, she started yanking my arm towards the tunnels. I pulled my arm away from her grip and stopped moving. "Why are we heading deeper into her lair? I am not going in there! She is dangerous Skye! We have to get out of here!" I pulled her arm towards the water. I didn't have a plan, but I thought we would have a better chance of surviving in the water than we did fighting Nãga in her own home!

"COME ON!" She yelled, yanking me back towards the tunnels, "Trust me." The expression on her face twisted into fear.

Skye was pointing at the water, which began to bubble ferociously. Something was coming up from the depths, and fear rushed through me thinking that Nãga was coming. Before I had time to turn and run, an army of those mutated crab-like creatures emerged from the water, like a swarm of ants across the forest floor.

Horrible sounds of high-pitch chatter echoed through the cavern as the creatures advanced. They were jet black in color and resembled enormous spiders with spiked exoskeletons that looked like armor. The bodies spanned over three feet wide, and their legs made them as big as a small car. Enormous claws viciously snapped in the air, as they advanced really quickly, covering everything in sight. The grotesque creatures stopped by the carcass Ryan had thrown and fought over it, ripping and tearing it to pieces and shoving it in their mouths. "RUN!" Skye screamed!

That was all I needed to see, I took off running, like a shot! "What are those things?"

"I don't know, but every time she leaves, they rush in and eat her leftovers and anything else in their path!" Skye screamed over her shoulder.

It felt like we were running forever. Torches speckled the

tunnels, but there were moments when we ran through complete darkness before the light of the next torch lit our path. We finally slowed to walk. There was a labyrinth of passageways down here, and it reminded of an ant colony for some reason.

Ryan became uneasy; he tugged on our clothes, and then rolled into a fissure under a large rock ledge and disappeared. Skye quickly followed him and so did I. A group of footsteps echoed through the tunnel as they approached. We remained still until they walked past us. When the sounds of their steps were far enough away, we shimmied out of our hiding spot.

"Come on." Skye whispered and motioned me to follow her.

We crept along silently for a ways, and then came to a stop at what looked like a dead end. A large pile of fallen rocks stood before us. It must have been a cave in. I turned around to head back the way we came, when Skye grabbed my elbow. "Wait," she whispered.

Ryan walked over to the pile and up to a particularly large rock. He grabbed a hold of it and lifted it up and out of the way. His strength amazed me, but when he turned sideways, I noticed that he had chiseled off the face of a huge rock to about half an inch thick, to create a secret door. It was very deceptive and very clever. We crawled into a hidden cavern and he placed the rock back, concealing our path.

"This is where he lives." Skye said.

It was pitch dark. Ryan struck the ground and created a spark, and then he lit a torch he had stashed between the rocks of the cavern. The ceiling was extremely tall; I suppose it had to be big enough for Nãga to walk through before the cave in. There was a bed in one corner that looked like it was made out of animal fur. I walked over and felt it; it was incredibly soft.

"Seal." Skye said. "Isn't this amazing? My little brother, he was

307

surviving all on his own, and fending for himself all of these years!"
Pride was written all over her expression. She went over to him, and
he took a big step away from her. I watched her slowly and
cautiously take his hand in hers. They didn't speak, and he seemed
uneasy being touched by his sister. She looked him in the eyes and
smiled. He nodded.

I had to admit, it was all very impressive. This boy, who was
younger than I was, took care of himself, and was very good at it
from what I had witnessed. There many tools and weapons lying
around made from shells and large bones. Ryan shoved his sister to
the floor. I made a move to help her, but she held up her hand to
stop.

"He appears to have lost his social skills, and he hasn't spoken to
me either," Skye said matter-of-factly. "He is just a little gruff, that's
all."

Abruptly, Ryan threw his hand over her mouth to silence her.
Skye nodded in agreement and the boy sprang from the floor, ran up
the rock wall, and grabbed onto a sharp outward facing corner of a
steep rock just above the entrance of the cave. He pressed his ear to
a crack in the rocks.

Skye quietly stood up and moved towards him. I heard noises
from the corridor. With a flash of silver, the rock rolled away.
Commotion grew from the dark corridor, another flash of silver and
a Piscisene child was shoved into the room. A girl child huddled to
the floor and curled up frightened.

Skye quickly scooped up the frightened child, hugged her, and
whispered assurances in her ear. The child slowly sat up and looked
around, wiping the big tears from her eyes. "You're safe now," Skye
said.

"What about my brother?" the child whimpered.

Skye shook her head slowly, indicating that he was lost. The girl immediately tried to protest, but Ryan threw his hand over her mouth and dragged his thumb across his neck to relay the message of death. The girl's eyes filled up with tears again. Skye just threw her arms around the child and held her tight. "We will get you out of here."

We sat silently in the dimly lit chamber and my brain was swirling. How did Ryan know so much about this place? He had to have been here for years. How else would he have had the time to find a hidden chamber, chisel off a rock door, and have the ability to distinguish between sounds in the darkness? He constructed his own tools…It was just then that I realized that Ryan was single-handedly trying to rescue as many Piscisene as he could from inside Nãga's own lair!

I must have been smiling when I made this revelation, because Skye turned her face to me and smiled warmly. Full of respect and adoration for the ten-year-old hero, I walked over to Skye, returned the smile, and she sat down next to the Piscisene girl.

Ryan disappeared off into a dark part of the cave and left the three of us by a small fire. Sitting next to Skye again made me feel stronger. We worked well together; our relationship has always been easy.

"I don't understand," I was trying to figure everything out, "How did Ryan end up here?"

"He hasn't spoke to me, but this is what I think has happened from watching the last couple weeks." Skye's face was glowing with pride, "The tornado that grabbed him was meant for me. I think that when Sukanar realized it had failed, he dumped Ryan in the ocean." Skye's face twisted slightly at the presumed evil. "Nãga has been forming an army of Piscisene for years. I think she must have sensed Ryan's Piscisene blood, and captured him."

Ryan returned to the small fire carrying four conch shells full of what looked like water. Skye grabbed one and thanked him. She held to pointy end to her mouth and drank. Nervously, I followed her lead. I must have been extremely thirsty, because I gulped down all of the liquid quickly. It was fresh water! It tasted so clean and pure. Ryan handed me his shell and walked back off into the darkness.

Skye continued, "He took me once, you know. To show me what Nãga does to them to make them follow her," Skye bowed her head and shivered, "It's a horribly cruel and long process. She uses magic to erase their memories and shoves them in a deep cave, sealing them in darkness. The children scream for days, trying to find their way out and then…they go silent." Tears welled up in the young Piscisene girl's eyes as Skye continued, "When they stop crying out, and they always do, Nãga leaves them there for a couple more days until she deems them ready, and she brings them out into the bright cave. She is disgustingly sweet to them, cuddling, pretending to be their savior, and treats them like her own children. It is sick brainwashing. They respond to her with love from delivering them from the darkness."

The Piscisene girl sobbed. "We will do our best to save him, but you must listen to Ryan or we will all end up in her army." Skye consoled her.

"So why is Ryan here?" I asked, still confused.

"I think it is because we are only half Piscisene. Nãga's spells didn't work entirely on Ryan, but as you can tell, he isn't the same as when he was taken from us."

Just then, Ryan shoved a plate made of rock under Skye's nose. It was filled with shrimp and crabmeat. Ryan grunted for his sister to take the plate from him.

"See?" she said as she accepted his offering. "Here, try this, it is really good." Skye placed the meal down in front of us

We all shared the meat, and Skye continued. "He pretends to be brainwashed when she is around. I think that is how he has survived so long."

Ryan suddenly kicked the plate of food out of the way and began drawing feverishly in the sand on the floor. Skye gave me a look, as if to say 'see what I mean?' He had quickly created a sand sketch of Nãga, showing her underbelly. He then plowed over me, knocking me down, and fetched a whalebone sword he fashioned. When he returned, he shoved the tip of the sword onto a spot on Nãga's underside.

I looked him in the eye, which flashed with anger and determination, "You want to kill to her?"

Then he banged his fist into my chest, and pointed to the sand drawing, shoving the sword back into the beast's belly.

"You want me to kill her." Ryan shook his head yes, but kept hitting the same spot on the underbelly of the drawing. "Is that where I need to kill her? Dragon scales are extremely strong; I don't think that is possible."

But just as quickly as he drew Nãga, Ryan dropped to his knees and drew sharp rocks. He then drew a tiny Nãga at the bottom of it and dragged his finger back and forth over the rocks. Then he pointed back to the underbelly with the tip of his sword.

I sat there, trying to analyze this weird game of charades. Ryan again dragged his finger back and forth over the jagged rocks, but this time he grabbed his stomach and faked pain; doubling over wrapping his arms across his belly.

"OOH! I get it!" I yelled excitedly. Ryan immediately threw his

311

hands over my mouth and looked over both shoulders. "Oops, sorry. Okay, I think I've got it. Her stomach scales are weak because of crawling over the jagged rocks. So that is my best place to try and kill her."

A smile grew across Ryan's face, and Skye clapped her hands silently at our communication.

"Okay, how are we going to do that?" I asked, but Ryan sat down to floor and shrugged his shoulders. "You don't have plan?"

Again, he pointed the sword to the underbelly of the beast and twisted one side of his face up, as if to say 'that's all I have.'

"She's not here right now," Skye interrupted the silence, "She's out feeding."

All of a sudden, I made the connection that my sister must be here, and I jumped to my feet, "Sofia! Where is Sofia?"

"What?" Skye was confused.

"Nãga has Sofia. She used me! She made me lead her to Sofia when she forced me to astral travel with her!" I felt my blood starting to boil. "She lured her from the house and took her. She has to be here somewhere! I have to save her!"

My chest grew tight with anger, and my breathing turned shallow. A thunderous roar grew from the dark corridor. "WHERE ARE YOU?" Immediately my dragon birthmark burned and my orb illuminated bright red.

"Nãga!" Skye and I said at the same time. Ryan's eyes grew large and his expression changed to determination. He shoved Skye, the Piscisene girl, and me towards the back of his cave. He stamped out the fire and tried to scatter his things to avoid detection. All the while, he was shoving us deeper into the cave.

"I CAN SMELL YOU!" Nãga roared from somewhere deep inside the labyrinth of tunnels, but her voice echoed off of every wall, sending fear down my spine.

"Nak! She can smell Nak in me," I realized aloud.

Ryan had pushed the three of us to a small pool of water. He motioned for us to dive in and swim away. Skye refused. He then plugged his nose and pointed to me. He pushed me into the icy waters, and then tried to push his sister in too. The Piscisene girl dove into the water without hesitation, and quickly swam away.

"NO! Ryan, I won't leave you!" Skye began to cry as she fought against his pushing.

"NAK! SHOW YOURSELF!" growled the beast. "I WILL TEAR YOU APART!" She was getting closer; rocks fell from the ceiling and crashed near the siblings.

Ryan threw his arms around Skye and hugged her tight. It must have been the first time, because she stopped fighting him and welcomed the hug, nuzzling her cheek into his hair. Abruptly he pushed her away and into the water. "GO!" he yelled.

His first words in years. They took him by surprise, as if her embrace triggered something inside of him. He looked down at us and smiled. Then very slowly, he found his words. "Go. I will be fine." Tears were streaming down Skye's face and a smile of confidence grew across Ryan's. "I love you."

Rock exploded everywhere! Ryan sprang from the floor again, and we saw him tuck behind a crack in the ceiling. He plugged his nose again and motioned for us to flee, just as the beast entered the room.

My ears filled with the sound of rushing water mixed with Nãga's angry roar. Skye was pulling me to the surface with speeds of a racecar. The same feeling as when Ryan pulled me into the Nãga's lair. That was what he meant. He knew I wouldn't be able to hold my breath long enough to escape on my own. He knew that I needed Skye. My heart smiled at his kindness.

We burst through the surface like dolphins. I took in a deep gulp of air and felt the sun on my face. I reached around, grabbed my birthmark, and screamed Khai's name, just as Aluvanim had instructed before. Then I turned to Skye, afraid that she would be sad.

A huge smile grew across her face and she leapt out of the water, performing a double flip. When she plunged back in, she grabbed me and swam us in circles. "He's back! I felt it in our hug! Something happened, and he is BACK!"

Something knocked Skye out of my arms and pulled her underwater. "Not again!" I yelled, quickly submerging myself to find her.

I opened my eyes under water, but the salt burned. I tried to look again, when a hand grabbed me. Instead of pulling me back down, it pulled me up to the surface.

"I told you I felt her!" cried Aluvanim, standing on top of Skye's shoulders, wearing the biggest grin.

A dragon roar called from the sky. I saw my majestic dragon partner soaring through the clouds. His bluish-green scales shimmering in the sunlight. "Over here!" I yelled.

Jock, too, emerged from the depths right underneath Skye and Aluvanim. Skye hugged her Imoogi and they bolted off to the east.

Khai scooped me out of the water. I was so relieved to be together again. We followed Jock's course just above them, and I spotted Ellida off in the distance!

Once aboard the dragon ship, all of our friends came running to greet us. Mateo, the bull-of-a-man, clutched Skye in his arms and swung her around. Brochara, Elia, and Fin all tackled me to the deck and each one hugged a different limb. Nak stood there laughing just beside us, watching our welcoming.

"Welcome back friendssss!" Nak laughed. I missed his lisp.

Screeching echoed through the skies. "Placessss everybody!" Nak hissed.

My friends darted to form a circle around me as I sat there on the deck, looking confused. *Come On.* I thought, *we just all got back together again…*

I glanced to the clouds and saw a Harpy circling the ship. Immediately, I was reminded of Ekadenc's assault on me. "Why is that here?" I shouted.

"You have been branded!" They will continue to hunt you down and carry you off to Tartarus until they succeed!" Brochara exclaimed over his shoulder, while he, Elia, and Fin encircled me.

"Branded?" I shouted, through the Harpy's deafening screeches, "How?" But, I already knew the answer. That creepy thing inside her satchel. Ugh, I was so stupid.

The Harpy made its move! It swooped in and grazed the heads of some of the Viking crew sniffing me out. Another pass and it snatched up a Viking and carried him high into the sky. Realizing its mistake, the Harpy released its grip and the Viking plummeted towards the water. Jock immediately dove in and retrieved the frightened crewmember.

The horrifying creature hovered above the ship, and just like Ekadenc had, it took a deep sniff and honed in on my scent. The creature let out a horrible sound of death, and dove straight for me.

Elia and Brochara through an enchanted charm over me, Nak shot light from his eyes, the creature burst into flames, and fell to dust over me.

"Well done everyone. Now, quickly get below deck." Nak instructed.

I just looked at him in amazement. "You shot beams from your eyes."

He just laughed and quickly ushered me below deck.

Chapter 21

Illustrated by
Laura Korn

21

THE UNDERWORLD

Back inside the belly of the ship, we all took our places around the round table. The captain's quarters were left untouched since Ekadenc snatched me up and broke through the side of the ship. The hole had mended but evidence of a struggle remained; chairs knocked over, steins strewn about the room, and papers lying all about. Before us the table, laid the scrolled map of The Underworld still open and riddled with talon punctures. Instinctively, I rubbed my hand where the satchel-demon clawed me.

"So, how do I get rid of this branding?" I glanced around the table looking for someone with an answer, but everyone's eyes shifted off avoiding mine. No one replied, "Am I going to be chased by Harpies for the rest of my life?" Still, no one would make eye contact with me. I guess that gave me my answer. "Great." I sighed.

"You will just have to learn how to defend yourself, dear," Elia cooed and placed her hand on my lap. It was a technique she used all of my life to calm my nerves, just by placing her hand on me.

"Thanks Elia," I smiled warmly at her.

Just then, a rather large Viking burst through the door. "Ttensir! A mermaid!"

"A mermaid!" Ttensir echoed back as he quickly ran from the room to catch a glimpse.

Skye and I looked at each other with confusion and moved at the same time. We ran topside and found the Piscisene girl that Ryan saved, trapped under the ship's nets, frightened, and struggling to free herself. She lashed out at curious crewmembers who ventured in for a closer look, defending herself.

"Let her go!" I yelled, but the crew looked to Ttensir for orders. "Ttensir, I know her!"

"Release her," he barked to his crew. The superstitious crew flung the net off of the frightened girl and quickly backed away, as if she would rip their skin off. I nodded a thank you to Ttensir and ran to the girl.

As soon as she was free, the girl looked up at us, frantically, and then buried her face in my chest. The others made a move to protect me, but I raised my arm to stop them. "It's okay, you're safe." I whispered to her, "What's wrong?"

"Ryan, he found me and told me to swim to you as fast as I could." Skye immediately dropped to her knees next to us; riddled with anxiety.

"Is he alright?" she asked.

"Yes, but Nãga has taken your Sofia." The Piscisene girl seemed frantic, "The army and her are all gone. Something about a Typhoon?" The girl was breathless; she had traveled very far in a short amount of time to find me.

"Typhon." Nak said as he looked to the ship's deck, "She's gone to get Typhon." Everyone gasped and the ship's crew immediately performed a superstitious ritual, in unison, of brushing their hands down their bodies while turning in a circle once, and then spitting on the deck at the sound of his name in hopes to ward off his evil. My face twisted with wondered, anger, and sorrow.

The Piscisene girl, who satisfied with herself for completing the task at hand, stood up, and walked to the side of the ship. She turned back, looked to Skye, and a smile grew across her face, "He saved my brother," was all that she said before leaping back into the ocean. Skye threw her arms around herself, giving a hug, and smiling proudly.

"It issss time." Nak said in a commanding voice. "We musssst travel to Tartarussss!"

Ellida's dragonhead let out a battle war cry! The Viking crew sprang into action. Ttensir shouted out, "Set a course to Hell!" The Vikings hooted and hollered, boldly accepting the quest. The ship lunged forward with great speed, and fear for everyone's fate crept into my brain.

We sailed for a day and a half. No one really spoke, except for simple niceties. I was trying to mentally prepare for what we were about to embark upon, and I am certain, everyone else was thinking about it too. I have never heard of anyone sailing into the depths of Hell and returning to talk about it.

"How does one actually sail to Tartarus?" I asked Ttensir.

He explained how Ellida, the Viking Dragon ship, was a gift by Aegir, the Sea Giant of the North and it possessed certain powers. I already knew of the regenerating powers of the wood, but he told me about the navigational tool, that is never wrong. Wherever they need to sail, Ellida would get them there one way or another. "We are headed back to The Devil's Triangle by way of Bermuda!"

The ship's dragonhead roared once again, and I thought it was in response to Ttensir's proclamation, but I wrong, dead wrong. "To your posts!" Ttensir commanded the crew.

Thunderous storm clouds appeared on the horizon, like a giant wall of evil! The crew flew into action, but fear lay behind everyman's eyes. The water started to churn, turning blacker as we approached the storm. I looked to my friends: Khai, Skye, Brochara, Elia, Fin, Aluvanim, Luca, Mateo, Ttensir, Jock, and Nak. Together we made twelve; twelve individuals, fighting to hold all things Pure and Light. It was our fate to end this darkness, before darkness ended us.

"Thank you my friend's," I stood on a crate near the main mast, "I appreciate your allegiance, but I will understand if this is a fight you are not willing to enter! I fear that not all of us will return!"

The storm started to pick up, whipping small things through the air, even my backpack lifted from my shoulders. My hair whipped around in the gusts and slammed it back against my face stinging my eyes. "We are going into battle!" but saying those words aloud triggered my memory and I paused. The last half of Dissyca's prophecy echoed in my brain, *you will return never in war will you perish*. Does the comma get placed before or after the word 'never'? Did she mean to say, *You will return, never in war will you perish, or You will return never, in war you will perish?*

"Giovani!" Skye's voice snapped me out of my torment, "Are you alright?"

"YES!" I had to yell now over the howling winds. "If any of you wish to leave, I will not judge you!" A large crate careened through the air, just missing Luca's head!

322

A Viking crewmember burst past Nak, pushing him out of the way, before he jumped off the side of ship. Three more followed his lead, "COWARDS!" Ttensir yelled after them, "I will judge!"

"Anyone else?" I shouted as thunder clapped over our heads.

Starting with Skye, each one of my Adrastai friends joined in a circle, touching the friend next to them. Hands were held or shoulders were touched, but they were creating a circle of solidarity. When it came to my turn, my turn to complete the circle, I stretched out my hands and smiled at each friend, individually. We were about to go to Hell, not many have ever returned from there. I loved each one of these souls standing around me and no words were strong enough to convey that. As soon as my hands touched Luca's and Nak's shoulder, a brilliant column of light shot from the center of all of us warriors of Light! Powerful and confident, it stretched to through dreadful sky, illuminating through the darkness just in time to for us to see the Harpy headed straight for me, talons protruding!

I hit the deck. Nak pushed Luca out of the way. Mateo flew across the circle, blades swinging, and managed to hack the beast out of the sky. Luca leapt on top of the creature and plunged her sword through it all the way to the deck, pinning the Harpy to the boards. Mateo high-fived his twin, plucked the beast from wood, and tossed it off the front of the ship.

The dragon figurehead let out a horrifying roar. We all ran to the front of the ship and peered over the side. Our own screams of terror would never be matched again! The turbulent waters just fell out from under us, as if we had reached the end of the world; a sheer drop off! Our ship was free falling, and there were walls of water surrounding us on three sides! "DEVIL'S TRIANGLE!" Screamed Ttensir in a drawn out manner as we free fell down this watery prism.

We all grabbed on to whatever we could find to keep us from floating off of the ship. Other Vikings fell upward, sucked off and into the wall of the abyss! Again, Fin started to slip through my hands. I struggled to hold on; the force of our drop was so strong. "BROCHARA, HELP!" I telecommunicated, and just in time.

I lost my hold on Fin and he started to be sucked off the ship! Brochara held my leg with one arm, and caught him in a charm with the other. We all sighed in relief.

Our descent came to a crashing halt! Ellida's dragon tail cracked off upon impact, and she roared in pain. Four more Vikings careened into the water below and immediately their screams were silenced. We all tumbled to the deck, and quickly took a head count to make sure all twelve of us remained. We were all there.

It was strangely quiet, too quiet. No more storm. No screams. Just silence. We were moving slowly, but now we were gliding on a river.

Peering over the edge, the water was as black as a starless night. I looked up to the sky, but there wasn't one. Endless darkness reached up as high as I could see. The river was as wide as a twelve-lane highway. Little light grew out of the darkness periodically, which was reddish-orange hued, reminding me of embers from a dim fire. The glow was enough to silhouette the shoreline with its creepy, gnarled trees, void of any green. Everything looked charred and dead.

We sailed along in silence. I stayed close to Khai, constantly scanning the air for Harpies. "You don't have to worry about those now," Khai gently spoke inside my head, "You are already here."

Khai gestured, with a sweep of his majestic head, for me to look forward. Before us stood gigantic iron gates as tall at skyscrapers and as thick as them too! The iron gates were bridged with large iron banner and scrolled across it, written in fire, was the word "STYX".

We sailed under the foreboding iron entrance and as soon as we passed through, something shifted in the air. I glanced around at my friends to see if they noticed it too. Mateo, who loved his sister so much he always tried to protect her, was glaring at Luca with hatred. I could see the rage building behind his eyes. They quickly sparked red and he made a move towards her.

I threw my body in between them, knowing that there was no way I could stop him from going Berserk. Nak, too, slid in his path. "Mateo!" Luca screamed, "Stop!"

He muscled his way through, and picked up the tiny-framed girl. Immediately, she shifted into a white dove and flew up out of his grip, narrowly escaping his crushing toss.

"What are you doing?" Skye screamed at him.

"SHUT UP!" Mateo snarled back at her.

"Everyone stop! Just wait a minute." I quickly recalled what Ekadenc growled before she turned and snatched me up, "hate and destruction will come our way."

"What? Seriously Giovani, sometimes I think you are such a..." Skye started, but Elia threw one of her bark patches over her Skye's mouth before she could finish.

"Why you little!" Aluvanim darted towards Elia with her hands poised to release a harmful charm.

"STOP!" I screamed and it echoed off into the darkness, "Can't you see? Ekadenc told us this would happen. She told us the River Styx would bring hate and destruction our way! It is exactly what she said would happen, now knock it off; all of you! This behavior is accomplishing anything!" I shot a look at Skye, trying not to show her that she had hurt my feelings.

Everyone stopped fighting and apologized to each other. "We need to stay strong, together, if we are going to succeed." I added and walked off, alone. "Keep a level head," I added with my back turned as I walked into the blackness. I stood silently for a moment, listening to the sounds of wood vines creaking over each other and a wry smile grew on my face knowing the Ellida was regenerating.

Suddenly, out of the darkness ahead of us, grew the most beautifully angelic voice. A lullaby of old was carried on the wind of angel's wings. I found myself closing my eyes and getting lost in the melody; swaying from side to side, like a mother cradling her sleeping child. I found myself singing the song. I knew the song! "Sofia!"

Ellida crashed onto a shore, unexpectedly. We tumbled around like fallen bowling pins. Sofia's singing stopped. Regaining our footing, we deployed the gangplank and exited the ship. The first step onto this cursed land was daunting. The ground was more of swampland than dirt. Our feet sank down into muck with every step. The Vikings, all except Ttensir, stayed on the ship refusing to go any farther and performed the same superstitious ritual as earlier to ward off evil. We watched as they slowly backed away from the edge disappearing into the dark.

The twelve of us slowly turned around. A disturbing forest stretched out in front of us, filled with more dead trees. Just like forest around Sukanar's lair, dark silhouettes darted through the shadows. "Stay close," I whispered.

With everyone's senses on high alert, we entered the dark forest. Upon our first steps, shadows scurried in front of us. An eerie howl traveled on the wind. Then strange shapes moved along both sides of the group in the shadows. We all turned around in every direction trying to defend ourselves, but no one could find what was out there, lingering in the obscurity. Again, something darted, but this time directly through the group.

Another streak of darkness shot through us from the opposite direction followed by another; they were toying with us. Then a shadow figure, black as tar stopped abruptly in front of Nak. It appeared to take a deep breathe, inhaling his essence. Nak swatted at it with his tail, but it only sliced through the smoke-like figure. The shadow figure shot up to the top of the trees and we watched it jump from limb to limb into the darkness.

"What was that?" Luca's small voice shined in the darkness.

"I am pretty sure Mother ssssent it," Nak hissed, "Look!" he pointed the tip of his tail towards a path through the marshy grounds. Trees bent off to both sides, broken and ripped from the ground, as if something large passed through. "Nāga."

We all picked up our pace, and sloshed through the forest with a purpose. A horrifying roar boomed through the air, stopping us all dead in our tracks, and sending chills down our spines followed by screams from a small child ringing through the skies.

"Sofia!" I yelled and I took off in front of the pack to save her!

Nak was much faster on his belly through the muck, and slid into my path tripping up my efforts! "Nak! I have to save her!"

"Not by yoursssself! We ssssstay together or die!" Nak hissed with angry eyes. The roars and screams continued and they did not sound far away.

"Then get everyone else and let's go!" I barked back. "She is my family!"

"Sssso are we!" He shot back at me. He was right, they were my family too, and we needed to do this together.

The soft angelic voice began singing again, but this time they sounded afraid. The roars quieted to muffled mumbles, and then the distinct sounds of something extraordinarily large snoring.

"Hekatonkheiressss." Nak whispered, "Ugh, I should have

known. That issss why she needed Ssssofia! Come on, but move silently."

"Heka-what?" I asked worried about the explanation.

"The guards of Tartarus," Luca answered, but with much dismay in her voice. "Have you not heard of them?"

I shook my head no, but answered, "I always heard there were giants with one hundred arms and fifty heads each," I half laughed thinking that my explanation was way off, but again, Dissyca's prophecy echoed inside my brain, *Golden Fruit shall quench your thirst and GIANT tasks are required...* "Wait? Is that what they're called?"

Luca shook her head yes. My sister was with them. "Why Sofia?" I asked.

"She issss a Ssssiren, issss she not?" Nak asked.

"Yes. Nãga needed her to lull the Giants, of course. Then she could pass into Tartarus and to your parents! UGH! Why did I not see that coming?"

"Because we are a team, and you require the help of others. That is what makes this work." Skye said as she pointed to all of us. "Combined, we have the strength to accomplish greatness!"

I was in awe by her wisdom and Mateo was too. He was staring at her with stars in his eyes. We moved forward with our confidence leading the way. Had we moved any faster, we would have marched right into the mammoth toe that jutted out before us!

I don't think that any of us were prepared for the size of these guardians of Hell. We found ourselves face-to-foot with a sleeping giant. The foot stretched three stories high; it was disgusting all full of cracks, calluses, and cuts. The foot was attached to a thick, hairy, meaty leg. We walked the entire length of the leg, which was as tall as the maple tree in our yard. It was when we reached the

Hekatonkheire's arm that I wanted to scream.

Clutched in his meaty paw was Sofia. Her body was slumped over the giant's pointer finger, faced down, and her arms outstretched and limp hanging beside her head. Her long brown hair lay across the back of its hand, only reaching the middle finger. She looked like marionette puppet, whose strings had been cut. I needed to know if she was alive. Did he crush her? I was about to climb up his shirt, when Mateo grabbed my shoulder and pointed towards my sister.

He whispered in my ear, "She's alive-ah, look at-ah her hands-ah."

He was right! Her hand was moving! I whistled a tune that I knew she would recognize. We made up birdcalls one year camping, and she giggled so hard all night, we got in trouble with Mom and Dad. I whistled my call.

Sofia lifted her head and looked around. I jumped up and down waving my arms! She looked directly at me and amazement lit up her eyes. She was wriggling her way out of his fingers to run to me, but the monster started to stir. We all motioned for her stop moving, but the giant's steady snoring stopped.

Sofia immediately began singing, the same lullaby that I heard earlier and he drifted back off to sleep.

"How are we going to get her?" Frustrated, I accidentally kicked my leg out, connecting with the Hekatonkheire's thigh.

A tremendous roar shook the very ground, followed by two more. Swiftly, three Hekatonkheires stood up, dwarfing our group to the size of rodents. They all roared at once, and the force of their sound waves sent all of us tumbling over ourselves in the muck. Regaining my balance, I looked at the beasts. They stood before the gates of Tartarus! Enormous pillars of jagged rock and metal that were blazing with over-sized flames.

Sofia sang frantically, but it wasn't working. The giant stuffed her into his shirt pocket that had to be the size of a king-sized mattress. I only saw two ginormous arms on each giant, not one-hundred. "Hey," I said encouraging the others, "Two arms, we can do this."

Just then, five more arms on each side stretched out from behind the first. "Okay," I half giggled sarcastically, "still not one hundred."

The giant with Sofia in his pocket, punched down towards us. One disadvantage to him was his height. We were able to anticipate the rate at which his fist slammed down, and we jumped out of his way.

The only problem was he had two more brothers. Chaos ensued. The gates to Tartarus flamed before us, and all we had to do was get past the giants and save my sister while trying.

I jumped on Khai's back, and Luca shifted to a giant white eagle. Fin climbed on top of her back, and four of us took to the air. Giant arms were flailing in every direction. Luca and Fin tumbled through the air and then they were slammed back in the opposite direction by another thrashing arm.

The giants stomped at the ground, trying to step on the remaining Adrastai. I managed to sink Servo into the calf of one of them, dropping him to his knee with the force of an earthquake. Every advance we made was met with thunderous blows.

Then, above all the roaring and screams, a shrieking voice I had heard many times before, stopping all movement abruptly.

Sofia had climbed to the top of the pocket and screamed. Even the Hekatonkheires were stunned by sound. All eyes turned to her.

Mateo took this silent opportunity to try to sneak past the giants, but another hand came out of nowhere and pinned him to the ground.

"ENOUGH!" screamed the eight-year old. "Sit Down!" she demanded.

Immediately, all three Hekatonkheires sat down, following her command, like a dog to his master. The rest of us stumbled around as the earth shook under their weight. I scratched my head, wondering how she was able to calm them, if she wasn't singing.

"You listen to me!" she wagged her finger at the face of her captor. "Why are you being nasty?" Sofia's voice was strict and unyielding. The giant cringed with every sharp syllable, like a child being scolded by a parent.

"No one pass." The booming voice made the dead tree limbs of the gnarled forest tremble.

"Why?" asked Sofia firmly? "Why can't they pass?"

"Bad, bad things kept in there," he answered, "Must stay in there!" The giant was gaining confidence and appeared to grow annoyed with the questioning. His two brothers nodded in agreement behind him.

"We don't want to let anything out!" I yelled from my harness on Khai's back. "A very bad serpent snuck in to release your evil prisoners! We must stop her!"

One Hekatonkheire with flaming-red hair, swatted at Khai and I, like a menacing bug. "Don't you touch him!" scorned Sofia.

The giant immediately pulled all twelve arms back into one extremely large pair, as if he was afraid of her scolding.

"Thank you," she politely responded folding her arms across her chest and nodding her head satisfied.

The over-sized simpletons were responding to Sofia, like children. I tried to urge her to keep going while we crept closer to the entrance. She was enjoying this; I could tell by the smug smile on her face. She was acting, like it was one of her famous plays, and she had the perfect supporting actors. She looked right at me and winked!

The gateway into Tartarus was only ten feet away; all we had to do was run. A twinge of disrespect for another creature crept into my soul, and I did not like the way it made me feel. I didn't even have to communicate to Khai, he already knew, "I know Giovani, I know."

Just as the others were about to cross the line, deceptively, I shouted, "Wait!" The giants turned their focus from Sofia and looked towards the gates. Each one of them slammed their fists into the ground, creating another earthquake and knocking our friends over.

Fury rushed across the face of each Hekatonkheire. Their gigantic arms split into fifty on each side, and many sets of eyes appeared all over their enormous heads! I saw the look on Sofia's face change to from smug to fear. We would be smashed to pieces!

"Listen, friends," I addressed the three brother, "We wish not to fight you! The High Mages of The Order of St. John have sent us on this quest. We must stop Nāga from releasing her father, Typhon. He will destroy the world as we know it."

Three hundred flailing arms quieted immediately and the sound of the word Typhon. The brothers gasped! The force of their combined inhales pulled Khai and Luca dangerously close to the giant open mouths. Both creatures fought against the forceful draw to stay in flight.

"TYPHON!" Yelled the brother with flaming-red hair!

"Nãga is already in there!" I yelled as I pointed through the gates, "She tricked all of you! She used a Siren to lull you all to sleep and snuck her army inside to release the monster!" I spoke nothing but the truth, and in giving respect where it was due, we gained their trust. We didn't have a need to quarrel; we could work together for the greater good.

Suddenly, the brothers plunked themselves down to sitting and their mammoth shoulders slumped forward in defeat. The giants, who were not holding Sofia, extended their pointer finger, like inviting a bird to land upon it. Both Khai and Luca accepted the invitation and nodded a thank you.

My heart smiled, and I continued, "Nãga used my sister, Sofia" I pointed to her, giving her a name. The ferocious giant, who held her in his clutch, drew her to his cheek and nuzzled my little sister, whispering her name, "I am Briareos." Sofia giggled as his whiskers tickled her.

"You do not need to feel defeated. Nãga is pure evil. She tricked you with the help of her monster parents beyond those gates!" I continued, "Let us pass and we will stop the beasts!"

The Hekatonkheires redirected their emotions back to anger. The brother with the flaming-red hair quickly added, "You must pass. Go and bring the intruder to me!" His voice boomed through the land.

"She is a sea serpent! The color of the middle-world's sky and silver combined." I don't know what made me think that they would understand this, but there wasn't any blue sky here. "Can you notify us if you see her?"

"Gyes will go with you. We will not be duped again! If you are lying, he will smash you all. If you are honest; then his strength will be a welcomed addition." The blonde-haired giant, whose name was

Gyes, stood and accepted his mission.

Then the flaming red-hair giant bowed his head to Khai and me, and said, "I am Kottos."

"I am Giovani, this is Khai, and we are all Adrastai!" Something lifted inside of me. My conscious was cleared, we told the truth instead of tricking the Giants, and the truth prevailed.

Kottos continued, "Not all of you shall pass. Only two Adrastai per brother may enter with permission. You must pick the six that will continue on your quest." Kottos looked down at the rest of my friends, squinted at Brochara, Elia, and Aluvanim and continued, "No elves allowed, tricky creatures they are."

Brochara took offense to that statement and was about to protest, when Elia threw one of her bark patches over his mouth. His shoulders slumped forward in defeat, and the giants laughed.

"Only six? We need all of us; we are meant to work together," my voice shook. *How were we going to do this with only half of us?*

"Rules are rules, and they are created to serve a purpose," every single one of Kottos' one-hundred eyes glared at me. "Question me again, and we shall send you all flying back to whence you came! Only six and no elves! The rest will stay with us to be destroyed if you are lying!"

"Only six," I repeated as Khai and I glided down to ground followed by Fin and Luca, who shifted back into her human form. That made our decision on who shall enter, slightly easier; no Aluvanim, Brochara or Elia. That brought us to nine Adrastai to choose from, but every remaining friend demanded on going further. Unexpectedly, the ground shook so violently, that the giants themselves stumbled.

"TYPHON!" Gyes yelled as all of his arms unfolded! "Hurry,

we must go now!

I grabbed Skye's hand, and she grabbed Mateo. Nak and Luca stepped forward. Khai, grabbed my backpack in his jaws, just like the first time we met at the river in The Enchanted Valley, and he flipped me up onto his back. I turned to my friend's that were ordered to stay behind, and smiled hoping to see them again.

Gyes and the six of us, quietly and cautiously, passed through the gates of Hell.

Chapter 22

Illustrated by
Tiffani Woods

22

SACRIFICE

As soon as we past under the gates, an overwhelming sense of despair filled my heart. The Underworld has never been described as a happy place, but I wasn't prepared for the immediate and heavy feelings of sorrow, pain, and hatred. Ghostly mists flew past moaning and crying; Gyes swatted at them like annoying bugs. It was a horrifying place of death and despair; exactly what I had pictured it to be.

Screams from tortured souls were a constant sound, as frequent as birdsong back home, but twisted in misery. Flames continuously burned casting an ominous red glow all around. Burning hot embers rained from an endless black sky and lava oozed from cracks in the ground. The foul stench of death and decay filled the stagnant air tainting my nostrils so that I tasted it with every inhale. Charred arms of wicked souls reached out of the shadows, grabbing at our ankles as we walked by; Luca flinched and hugged her brother's arm for protection.

"Sssstay the coursssse!" Nak yelled detecting the angst among our friends. "They cannot take from you what you do not allow them too!"

Black unrecognizable creatures slithered across the ground. Khai and Gyes stomped on a few of them, but they just burst into a black cloud, reforming a few feet away. One ghostly ghoul wrapped around Luca's waist and slithered up her torso, creeping under her white-blond hair. Mateo tried to grab at it, but it struck out at him, inflicting a dark bite on his forearm. Nak quickly slid over and pulled the demon from Luca's tangled tresses.

"Just go!" Mateo growled as Nak tried to address his wound.

More shadow figures, like the ones we encountered in the forest, darted in between the members of our group. Their touch felt like ice in this place of heat and flames. They were more attracted to Nak, Luca, and I over the others seemingly looking for something in their actions. Khai snapped at them with his jaws, but this place is full of the dead. How were we going to defend ourselves against something we couldn't kill?

A sinister laugh grew from the shadows and echoed in the darkness. Everyone was immediately uneasy upon hearing it. The laughter suddenly came from behind us, quickly it moved to the shadows on our left, and then again from the front of the group. We were turning around in circles unsure of how to defend ourselves, but Nak calmly stood strong. It was the sound of pure evil, full of hate, poison to any heart.

"Hello, Mother," Nak simply spoke staring off into the shadows in front of us. *Mother?*

A giant form began to take shape in the darkness before us as Nak's mother, Echidna, slowly emerged, pompous and full of arrogance. Her half-woman, half-snake form towered over most of us, standing as tall as Khai.

"Mother is such an endearing title for one who would rather kill you!" The creature lunged forward towards Nak, who stood tall and did not flinch. Startled, the rest of us jumped.

I shook my head in amazement; she was absolutely stunning and horrifying at the same time; beautiful even. Echidna had the face and torso of a giant supermodel, which swayed and rested on top of an enormous snake's lower half. Her long golden hair billowed in front of her chest glistening in the soft glow of the flames, but upon closer inspection it was entangled with serpents. Her beauty entranced me, but the feeling was short-lived.

Echidna quickly unfurled enormous wings and lifted her oversized serpent body from the ground, hovering, and glaring down at Nak; upset over not intimidating her son. Nak held his ground staring blankly back at the beast. The Oracle, Dissyca, inherited her mother's wings as they majestically reflected the glow of the fire, causing us to shield our eyes.

"Tisk, tisk, where are my manners? A surprise family reunion and me without any snacks!" Without warning, the creature struck out at Skye. Khai quickly flicked his dragon tail and knocked Echidna out of the air. She rolled across the charred ground, up-righted herself, and cackled a sinister laugh.

"I shall enjoy the taste of dragon tonight!" A demonic voice grew from her throat as she snapped in our direction.

Nak's eyes abruptly changed and the same powerful light that killed the Harpy on the ship, shot like lasers from them hitting his Mother's wing instantly burning a hole through it. She roared in pain and whipped her tail, cracking Nak in the back. Screams of agony were muffled by the ground as Nak fell forward into the ash. A cruel smile grew across Echidna's face and she lashed out again, crushing the tip of Nak's tail; the twisted, evil Mother enjoyed inflicting pain upon her son.

Servo leapt into my hands, the distinctive sound of metal sliding through the sheath echoed in the darkness and determination filled my body. I ran to end the beast, but unexpectedly the ground shook ferociously. Everyone was stumbling knocked from his or her feet, including Echidna, who immediately tried to fly but her wounded wing sent her crashing to the ground. She rolled from side-to-side, creating a cloud of ash, and laughing manically, "You are too late! Daddy and I shall destroy you and everything you have every loved!"

A horrifying sound rang out of the darkness; the sound of one thousand deathly screams that sent shivers down my spine and filled me with terror. Then, like a candle at the end of a long dark tunnel, a light grew from the darkness. Everyone focused on the dim light that quickly grew brighter. Suddenly, a stream of fire over two stories tall shot through the air above us, knocking everyone to the ash.

Echidna rolled on the ground, giggling psychotically, enjoying what was transpiring. It was happening. Nãga was freeing Typhon!

Gyes quickly scooped all of us up in his meaty hands, jumped to his, stomped on Echidna's tail with his giant foot, and took off running into the darkness where the fireball came from. Echidna howled in pain and struck out at his heel with her venomous fangs.

Gyes stumbled, but continued to run forward into the pit of darkness; each giant step longer than a city block. Another fiery flame shot past his face, burning his right shoulder. Gyes tilted his cheek to his shoulder, extinguishing the fire and growled, "You will not escape!"

Suddenly Gyes momentum came to a skidding halt as rock rubble sprayed onto the scene before us, like a skier on fresh snow. A horrifying sight grew out of the darkness. Nãga and her army of Piscisene children were at the base of Mt. Etna, some of them careened into the black abyss that surrounded the volcano as the rocks pushed them over the edge.

Nãga and her entranced soldiers tirelessly worked an enormous trident, fit for Poseidon that was wedged under the volcano's edge. They were prying Mt. Etna off Typhon and they were succeeding! The volcano tilted off its base and one of Typhon's grotesque serpent arms with a handful of vipers as fingers was growing out from under it. Each snake digit was as large as Nãga, gripped the base, and lifting the mountain off his terrifying frame.

Gyes growled a horrify sound, threw us to ground, and jumped on top of the volcano to force it back down! Typhon screamed in pain and spit lava up through the mouth of the volcano! Our giant friend roared in agony as the molten rock spewed in his face. He held strong, jumping up and down, attempting to force the volcano back down.

"NO!" Nãga growled! She spit fire towards Gyes, catching his leg.

We needed to do something. Gyes would surely be dead if we just stood watching. All of us sprang into action. Mateo, Luca, and Skye took to the Piscisene, knocking each one of them from the enchanted trident that was prying the mountain off the demon. An epic battle ensued. Flashes of silver and molten lava streaked the air.

Khai, Nak, and I focused on Naga! "I WILL KILL YOU!" Nak screamed as he slithered over to his twin and opened his cobra jaws. He bit down on Nãga's neck. The sound of crushing bone and agonizing pain filled our ears.

Nãga swiped her tail and struck a blow to the back of Nak's hood. He rolled down the side of the volcano, and one of Typhon's viper digits caught Nak in its venomous jaws. Nak's eyes grew larger than I had ever seen them, and then quickly shut. His body went limp, the snake finger released its grip, and my brother rolled off the mountain into the darkness. Nãga's sinister laughter echoed inside my skull.

"NO!" I cried. "NAK! NAK ANSWER ME!" Everything was moving in slow motion around me as I tried to rush to Nak's side. Tears were streaming down my cheek as my brother disappeared from my sight, and his twin sister cackled from behind me, and mimicking my pleas, like a bratty schoolchild.

Rage filled my heart! Evil will not win! "By the power of the High Mages, I WILL END THIS!" I cried.

My dragon partner inhaled deeply and, instinctively, we banked left and shot a stream of fire right into Nãga's side. She roared in pain and returned the deadly fire. My shield leapt from my pocket and opened, in a spiral manner in front of Khai's body, deflecting her fire breath.

I watched fear grow behind Nãga's eyes at our defense tactics, and I took pleasure in it! Hatred was consuming me. I felt my heart harden, and I wanted to inflict nothing but pain and torture upon her.

A large object flew past us, narrowly knocking us from flight. The enchanted trident coursed through the air, bounced of a jagged rock wall, and plummeted into the pit of despair. The sound of metal bouncing of rock echoed, as it descended into the abyss accompanied with cheers from my friends.

"NOOOOOO!" Nãga growled again, and snapped at her own army, ripping many of them in half and spitting them into the gaping darkness. She was losing her fight. With the trident removed, Gyes shoved Mt. Etna back down, pinning the Father of All Monsters beneath it, again slicing off two of the viper digits. Gyes leapt from the volcano and tumbled across the ground, injured and exhausted.

The battle continued between the Piscisene army and my friends. I turned my sights back to Nãga. She was losing her twisted sanity, and I was enjoying it. She has cause pain and tortured to so many

342

families; watching her writhe in pain and defeat made me smile. A sudden fissure burst open the side of the volcano she clung to, oozing lava in her direction, and sending Nãga sliding down the mountainside. She leapt off just in time, catching the cliff at the edge of the bottomless pit of despair. Nãga grabbed more Piscisene tossing them into the abyss to satisfy her father's rage, as she struggled to clamber onto solid ground.

"You have failed me!" Typhon growled from the pit of darkness, the sound of his voice shook the ground and filled me with hatred. Lava exploded into the air like fireworks. My senses tingled and my focus drawn to the depths of the abyss. The glow from the eruptions cast off light, illuminating the grim scene at the mouth of the pit of despair. Piscisene warriors, children, lay lifeless scattered among the rock ledges that flanked the mouth. Through our bond, Khai saw what I saw and sighed at the horror. A flash of bronze caught my eye, "NAK!" He was there! Nak was clinging to life, on the side of the very volcano that imprisoned his father in Tartarus.

Something happened inside of me. I looked at Nãga, who had successfully pulled herself onto solid ground, and was laughing. "I don't need you!" She cackled into the pit! "You needed me! Well, look who is walking away, and who is still pinned under a rock, and I failed you?" Her maniacal laughter grew stronger! She became completely unhinged, and blew fire in a circle all around her; burning everything in its path. I no longer hated her; I pitied her.

Piscisenes scattered into the darkness, some with their skin flaming. I cringed at the thought of the pain. Instinctively, Khai shot another fiery blow at the evil serpent. She howled in agony, and fell on her side. When the flames dimmed, a small figure stood directly in front of the failing Nãga. One shining, silvery Piscisene boy with dark hair and silver eyes silently stood before the wounded beast. His arm extended presenting something and in his hand…a Golden Apple.

"RYAN, NO!" Skye screamed and it echoed through the eerie silence.

Nãga opened her fiery-colored eye and spied the Golden Fruit. A sinister voice gurgled from her throat, "That's a good boy," she cackled again. "Bring it to Momma!"

Ryan looked at Skye and sent a message of sorrow to his sister with just his eyes. The beast would surely snap her jaws down upon him as he delivered the Golden Apple to the unsuspecting beast.

I had forgotten that no one besides Nak and Elia knew that the Golden Apple was a decoy full of poison. Everyone else thought it would give Nãga immortality. Ryan slowly walked closer to the beast. Nãga was struggling to inch herself towards him, dragging her charred corpse across the ash.

"Grab Him!" I screamed, and Khai took off like a shot!

We swooped down, and grabbed Ryan by the shoulders in Khai's talons. Skye screamed in disgust, thinking that we would toss her brother into the abyss. She lunged to stop us. Nãga spit fire at the advancing commotion and Skye! Mateo jumped in front of her, and the flames consumed him. Luca's screams of horror filled my ears.

"NOW!" I screamed and Ryan released the Golden Apple into Nãga's open jaws. She spit fire in our directions and we tumbled, out of control, through the darkness.

Khai dropped Ryan, but he rolled onto solid ground. Skye ran to his side. He was writhing in pain, grabbing his leg.

Luca watched in horror and Mateo burned before her. Gyes suddenly conscious again, threw his giant hand over Mateo, smothering the fire.

Revived, Nãga sprang to her feet and let out a tremendous

victory roar. An evil grin grew across her scorched face. She opened her mouth and began to laugh once more, but her expression changed drastically as the poison quickly ravaged her body. She drew in a deep breath, and everyone around ducked to avoid her fiery spew, when instead of burning everyone around her, the powerful Nãga exploded raining charred remnants of beast into the abyss.

Typhon roared with laughter from under Mt. Etna, and the ground shook like an earthquake. Lava shot out of the mouth of the volcano as he belly laughed out of control at the demise of his daughter. Gyes, once again, grabbed my friends and Ryan and took off running towards the gates.

I tapped Khai's shoulder. "I can't leave him!"

"I know! Where is he?" Khai's voice boomed into my head. We searched frantically, but could see him anywhere. Typhon continued his raging laughter and molten display. It was too dangerous for us to stay in the air; lava was flying everywhere.

Then I closed my eyes and willed myself to him, just as Laurina had told me to do before. The familiar feeling of my essence leaving my physical body took over me, and then, once again, I found myself on a charred mountainside only this time, Nak lay lifeless before me. I knelt down beside him on the edge of Mt. Etna, and held him in my golden arms. My heart filled with sorrow and my essence shined through the darkness.

"I WILL END YOU!" growled Typhon from the depths of Tartarus, and the volcano shook, violently.

The trembling ground sent Nak and I sliding, careening towards the depths of despair. There wasn't anything to stop our descent! I tried to hold on; jagged rocks ripping through my golden fingertips. I couldn't leave him here, not in a place so full of hatred. Nak was a creature of Light. Nak fought for everything Good in our worlds.

Nak was my brother!

With a heavy heart and a swirling mind, we slipped off the edge. The weight of his body was too much for my essence form, and he fell out of my arms.

"NOOOOO!" I screamed as I watched him fall faster into the pit of despair.

Typhon bellowed, and molten rock shot everywhere! One large droplet shot through my left shoulder and the pain was immense, blurring my consciousness. Then, like a beacon in the night, Khai rose out of the depths, catching me. I rolled onto the harness and blacked out. Typhon's roars were the last thing I heard.

When I opened my eyes, Khai gently glided to the ground for a soft landing. We were just inside the gates of Tartarus. I saw concern on the faces of our friends on the other side, held by Hekatonkheire rules, and unable to get to the six of us to help. I felt my body re-inflate, and I slid down Khai's side.

To my surprise, Nak was lying on the ground at Khai's feet. He had caught him, "Thank you friend." I managed to sigh.

Khai nodded majestically. I was in awe of his never-ending commitment.

Gyes was sitting on the charred earth with his back against the gates of Tartarus, cradling a badly burned Mateo, with a sobbing Luca sitting on his knee. The giant just nodded his head in a no-like fashion, looking dismal.

Ryan's head was in Skye's lap, and she too, was crying as she tangled her fingers in his dark hair.

I felt immense sadness. We had been successful, but we all had lost so much. Suddenly, all of the hairs on the back of my neck stood straight up. Immediately, I reeled around and stood tall, just as Nak had instructed me to do before.

"Show Yourself!" I growled.

Echidna cackled as she dramatically slid out of the darkness. Khai growled and snarled at her. She stared him down and his efforts silenced by an evil charm she cast with her eyes.

"You didn't think it was going to be that easy did you?" The Mother of All Monsters chortled.

"We succeeded with our quest," I answered. "We are not here for you, hag."

I felt Nak's hatred for his mother inside of me. She slithered closer and towered over me. "Well, well, do you wish for a metal or a chest to pin it on?" Sarcasm filled her voice, "Silly little boy, I am here for you!" she hissed. "You have killed my daughter, doomed the fate of my husband, and foiled our plans. There is no way in Tartarus you will escape me this time!"

Something grew inside of me, but it wasn't anger; it was more pity. Luca jumped from Gyes arm and landed beside me. Her bright white skin glowed more than ever. She grabbed my hand, and at the union of our skin, Pureness filled my heart. Suddenly, beams of light shot from both of our eyes hitting Echidna squarely in the chest! Injured and wounded by love, the beast recoiled in fear, and slithered off into the darkness.

"What was that?" Skye asked.

"Dearesssst love," answered a weak Nak. Luca and I ran to his side. "Ssshhh, my lovessss. I will be alright." Nak looked up at Khai and me and whispered, "Thank you, now let's go home."

Gyes let out a horrible cry, like a toddler having a tantrum, and it started raining huge Hekatonkheire tears from one-hundred eyes.

Luca gasped! She immediately transformed back into a white dove and flew up to Gyes hand, fearing Mateo's death. She peered over the side of his thumb, a girl once more, and relieved, she gave us a thumb's up.

"What is wrong, friend?" I called up to Gyes, avoided huge falling tears.

"One mortal soul must stay!" he blurted out. "That is part of the deal…one must sacrifice themselves to save the others." Geyes was sobbing uncontrollably now, "A mortal stays behind to free the rest; destined to be trapped in Tartarus forever." The giant sobbed even harder. "I am so sorry!" and he immediately walked through the entrance still cupping Luca and Mateo in his hands.

An invisible barrier stuck to his giant form and, bounced back into place as the three of them passed through. Luca had leapt from Gyes giant hand and was pounding on the invisible barrier, trying to get back inside. We all stood silent, with our mouths gaped open, and looking around at each other, horrified. Skye, Ryan, Nak, Khai, and I remained. The answer came to me, like a message from above, or from the knowledge of an ancient Elven High Mage.

"I will stay," I calmly stated and peacefulness washed over me. Cries of turmoil and disagreement rang out from my friends, but I just knew that it had to be me.

"No, it's not fair!" Skye screamed. "They should have told us that in the beginning!" She threw her arms around me holding on with all of her might, "There has to be something that we can do? We just need to think…you know, work together." Tears of frustration were streaming down her face.

"If you had known that one of us must stay behind, would it have changed your mind about entering?" I asked her, to which she shook her no. "Trust me," I winked at her and then repeated, "I will stay, and it must be so."

Luca screamed in terror from the other side, and she flew up to peer inside Gyes hand at her brother. Confused and upset, myself, Skye and Ryan picked up Nak and we carried him to the entrance. Brochara and Elia stared at us through the barrier, and concern was written all over their expressions. I laid Nak down and hugged my dear friend. He smiled with his eyes closed, too weak to look upon me. Skye and Ryan pulled him through the gates as the invisible barrier stuck to the group and sprung back into place.

My dearest friend, Khai, sat back on his haunches, turned his gaze away from mine, and refused to go. I walked over to him and he bit down on his lip, which was quivering fighting back his fear and concerns. "I will not leave you." He stated, defiantly, still unable to look me in the eye.

I threw my arms around his neck and snuggled my dear friend, not wanting to let him go either. I secretly hoped that my plan would work, but I could not be certain; I was acting on a hunch. "I love you, brother." I wept as I pressed my face into his shoulder, praying that I would see him again. He nuzzled my shoulder, as he had many times before, and held me tight against his chest with snout producing the best dragon hug.

"I am honored to be your brother," Khai whimpered, "but I am still not leaving. Whatever must be done, it will be done together."

"You know this is the only way. They need you. I need you to help them. Now GO!" I shouted, "Leave me!"

Khai still refused to go, stubbornly sitting back on his hind legs; he would not budge. He was shaking his head from side-to-side, still refusing to leave me and tears pooled in his eyes.

"It has to be this way; rules are created for a reason." My hand trembled as I placed it on his shoulder, "We will ride again. You must go help the others."

"I will not." Khai simply stated, without making eye contact.

"LEAVE ME NOW, I COMMAND YOU!" I screamed through my tears. An Adrastai's dragon must always obey his rider. Khai roared out in protest, and he sunk his claws into the ground to stop the invisible force, which was dragging him to the gates of Tartarus.

"NOOOOO!!!!!" Screamed my dragon and I felt our bond being stretched thin as he was forced through the gates of hell.

Emotionally and physically exhausted, I fell to my knees and lifted my eyes to glance at my family on the other side. Everyone was hugging each other and weeping. Sofia ran to entrance and pressed her hands against the invisible barrier, and Skye cradled her in her arms. My heart sank to see such sorrow. Instantly, I watched their expressions turn to fear.

"Tisk, tisk. A brave silly boy offers himself as a sacrifice. How sickening sweet! Now I will end you," Echidna barked from behind me. "I have the rest of eternity to cause you pain and torture. And I shall gladly enjoy it." She tossed her beautiful head back and laughter boomed out of her. Echidna continued in a sarcastic tone, "Today must be my birthday, because this is quite a gift you have given me." With a quick swipe of her serpent tail, my feet were knocked from under me without any time to react. I fell to the ground; bashing the side of my head onto a rock. Pain coursed through my skull.

"A gift I have, but not for you, hag!" I replied smugly as I pulled the half of an orange from my backpack, and brought myself to sit against the rock.

Echidna roared with laughter. "An orange? Really? Do you plan on squirting it in my eye?" she mockingly retorted, swiping her tail again. This time I ducked and caught myself before my head crashed to the charred ground.

"No, I simply plan on eating it," I arrogantly proclaimed. I proceeded to pull out a bandana from my backpack and spread it across my lap as a napkin; casting a mocking look in her direction.

"What are you getting at, fool?" she asked. "Your mind games do not bother me! Go ahead; eat your orange. I have an eternity to torture your mortal soul!" she growled as her excitement bubbled up with the tone of her voice. The ground began quiver and shake. Echidna's grin grew larger with pleasure. Then she yelled over her shoulder into the darkness behind her, "Yes Dear, I have a present for you!" in a sadistic evil song.

An explosion shook the ground so violently that Echidna herself stumbled over but not without laughter. "Oh, he likes that." She looked squarely at me and growled raising her eyebrows. "You foiled our plan, and now, we have an eternity to punish you for it!"

Immediately, large fissures began to split apart the ground that I sat on, and molten lava, formed enchanted hands of death, and started to seep up towards me. Stunned, I shoved myself backwards to avoid being burned, when the orange fell from my grasp. Like a child's spinning top, the fruit teetered at the edge of the fissure, poised dangerously close to falling into the abyss. I held my breath, hoping somehow to keep the fruit from falling into the lava. Echidna's menacing laughter echoed from all around me.

Typhon roared. The ground shook ferociously, sending Echidna retreating into the shadows. Lava shot ten feet into the air from the growing cracks in the earth. The Golden Fruit ejected from the force of the eruption, arching fifteen feet above me. My eyes followed the semi-sphere's trajectory as it flew through the darkness.

Instinctively, I shoulder-rolled in the same direction. Servo flew into my hands. Echidna also made her move; her once pretty smile replaced with a terrifying mouth full of fangs gaped wide open, to intercept the flying fruit. With the skill of a Samurai swordsman, I sliced through the air, piercing the fruit just before Echidna bit down into nothing. Her disgusting chin, split open by the tip of my cool steel blade. She howled in pain, as she rolled across a small island of rock and tumbled over the edge. Typhon grew fiercer.

Jagged, charred rocks fell from above, narrowly missing me. More fissures snaked their way through the blacken earth heading right for me, with the pinpoint. The ground split apart, like the dried mud from a puddle. Sheer drops into a fiery abyss below surrounded me, with rivers of molten lava spurting out of the severed earth.

I glanced to the Gates of Tartarus. My helpless family watched in terror. The ground continued to shake. Islands crumbled like sandcastles and I stumbled to edge. Servo knocked from my grasp and slid to the edge, teetering on the brink. The memory of hanging upside down in the snare on the outskirts of Sukanar's lair sprang into my mind. I had named my sword that day, by calling out it aloud. It flew to my hands. "SERVO!" I screamed just as it slipped off into the molten crevice.

The orange and red glow reflected off the cool steel blade as it coursed up into the sky, through the darkness, and into my hands. The rotation of its path caused the Golden Fruit to slide off the blade and into the air. I reached out to stop it from falling, just as I had the love-filled tear that dropped from Aunt Evangeline's cheek carrying the memory of the boy I used to be. My brief life played before me in that split second; laughter and love filled my brain. Something powerful happened. The smiling faces of my family and memories of my childhood filled me with a strength I cannot describe.

I caught the fruit of immortality, and shoved every bit of it into my mouth, at the same time I sprang from the cracked earth beneath me, just before it crumbled into the molten abyss.

I tumbled hard onto another island of charred ground and rolled to edge. I turned my face to the Gates and spied Elia, her hands clasped over her heart, and she was grinning with pride. Three more rocky islands stood between the invisible barrier of the Gates of Tartarus and me.

Horrifying screams from my friends were muffled by the invisible barrier, all except for Elia, who shared my secret. Echidna was darting across the remaining jagged rocks that stood where the ground once was. Hatred filled her eyes as she focused on me, but she was much faster than I. Her massive, venomous, fangs jutted forward, she was instantly on top of me, and plunged her fangs into the top of my head. I felt the crushing pressure, but no pain. Bright light shot from my wounds, but there was no agony. The monster stood before me, and I watched the hatred in her eyes drain, as fear and confusion replaced it.

She lashed out at me again, and again, met by the same mystical response. Her fangs made their mark, yet they had no effect. My body began to glow, just as it had when I astral traveled with Nak and the Mages. Echidna stumbled backwards, terrified, trying to retreat from me, unsure of what was happening. The crumbled beneath her and she tumbled over the edge. I stood there silent, glowing, and unharmed.

Typhon's guttural roar echoed through Tartarus and even the darkness shook. Glowing or not, I knew I had to get out of there. I leapt from rocky crag to crag, as they crumbled into the fiery abyss beneath me. Using Servo like a pole, I plunged the tip into the last cliff and vaulted off, just in time to tumble through the once impenetrable barrier of the Gates of Tartarus, and into the arms of my family.

There was no time for a reunion; even outside the Gates, the ground beneath us began to crumble with Typhon's fury. Ttensir flung Mateo's badly burnt form over his shoulder and took off running back to Ellida, the dragon ship. We all scrambled towards the dark forest, but the earth shook even more violently than before, causing us to stumble and fall falling into the muck.

The Hekatonkheire giants unfurled their hundred arms and began pounding the ground to fill in the fissures that grew from the Gates of Tartarus. "Sofia!" I screamed as I saw her turn and run towards Kottos, the giant with flaming red hair.

Kottos immediately stopped his fury, and gently scooped up Sofia. He nuzzled her gently with his enormous cheek and smiled fondly at her. Then, without any need for words, he left his brothers and ran in our direction. The gentle giant scooped all of us up, using many hands, and with giant strides, we were at the water's edge.

Kottos placed all of us on the deck of Ellida and picked her up, like a toy boat. He took off running through the River Styx and stopped at the triangle tunnel of black water that led up to sunshine. He pulled us back over his shoulder, bringing us to a brief stop eye-to-eye, "Hold on!" he winked as he flung the entire ship. Ellida's dragon wings unfolded and we soared, like a paper airplane, up to the Earth's surface.

"Thank You!" Sofia yelled back to Kottos with tears in her eyes.

Typhon's anger was mounting. An angry sea awaited us, with fifty-foot waves reaching out to grab us. Ttensir leveled Ellida off, but not on the water. We continued to sail through the sky, gliding on the wind, until we came to calmer waters.

The air was crisp and the sun was warm and welcoming. It was then when we all stood, on the hull of an enchanted dragon ship, holding each other up, and smiling arm in arm, united in Pure Light. "We did it…We stopped him," was all I could manage to say.

Everyone stood arm-in-arm, reveling at how beautiful and bright the world was, squinting through eyes not yet adjusted from the eternal darkness below. No one let go for a long time as we stood, united. Together we were strong; together we saved the world.

Skye nudged my elbow and pointed to the water's surface. Many Piscisene were breaching the water alongside Ellida, like pods of dolphins to sailing ships. Then she pointed up ahead of us to a large group of Piscisenes and I recognized the family that helped me. We slowed our course and I waved to the family. Just then, the Piscisene who were traveling alongside of us, leapt in the awaiting arms of their families. There four of them, reunited and arm-in-arm, waved back at us with smiles on their faces. Nãga's spell must have been broken upon her death; their children had returned. Other Piscisene families waved up at us as well. My heart welled up with pride.

Sofia had tucked herself under my arm and whispered, "Let's go home."

I hugged her tightly and nodded, "Yeah, let's do that."

I sat down on the deck of the enchanted Ellida, exhausted. All of my friends were too. Brochara and Elia were tending to Mateo while Luca held him in her lap. Nak, Fin, and Khai were sleeping in the front of the ship and Skye was holding her brother's hand staring off into the horizon.

I was so proud of each and every one of my friends, and of what we accomplished together, but I was also very aware of what lay ahead of us. We must rebuild our forces. I was unsure of just how many of our Adrastai were destroyed, and found myself contemplating what our next move would be. Evil won't rest for long. There will always be a constant struggle between Light and Dark, but for now, maybe we will get a break.

Sofia and I cuddled up against the main mast, and I felt her body relax against mine as she drifted off to sleep. A smile grew across my face as my thoughts floated off to home.

Just then, horrible sounds of death screeched through the sky! "Harpies!" I shouted.

My protectors sprang into action, but a sharp pain shot through my torso. The force of the Harpy's attack crushed me into the deck of the ship; splinters of Ellida flew up through the air. Pain consumed me. I was fading in and out of consciousness. I heard the faint screams of my friends followed by the sounds of swords being drawn, but then the darkness overtook me, again, and everything went black.

To be continued…

ABOUT THE AUTHOR

Book Two of the Dragon Birthmark Series, Threats of Tartarus, continues our journey with The Adrastai warriors. Author Jennifer Phillips Russo held a student artwork contest for her second book of "The Dragon Birthmark" series. This challenge promoted visual literacy and confidence, as well as provided student artists with the opportunity to have their personal artwork published at no cost to them, if chosen.

"Threats of Tartarus", Book Two of "The Dragon Birthmark Series, follows the story of an 11-year-old boy's journey to self-identity through a fantastic adventure, speckled with legend and lore, and offering a few great lessons and themes throughout the story. "'The Dragon Birthmark: World in the Shadows' is an entertaining, thought-provoking book that takes the reader into the world of imagination and fantasy through the eyes of an 11-year-old boy," said Amy Piper, Fredonia Elementary School Principal.

Russo, a local resident of Fredonia, possesses an insatiable desire to spark imagination and creativity in her readers, she created the art contest for students across the state and nation. She believes that imagination sparks innovation, and our world could use some innovative thinkers. This contest provided the opportunity to sketch characters or scenes from the second book, which the chosen winners are featured and published in this book. All middle and high school students were eligible to enter the contest.

Students were able to submit their artwork pieces through the novel's website. An online gallery is also available through the website, which gave contestants the chance to see examples of artwork that other students have created and submitted. A description of the characters to be sketched was provided at www.TheDragonBirthmark.com, as well as detailed rules and entry guidelines for this free contest.

www.ingramcontent.com/pod-product-compliance
Lightning Source LLC
Chambersburg PA
CBHW020821180626
46814CB00001B/59